Looped

A Novel

ANDREW WINSTON

AGAT

CHICAGO

D1082458

Printed in Canada.

Library of Congress Cataloging-in-Publication Data
    Winston, Andrew.
    Looped / by Andrew Winston.
      p. cm.
    ISBN 0-9724562-9-5
    1. Chicago (Ill.)—Fiction. 2. City and town life—Fiction. 3. Sexual orientation—Fiction. 4. Race relations—Fiction. I. Title.
    PS3623.I665L66 2004
    813'.6—dc22

                                                                2004017188

10 9 8 7 6 5 4 3 2 1

Agate books are available in bulk at discount prices. For more information, go to agatepublishing.com.

For Kate, whose passion and belief make all things possible.

January

Saturday the 1st (New Year's Day)

As their Ferris wheel car rises, Alice watches the Chicago River spread its banks and split the sparkling city wide open. The glittering streets and avenues part like a jeweled crust cracked open by a surging artery of coal black ink. She shudders.

"What." Brad nudges her. "Cold?"

"No, it's nothing. Just, it's weird, you know? This millennium thing? Two thousand years. Criminy." She shakes her head in awe. "Makes you feel small." Alice pulls the jacket collar over her ears. A wisp of blonde hair waves in the breeze, antennae-like.

"Look at it." Brad leans over the edge of the car. "Almost looks like a big city."

"Almost? It *is* a big city. Nine-something million? That's no Cleveland down there."

"It's no Paris, London, or New York, either."

"Oh, so now it's too small for us to get famous, Mr. Big Time?"

"Hey, listen," Brad interrupts. "It must be midnight."

Dangling high over Navy Pier, they can see fireworks squirt around the edges of the city, bursting and flaring briefly in the cold air. The faint cacophony of explosions, horns, whoops, and gunfire reaches them in the windblown car.

"Thank god. Now we don't have the listen to that freaking song anymore. It'll never be nineteen ninety-nine again," Brad sings. He bops, and the car sways.

That's my Brad, thinks Alice. Always the big picture.

The Paulina Street platform is nearly empty as a southbound el train rocks and sparks its way to the platform. No station attendant even; rides are free tonight. Four cars arrive with a screech of brakes. The doors whoosh open.

The station's speakers crackle, and a voice says, "Welcome to the year two thousand. All aboard the love train."

A couple standing in the shadows smile at each other and step aboard. One woman touches the other's face.

"I'm drunk."

"I told you to be careful, Ellie. Five chocolate martinis? I swear you have a death wish."

"But I want to *celebrate.* What better way to mark the end of the millennium?"

"I can think of others. I'd rather have you sober in bed, for instance."

"Soon, Megs. You heard the man. This is the express love train, next stop happy valley."

Megan leans forward, kisses her on the mouth. Ellen's head swims. The flashing lights flutter against her closed eyelids like moth wings. Too much vodka and too much Megan. She feels herself begin to slide down and off the slick seat. Whoopsy-daisy.

Viewed looking west at midnight from the forty-third floor of Lakepoint Tower, Chicago unfolds itself from the rumpled downtown through neighborhoods and suburbs, rolling out and out like a smooth old comforter stitched with light.

Like the knots on our chenille bedspread, thinks Florence. Her breath clouds the window. *Our.*

Suddenly the hostess arrives with a silver tray of crustless sandwiches. "We're so glad you came, Mrs. Finkel."

The old insurance men, comb-overs striping their gleaming heads, look swollen with contentment. Only her presence disturbs them. Sometimes they meet her eyes and quickly turn away. All of Arnie's old friends worry about her, but what can they do? She's alone in being alone.

Florence thinks of the taxi ride home, the empty apartment, the fitful sleep to come. Silently, colored lights shatter the sky. Stunning even without the booms. The glimmers sprinkle down above the distant hamlets. Her lungs tighten. She sways, but there is no arm around her.

A shirtless man straddles the chair, trapping Nathan's arms and rubbing a large silver belt buckle against his shirt. Nathan smiles and looks away from the sweaty abdomen. Where's Robin? Lost in the sea of hips and torsos.

The lap dancer departs, disappointed.

If I don't make him leave, he'll stay all night. Nathan wades into the disco melee. He sees Robin in a crowded corner, bouncing to "Disco Lady." He laughs. Robin bounces over and grabs him by the waist.

"I knew you couldn't resist K-Tel Hell!" His hair is curly and wet. The silk shirt clings to his chest. Robin's smile, the full mouth, the dark, darting eyes are so alive—it's like standing near a generator humming with menace and promise. Nathan swallows the saliva that rushes to his mouth. Still the taste of cologne on this tongue, a residue of their sleepless disco nap. He savors the ghost of musk lapped from clavicle and abdomen.

Robin throws his arms around Nathan's neck. "Come to kiss me under the mirrored ball?"

"I'm tired."

"Don't fight it! Stay and celebrate!"

"Please, let's not—!"

But Sly and the Family Stone kick in and swallow his words. *I wanna thankyou falettinme be mice elf again.*

At midnight they pause to kiss while flecks of light dance across their bodies.

Just after midnight, the Jeffrey bus stops at 71st Street and disgorges a dozen tired partygoers onto Stony Island Avenue. Two sharp voices emerge as the small crowd disperses.

"I just *know* I didn't marry a man stupid enough to go out in the street at night and shoot off a pistol."

"Elvin said it was registered."

"Alph!" she cries in amazement. "Who you think's gonna ask that before they blow your fool head off?"

"Damn, woman. Nothing happened, okay? Forget it." He rubs his stomach, feeling sour with champagne.

"You don't even know where that bullet fell. Might kill someone. Kill your own daughter somewhere out there."

Everything, everything comes back to that. What about our son, he wants to say. Don't forget we can still save Tony. But he says nothing, watching Eloise storm ahead without him, muttering a small fog into the air.

His jaw bulges with tension. The bus driver said nothing about love, only, "No smoking, drinking, or radio playing."

And a happy damn new year to you.

The boy just sits in the corner booth and draws. Whenever Elias comes near with the mop, the boy turns to shield the paper.

He hadn't said a word. The diner closed two hours ago and the boy didn't budge, daring Elias to throw him out. The dinner rush had slowed around nine and Elias let the waitress go early. Then Luis, the cook. When he picked up the boy's dinner plate, the boy glanced at him but didn't move to leave. He looks Asian. High school age. Lonesome. Elias is used to seeing lonely people in his diner, but not often one so young, and on New Year's Eve, to boot.

Elias turns off the neon Sophia's sign. He locks the door and cleans the kitchen. The boy is still there. Elias hums, sweeping around the booths and stools. The boy draws.

At midnight Elias brings two glasses of cola.

"Happy New Year. I'm Elias Kanakes."

"Ng," the boy says. They clink glasses. The boy bobs his head slightly. Elias isn't sure he's heard the boy's name right, but lets it pass.

"Don't you have a party to go to?"

The boy, Ng, shrugs.

They drink their sodas in silence, watching people dressed in party clothes walk gingerly on the icy sidewalks.

"Your name, is that—"

"Vietnamese. I'm half."

"I'm Greek," Elias says to even things. "Been in Chicago thirty years, though."

The boy finishes his soda, grabs his backpack, and walks to the door. "Thank you." He bobs his head again, unlocks the door, and lets himself out.

Elias picks up the placemat. There is, as he hoped, a drawing on the underside. A huge-torsoed man with bushy hair, wearing a cape and superhero costume, flies a banner that reads, Welcome 2000. In the corner of the picture a small boy and his mother look up and wave.

Elias stares at the picture. It's me. He drew me.

Monday the 3rd

The last year of the twentieth century began miserably for Alphonse Duchossois. Eloise all mad at him for reasons other than what she says, which is that he fired a pistol in the air at midnight New Year's Eve. What she's really mad about, all the time, is Giselle. He's mad too, but right now his problem is how his mail truck is stranded on a snow bank and no one will stop to help him push. Why these things got such damn little wheels? For ten minutes he revs the engine, rocking the truck back and forth until he feels sick. Clouds of exhaust mingle with his steamy breath.

Finally the top-heavy rig slews forward, begins to slide down a little mound of hard-packed ice. A Volvo's back end comes zooming toward him. Man, I'm gonna buy it now, he thinks. Just then the treads catch some salted pavement and the truck stops and rights itself. "Jesus H.," mutters Alphonse. He blows on his cold-throbbing fingertips. I don't mind winter, but enough hell-freeze already.

Then Mrs. Finkel meets him in the lobby of her building, looking upset. "Have you got that package from my sister-in-law?" she says. Her look says the question is merely a formality.

He searches his bag. "What was it again?"

"Grapefruits. From Florida. A dozen."

"No, ma'am," he shrugs. "It don't look like it."

The old lady's narrowed, angry eyes make him think of a copperhead he'd killed with a shovel back in Baton Rouge. At age twelve, mind you. Cool as a cucumber. But Mrs. Finkel's something else. Not shovel-sized, anyway.

"Louise mailed that package on December tenth. You tell me what's happened to it."

"I don't know, ma'am. It hasn't showed up in my delivery yet. Alls I can tell you."

"First it's bills, then catalogues, and now whole entire boxes I don't get!" bursts Mrs. Finkel. Her tiny, gnarled fingers worry a handkerchief.

"Now listen here, ma'am—"

"Don't you 'listen here' me!" Her face is going red under the beige powder. "I want the name of your supervisor."

Anticipating this turn, Alphonse cuts her off. "Elvin Wrightwood, and here's his card." This sort of thing has started to wear him out.

Mrs. Finkel, clearly winded by her outburst, falls heavily onto the lobby's only piece of furniture, a cream vinyl banquette, and dabs at her upper lip with the handkerchief.

"You okay?" asks Alphonse, despite himself.

Mrs. Finkel stares straight ahead of her and shakes her head slowly. She has a large, old lady's bosom, Alphonse thinks, but a nice enough face now that it has smoothed itself out. She sighs and says, "Arnie wouldn't have stood for this."

Alphonse knows that mail addressed to Arnie slowed to a trickle several months ago. He is aware of the slant of sun falling through the lobby's glass door. Most of his route still lies undone before him.

"Arnie knew how things worked," Mrs. Finkel says. "He always got the car fixed for a good price. He could get a good table at busy restaurants. He knew how to get things done." She looks at Alphonse. "I don't get how you people think."

Alphonse narrows his own eyes at this. "Us people?"

"You men."

The rest of the day was the usual slog of a winter run, Alphonse's mood dark as the lake water chugging out there under the snow and ice like a billion gallons of fish Slurpee. He lingered in the lobbies of the high-rises, chafing his hands for relief, snot glistening on his upper lip. He stepped around argyle-sweatered lapdogs soiling the snow. Everyone in some way angry at the world because they fell, twisted an ankle, dropped the groceries in a parking lot. He'd seen eggs frozen to the sidewalk. Then everyone goes home and yells at the kids or the old parent who just sits quietly in front of the tube all day. What's got into you? they'll be asked. And not know how to answer.

Dang gloves not up to the job any more. Oh, and the final straw: it was Tweeds catalogue day, and his back was numb and sore all at once. How can they expect me to hump all this stuff across the ice? I'll have to finish delivering the rest tomorrow.

Need something warm, he thinks. The sun'll be down soon, and it's a long, cold drive back to the station. He stops at a little flower shop where they sell coffee, too. Everybody up here sells coffee now. Gas stations, grocery stores, dry cleaners, pharmacies. Fancy stuff. Arabian this and Costa Rican that. The air is warm and rich with a smell somewhat like a distant campfire. He orders a decaf mochaccino. Why not?

The long-haired boy behind the counter begins measuring coffee and turning dials on a large machine.

So what if I don't deliver all the mail? thinks Alphonse. He had delivered everything yesterday, right? And the day before? But still, the trunk of his Oldsmobile is almost full. And there's the bags in the garage, still from the summer and fall, when he'd begun to shave his rounds a little short so he could go out looking for Giselle. And after he found her, and couldn't get her to come home, it never seemed important to break the habit. And there's never been time to catch up.

Okay, it was stupid to keep that old lady's grapefruit. But for the rest, she don't need all those damn catalogues anyway. Bunch of gardening crap and kitchen crap, and she got no garden and probably eats out every night. The real mail gets through like always. Leastways, when I get it, I deliver it.

"That's kind of slippery."

"What?" asks Alphonse.

"I just said, be careful, the floor's kind of slippery there," says the coffee boy.

Alphonse looks at the puddle around his boots. "Thanks."

He takes his coffee to a little table. Sips. "Jesus H., that's hot!"

The girl wiping down tables wears a little tee shirt that says LOVE IS BIND. Alphonse shakes his head.

Gonna be a tough year, he thinks. Even love taking it on the chin.

Thursday the 6th

Brad has really been a prick lately, and you can't blame it all on the weather, thinks Alice O'Leary. Look at him storming around behind the counter like a java-hopped Hitler. Wipe those tables, clean those windows!

"Like to, but the windows are all iced up on the inside."

"Well then clean up the melt along the bottom. The sill's warping from all the water."

She sniffs and gently touches her nose-stud. Why'd she let Brad talk her into it? Well, she knows why. Brad's got this thing about if you're in a band you have to look so counterculture. As if anyone in the band really is.

But underneath that is the fact that her and Brad's relationship has entered the phase she calls morphing time, when you stop simply dating and either mutate into a couple, or back into two singles. The nose ring is her bid for coupledom. But right now it doesn't seem like enough. She just feels silly, and every sneeze is a major production.

As she squeezes icy water into a bucket, she sees Mr. Kanakes across the street throwing pink ice-melting pellets onto the sidewalk in front of his diner.

There are only two customers at Mr. Kanakes's counter. An old lady hunched inside a huge tweed overcoat and a young woman with dark red hair and wire-rimmed glasses. Mr. Kanakes sees Alice. He waves and comes across the street and scatters some pellets in front of the window where Alice squats, swabbing underneath the painted name of the store: *Urbs in Horto*.

She smiles at Mr. Kanakes. He waves.

Brad watches her dump the bucket while he hums his new song to himself and sloppily wipes down the grill on the espresso machine's spill tray. Whenever he has a tune but no lyrics, he sings the band's name—his name for it—Lather Rinse Repeat.

Brad calls out, "Customer in flowers."

She walks over to the arranging table. A handsome guy, nice suit. Is that what they call herringbone? Next to him she feels suddenly frowsy, unkempt. She pulls her long blonde hair behind her ears. "Can I help you?"

He smiles. It's a good smile. This puts Alice on the defensive. She smirks, just a little. With the nose-stud, she looks fierce.

"I'd like a bouquet for about, I don't know, thirty-five dollars?"

"Do you want anything in particular?"

"No, I trust your judgment."

He trusts my judgment? She thinks. Hello.

"No roses, though." He peers into a peony. "I really like the flowers you have in here. Do you do the buying?"

"The owner does most of it. But I order the exotics. Like those birds of paradise."

"I like them. Can you use a couple in the arrangement?"

"Sure. And I'll use some of this dried holly here for contrast, and this fern, and these anemones. Black-eyed susans?"

"Yeah, I like them. They're honest."

Alice smiles. She's exposed now. The head-banger who spritzes lilies and likes it. She selects the blooms and a few feathery greens, gathering them in one hand. She feels the man watching her.

"What's your shirt mean? Love is *bind*?"

"Oh, that's a club thing. A guy at the Fusebox—you know where that is? In Wicker Park? He silk-screened a bunch of these and some other stuff, too. I guess it means love's like blind and a trap and everything? It's dumb, but I like the colors."

"It's eye-catching. And kind of ambiguous."

Alice shrugs. She lays the flowers down with the greenery on butcher paper. "Need a card?"

"Sure." He takes one and pulls a fountain pen from his coat pocket. Mont Blanc. Christ. Half a week's pay. Alice peeks at his hesitant scribble while she wraps the flowers. He's careful to say something just right. She can just make out the name Robin. And the word Sorry.

He seals the card into its tiny envelope and draws a heart on the outside. This intimacy makes Alice feel ashamed, and she turns her eyes out to the street where a new snowfall is beginning to drift down. She suddenly feels like crying.

He takes the flowers and props the card into a cleft of the fern. "These are lovely. Thank you very much." He holds out the money. He has beautiful hands.

"Here's your change."

"Thanks." He's smiling again, but directly at her, looking into her eyes. Alice feels her face heat up and her mouth draw tight.

"Bye-bye," he says.

"Come again," she says. Her face burns. Why does she have to talk like a shop-girl robot? Stupid! She begins to straighten up the flower shop, staring at the broom as it sweeps fern fronds into a soft pile. She hears the jingle of the door.

There's some tables to bus. Brad has switched the music to the all-70s-all-the-time station. *I believe in miracles since you came along, you sexy thing, sexy thing you...*

She doesn't want to see Brad right now. She fusses with the flower buckets, turning all the bright faces to the front, like choirgirls above the neatly lettered signs.

"Hey," says Brad, coming over to the arranging table. "You okay?"

"I'm okay." She is alternating the colors of the Gerber daisies—yellow, fuchsia, scarlet, yellow.

"You sure?"

Alice shrugs. Brad goes back to the coffee bar and begins frothing some milk with syncopated bursts of steam.

The flowers seem to give off a kind of heat. She wants to stay near them for now. Until the streetlights pop on and the café becomes its own zone of warmth against the dark night.

Tuesday the 11th

Ellen Kovacs watches the snow from her bedroom window. Enough snow has fallen by nine o'clock to turn the parked cars into pure white dunes of no clear origin. A bundle of dried lilac burns in a copper bowl. In her lap are a highlighting marker and a book on film technique by Eisenstein.

How relevant is this? Who would use a montage these days? Ridiculous.

Speaking of ridiculous, how about wasting another afternoon watching that flower shop girl who I don't even know her name and is probably dating that guy. It's a farce, a bedroom comedy without bedrooms. She's so beautiful. Why else waste my time like I'm some freakish bird watcher on urban assignment. The golden-tressed Lakeview hummingbird. Since I discovered her, I get to name her. Rara avis florist. Okay, for now, at least, she's Avis. To me.

Megan doesn't count. Megan is a recurring fever. Like malaria. Anyway, she's on the cutting room floor tonight. I need a break.

The mix tape segues from the Indigo Girls in seamless harmony to Hole grinding it out.

Back to the book. Paper due next Wednesday and I need the highest A ever given. Another C, Dad pulls the tuition plug. Again.

Courtney is wailing about pain and all the while you're thinking that Kurt killed himself and still she goes on. Tell it sister.

All these Russians get together, kind of like the Little Rascals, and decide to film the October Revolution. Or *Battleship Potemkin.* Watch the little baby carriage bouncing down the steps while bullets fly all around. Metaphor shmetaphor. Will we be tested on this?

Try this montage: Me in a white gown, standing in a field. On either side, in separate frames, Megan and Avis running—toward me? Away from me? Stupid Russians and their enigmas.

Faintly, then, she hears: "El-len."

No. No, no. I'll go make some tea. No more caffeine though, I've had enough trouble sleep—

A snowball thumps against the glass.

"EL-*LEN*!"

I will not go to the window, I will not go to the window, I will not—

Ever since New Year's, Megan has been back on her riff about how Ellen won't commit to anything and how she has to see that Megan's got this pure emotion welling up for her. It makes Ellen feel trapped. But then again, the pursuit always has certain pleasures.

THUMP.

Ellen drops her head into her hands. The small hairs of her nape crackle. Goosebumps fizz down her arms.

"Goddamn it, Ellen! I know you're in there."

She creeps over to the window and peers around the side. It feels like espionage. Under a cone of lamplight Megan is scrunching together another snowball. Her long black hair is starred with snowflakes. She stands and Ellen sees the glint of glasses and the wide slash of her full mouth. The pointy chin lost in swaths of argyle scarf.

Suddenly a white blur and then *WHUMP*! Ellen stumbles back against the bureau, knocking over vials of essential oils.

"Damn!" She scrambles to right the bottles and replace the glass stoppers. Cedar. Jasmine. Patchouli. It's an unholy combination.

"I see you! I know you're there."

Ellen flings the window open. "Well come up then!" she shouts. "What are you, Stanley Kowalski?"

Megan falls to her knees and leans back, her arms raised in perfect Brando mimicry: "E-L-L-L-L-E-E-E-E-N-N," she wails.

A few flakes whisk into the room swirling madly in currents of warm air. "I'll buzz you in." Ellen smiles, and is only vaguely aware of the microsecond chill of flakes falling against her lips before she shuts the window.

The mugs send up a thin curtain of steam between them. Megan is glaring at her. Now that she's inside, it's the silent treatment.

"Hello? I said, honey?" Pretend everything is fine. Just a friend dropping over.

"Sure. Fine. Arsenic, too. Three lumps."

Ellen laughs.

"Don't laugh," Megan says, but smiles. "Did you get my card?"

"Yes. I didn't know what to say back."

"Hmm." Megan holds the teabag, letting brown droplets plop into the cup. "I don't know how to take that."

"I don't have anything to say. It's all been said."

"Come on. Everything? I'm sure there are a few things left. I'm sorry, for instance. I screwed up, for another."

"Are those my lines or yours?"

Megan stands up and strides into the bedroom. "What's been going on in here?" she shouts back to Ellen. "Whoever she is, she wears a crappy perfume."

Ellen reluctantly follows. "It's not perfume. I spilled—"

In the dim light she sees a lump in the bed and Megan's clothes on the floor.

"That was fast."

"Mm-hmm. I got sleepy all the sudden."

There is a silence then. The tape has ended and the cassette player clicks off. In the distance, whirring tires and the voices of couples laughing. Why is it, Ellen wonders, that sound carries so clearly during a snowstorm?

"Come on then. It's cold in here."

"Not that cold."

"Let me feel your fingers. You're always an ice cube." Megan's naked arm emerges from the blankets.

The fingers hot on her palm, entwined with hers, insisting.

Here we go again, thinks Ellen, falling.

Friday the 14th

As a consequence of his mother's preference for impeccable cornbread over personal safety, Robin Schafer was saddled for the rest of his life with a ruthless culinary perfectionism.

Even though it is the middle of winter, as he slices gnocchi batter with a wooden spatula, Robin can taste the humidity in the still air and the metallic fear in his mouth as the sky turned green over Texarkana, back in May of 1971.

"What is it, Momma?" The county sirens wailed mournfully, meaning a twister was on the ground somewhere not far away.

His mother laughed as he tugged on her apron. "Don't be a pill, Robbie. Momma's just going to finish up these corncakes and then I'll be down in the cellar with you. Now you take Janie and get on down there."

Darkness can be kind. Nighttime darkness or closed-in darkness. Unless you sense something else sharing the darkness, something unknown, which becomes whatever you fear most. Is that what it's like for Nathan in his closet? If he'd ever been in real darkness, Robin thinks, he wouldn't stay in it. He'd want out.

The sirens made him feel alone, helpless. He wanted his mother in the dark with him, holding him close, crooning "The Old Gray Mare," or "My Bonny Lies Over the Ocean."

"Now, now," said his mother, leaning down to wipe his cheeks with a floury thumb. "I'm baking these just for you, darlin'. When this is all over, I'll make some chocolate milk and we'll have us a fine snack before Daddy comes home, just the three of us. Now be a good boy and take Janie downstairs."

Robin, panicking, obeyed. He found Janie curled into a ball behind the sofa, grabbed her arm, and pulled her down the wooden stairs into the moist darkness of the cellar. He sat her on a stack of paint cans, where she stayed, sucking her thumb.

A freight train roared through the house. The world shuddered and cracked. Janie's eyes round and white. "Momma!" Robin leaped up the stairs, two at a time in his heavy orthopedic shoes. He stood in the doorway watching as his mother, impossibly, hovered above the ground, anchored by her white-knuckled grip on the handle of the oven door. With a soup ladle she batted away a shoebox, a hubcap, her sewing box, as they flew at her head.

"Robin! Get downstairs, boy!"

But he was mesmerized. He watched the sofa rise up on one end, jog across the room and somersault out the bay window. He saw his bicycle cartwheeling in the yard. Momma's skirt blew over her head and he saw her long legs, white as chalk, and her bare feet rise up until her toes brushed the ceiling.

Then he saw the trunk of the old pine tree replace the doorway to the garage. Then a heavy branch, bristling with cones and needles, rushed into the room and shoved him back down the stairs.

Robin finds a chair and falls into it. He wants to call Nathan. No, that just makes him angry. I can wait it out, he thinks. He grabs an old blanket, rolls into it, and shivers.

When he awoke everything was silent. Janie was touching his face. He felt stickiness there, sniffed the sharp smell of pine resin. Needles in his hair. "Momma?"

He slowly climbed the stairs. He felt dizzy in the eerie silence, climbing up to the light that glowed where there should have been the white-painted ceiling and overhead fan of the den. Janie held his shirttail. Upstairs, rain fell through the window frames. Robin stepped gingerly on glass shards. He called "Momma" all through the house until, looking out where the front porch had been, he saw her lying on the couch in the yard. As though napping. One arm was thrown across her face. One hand still held the ladle, the knuckles white with tension.

"Momma," he whispered, moving her arm away. Her bangs were pasted to her forehead with blood.

"Robin," she murmured.

Janie crawled onto the couch and held her mother's skirt.

He almost cried. Almost. But bit his tongue and said, "Yes, Momma."

"Be a doll and get those cakes from the oven."

"Okay, Momma."

"And use the oven mitt, darlin'."

Nathan senses sadness the moment he opened the door. He sets his briefcase down and walks through the house holding the flowers, which now seem gaudy and maybe ill-timed. The rich and mingled smells of cooking. But no cook clanging about.

Robin sits staring out the window, the clutter of food-in-progress all around: a bulb of dough, parsley, tomatoes, sausages lounging in butcher paper.

"Robin?"

A listless wave of the spatula.

"What...?"

"Never mind." Robin rises, gropes for an oven mitt. "I have to get the corncakes out of the oven."

Nathan watches Robin walk to the oven, open the door and stare into the cold interior.

"Did I say corncakes?"

"Well, yes."

Robin puts his face in the oven mitt. "I am so-o-o-o screwed up."

Nathan puts the flowers down and sniffs. "Is something burning?"

"Jesus!" Robin lunges for the saucepan with the rattling lid. He lifts the lid, releasing a cloud of foul, black smoke. "Anyone for scorched ratatouille?"

Nathan touches his shoulder. "How about instead let's have a quiet dinner out?"

"Okay. But only if I can tell you about the corncakes."

"I'm all ears, lover. Blab away."

Monday the 17th

Elias Kanakes wakes suddenly in the silent darkness. He looks at the clock. Four a.m. on the dot. Most mornings he simply finds himself conscious, with no alarm, a natural evolution of wakefulness out of sleep. The result of an orderly life. Never this bolting awake. What was it? Oh yes.

He had dreamed all night of children. A gaggle of them in a playground. He was flying over them, his children, their bright faces turned up to watch him. Their beckoning hands. Grandpa, they cried. Or Daddy. They needed solace of some kind. He just kept flying, unable to reach down to them.

He flicks on the bedside lamp. A thick sheet of ice inside the storm windows reflects the light in fuzzy crystalline refractions. He pulls the boy's drawing out of the nightstand drawer. Superman. But he had saved no one. He could forgive himself for that, had forgiven, in fact. But this boy, what did he see? Was it a whim? Or was Elias actually faster than—what? Stronger than sleep, for a while.

He shuffles to the kitchen and puts the drawing on the refrigerator door with a magnet. Next to the drawing of him that Elana had made in her preschool class. Always the wiry hair and the turnip nose—his best features. His cartoon self is holding Elana's little balled fist. Holding her other fist is her father, Jonathan, like a black-haired pencil with a beard. And holding Jonathan's hand, Sophia. A cigarette pokes out of Sophia's free hand. All of them have huge smiles with teeth like stacked sugar cubes. It looks happy enough. He turns on the coffeemaker.

But there is something about his daughter's family that doesn't ring right to Elias. Maybe it's just how far away they are, in Boston, near Jonathan's family. Elias feels like an intruder on holidays. Sophia never wanted to come back home, he knows that. The wealth and prominence of Jonathan's family must have made the choice easy for her. Elias almost feels guilty for wishing they were closer.

As he shaves he tries to see the crowd of children in his dream again. Was Elana there? She seems to love him, in the distracted way four-year-olds can, but how could she really know who he is?

Bundled up, and sipping from his silver thermos bottle, Elias sits in his 1990 Taurus while it warms up. The boy, Ng, hadn't come back since New Year's Eve. He will, though, Elias is sure. Who knows what fills the days of young people? On a whim, Elias leaves the car idling and goes back in the house. He takes both drawings off of the fridge. He'll put them in the diner, by the cash register.

On the way out, as he never fails to do, he touches the frame of his wife's picture. It is part of opening the door, as much as the lock itself, part of every coming and going.

He drives through the dark streets. Snowplows block his way. Rock salt pings on the car's undercarriage. Faster than a short order cook? More powerful than Turkish coffee? Able to leap city health codes in a single bound?

Health codes. "Remember to check the rat traps," he says aloud.

Luis is waiting by the door, stamping his feet for warmth.

Elias juggles the keys with mittened fingers. "Morning."

"Too effing cold, man. I'm going back to *pinché* San Miguel you know?"

"Greece, too. Always sun on the white houses. Make you feel warm just to see the light."

"Don't remind me."

"You have to embrace the cold, Luis."

Able to leap frozen lakes in a single bound. That's me.

They trudge through the morning routine. Retrieving the bundled newspapers, setting up the coffeemakers, prepping the kitchen. Elias checks the rat traps. Nothing.

At six the waitress arrives. He lets her in the front door, flips the neon sign to open.

After a slow breakfast rush, Elias goes to the Y for a swim. In the mid-morning he is, as usual, alone in the old, tiled pool. Forty laps of slow regular strokes. It gives him time to think about Sophia's reluctance to come back to Chicago. She was one of those children who wanted to be whatever her parents were not. Not to be Greek, not to be middle class. He still hopes that having Elana will change Sophia, soften her hard edges, though it hasn't happened yet.

Before he gets out of the pool, he pushes off and glides as far as he can underwater. He never makes it all the way. It's a small superstition: the distance he travels foretells the quality of his day. Today he makes about three-quarters of the length.

Faster than a speeding smelt?

When he returns to the diner the young redhead is in the front booth staring out the window, as she is two or three times a week. The sidewalks have iced up, so Elias takes the bag of Ice-Away and sprinkles it in front of the diner. Then, he decides to keep sprinkling. He crosses the street to the flower-café and sprinkles some there. Alice waves at him through the glass. He mouths, "Hello," and gestures with the bag.

"Thank you," mouths Alice.

Crossing back, he notices an older woman hesitating at an icy curb. He takes her arm.

"Thank you. I'm going in there, to that diner."

"That's perfect. I'm the owner. Come inside, please."

He seats her at the side booth and brings her a coffee.

"I'm not sure this was such a good idea. I might have fallen, and my lungs aren't so good."

"Now, now, you're fine here. Take a minute to warm up and I'll be right back."

Elias goes to the service island and pours himself a cup of coffee. He watches the woman as she fusses with her scarf and coat. She looks very alone.

Stronger than—well, only stronger than sadness, maybe. But that is something.

Thursday the 20th

When she wakes, Florence can't shake the idea that she had been bowling with Arnie the night before. She didn't look for him when she got up—that would be crazy—even though she could still feel a residue of his dream-presence in the room. She lies in bed for a long time. There is no phone call, no reason to get up. Nothing.

Some mornings are just like this, thinks Florence. You wake to the sound of your own breathing. Nothing else. A sound so helpless and persistent, it makes her want to stop breathing altogether.

"So the grapefruits never arrived?" asks Louise.

"No dear, but don't you worry. It's the thought that counts." Something about Louise's voice makes the phone hot against Florence's ear.

"Well, I want to do something about it. I'm going to complain to the post office."

"Why don't you just try again next year?"

"Why don't you come down here for a visit? We'll feed you daiquiris and shrimp for a few days. Jimbo could even show you around some of the new developments. You know, if you wanted to."

I was waiting for that one, thinks Florence. "I don't know," she says. "I think the trip is a little more than I can manage right now."

"Getting away might do you some good." Louise is snappish now. "You can't go on like this, being all alone, can you?"

Florence wants to say, only if I want to go on at all. Instead she says, "Well, what choice do I have?"

It begins while she dusts the trophies. She pulls down the largest, second place from the 1998 Willow Bluffs Insurer's Cup, Senior Division. It was the one Arnie got out late on poker nights when all the men's voices got loud.

She looks at the little gilded man about to swing down on the tiny golden ball at his feet. He looks melted, yet perfect. I'd like to see one like Arnie—a shining, potbellied man with shaggy eyebrows, frozen in the act of breaking a putter over his knee. She stopped playing golf with Arnie after he got into a fistfight on the course. On the twelfth hole at Bonny Mead, a bull-necked young man badgered them to let him play through. He cruised by, shouting from his golf cart. Arnie picked his ball up from the green, pitched it. It careened off the young man's skull. And that was that. Fist city.

She rubs the golden man's head. And then she feels the pain, like a needle pressed behind her ear, echoed by a larger pain in her forehead. Like the sound of a gun fired into a canyon, the pain throbs and spreads. She closes her eyes and feels her way to the couch.

After the pain passes, she picks up the trophy from where it fell to the carpet. The golf club has snapped off. This seems like a good time to cry, she says. But she doesn't. She takes a nap instead.

She is roused by the intercom buzzer. It's the super, Les Potamkin, calling her down to get a package. She cajoles him into bringing it.

The package is a dozen grapefruit. Texas Ruby Reds. Not Louise's. No note, no address.

"Who brought this?"

"The mailman, who'd you think?" Potamkin hitches up his pants. He is a large, shy man who, Florence thinks, needs a belt.

She finds the card the postman had given her and calls the number on it. After a few gruff transfers, she gets the man on the card, the supervisor.

"Wrightwood." The voice is tired.

"Yes, hello. I'd like to speak to my carrier."

"Is there a problem?"

"No, I just had a question. I mean I'd like to thank him."

"What's your address?"

She tells him. After a minute, he says, "That's Mr. Duchossois."

"Is he in?"

"He's not back from his route yet. Would you like to leave a message?"

"No, thank you. I'll see him tomorrow."

"Has your service been satisfactory?"

"Well, yes, I suppose so." It isn't entirely convincing, but she doesn't feel like getting the man in trouble right now.

"That's good. Thanks for your call."

After she hangs up, Florence feels a rush of happiness. She sniffs the spicy skins of the grapefruit. And then she cuts one open and eats half, scooping out the gem-like flesh with a serrated silver spoon.

Pleasure wells up inside her. I need to get out. I need to walk. And she bundles up in sweater, jacket, overcoat, hat, gloves, two scarves, and rubber boots, and marches out into the slushy streets.

The early dusk makes the shops look so inviting. The yellow warmth beckons. She walks by the diner and waves to the owner inside, that nice man.

A Yorkshire terrier in an argyle sweater, tied outside the White Hen Pantry, yaps at her. He is eager even in the cold, wiggling happily as Florence pets him. His whiskers are crispy with ice.

She walks as far as the Drive. The lake is still ice as far as she can see. The momentary pleasure of the grapefruit is fading. It will be dark soon, and time for her TV shows.

No matter how happy she feels walking home through the shining wintry streets, misery returns as soon as she steps inside the apartment. Check your happiness at the door.

Sunday the 23rd

The lake is a black brooding backdrop for the winter's evening. Ice has melted and refrozen to a high polish in the harbors, the winter sun working like a slow Zamboni. The piers are desolate. The sailboats rest in drydock far inland, in old feed lots and the lading aprons of abandoned factories. Traffic swishes along the Drive, carrying the city's blood out to the limbs, the bedroom communities, the phalangeal districts. The lake is shingled with plates of ice that slowly swell and drop with the muffled waves blown in from the far, unfrozen reaches, if there are any such places between here and the dunes on Michigan's far shore. And a few seagulls still circle, hoping for some belly-up alewives or a taco shell to tide them over until daylight.

Farther out, the water intake cribs become mysterious islands, disappearing in the oncoming darkness, and the skyscrapers enjoy a last pale blush on their western faces as the sun sets somewhere beyond the el tracks' end. Beyond the beltways and tollways, subdivisions and shopping malls. Perhaps it sets in the mythical land of cornfields and hog farms where the city is felt only as a dark and complicated presence, like the approaching night. The night that creeps in from the east.

Eloise watches Tony playing in the yard. Her fear for him is a perpetual state. Crazy for her and Alphonse, at their age, to be raising a child now, especially with the dangers that surround him. But that's what you get when you have an oops baby at thirty-five. God's blessing and god's challenge all wrapped up together.

"I'm taking you out tonight," Alphonse says, walking in as full of cheer as she's seen him in months.

"What got into you?"

"You're looking at employee of the month," Alphonse beams.

"You?"

"For service above and beyond. You remember those grapefruits?"

"Yes. That mean woman."

"She called Elvin and gave him an earful of how wonderful I am. And so." He grabs Eloise by the waist. "We going out to celebrate."

The battering of a city in winter is calculated in miles of ruptured asphalt, tons of salt, acres of ice-broken trees, lengths of power outages, the dollar-cost of fender benders, and the simple numbers of infants and elderly dead in unheated apartments. And most importantly, in the response time of snowplows. It is also reckoned in the small agonies, the extra grind of the day that, at night, makes people lean toward the TV commercials about Key West getaways. But, like whispers, the city doles out winter's small and secret pleasures. The parks after snowfall, smooth and flawless before the first footprint of jogger or vagrant. The lights of the Loop against the certain crisp black of a clear winter night. The plumes of smoke and steam from factories and high-rise apartment buildings.

One place to find such beauty tonight would be the soccer fields of Jackson Park below 60th Street. Near the fields there is a small shed, a public bathroom where Giselle Duchossois awakes, her cheek pressed against a pile of free newspapers, shivering with the cold that comes right up from the floor. She gathers her coat around her. Where'd Jimmy get to? She'll have to hitch a ride home. If she even decides to go home. But where else would she go? She feels the beginnings of nausea. Water, a tall glass of water would save her at this moment.

She pushes open the door of the shed and scoops a handful of snow from beside the doorway. The cold burns her already numb fingers. She stuffs the snow into her mouth, and it sits there, dry as straw for interminable moments before the first trickle of thaw slides back toward her throat. She raises her head and looks across the park. New snowfall is at that moment covering the gouged and trampled ground. The streetlights fire the infinitely small lattices in the flakes and a warm light comes up from the coat of snow. There is a hush, as though traffic has ceased, and the horns and shouts of everyday have paused for a moment of respect.

The pain behind Giselle's eyes is knife-like, her tongue rough as bark.

She thinks of her mother looking out the living room window at this very same snow.

"Still proving she's tough as any boy," says Eloise into the phone, "that's what it is." She looks out in the yard, where Tony and the twins are making a snow fort. Snow has started to fall once more.

"She had to outrun them, outfight them. Nothing gone bring her down."

"Well that's too bad when she meet Mr. Crack," replies Eloise's sister, Germaine Cochran. "Can't fight that."

"What she gone do?" says Eloise quietly. She will not cry now and ruin her night out. "What *we* gone do?"

"Wish I knew, baby."

"You ready?" yells Alphonse from the bedroom.

"In a minute! I gotta go."

"You send Tony and the twins over here, then go have a nice time. Can't keep worrying about that girl. Life goes on."

Alphonse appears with his overcoat on, car keys jingling in his hand.

Eloise looks at the boys. "We'll drop them off. It's getting dark."

The house is quiet when the knock on the door comes.

Wednesday the 26th

Even before Bucktown peaked with rents to match Lincoln Park, the painters, musicians, and the transient bohemian mix had already established beachheads in Logan Square, Pilsen, and the South Loop. Grotty spaces with rotten floors, the streets all taco stands and currency exchanges. By the time Brad moved in three months ago, his building was one of the few remaining unrenovated lofts on South Michigan. The building next door has just become deluxe condos above a first-floor boutique called Riffs, selling souvenirs and memorabilia of Chicago's blues heritage—bar stools from the Checkerboard Lounge, old Chess singles.

Brad's place is two-thousand square feet of raw space. No running water. You have to walk down the dim hall to a locked bathroom. The key is attached to a toilet plunger, like at a gas station, so no one forgets and walks off with it. The nice thing about it, Brad says, is that it stands up on its own while you do your business. No insulation either, just concrete and brick and single-paned windows between you and the icy gales that whistle down the avenue. Alice hung white sheets across all the tall windows to baffle the drafts, but in the evening, Brad pulls the sheets back to get a little atmosphere for the rehearsal. The northwest corner holds the bed and Brad's piles of clothing. The kitchen consists of a dwarfish dormitory fridge, a hotplate on a table, and a plastic bin for carrying dirty dishes down to the bathroom for washing. Chipper's drum kit and the amps stay in the southwest corner, where two banks of windows converge. Chipper complains that the cold is making his drumheads too brittle.

Brad is unsympathetic. "It's making *me* too damn brittle," he says.

Alice arrives early. She and Brad make love, huddled under the blankets. They squirm around and then lay entwined, breathing each others' trapped scents.

"Remember when you showed me this place? You said, just imagine it, a giant bed in the middle of this room, and we're making love with the sun streaming all around. Is that ever going to happen?"

"Meteorologically speaking, I'd guess there'll be a four or five month wait on that one, little missy."

"I don't mean is the sun ever going to shine. I mean when it does, will we be making love?"

"Oh, I see. You mean are we going to break up."

"Yeah, I guess so."

"Why? Why are you asking that?"

"'Cause I'm wondering. It just feels like."

"What?"

"Ever since you moved down here, I hardly see you except at work or rehearsal and I—I don't know."

Brad grabs her head and kisses it. "Come on, Allie-pie. Don't get worked up. It's winter, hunker-down time. Everything will speed up again in the spring." He stops short.

"What?"

"That could make kind of a nice song, don't you think?" He moves away. "Slow winter, quick spring. Spring forward, fall back."

"Hey," Alice reaches for him. "We were talking."

"Just a minute, okay?" Brad pulls on a sweatshirt then sits in bed and plucks out a melody. A few false starts before he gets something to work with.

Alice lays there listening and then, when her anger has subsided, she helps Brad with the refrain. Then she writes the bridge. It flows out of her, it's easy. It sings.

"I like it," Brad says. He sings her lyrics. "That's good."

Brad gets up. Alice watches his lean haunches in the weak light, and she wants him back in bed with her.

"Hey, you've got some unfinished business here."

Brad pulls on his jeans. "I want to polish this. Maybe we can expand it tonight at rehearsal."

Alice slumps down into the bed. She hugs herself and feels the desire ebbing away. Go ahead, she thinks. Be a rock star.

Everybody's edgy, driven to nervous fidgeting by the need to stay warm. Chipper is printing Lather Rinse Repeat on his bass drum with a magic marker. Alice notices that he's growing his sideburns together across his chin. Shanklin drinks a beer and flips through *Rolling Stone*. Five more beers are cushioned in the snow out on the windowsill. He sticks out his tongue and taps the silver stud against his teeth. His face in the shadows looks like an inverted teardrop with a cap of black fuzz. When Alice glares at him, he stops tapping, looking sheepish.

Molly is the last to arrive. She takes off her red-checked hunting cap. Underneath, she is wearing a knotted kerchief over her black buzz cut.

"Dig the flannel do-rag," says Alice.

Molly takes off all of her outerwear, then her thick, cable-knit sweater. Under her T-shirt is a clarinet, the two pieces tucked into the waistband of her tights, nestled against her skin.

"What, are we a klezmer band now?" Brad snorts.

"Don't knock it till you've tried it."

"No way," Brad says. "We're power pop all the way. I thought we decided that."

"Yes sir," Chipper says.

"Power pop," Shanklin agrees.

"I asked her to bring it," Alice says. "In case we want to vary the instrumentation."

"Whatever," Brad says. "In the unlikely event."

"Let's get going," says Chipper. "I got to meet someone later." He taps on the snare for emphasis.

"Okay, I got this new song," says Brad. He plays a few bars and talks through the lyrics. "Give it a try?"

"I don't know," says Shanklin. "It's kind of like...stupid. To me, anyway."

Molly gives Alice a knowing look. "I like it." She wets her clarinet reed and extemporizes a harmonic line.

"That gave me goosebumps," says Alice, smiling hopefully.

"Probably the Siberian Express," says Chipper. He crosses his arms. "We don't need anything new right now. Let's work on our set."

Brad looks at Alice and shrugs. "He's right. Auditions aren't for new stuff. We'll make time for it later."

"Fine," says Alice. "God forbid we should play a love song. How dated."

"Come on, Allie-pie. Be good." Brad ruffles her hair.

Chipper sits down at the kit. He has combed his hair forward. "Who am I?" He frowns.

"Charlie Watts?" says Shanklin.

"Right-o, mate." Chipper hits a rimshot. "Now let's see what you wankers can do."

Saturday the 29th

"God is a run-on sentence. And we are but commas, brothersisters, hesitations of no significant weight. The earth, our existence, is a pause, a long breath before the next paragraph. The millennium which is now upon us is a paragraph mark, or as they say in the computer age, a hard return. A hard return. Ain't that right! We wish to return to the embrace of the Lord, and the way is hard, yes it is.

"Look closely at the good book, people. You think you know the word of God? Look closer! See how God's word is cluttered, is filled to the brim with the word And? These Ands are as seeds upon the soil of the divine word! John 3:16, 'And God so loved the world.' Ezekiel 1:14, 'And the living creatures darted to and fro, like a flash of lightning.' Revelation 22:7, 'And behold, I am coming soon.' Yes, brother, soon.

"But what of it, Brother Even, you say? What light should find us through this lens of syntax? This is the *Bible,* brothersisters. I'm telling you—thank you sir God bless you—there is no word too small to carry the weight of the Lord's meaning. Think about it. And. A word of linkage, of connection. Just as the Bible is our connection to God. Ain't that right, sister? And connects everything in the great story of God's glory to every-thing else. It connects the low to the high, God bless you, the weak to the strong, the rich to the poor.

"Notice, too, my children, that every report of God's word begins with And. And the Lord spake. And God said. For He is forever in mid-thought. Lord, you know the scribes had some mean shorthand. What cramps they must have suffered in trying just to keep up with the Lord God's outpouring of the Word!

"God's voice plunges us into a river that contains everything in the universe. Do we get a word in edgewise? Maybe like Job we can stand petitioning the great wind and make it reply. But how many times, I ask you, how often in a millennium does that happen?

"The only exception to this rule of And, and the one which I mention only to prove the rule, is the Bible's first line. In the beginning. No And. From darkness to light. Bam-boom, brothersisters.

"If you accept Christ Jesus as your Savior, then God will make the next paragraph a story of his love, not his wrath, a comedy, not a tragedy. That story will be written, my friends, so make it a happy chapter for yourselves. For there is no end to the word. Amen."

To Ng Pran-Markowitz, being half-Buddhist-half-Jewish by birth was a non-event. Jesus or no Jesus, Buddha, Mohammed, Allah, or Confucius, it makes no diff. He doesn't know why he doesn't care, he just doesn't. He's lapsed any way you slice it. All the same, somehow the street preacher makes him self-conscious about his apathy.

He watches the preacher from the shadows of the Tower Records' entrance. He enjoys the rhythms and the melody of the man's chanting sermon. He enjoys the dance of his thin, black-suited frame as his voice splits the crowd and drives it around him like a rock in a stream.

Ng fingers the change in his pocket. Not enough for a taco anyway. He puts the new comic books inside his coat and zips it up. He drops the coins in the preacher's dusty black fedora as he heads to the subway entrance on State Street.

"God bless you, son, and thank you," says the preacher.

"De nada," says Ng. "Amen."

The overheated el train car puts him right to sleep. He dozes even as the train emerges from the subway and angles skyward, joining the trees below the sky turning salmon over the cold and steaming city. His head bounces against the window. He wakes up at Belmont and debates going to the diner. He's thought of it everyday since New Year's Eve, but when he remembers his corny sketch, he is filled with embarrassment. While he ponders, the doors close and he rides on, emerging groggily when the train pulls under the red tiled pagoda-style roof of the Argyle Street stop.

He walks down Carmen Street to a white, two-story building squeezed between two Vietnamese grocery stores. The door reads Chicago Best Silk-screen. Even though it is late on a Saturday afternoon, the second-story shop is filled with women. Benny Lee, the supervisor, curtly jabs his thumb toward the back of the shop. Ng walks to the back of the shop and finds his mother applying red ink to a pile of baseball shirts. He looks at her small, dark head and her thin neck. The screen reads, *Park Ridge Pumas*.

"Hey," says Ng.

His mother leans up to kiss him on the cheek without stopping her work. "You have nice day?" She has a distracted smile in her eyes.

"Yeah, it was okay. When are you coming home?"

She stops for a moment and rolls her neck around to loosen it. "Not much soon."

Ng is silent.

"I know, I know. You get something for dinner?" She pulls her purse from under the workbench. "Here is ten dollar. Get nice chicken or something. I bring home video, and we watch later, okay?"

"Sure, fine. But something in English, please?"

Soo wrinkles her eyes. She prefers videos in Vietnamese, especially ones about Vietnam—no matter how bad or old the film, or how objectionable the politics.

"Something funny," Ng insists.

"Okay, then you no buy Mexican food."

"All right," Ng relents. "Deal."

Ng stops at the store downstairs and buys a roasted chicken from the window. His mother will make meals from it for the next five or six days, stir fries, soups, using everything, even the feet, which are still attached. The thought of it makes him hungry. Despite the deal he has just made with his mother, he walks four blocks to a taco stand and scarfs two beef tacos. It comforts him the way his mother's cooking never has. Am I part Mexican, too? He wonders, and the thought makes him laugh.

February

Tuesday the 1st

Lake Shore Drive's abrupt swan dive into the intersection of Hollywood and Sheridan always strikes Tyler Kovacs as a melancholy event. The end of speed and bright stretches of lakefront, the beginning of congestion and shadows. His hands tighten on the steering wheel as he turns off the Drive and heads up the Sheridan Road bottleneck to Rogers Park.

As he nears Ellen's apartment, he starts to feel claustrophobic. The streets aren't wide enough. His car feels obvious and loud among the four-cylinder rice wagons and listing old Chevys with grime-clogged Cleveland eights.

Ellen's building is Tyler's nightmare image of a tenement. Peeling paint and powdery mortar. The courtyard is piled high with snow, dirty and trampled every which way. A fallen birdbath rests among long-dead, snow-hooded marigolds. Why would Ellen want to live here? It's probably full of drug dealers and convenience-store clerks. A last stop before homelessness or prison. For this she refused his offer to buy her a condo in River City? He steps gingerly across the slick walkways, imagining just how much money he'll demand from the landlord after he breaks his ankle on the steps.

He pushes a calfskinned finger against the bell.

"Hello?" Ellen's voice in the speaker garbled and staticky.

"It's Dad." Tyler places his hand on the door, waiting for the entry buzzer. Nothing happens. Don't get angry, he thinks. He takes a deep breath and rings again, jamming the button down hard. She can't hide from me. I've indulged her all I can. That's it. Her transcript is the last straw.

The lock finally buzzes, and Tyler pushes the door open more forcefully than necessary. The carpet on the stairs is rank.

"Hi, Dad." Ellen opens the door looking sweet and flushed in a robe, her hair wet. "I was just in the shower."

Tyler reddens slightly, feeling foolish. "Sorry I didn't call first. I was up this way."

"Come on in. Have a seat." She rubs a towel across her shower-darkened red hair.

He sees the rumpled bed through a doorway. Was she just getting up? At this hour?

She leads him into the living room. The radiator is hissing fiercely. The windows are sheened with ice. "So what's up?"

"I was in the area, decided to stop by." He fumbles a paper from his suit pocket. "This came today."

Ellen looks at the transcript in her father's hand. A death warrant. Finis. Roll credits. She sits quickly, her knees weak. "Dad, I can explain."

"I don't think so. Not anymore." Agitated, he stands and takes a few uncertain steps. He can't pace, doesn't belong here, doesn't know his way around. "Ellen, it's—" he takes a breath, "time you got a job."

She flinches as the sentence comes out and crumples into a slack lump at its conclusion. "Daddy," she whispers. "Don't." Her pale neck, the thin shoulders.

"You said this semester would be different. It was your promise that got broken, not mine." He knew it would happen, but it he still wasn't prepared for the welling tears, how she abandons herself to the instant despair. "You think I like this? I want to support you, but how can I when you don't take it seriously?"

"I can't, I *can't* stop now. I need one more chance. I had some personal stuff. And the teacher doesn't support me. No one does." She falls into the cushions.

Tyler finds himself, still in coat and gloves, kneeling on the floor beside his daughter, stroking her head. He sighs.

"Okay, baby, let's talk. We need to make some changes, right? We can talk this through." How does this happen? Why is it his talks with Ellen always end up like this? Ellen's tears and mucus darken the sofa pillow. He pulls out his handkerchief wondering, What personal stuff?

Thursday the 3rd

Nathan keeps on buying flowers for no specific reason. Just because. For the sake of beauty. Sure, he likes the flower girl, with her nose piercing and cynical wordplay T-shirts. She smiles when he walks in and, along with the intrinsic value of the flowers, it seems like a good enough reason to stop by, especially after a lousy day like today.

So, women affect him. He may be gay, but he's not dead. The flower girl leaned over in that bowling shirt, reaching for a sheet of butcher paper, and yes, his eyes wandered and he saw the little peeping nipple, pink and feisty. There's a reason it haunts him. But he'd never. He was with plenty of women before Robin came along; there's still a well-trained part of him that responds. But things are different now. If Robin only understood that.

For some reason, Nathan's stepmother Maddy calls him at work, never at home. As though there is some kind of understanding that their conversations would be easier out of Robin's earshot. But she doesn't know anything. How could she?

"Nathan, sweetie, how are you?" Maddy is only five years older than Nathan and relishes her role as the matriarch, planning events, negotiating the uneasy ground Nathan and his father had staked out as their DMZ after his parents' divorce.

"Real busy," Nathan says abruptly. "What's up? How's Dad?"

"He's fine. Well, actually, he's still put out that you didn't come home for Christmas."

"Still?"

"He just loves you so much, Nathan. He feels like you've been distant lately."

"Is that why you're calling?"

"In a way, yes. He didn't think he could ask you for a favor, so I decided to ask for him."

"What favor?"

"His Uncle Peter—the priest, you remember him, I'm sure—is coming to Chicago for a few weeks, and your father thought he should stay with family rather than at some priest's dormitory."

"Uncle Peter?" Nathan laughs involuntarily. "Are you kidding?"

"Of course not. Why is that funny?"

Nathan strangles on all the reasons why this is funny, but not ha-ha funny. Any family visit would pose a problem, but Uncle Peter—a scolding, deeply conservative presence since Nathan's childhood? Uncle Peter and Robin in the same house? It's too ridiculous for words. Nathan often thought Uncle Peter would have been happier as a fire-breathing Southern Baptist minister—or a Moral Majority paratrooper—if he hadn't been raised in the Church. He was an interesting nature versus nurture case. But one best studied from a safe distance, not as a houseguest.

"I'm sorry," he stammers at last. "I just don't think that would be such a good idea."

A beat of silence. "That's what your father thought you'd say. It's all right. I'm sorry to bother you."

"Wait, Maddy. I'll think about it, okay? Let me talk to my roommate."

"Why do you always say roommate? Just say Robin. I know who he is."

"Right. Okay. Let me talk to him about it."

"He won't mind, why should he mind?"

He won't mind, thinks Nathan. He'll try to talk me into it.

If you look at it a certain way, thinks Robin, you bring flowers home to watch them die. He pours the foul vase water into the sink. We're like a hospice for periwinkles cut off in their prime. We make their final days comfortable. He scrubs out the vase. The softened flowers with their rotted stems crumpled in the trash.

At first it was fun and nice when he thought they were for him. But now that he knows Nathan's just crushing on the flower girl, every pretty bundle that he brings home makes Robin say something snide, like: "And how's Courtney Love today?" Or: "What quoth her shirt today? 'Love is a many splintered thing?'" I mean, is he or isn't he? Does he think the closet is a halfway house? It's not Robin's best side, jealousy. But what's worse is how Nathan pretends he's not, and takes the opportunity to say, "Today she was wearing a bowling shirt with the name Rocco stitched over the pocket." Or,

"She was wearing a magic eight-ball earring and I asked it if you were going to be testy when I got home and the answer was, 'Bet on it.'"

"Never fault the magic eight-ball for brute honesty," was all Robin could say.

As Nathan expected, Robin was in favor of Uncle Peter's visit, knowing full well that the façade Nathan kept up for his family would crumble. But this isn't the way to do it. How can he explain it to Robin, who sees every hesitation as a betrayal? Nathan left his office and wandered out into the galleries, wondering why he had bothered to go through the motions of considering the visit. Guilt, maybe? The nice thing about working in a museum is that there are hundreds of small, dim rooms where you can stand in front of a painting and people will leave you alone with your thoughts. Even when your thoughts aren't on Monet's brushwork, but on how to keep your lover from welcoming your hellfire-minded uncle the priest into your home. Robin doesn't understand it would be a fox invited into the henhouse by the chickens. He thinks it's all about my un-out-ness. But it's not that simple.

He'll probably bring flowers tonight, too. After the phone-fight over Uncle Peter. Bring him on, thinks Robin. Let the cat out of the closet. Wear that triangle shirt I bought you for the gays-in-the-military party. There's more to this than just fucking me. And you've got to stop making women want to screw you. Get over it: you're gay.

The speech Robin'll never make. At least he thinks he won't. He didn't want to be Nathan's first, and he knows he should have listened to that little voice. But that voice didn't have anything to say when I saw his bare ass for the first time. Whoops, there's the door.

"Darling, you brought flowers. How—*sweet*."

Wednesday the 9th

Since the first episode, Florence has gotten used to the pain she calls the needle. The needle comes at odd times, washing out everything in her mind like a light turned on too bright to comprehend. Since it tends to come in the afternoon, she takes long naps after lunch. But still the needle finds her reading the newspaper or chopping lettuce in the kitchen. You can't sleep forever. She believes the needle is a sign from god, from whom she has kept a suspicious distance since Arnie's death. And god is saying, "change."

Since Alphonse brought her the replacement grapefruit, the receipt of mail has risen to the status of a mixed blessing. Now Florence waits in the lobby with a thermos of tea or hot chocolate and chats with him as he tosses envelopes into the mail slots.

"Mornin', Miz Finkel," he always says.

"Good morning, Alphonse," she'll say, and make a sympathetic remark about the brutal weather. "It is so dreadfully cold today." Or, "I'll get after Potamkin to make sure the walkway is clear for you tomorrow."

The sourness undercutting the pleasure of Alphonse's visits is the mail itself. Almost daily a new piece of mail arrives for Arnie. Magazines aimed at his Republican heart. Five-dollar burial insurance policies. "Act now," shout the envelopes, "Don't delay."

Arnie wouldn't have delayed. He took junk mail seriously. He stacked it on his desk and every evening read through the letters from the presidents, appeals from the council heads, alarms from the conservative think tanks. Often he sent them checks. Florence often wonders how much money went out in those prepaid envelopes and never generated a magazine or stock share or bowl of rice in a developing country.

I've got the checkbook all to myself, she thinks. And nothing at all to do with it. She receives no solicitations. She never paid by name for anything in her life. Until the funeral.

In the evening she goes to Sophia's Diner and has a Greek salad and chicken soup in a front corner booth. Mr. Kanakes waits on her himself. She feels herself relax as she blows on the hot soup in her spoon.

That nice Ellen is at the counter, sipping coffee and reading a book. She wants to make movies, the sweet thing. And so pretty!

"You should be in *front* of the camera, dear," Florence says. "Look at your hair. There hasn't been a decent redhead since Rita Hayworth."

Ellen blushes brightly. "No way. I would die first. Besides, I want to say things I don't know how I would say in front of the camera."

"I'm sure you have some very interesting things to say."

Ellen shrugs.

"I know you must love beauty, you're always looking across the street at the flowers."

Ellen coughs. "Well, yeah. Who doesn't love beauty?"

Arnie taps Florence on the shoulder. "Why come to a Greek for chicken soup? There's a kosher deli not one block away from here." Arnie's bright eyes are wrinkled with mischief. "Arnie?" Florence turns with the soup spoon raised to her lips.

"Florence?" Ellen says.

Blood roars in Florence's ears and everything grows white.

She feels herself being tugged at, and hears voices speaking softly, kindly. She is lowered, blinking, onto the cushioned bench seat. Mr. Kanakes and Ellen look into her face and soothing sounds emerge from their mouths. She looks around. No Arnie. Well, of course not.

"I'm fine. Really. Just. A glass of water."

There is nowhere for her sudden sadness to go. She looks up at Mr. Kanakes, whose image begins to wobble in the swell of tears. "I'm just an old woman."

"You go ahead and cry," he says, patting her arm. As if she had a choice in the matter.

Tuesday the 15th

He tries to make last night romantic for Eloise, and she spends half of it shouting and the other half crying. A dozen tulips plucked bare as she sat sobbing about Giselle and how Alphonse doesn't care enough to spend all day calling her name up and down every street in Chicago.

He swallowed so many words he started to feel sick. But maybe it's just fish sticks on Valentine's Day that makes his stomach turn. Holidays, when your life is full of holes, have a way of blowing up on you. The worst part is Tony hiding in his bedroom, afraid of them fighting. He thinks the day is all candy and fun, exchanging those cartoon cards full of "Buzz-Buzz, Bee My Valentine!" and "I'm Not Lion, You're the Cat's Meow!" He doesn't understand that holidays are when you find out just how far short of happiness you've fallen.

A whole entire box of chocolates scattered in the dirty snow, two halves of the heart-shaped box lying in separate bushes. Crazy woman.

Alphonse feels like a badly wrapped package stuck into a mailbox and fed into the post office every morning. He hates the endless bustle, moving things around, breaking big piles into little piles and sorting the little piles back into big piles. The whole building churns and churns and nothing ever changes and nothing ever happens.

Elvin calls it the belly of the beast.

Alphonse replies, "You know what comes out of a belly, don't you? Gas and turds."

Elvin looks hurt and says, "It's just an expression. Maybe you should think of us as blood, like, moving oxygen where it does some good."

Alphonse picks up a handful of shampoo samples in plastic envelopes. "This ain't no oxygen, Elvin. This is crap."

"What about the other stuff, love letters, checks—grapefruit?"

Alphonse smirks. "About two percent of my load. Make that one pound of the fifty on my back."

"I'm your friend, Alph, and even I don't like your attitude. You got one fan in that old lady, but there are complaints, too."

Alphonse senses the warning. "So?"

"So go do something else if this makes you so unhappy."

"Right, throw away fifteen years civil-servant tenure, pension and all that."

"Other jobs have pensions. And more perks maybe."

"Do I look like a man about to get a private parking space for his company Lexus?"

Elvin shakes his head. "Things don't change just 'cause you aren't happy, Alph. Something'll give way, and it won't be the U.S. Postal Service."

A late snow is falling, taking the city by surprise. The salt trucks emerge in a panic. They slur into traffic and then slow to a crawl, spraying out fantails of dirty crystals. Trapped behind one, Alphonse watches salt pellets ping off the truck's grill. He imagines driving his route, throwing the mail out the window like a paperboy. Old men in bathrobes shaking their fists at him as they fish their *Reader's Digests* out of the snow.

Since he can't roll his cart across the ice-rutted sidewalks, Alphonse is forced to use his blue canvas mailbag.

Third Pottery Barn catalogue this week. By one o'clock his back feels knotted and lumpy, like it's been implanted with baseballs. He starts leaving the mail in unsorted piles in the high-rise lobbies. He looks at the half-full pouch. Fat, wet flakes pat his cheeks like moist baby hands. Close enough. I'll get the rest tomorrow.

Back in the post office parking lot, he looks around. No one. He dumps the last of his deliveries in the trunk of his car. The envelopes slip across others from the week before and the week before that. The accumulation of undelivered items stops him for a moment. He makes a mental note to sort through it. Still, it's a good thing he'd made room by dumping that box of Lillian Vernon catalogues behind a taco stand in Pilsen last week.

He drives slowly toward home, fishtailing around more plows and salt trucks. Finding himself on Jeffrey Avenue, and with a little time to kill, Alphonse turns west on 73rd Street. After a few minutes, he turns south again and after a few blocks parks in front of the brick three-flat with a weather-worn porch and cockeyed wooden steps. He is glad to see they've put sheet plastic over the windows and crammed socks into the gaps in the window frames. He sits and watches no lights come on in the early darkness. He wonders if the water is still on.

Wish I had enough control to go up to the door and ask to see her. Probably do more harm than good.

The light from the porch casts a blond pool onto the snow in the yard. He can make out the gothic X of Tony's White Sox coat before he can see the shape of his son, obscured in the shadows of another snow fort. He loves making forts. Wants to build fires, eat dinner, sleep in them.

"No, son, you can't spend the night out here." Alph tried to hide the tiny smile on his lips.

"But Dad, the Eskimos do it. They live in igloos all year!"

"Eskimos don't live in Chicago."

"But it's even colder at the North Pole, and they don't freeze."

"Tell you what. You draw up the plans for an igloo, and maybe I'll help you build one good enough to live in."

Tony had run for paper and pen. Now, it appears that Tony is ready to make his dream igloo a reality.

He comes running across the yard. "I made a plan, Dad! If you help me, we can build an igloo tonight." The boy's eyes are bright and the breath clouds around him like an aura of energy.

"Well, I don't know if we can finish it all tonight, but we can make a good start before dinner." Alphonse looks up and sees Eloise's silhouette at the living room window.

They've got one child left, and he isn't going to make any mistakes this time. A promise that would be easier to keep if he knew exactly what had gone wrong the first time.

He waves at Eloise, and then sits down and starts packing the heavy snow between his two gloved hands.

Friday the 18th

Megan hits the snooze and spoons herself against Ellen's chilly bottom. She moves her hands up and down Ellen's body, teasing the little muscles of her abdomen and the ticklish hairs below. Ellen lies inert as though still mired in dreams.

"You know it's been a long time," Megan whispers, cupping Ellen's breasts. "Are you still bummed about your grades?"

Ellen turns away from Megan and twists herself tightly into the blanket.

Megan rises on one elbow. "Come on, you know, it isn't like your whole life is over. You don't need your dad's money or his approval."

"Wrong. I need his money. I can't pay the rent, much less buy film or studio time."

"Well, working wouldn't be the worst thing that could happen."

The blanket twists tighter, a woolen cocoon. "Speaking of jobs, aren't you late?"

"Whatever, Daddy's Girl. Don't watch too much Oprah today." Megan crawls across Ellen and begins tossing clothes around, picking out her underwear and socks from the tangle on the floor.

Watching TV would be preferable to what Ellen must do today, which is to meet with the dean of the college about her falling grades. She wants to talk to Megan about it, but there's so much tension. They're on each other's nerves all the time. Not like when they first met and everyday was talk and sex, talk and sex. She can still remember the Megan that had overwhelmed her—the fully out, opinionated, horny, and let's not forget beautiful social worker who had thrown herself at Ellen. The come-on was full bore, like everything Megan did. Megan devoured the world, and Ellen loved seeing her crack it between her jaws. Part of her believed that being with Megan would help her shed her ambivalent, uncertain self and attain a little of Megan's passion. But Ellen now knows that passion has a flip side.

She opens one eye to see Megan reduced to a curtain of long black hair and a white, narrow-hipped rump rummaging on the floor. When Megan stands up and looks toward the bed, Ellen quickly closes her eye.

Megan storms out of the room. In the bathroom she blinks back the sting of tears. Adrenaline tingles in her hands. Blindly she grabs her hairbrush and throws it against the tiled shower wall. The handle snaps off and caroms against the sink. The brush head clatters on the bottom of the tub and comes to rest under the leaky faucet like a fat, bristled caterpillar.

Ellen sits up on creaking springs. "What was that?"

"Nothing. I dropped my brush." She hears Ellen huff back on the bed. "Well, I didn't hit you, did I?" Megan shouts.

Later that morning, Megan sits at her desk and remembers last April, during their first fight, when she slapped Ellen so hard it knocked her to the floor. Ellen had picked herself up and walked through the kitchen and out the back door. It was a late spring with black snow still crusting the gutters, and Ellen walked out without shoes or jacket. After the door slammed, Megan had stood, holding her throbbing hand, shocked by the shape her anger had taken. She found Ellen blocks away, sitting beside a basketball court. Her socks black with mud.

Ellen was hugging her knees, tears coursing down her face. Megan sat down and held her. There was nothing she could say. They rocked together, sobbing. Ellen had forgiven her, but the slap still hummed between them, dampening the good moments and sharpening the bad ones.

"I wish it didn't come down to something as trite as grades," Dean Hollis, says, "but there you are."

Yes, here she is. Out of school, with no job, and worse, the humiliation of telling her parents that all the slack they'd cut her had run into one final barrier that wouldn't budge. It could be a funny scene, if it were in a movie. But Ellen finds it hard to laugh. Her father had succumbed to her pleading and agreed to pay for one more semester of classes. Only the school wasn't quite so generous. How fucking ironic.

"But I'm so close with this project," Ellen moans. "Can't I keep my studio privileges? At least for this semester?"

"You'd have to finish your incompletes first," Hollis says. "I'm very sorry."

The finality of his polite apology, if you can call it that, stings her. "Don't you care that I'm one of the few students here who has actual talent?"

He pauses. "Of course I care," the Dean says evenly. "Do you?"

Ellen cleans out her locker, wishing she had someone to talk to besides Megan. But there is no one else. Maybe she shouldn't have been so hard on her this morning. Only Megan doesn't make it easy to be nice. Nothing runs a simple path with her—it's almost as though if the waves aren't slopping over the bow of their boat, they won't be moving forward.

Full of her books and cassettes, Ellen's backpack weighs about thirty pounds. She considers apologizing to Hollis for her outburst, but mostly so he can say something hopeful like see you next term. Never mind.

Driving back from work, Megan pulls off the expressway and uses the pay phone outside a gas station. Ellen isn't home, so she leaves a long, rambling message, nervously jingling coins in her hand. She has to call twice to get it all in. As she talks Megan looks down on the taillights of the cars gathering like radiant blood cells being sucked into the heart of the city.

Hi it's me I wish you were home. I wanted to say I'm really really sorry about this morning. When you shut me out I feel like this tiny speck floating off into space that you're not even noticing get smaller and smaller. Maybe that's okay. I don't think it really is though. But me saying that about Oprah was mean and I don't know why my anger, why I get so angry. I know things are—

The machine clicks and then a second message begins.

Oops. Ran out of time. I know things are bad for you right now but I don't know what to do, what you want, what you need, or if I can even give you that. I feel pretty shitty about everything and my hair's a mess 'cause I broke my brush and then I didn't say goodbye when I left which is just like hanging up on someone god I'm running out of time loveyoubye.

Ellen stands over the answering machine flooded with relief that she didn't have to make the first move. And how could you help but like such a terrible apology? She picks up the phone and dials.

Monday the 21st

Alice stretches like a pleased cat. She and Brad have made love in the predawn, bathed in the space heater's muzzy light. Such moments were common before he moved down to South Loop. But it's like when he moved farther away, he grew away, too. He has time for nothing but Lather Rinse Repeat. She finds herself resenting that she helped him put the group together. But he was so earnest and so handsome, she would have been a groupie if not a bandmate. And the unflattering comparison, as it occurs to her, is a little too close for comfort.

"You know," says Brad, tracing the orangey crescent of heater glow along Alice's ribcage with a callused finger, "we should get matching tattoos."

"Oh yeah? What kind?" asks Alice, sleepily.

"I don't know. Something passionate or mystical."

"Like what?"

"A yin-yang?"

Alice laughs deep in her belly.

"Okay, maybe something decorative. A braided ankle design, something sort of Celtic, Miss O'Leary."

"Celtic?" Her limbs are rubber. She can barely focus on his voice, but whatever he says sounds fine. "You should let me be on top more often."

"Oh, did you like that?" he asks in mock surprise.

"Well," she rolls over to meet Brad nose to nose. "It was when you did that, um, thing with your finger?" She grins. "Where'd you learn that?"

"In de jongle," he laughs and disappears beneath the sheets. She feels teeth on her belly. Maybe things will be all right after all. They are partners, after all, in work, in the band, in love. She still melts when he leans toward the mike with his eyes closed, as if he's going in for a kiss. That's his charisma. She holds his head against her as his bites become kisses and floods her with sleepy sexiness that disengages her mind from further coherent thought.

"Do we have time before work?" says Brad's muffled voice.

"Mmmm," says Alice. "What work?"

He mentions the tattoo again after the morning rush.

"You're serious?" says Alice, kneeling among a disarray of fleshy tulips in the window. She catches Mr. Kanakes's eye and waves.

"Well, yeah, why not?" Brad shoves a water bucket into the middle of the café tables.

First the nose ring and now this. "Why tattoos all the sudden?"

"It's not all the sudden, I've always liked them. Just seems like—" He wrings dirty water from his rag. "Look good on you."

"They hurt, you know. And you have them forever. For-ever, Brad. Not a nose ring you can pull out."

"But if we both get one?"

Alice bristles. "It's more permanent than marriage, Brad. Are you sure you're ready for the commitment?"

"Whoa. Never mind." Brad scrubs a table extra hard. "Forget it."

"I'm sorry," Alice says, immediately regretting her sharp tone. "Let me think it over, okay?"

"All right." Brad looks hurt. "I just thought it might be fun."

The phone rings, calling Brad into the back room. Alice looks out into the icy world. The redheaded girl is walking toward the diner. Sunlight turns her glasses into inscrutable blanks. She starts to cross the street toward Urbs, then veers back and enters the diner. Odd bird.

Brad comes back to the counter. He flings a rag into the air and spins around before catching it. "I'm going over to the Fusebox after work. Want to come?"

"Nah. I've got to run some errands. I don't have time to hang."

Brad starts the coffee mill. Alice cuts flower stems with the high whine in her ears. A blue vase full of yellow tulips is close enough to spring for now. She cuts another fleshy tube on the bias. Suddenly, her ears ring with silence.

"By the way," Brad adds casually, "I'm not going there to hang." He makes quotation marks around the last word with his fingers. "Chipper's friend Lori got our tape in there and they liked it." He starts the mill again.

"Say what?" cries Alice, jumping up.

Brad does a jig behind the counter and holds up his thumbs. "It's gig city, baby. Gig fucking city!"

At dusk, Belmont Avenue looks almost glamorous in the dark-blue light burnt through with neon. The sidewalks are crowded with white-collar commuters in tennis shoes and long, belted overcoats. There is brisk trade in ready-made pasta, white boxes of Thai and Indian curries, and pizza slices in wax paper.

Alice and Molly scan sheet after sheet of possible tattoos. One-quarter cartoons, three-quarters motorcycles, women's bodies, and occult symbols.

"I don't see anything that's really me," says Alice.

"I wouldn't rush into this," says Molly. "Not on Brad's account."

"Maybe this daisy—oh my god." Alice grabs Molly's arm and whispers,

"There he is." She points out the front window at two men standing in front of a Swedish restaurant.

"Who?"

"Nathan. The guy who buys flowers I told you about. The tall one."

"Who's the gorgeous thing he's with?"

"I don't know. Let's find out."

They hurry across the street and Alice pretends to have just noticed Nathan.

"Oh, hi!" She blushes gamely.

Nathan startles. "Oh, hey. Hi." He scans the street beyond them helplessly. The four of them stand looking at each other.

The gorgeous thing puts out his hand and says, "You must be Alice."

"How'd you know?" She reaches out and shakes.

"The shirt." His smile is dazzling. "Nathe talks about them all the time."

Alice looks down at her shirt. Through the gap in her coat are the letters OVE IS BIN. "Alice, this is Robin," says Nathan briskly. "Robin, Alice." He keeps his eyes far down the street.

Alice stands frozen a moment before her smile kicks in. "Robin! I'm so pleased to meet you. This is my friend, Molly."

Molly and Robin shake, too, but Nathan's hands stay rooted in his pockets as he stands, half-turned from the rest of them.

"Well," says Nathan. "We were just. On our way."

"Home," Robin interjects. "We were just going home." He hooks Nathan's arm, and they turn away. "Nice to see you!" he calls out over his shoulder.

Alice and Molly watch them walk down the crowded sidewalk.

"God," says Alice, finally. "That's *Robin*? How did I miss that?"

Molly bites a fingernail. "Guess love really is bind."

Saturday the 26th

Robin regards the weekend as a bon vivant's canvas. He measures Saturday morning as the first critical pencil stroke, weighing in his mind the best possible first line that will launch his forty-eight-hour diptych. He makes these calculations while lying on the couch in a striped terrycloth bathrobe, eating a leftover flan and watching Heckle and Jeckle cartoons.

Nathan used to follow Robin's lead, lounging through afternoons, making love, eating Friday night's leftovers as Saturday's brunch. But lately, he's been too restless. This morning he stands with lists, checkbook, scarf, and hat, saying, "I'm going out, I'll grab a bagel, see you at five or so."

Robin looks up from the couch. "What? Just like that you're bolting out the door? I'll come too! What are you doing? What about tonight?"

Nathan squares his shoulders against the assault. "There's too much to do. You just plan tonight. Do whatever you need to do and I'll see you back here later." He sees the hurt look in Robin's eyes and softens his tone. "For cocktails?"

"What's wrong with us going out together?"

"Nothing. Nothing."

Robin jumps from the couch, robe flying behind him. "Five minutes! I'll be ready!"

They compromise. After a late breakfast, they split up—Nathan to the dry cleaners and hardware store, Robin to Treasure Island for staple goods, to Whole Foods for vegetables, and to Devon Avenue for Indian spices. Mixed into this are a wait at the post office, a late video return, a shoe repair, two lattés, a thirty-dollar haircut, a bakery, and a liquor store. The city is a hypermarket and their life a string shopping bag.

Robin returns first. He opens a small tin of caviar and puts a couple of vodka glasses into the freezer. He chops onion and boiled egg and capers.

Then he sits and looks out at the slate-blue lake falling into blackness. To the south, he can see the glowing circle of the Navy Pier Ferris wheel turning slowly.

The end of a weekend day carries a melancholy weight, and Robin lets it filter into his soul. To add further ballast, he imagines his mother in her invalid's bed, and then makes this image wonder where on earth her little Robbie can be? It's time for him to come for dinner. And then he makes her eat strained peaches from a rubberized spoon.

"I'm a lousy son," he says to the air.

Nathan returns grumpy and unloads his packages. It is not until he has put the new picture frames on a table and filled his re-soled shoes with their shoe trees that he notices Robin's inert form on the couch.

"Robin?"

No reply. A vodka glass stands empty on the coffee table. Nathan has seen this before. Left alone, Robin tends to fall into general disrepair.

He sits down and strokes Robin's hair. "You okay?"

Robin turns a bleary, red-rimmed eye at the room in general. "You win. You came home flowerless." His voice is croaky.

"Why is that winning?"

"You avoid compounding my misery with jealousy. For the moment."

Nathan purses his mouth tolerantly. "I like her taste in flowers. That's it."

"Flowers." Robin flips the idea away with a gesture. "She has a crush on you, you know."

"I can't help that," Nathan says quietly.

Robin touches his cheek. "You could try to be less beautiful."

Nathan smiles, recognizing the peace offering. "Let's eat in. I'll cook."

"God, no. I'll cook. You wouldn't know what to make. We're out of *bologna*."

Over dinner, Nathan turns the tables and presses Robin about what happened to his father after the tornado.

"You're always talking about your momma and how you should visit her in the nursing home. What about your dad?"

Robin thinks a moment. Then deliberately: "I am. To my father. What the. Neutron bomb is to. The H-bomb." He sits back with a satisfied smile.

Nathan's eyebrows say, "What?"

"OK." Robin leans forward again with greater energy. "I am to my father...what chicken Vesuvio is to chicken fried steak."

"Let me see," Nathan plays along. "You are to your father...what a Yorkshire terrier is to a Rottweiler?"

"Not exactly. I am to my father what the Cubs are to the White Sox."

"What year?"

"Any year."

"Then you are to your father what Hair Cut 100 is to Abba?"

"Exactly!"

"What Marcel Marceau is to Francois Truffaut?"

"Sure."

"What Abbott is to Costello?"

"You asshole!" Robin's face glows with laughter.

"You didn't answer my question."

"Didn't I? Oh, didn't I really?" Coy, regarding his lover at arm's length, Robin studies the furious blue eyes, freckles, the purposeful, nimble lips.

"Did you?"

"Come to bed."

∞

Sex, thinks Nathan, as he lies next to Robin, still hot where their bodies touch beneath the blankets, tricks you with its recoil. After all that groping toward each other, you realize how separate you remain. If not this together-ness of oddness, then what is there between us? It is a silent question that vibrates in the air like the sonic tone of a muted TV in another room.

He speaks over the hum: "Honesty is the hardest part of living, don't you think? I mean, we have no good way of living with truth." Now that he's said it, it seems to address everything. Too much.

He thinks what he has said will just hang there, unanswered, but finally: "You don't have to live with it. It's out there, like the weather. It just exists."

"Speaking it can be cruel. But to avoid it is always crueler. Self-indulgent. Mean."

"Are we talking about something?"

"That's just it. Everyone always is talking about something by talking about other things. How do we survive ourselves?"

"That's just pretentious."

"You don't agree?"

From under the pillow: "I didn't say I didn't agree."

"Well then."

"Let's have some truth then, Mister Honesty-At-All-Costs."

"Not tonight, please?"

Again, a large, open-ended pause, before at last Nathan adds: "This is how we survive ourselves."

Turning, they accidentally catch each other's eyes and then glance away. They haven't got the stamina to unload all the unspoken they carry between them. The TV hum grows louder. An actual ringing in the ears.

Lying face to face, breathing the exhalations of the sweet familiar mouth, feeling the twitch of fingers as one drops into unconsciousness. And the other quickly follows.

Tuesday the 29th

Sometimes, from his bedroom window, Ng looks east across the Uptown rooftops and imagines that he is in Saigon. Twenty-five years ago, his mother was the age Ng is now. The Saigon experienced by the child Soo Pran, and related to her son as bedtime stories years later, fell to the Viet Cong three years before her family arrived from their failing farm in 1975. It had become, for many country people, a halfway point between the ongoing agony of farming their destroyed, mine-filled land and the more desperate but finite torment of a probably fatal boat ride across the China Sea. He never knew how she had gotten the money for the trip.

She would show him the map of Saigon painted on the wall of the old Pasteur restaurant on Sheridan, before it burned down. "Here is where I live with Uncle Nguyen. I robbed, lose all money over here. We had come way down here, away from harbor police to get on boat."

What she told him of the boat haunts him.

Ng misses that map. He misses visiting his mother at work in the Pasteur kitchen. He loved watching her cook, handling the wok in a cloud of ginger-garlic steam. He liked as well the lovely, shy waitresses who would tease him and bring him little cups of iced coffee. It's all gone. The restaurant re-opened as a far more upscale version of itself further north, on a gentrifying stretch of Broadway. Soo was never called back by the owners. And she never called to ask them for her old position. Now she sits hunched in a dark, fumy room all day, and sometimes all night.

He hears clanging. He goes into the kitchen where the small, sharp-shoulder figure of his mother is hunched in front of the open oven door. He stands and watches, silent, as she turns back to the table and sits down to consume a cup of coffee and a croissant. What does she think about, he wonders.

He raps his knuckles on the door frame. "Did you know more people kill themselves in February?"

"Good morning, Mister Happy," says Soo. Her eyes wrinkle with a smile that her mouth doesn't show. "Why February so good for die?"

"I think it's because you don't get any holidays for like three months. It's dark all the time. In January you can at least remember Christmas. By February, all you want is spring. And it never comes."

"Spring come soon." Soo wipes at the flaky crumbs around her mouth. "You so impatient. Don't think about kill you self," she says, knowing very well her son hasn't that kind of despair.

Ng pours himself a cup of coffee and creams and sugars it heavily. "Don't worry, Ma. You home tonight?"

"Maybe late. Benny say we got one day big order basketball jersey." She glances at the wall clock. "You be late."

"I'm going," Ng says, swigging down the sweet coffee. "I'll see you later."

He walks to school in darkness and waits by the door until the janitor unlocks it. Then he sits in the empty cafeteria, listening to the building come awake and fill with people. He sits quietly through the first two periods, until he is forced to switch rooms for art class. He feels he is entering a minefield. The streets of Saigon, so his mother tells him, were crowded with crippled villagers from the countryside—one-legged men on crutches and legless women in hand-built carts pushing themselves with blocks of wood smoothed to fit their hands. Tiny oars for little boats that went nowhere fast.

Ng goes everywhere fast, walking close to the walls, eyes down, watching his feet. He has mapped out a route of minimal danger, but this doesn't prevent trouble once or twice a week. Sometimes, like last week, he cuts out early. But then he misses his favorite class, art. He's not so lucky today. Today he steps down the wrong corridor and feels a slap on the back of his head. He turns to see Ivan Pak. With five of his gang glowering behind him.

"Hey, come on, Little Too Good. We going to my office." Ivan's black eyes glisten. Ng feels ill and pulls back, hunching down into his jacket.

Ivan has selected Ng to hate out of the whole school population. It was like Ng somehow drew Ivan to him, like a magnet. Opposites attract. Ivan is new in the country and has a feral anger that takes unpredictable forms. On New Year's Eve, it was Ivan's roaming terror of the streets that sent Ng scurrying down to the Lincoln Park diner—a lighted, safe place to hide.

"Come on." Ivan pulls Ng by his coat front down the stairs.

The boy's bathroom on the basement floor is the gang's office. It is clean, since no one else will go there. It is also cold, with the transom windows cranked open, and the garbage barrel contains only empty plastic bags, soda cans, and the occasional wad of bloody paper towels. The boys line up with their backs against the sinks, arms crossed over their jackets appliquéd with a tacky gold dragon. Ng looks in the mirror at the innocent, vulnerable backs of their heads, and then at their hard eyes.

"It time you become part of us," says Ivan. "We test you."

Ng swallows. "I'm not interested, Ivan."

Ivan places his palm across Ng's face and drives his head against the tile wall. Ng gasps involuntarily as streaks of pain shatter the inside of his skull.

"I not asking," Ivan says bluntly.

Through stars and bleary eyes, Ng sees the mirror image of himself standing behind Ivan's reflected head. He imagines this reflection coming up behind Ivan and lacing mighty fingers around his throat.

"You take this package." Ivan tosses him a small rectangle wrapped in plastic. "We tell you where."

Ng touches the back of his head and feels a patch of blood matting down his hair. The package in his hands looks benign, innocent.

Unsure where to go, Ng returns to the diner where he had lingered on New Year's Eve. He feels awkward about returning when the door jingles, announcing him.

The owner's bushy eyebrows leap up in surprise. "Hello, my friend! I thought I'd seen the last of you."

Ng blushes and dips his head. "Thank you. I meant to come before. But—"

"That's okay," says Elias, clapping him on the shoulder. "You're welcome here anytime. Do you want something to eat?"

Ng hesitates. "Maybe a Coke?" He glances at the cash register. "You put up my drawing." He can barely remember drawing the Superman sketch. It was a doodle, and the old man kept it?

Elias laughs. "How could I resist showing everyone my secret identity?" He pauses, watching Ng's reaction. "Do you mind?"

Ng shakes his head. "No. It's just—strange to see it out in public, is all."

"Hey." Elias's eyebrows bunch together. "Shouldn't you be in school?"

Ng drops onto a stool at the counter. "School was a little too much for me today."

"Test? Or something else?"

"Long story."

The phone rings. "I'd like to hear it," Elias says. "Just a moment." He goes over to pick up the phone. The boy watches as Elias talks, eyebrows bunching and unbunching. He watches the corners of Elias's mouth turn down and, embarrassed, Ng picks up a menu and scans the several pages quickly. Breakfast Served All Day. Mile High Corned Beef. Greek Salad. The Francheezie. Souvlaki. Butt Steak. Denver Omelet.

Elias comes over and sets a glass of Coke on the counter. "My daughter, Sophia. Canceling her visit for Easter."

Ng rips the end from the straw's paper sleeve and blows it free. It describes a broad arc toward the ceiling before plunging behind the booth.

"I haven't seen her for over a year. Any excuse, she cancels. Too much work. Bad weather. My granddaughter—Elana—coughs, they stay home."

Ng tries to look sympathetic, thinking that it was a mistake to come back here. It is so complicated to make friends, getting close enough to strangers to see the troubles they have.

Plus, this is not the right time to ask him for a Mexican omelet. He makes an excuse and leaves quickly.

The storefront windows of Stimpy's Strip Shop are like a forcefield barely containing the leaping figures of the X-Men, Spider-Man, and the Silver Surfer. Their sculpted figures rage against the glass in bold colors. Ng hurries toward their loud voices, their certainty, their righteous strength.

Stepping inside feels like the first stages of sleep, a time when Ng feels safe enough to let the dreamworld descend and engulf him. He stands inside the door, shaking. Comic books call out from every crowded corner of the shop. The counter girl looks up from her comic and peers at Ng through her hair.

She looks at him curiously. "You okay?"

Ng nods. She is beautiful.

"Leave your backpack at the counter." She looks back down.

Ng wanders along the shelves. He stops at his first loves, the Marvels and DCs with their parallel and alternate and exploding and revived worlds. Spiderman and Batman still leap across high-rise rooftops. Ng picks up a couple of the latest adventures.

Is she really that beautiful?

More and more he has found himself drawn to the back of the store, where the nonheroes and antiheroes reign. He thumbs the thin newsprint looking at unbelievably curvaceous women, drooling and bug-eyed cats, self-lacerating whores, hollow-eyed Holocaust mice. The anger blazing at problems without solutions excites him. He picks up a new issue of the *Acme Novelty Library* and a small, hand-stapled pamphlet, *Globbo's Amazing Nickel Wonder-Lust,* and goes to the counter. He slips the magazines across the glass and clears his throat.

"You got a bathroom?"

She looks up again. "Not for customers, sorry."

Yes, she is that beautiful.

"Please? I'm not feeling well."

The beautiful girl pops her gum and sighs. She points to the curtain at the back of the store. "On your left. It don't lock."

In the cramped and cold bathroom, Ng takes the package out of his sock.

It is the size of a new gum eraser, but heavier. It appears to be faintly brown through its many layers of plastic wrapping. Before he can reconsider, he drops the parcel in the toilet and flushes. He watches as the vortex of water gargles away the package, and clean water fills the bowl as if nothing ever was there.

He drops his head into his hands. Now he's done it.

March

Thursday the 2nd

Florence leans back against the sofa, looks across her lap and down her legs to her feet. The bunions, the creases, the toes bumpy within the dark double-knitting of her nylons. See how all of the toes are angled toward the invisible tips of her sensible pumps, the daily shoes of her almost sixty adult years, now removed and sitting beside the coffee table. Might as well have been foot-bound like those poor Japanese women. Sore feet. Loneliness. Louise with her harping.

"I heard about that drive-by shooting." Louise is on the cell phone, static sizzling as she claps across the patio in her sandals. Louise thinks everything bad that happens in Chicago occurs within a hundred yards of Florence's apartment.

"That wasn't near here, not that I know of." But a little fear insinuates itself inside Florence's chest just the same.

"That picture in the paper looked just like your neighborhood." There are sounds behind Louise's voice. Splashing, laughter, the tinkle of ice in a glass. Florence feels herself pulled toward the warmth, the bustle.

"Listen, Flo, another unit just opened up down the block, and—"

"Oh, Louise, wait. I think someone's at the door."

"At least come down and visit. We won't tie you up and keep you!" Louise's laugh crackles through the phone.

Suddenly Florence snaps, "Sorry Louise, I have to go," and hangs up the phone. Without a goodbye. One doesn't do such things. But she had to. She'll call back and apologize. Later.

She wants Arnie to come again, tap her on the shoulder like he did the other day. She won't faint this time.

She shakes herself, rises, and goes into the bedroom closet, looking for her paints and brushes. Something to turn her hand to. She painted once, in school. A roomful of girls in pastel smocks looking at a model—a hard, booze-faced woman, nude and unashamed. It was part of being an Artist not to be shocked by the brazen nakedness and turn it into something soft, round, colorful with the paints. That was before Arnie. It was another life.

A rack inside the closet holds Arnie's hats. She picks up his favorite soft, gray fedora and buries her face inside it. Already his scent has faded. The hat now just smells old and kept. It doesn't make her think of Arnie, his physical presence. His thighs, his gorse hair, his flattened buttocks—his penis. Instead she thinks of giving the hat away. She gets a shopping bag and loads it with several of the musty old hats.

The damp, gusty wind toys with her light shopping bag as Florence walks to the diner. Her face feels tight and swollen, and the wind extra sharp.

She becomes aware of a declamatory voice bouncing off the buildings and the bare, frozen ground. As she nears Broadway, the words become clearer.

"What is inside the word repentance, brothersisters? Look inside it. The Bible is a wondrous lexicon. Repentance! Savor it, brothersisters, let it roll about your tongues and into your hearts. Ask God to reveal and expel the evil that is pent up in your hearts! Oh yes, it is pent up, like hogs wallowing in a pigsty. You, brothersisters, are the gatekeepers. The devil boards his filthy swinish sins with you, and you feed and nurture them."

The rail-thin man is hopping as he releases a torrent of words from a face turned upward to the sky. Florence can hear the propulsion of the man's breath as he exhorts the passersby, his voice rising in timbre.

"Open up that pen, brothersisters. Kick those swine from your heart. Get out the muckrake and shovel out the devil's filthy droppings. Then, brothersisters, get yourself re-pent. Get pent up like a lamb in the corral of God's love. Let him shepherd you. Shed the pen of mud and reap the pen of God's green meadow."

Florence stands listening. She can see the diner from where she stands. She turns away, no longer feeling the wind. Elias would like these hats.

Saturday the 4th

The lone window of the front second floor bedroom in the house on Kimbark consists of a quarter pane of grimy glass. The iron-colored light sieved through that opening falls on Giselle's round and trembling eyelids, drawing her into wakefulness. Her shins are numb from the cold, exposed between her thermal underwear and the tops of three pairs of socks. She is only half covered by the blanket, the rest being wrapped tightly around Jimmy. In half-wakefulness, Giselle stumbles out of the room and down the stairs.

At least she is only fighting with one other person for the covers. Every other bed or couch is at triple or quadruple occupancy. Jimmy commands this vast bed by virtue of paying the house's nominal rent. But not the utilities. There is a kerosene space heater in the living room and people are crowded around it, lying everywhere, as though knocked flat by a bomb. Giselle steps over the bodies without caution. She steps on one or two and they neither mumble nor wake.

In the bathroom she finds the flashlight and slaps it against her palm to strengthen the wavering beam. Roaches scurry away from the light. Her urine spatters onto a clog of toilet paper and she remembers the night in January when she woke up in the park bathroom. The humiliation of it almost drove her home. It still rankles, but she has no energy for anger. Anyway, Jimmy had made it up to her. She got a rhinestone anklet and a sirloin dinner at Shug's. She feels weak, her stomach queasy. She crawls back into bed until the afternoon, when the front door begins to open and close with the day's traffic.

Jimmy takes her out for breakfast. He orders the steak and eggs with hash browns and a side of bacon. Giselle orders oatmeal and wheat toast.

"You okay, baby?" Jimmy says around the wad of steak in his cheek.

"I'm all right. I don't feel too good." She plops the spoon into the bowl. "Maybe I'll just have tea."

Jimmy cleans his plate, wiping up the egg yolk with a buttery English muffin. He wolfs the bacon down as a dessert and smacks his lips happily. "Man, I feel good."

Giselle is quiet.

"Damn, you are no fun today. Maybe I'll put you back in bed."

She looks up and forces a smile. "Take me for a ride by the lake."

"You got it." He grins, and his thin moustache almost disappears as his lip curls up to reveal his gleaming teeth. "A-One Limo at your service."

The lake is mostly water again, with only a rime of ice along the shore and a few stubborn chunks still bobbing in the harbors. Jimmy drives his convertible LeBaron down past La Rabida hospital. Giselle sees a pale child in a stocking cap being moved carefully from a wheelchair to the backseat of a minivan. She does not like to think about children. Instead she looks at Jimmy's fine profile. Sharp nose, good chin. The nails of his hands are polished and clean on the steering wheel.

Jimmy catches her looking and smiles. A thought crosses his face, and he says, "Hey, baby, you remember Scout?"

Scout is a name that always accompanies something unpleasant involving money.

"He did that Super Bowl thing, right?"

"Yeah, that's him. He's on my ass again about that little bet."

"I thought you paid him."

Jimmy laughs. "I was going to, you know, but there was that thing with Lem and the Bears tickets? It soaked up my free assets."

They are passing the South Shore golf course. She remembers going with her father to pick up lost balls outside the fence. Then he would take her over to the Jackson Park driving range and pound balls way over the trees. She had a little plastic club. He showed her how to hold it, and she can feel his arms alongside hers, and her fingers all tangled up on the handle, and hear her father laughing.

"So," Jimmy continues, "it's just I have this liquidity problem."

"Yeah, so?"

"So?" Jimmy wrings the steering wheel in his hands. "So you want to keep sleeping in my house? You eat and sleep and snort. What you contribute?"

"I fuck." A fatigue settles over Giselle's eyes. "That's my little contribution."

"Yeah, well, you did. And you ain't the only one who could provide that service."

"Go get yourself a whore, then." She almost yawns.

Jimmy jerks the car to the side of the road and slams on the brakes. He looks straight at Giselle and says, "I already got me one."

Where is my anger? She sees his hand coming at her. Why don't I care?

The sharp sting of his palm feels almost good, like a clear, resolute wakefulness that she hasn't felt in a long time.

As they get near the club, Jimmy removes his hand from Giselle's shoulders and shifts so that her hand slips free of his back jeans pocket. She rubs the side of her nose, where it tingles. She feels cool all over, like she has been rubbed in mint. But the sensation is slipping away.

Neon loops of the Shug's Haven sign lay across Jimmy's sunglasses like cake icing. Giselle's face is still swollen, but her eyes are dry.

"Come on, baby," says Jimmy. "We all right."

"Yeah, fine. Let's go in."

Jimmy yanks open the steel-plated door and steps into the stale-smelling din. Giselle follows, wincing as her pupils flood with darkness.

"Jimmy in the house!" Jimmy opens his short, belted leather coat, and shakes himself all over like a dog let inside from the rain. "Do you feel the love?" he croons.

The other men laugh. Giselle sees over Jimmy's shoulder outstretched hands glinting with gold rings, and faces unsmiling behind sunglasses. "How's business?" she hears.

The only other women in the bar are two waitresses in stretch pants busing tables. Giselle suddenly feels weak. The smell of old beer is like puke.

"Jimmy, I need to sit down," she says behind him.

In reply, Jimmy hooks a finger in her belt loop and pulls her to his side. "Hang on a minute, baby."

The men turn their attention to her. She feels eyes travel up and down her body. She sees teeth flash and a bit of gold.

Jimmy puts his hand on her neck, as if to prevent her from bolting. "As I was saying, the action over Cottage Grove been a little off lately."

As he talks, Jimmy's right hand slides from her neck, down her back, and settled on her ass. His left toys with the chain that connects his wallet to a belt loop.

Giselle's mind wanders. She hasn't been able to focus well lately. Some of these men are her father's age, but they look older. Or even alien, as though they aged at different rates, making them somehow older and younger at once.

Father. It's about time to face him again. Find out how Mom and Tony are doing. Maybe Dad would have a little something set aside, a fifty, a twenty. Something that could get her and Jimmy over the hump. Just this once.

She shivers, and Jimmy pulls her closer.

"Naw," she hears him say, "she just got spring fever, ready for the big wood to sprout leaves."

As the laughter of men washes over her, she imagines calling home, and Eloise answering. Her throat contracts. Why is it that home seems like a place in a story now, and no longer a place where she ever could have possibly lived?

Thursday the 9th

A back can be friendly, an invitation to spoon, or downright hostile, Brad thinks, looking at Alice's thin shoulders pulled tight, the ripple of her spine, the slight impression of her ribs against the skin. A fortress.

A new tension erupted the moment Alice decided to go back home for a visit. For some reason, the impending separation had widened the tiny gaps in their relationship into fissures.

Even before Alice had booked the flight, she was in a full-blown dither. She began to talk in a distracted monotone, and her singing voice was suddenly brittle and full of squeaks. She hadn't been any help in finishing songs, and at work she lost the credit slips for flowers and screwed up coffee orders. Coffee orders!

Brad had chewed her out when the second flavored cappuccino of the day came back, and now he wonders whether it was that or the impending trip that accounts for the iceberg that has moved into his bed for the last two nights. Sure, Alice doesn't have the best relationship with her mother, but who does? He can't figure her out.

He looks over at the mute blank oval of Alice's back. In response, he turns to his side of the bed and makes sure that neither his heels nor his ass makes contact with Alice's. It is small satisfaction.

"My flight's supposedly on time," says Alice, hanging up the phone. They are her first words of the morning. "I'd better get going." Alice checks her coin purse for tokens.

"Why don't you just take a cab?"

"Why should I? The el's easy."

Brad sniffs. "If you like sitting with homeless people for hours."

"What's with you? You've been a jerk for the last couple of days."

"What?"

"If you don't want me to go, just say so."

"You're the one who's been so crabby lately."

Alice looks at her watch. "Listen, I don't have time to fight right now."

"Did I ever say I didn't want you to go? Of course go. Why not?"

Alice flicks her nose ring, thinking. Oh, never mind. When she notices what she is doing, she slaps her hands down into her lap and glares out the window.

Alice rides the blue line out and out to O'Hare. How can the city go on like this for so many miles? Malt liquor billboards in English and Spanish, tarpaper shingles, back porches, and fire escapes rattle past.

The el goes underground and comes up in the middle of the Kennedy Expressway, and then Alice feels herself hardening, the dread locking her bones into rigid defensive postures. Let's see, nose ring, a non-job job, raunchy loud songs, messy apartment, unreliable boyfriend with stringy hair. How many reasons for Mom to go apeshit?

This is so typical. Disappointing daughter, frustrated mother. Why do I hate more than anything that this is so typical?

Everyone is late for rehearsal. Brad sits on an amp, plucking at his guitar and getting angry.

The Fusebox in a few short weeks and the band isn't ready. Everyone has other shit going on. Plays, school, some half-assed career thing. And Alice with her trip. It's pissing him off.

Molly staggers in, carrying her bike, followed by Shanklin.

"Sorry," they say in unison. When Brad doesn't reply, they begin to fiddle with their instruments.

"Where's Alice?" asks Molly.

Brad looks up. "Went to see her mom."

"Oh right." Molly grimaces. "Was she so dreading it?"

"How should I know?"

"Of course. Why would I ask you?"

Shanklin rolls his eyes at Molly. He thumbs three booming notes out of his bass. "Can we get started? I have to leave in an hour."

Brad stares a hole through Shanklin.

Chipper struts in with Lori on his arm as though pulling a wagon laden with treasure.

"The Queen of Bookings," Shanklin salaams.

"Hey, girlfriend," Molly sings out.

Lori gives her a high-five.

"Hey, mateys," says Chipper brightly. He still enjoys affecting a droll Charlie Watts demeanor, although he drums more like Keith Moon, Shanklin says. A monkey on meth.

Brad hops to his feet and straps on his guitar. "Let's get started," he snaps.

"Hello to you, too," laughs Lori.

Brad stops and doesn't know where to go with his irritation. "Sorry. Hi," he mumbles.

"Lori gave me a ride, and we got caught in the commuter-zoo stampede," adds Chipper.

"It seems you have to be both insane and belligerent to drive on the expressways at rush hour," quips Lori.

Everyone laughs.

Lori catches Brad's eye and, for a moment, it seems to Brad that Lori twinkles at him. Not a wink, a twinkle. However she manages the effect, it is mesmerizing.

"Hey, Brad!" Lori is close behind him. Her breath is on his neck, washing him in mint gum and patchouli. "I was going to hang out at the Rainbo later," she whispers. "If you're free."

Brad makes a quick calculation. If Alice needs space for her issues, he can have some, too, right? "Sure, what time?"

"About ten?" Her smoky voice is conspiratorial. He feels her hand brush the small of his back. "See you."

Brad feels a slight erection rising. How is it that Lori behind him is more inviting than Alice in front of him?

Alice hangs up the phone after twenty rings. She feels like a stalker. But she can't help calling just one more time. She needs to talk to him, lonely here in her mother's house at night. It's after midnight. Where could he be?

Sunday the 12th

As she pulls Megan's car into the semicircular gravel driveway of her parents' house, Ellen feels the familiar erotic tingle of being an unsupervised adolescent alone in the house on her parents' opera nights. Those nights were like Christmas Eves on which the giant mysterious package marked Sex was shaken and peeked into and then opened.

She walks toward the house, her steps echoing loudly. The dark windows reflect trees and grass whispering in the silence far from the city. There's a calm in the secluded yard that she never noticed until she'd moved away.

The kitchen resounds with silence. She remembers leaning against the butcher block island under the canopy of copper pans, waiting in the kitchen for Jamie Hagel to ride his bike over after lying to his parents. She was what, fourteen? And nauseous, her hands almost too weak to pour out the vodka filched from the wet-bar. The highball glass, etched with golf clubs, rattled against her teeth, and the alcohol burned in her throat. Yet when Jamie arrived, instead of vomiting, Ellen led him to her room.

Now she stands in that room remembering how wild she felt, as light-headed as when she puffed her first cigarette. Only, when their thin, naked bodies were on the bed, all knees and goosebumps, her excitement devolved into a disembodied inventory of sensations. Is that his smell? Does he think my boobs are impervious to pain? Is he whimpering? Why did the sight of his blunt and searching cock make her feel like laughing? So different from when she and her first girlfriend had gone home that night from Paris Dance. Which was like, oh, of course.

Ellen stands on her little princess desk chair and pulls down three shoe boxes from a shelf in the closet. She lays them on the bed and takes a deep breath. Maybe I *am* crazy, she thinks. Then Megan and I are perfect for each other.

A photo lies on top inside the first box: Grampa Kovacs in his Adirondack chair in the back yard of his Lake Forest mansion, holding on his lap an earnest ten-year-old Ellen who is patiently explaining why she has decided to become a famous film director.

In the superior and indulgent way Grampa Kovacs had with everything, but especially the ideas of ten-year-old girls, he said, "And how do you know that?"

"'Cause I'm going to make *The Wizard of Oz*."

His white eyebrows jumped with amusement. "But it's already been made."

"I'll make mine better, and Toto will be the star." Her specific but never stated intention is to recast Toto with a collie just like Lassie. And Dorothy gets to ride a Horse of a Different Color down the Yellow Brick Road, vaulting over the Lollipop Guild like National Velvet. A cavalcade of preteen sublimations, thinks the ironic older Ellen as she wipes dust off the boxes.

Grampa Kovacs gave Ellen an old 8mm camera and a box of film. She immediately shot five reels of her cocker spaniel Libby and put the camera away. Now she lifts the camera out of the box and turns it over in her hands before gently blowing the faint coat of dust from its pebbled cast-iron casing.

The other two boxes of her bequest include a projector and a dozen reels of silent comedies. Stan and Ollie chasing an upright piano down a million steps. Harold Lloyd hanging from a clock face. Even into high school she would sit in her room watching these films over and over, with only the chatter of the projector for a soundtrack.

One of the first things she told Megan was, "If I could ever film anything as sublime as the scene where Buster Keaton stands scratching his head while the house falls down around him, I would be happy."

Her parents never found out about Jamie, or her other night visitors. She remembers Gary Lester, a linebacker with flat feet, climbing out the window while her father pounded on the bedroom door. She could still see his white briefs bounding like a roebuck's hindquarters across the darkened lawn.

Her insulted rage had thrown her father off the scent. "Of course not, Dad! What do you think I am?" The boys themselves were less discreet, and Ellen became famous as an easy mark for big, muscular guys. The more testosterone the better. Pick her up at the McDonald's and pow.

She carries the boxes out in a Bloomies shopping bag. In a way, she thinks, it feels like I'm sneaking another lover past them all over again.

Megan holds up the tiny camera. "You're going to shoot with this? I mean, why not at least video?"

Ellen takes the camera from Megan, feeling foolish. "Because I can't get equipment from the school anymore. They took my key."

"I thought Tyler gave you probation." Megan flips through the film reels. "Wasn't Fatty Arbuckle a rapist or something?"

"Anyway, even though the school was less forgiving than Dad, it really doesn't matter—this academic suspension would be the last straw for him."

"So what are you going to do with that thing? Can you really shoot your film with it?"

Ellen shrugs. "Don't know. I don't know anything." She flops down onto the bed. Fatty Arbuckle is knocked onto the floor, where he unspools into the hallway.

Later, after Megan leaves, Ellen watches her old films of Libby chasing a ball, or trying to lick the camera lens. The shadows wobbling across the bedroom wall have the force of memory. She finds herself crying uncontrollably.

To cheer herself up, she runs backwards some of the reels she and Megan had watched together. In the last one, Harold Lloyd jumps from a boxcar to the front seat of a driverless roadster which suddenly appears, bouncing backwards up from gully beside a train trestle. He drives madcap in reverse, the tires swallowing dust as they go. In the end, he retrieves his sweetheart, and then they part after the first loving glance, wandering backwards into separate crowds, never to have known one another.

If it were only possible to un-know someone that way, thinks Ellen, I'd throw myself in reverse tomorrow. I would un-know Megan, my parents, Jamie and Gary. But where would I stop?

The film counts up to five and then snaps loose of the sprockets, clucking like a disapproving tongue.

Friday the 17th (St. Patrick's Day)

Brad is late. Alice looks up at the Wrigley Building clock. Really late. He's developed this strange habit of suggesting that Alice meet him somewhere and then forgetting to show up. I flew back especially for this? It's not like a week with her mom isn't enough, but to get stood up after a trip of several hundred miles is an insult of the highest order.

She leans against the Tribune Tower beneath a rock heisted from the Great Wall of China, chewing a fingernail and going back over her who-do-you-think-you-are speech in her head. Giving up, she decides to work her way over to Dearborn and the parade route. She crosses over a river the color of anti-freeze.

"I'll buy you a green beer, laddie," says Elvin.

"No, I don't think so."

"Come on, Alphie O'Duchossois. Just for an hour. It's a nice day." Elvin gives the jocular approach one last try. "How about a plain yellow beer?"

Alphonse keeps going through his package slips. "Why you want to watch a bunch of fraternity boys get drunk and fight in the street is your own business."

"They got some good marching bands."

"No."

Elvin shrugs and walks away. "Oh Danny Boy," he croons. The other workers laugh.

It's not that Alphonse minds the green beer, really, or the red-faced Irishmen. It's been two days since he left a note at the house on Kimbark and he wants to stay near in case Giselle calls.

He's keeping lunchtimes open so he can see her without Eloise knowing. It's a bad thing, but at least this way he gets to see her. Maybe.

"Get a move on," Robin says. "I've got a parade to catch."

"You're not really going to do it," Nathan says. "Are you?"

"It's my duty as a leader in the community. Until they admit us to the parade, it's guerilla action time."

Nathan covers his face with the neck of his sweatshirt. He can still remember when St. Patrick's Day was a family holiday, when all the Carmichaels gathered at a restaurant or rented hall to sing "Barbara Allen" and eat corned beef. And get drunk, of course. But this new way of seeing the day, as a battleground for inclusion—it makes him wish for the old simplicity of being, however uncomfortably, straight.

"I don't have all day," Robin says. "I'm supposed to meet those lesbian activists I'm marching with at eleven."

"You mean Erin Go Bragh-less?" Nathan winces.

"You are such a titty man," Robin smirks.

Ng feels sick. Sick and happy. Since Leda Villareal said yes, she would come to the parade with him, he's been woozy. He left for school as usual that morning and, before Ivan could find him, he ditched. He's been avoiding the gang at all costs. He still doesn't know if they've found out about his flushing the package. Obviously not, he reminds himself. I'm still breathing. And waiting for Leda. The Marshall Field's window is filled with a giant heart made out of knotted red silk ties.

Maybe waiting forever. When he asked, standing in a nervous sweat before the counter at Stimpy's, if Leda would maybe be interested in going to the parade, she looked up from her copy of *People* and stared at him for a very long time, popping her gum, before she said, Sure. Two syllables, like sugar without the g. Was there any flicker of expectation in her eyes? Maybe it meant nothing. Maybe she didn't mean it at all. Just get the little punk out of the store. But she had also said, "I don't even know your name." And so she had learned his name. And he had learned that she was named Leda. He can't get the sound out of his head. Leda. He mumbles it to himself, a reassuring mantra. "Leda."

A tap on the shoulder and Ng squeaks, whirling around.

"You called?" She is really there. Big jacket, big pants, big hair, and those red lips and sweet brown eyes.

"Hi," Ng whispers.

"What's the matter?" Leda pops her gum. "You okay?"

"Yeah," Ng almost laughs, but stops himself.

"Well? Don't you want to see the parade?" Leda smiles, and Ng's stomach trembles. Sick and happy.

"Yes, I do." Ng searches for something to say. "I heard there's a Batman float with lasers."

"Woah," Leda grabs his hand. "*Vamanos,* man!"

This little camera is kind of fun, thinks Ellen, aiming her 8mm down the length of the river. Her black and white film can't capture its green, but maybe it will get the strange fluorescent dye glow, how it seems to be a green glass table top for playing with toy boats.

She wheels back toward the parade. The frame fills with moving bodies, faces blurring past. And one face—wait. Ellen lowers the camera. It's her. She raises the camera again, tracking the flower shop girl as her blonde head weaves through the crowd.

Here we go a-birding again, Ellen smiles to herself. She follows Avis as she steps up onto a large planter and peers over the crowd to see the parade. Even at a distance, and through a tiny lens, Ellen sees her turn pale.

Panning to a gap in the crowd, Ellen searches for the object Avis's gaze. It's the guy from the coffee shop, with another girl on his arm. He looks at his watch uneasily. The other girl is laughing and pointing at a unicycle clown. She has a pinwheel in her hand and short brown hair. Ellen hates her instinctively, on Avis's behalf.

When she pans back, Avis is gone. Well, Ellen sighs, it looks complicated, whatever it is. I'd better stay clear of that. Right?

"This is quite a nice view," says Elias. "I should get out more." He's impressed by the spread the insurance men put out, and that they can commandeer this vast space of large-windowed rooms on the river, looking right down on the vivid water.

"Oh yes, they do this every year," Florence says. "I never get used to that green color. It's kind of horrid."

"It's a great big party ribbon tied around the city. You should enjoy it."

"Why, Elias," says Florence. "You're quite right to see it that way. How poetic."

"Why doesn't the green dye flow into the lake?" asks Elias. "It flows inland."

"Oh, Arnie told me all about that," says Florence airily. "They turned the river around. A long time ago."

"Is that possible?" says Elias, shocked that such a thing could be considered. "How can they do that?"

"They used locks and levees and things. Anyway," Florence turns back to the window, "Arnie always said it's important to know these things, so that you're not just living anyplace, but living some place."

"That's a nice thought," says Elias.

"Yes, I think so, too," says Florence. "What a lovely day."

Thursday the 23rd

"So you haven't talked to him yet?" says Molly.

"Well, I've seen him, obviously," Alice says. "I worked two days this week. And at rehearsal."

"But you didn't *say* anything."

"What could I say after seeing him with her at the parade? I saw how he looked at her. And he didn't even apologize. I don't think he even remembers asking me to meet him at the parade."

"So it's been over a week. Christ, you must be about to explode."

"I think I already did. Like one of those underground nuclear tests. The surface looks normal, but there's a big invisible hole way down there somewhere."

She hadn't told Molly the whole truth. Brad had been trying to make up in that pathetic way of his that made not-trying look almost heroic. He looked sad and mournful. He tried to be nice. He tried getting angry about her silence. But she couldn't confront him. Unless she told him what she'd seen he would never come clean about Lori. But damned if she wants to be the one to put that on the table.

She calls in sick. She's had enough Brad for a while. She takes the bus down to the Museum of Science and Industry. It's a school day, and the cavernous building is crawling with school children.

They surround her as she walks through the hall of gems. She tries to concentrate on the unearthly glow of the stones in the dark rooms, but the clamor of children drowns her concentration. She is adrift in a sea of small bodies as they travel through the coal mine and submarine and watch the Tesla coil make everyone's hair stand on end. She begins to enjoy the jostling crowd. The kids don't care about who she is. She's another big kid for the moment.

Finally there is a general ebbing of noise as the children get loaded back onto their buses. Alice's ears ring with the almost-silence that seems to suddenly pour through the exhibits like an aural fog. She finds herself alone in the anatomy section. She follows a blood cell the size of a breath mint on its perilous journey. She watches lungs inflate and deflate like a kind of grotesque butterfly stretching its wings on a sunny wall. Then she climbs awkwardly into the chambers of the giant heart. It is dark and cozy—almost too small, actually—strangely womb-like as she sits hunkered, knees to chin in the left ventricle. She closes her eyes. The only sounds are distant, echoey. No one knows she's here. She feels suddenly light, free. No one can touch her, not Brad, not Lori. No one.

"Hey," a small voice says. "You stuck?"

She turns to see boy, eight years old, maybe, eyes bright with amazement to see her jammed inside the plastic structure in a very un-adult posture.

"No, I'm okay."

"I got stuck in the chimbley sweep exhibit," the boy says. "They had to get a man to pull me out. Want me to get him?"

"I can get out," Alice says. "I'm just not ready to go yet."

The boy looks suspicious, as though he knows a fib when he hears one. "Okay. I'll be over by the taste buds if you need help."

"Thanks," says Alice. But she doesn't move for a very long time, even though the boy checks on her regularly until she finally crawls out of the ventricle with stiff knees and one foot asleep.

The ride back uptown lulls Alice into a kind of trance, putting her brain in neutral. That's the only way she can explain how she ends up knocking on Brad's door an hour later without any clear idea of what she intends to say.

Brad's face lights up, and then collapses on itself. "Hi," he says, tentatively.

"What's the deal with this Lori?" Alice pushes past him and sits herself on the edge of his bed. "I saw you at the parade."

Brad's mouth falls open. "Oh my god, oh my god. Jesus!" He grabs his head and leans back, wailing, "Why didn't you say something?"

"Right. In front of the whole band? I didn't want any witnesses to me breaking your neck."

"Look, I just ran into Lori. We talked about the band, and suddenly the parade was there. I looked, but I couldn't find you."

"You didn't look like you wanted to."

Brad stops and looks at her. "Well, if you saw me, why didn't you wave or something?"

"Get real, Brad. I saw you with Lori, and she was hanging on your arm."

Brad stands with his mouth open.

"Just fuck you, okay?" Alice falls onto the bed and begins sobbing.

Brad kneels beside her and strokes her head. Alice shakes his hand off, but it is exactly what she wants him to do. And when he starts again, she fights her wanting not to want him to touch her, and remains still.

"God, I've missed you so much," Brad says. "It's been such a long week."

"More like two weeks," says Alice, muffled by the bed.

Brad begins to rub her back. "I'm sorry," he says. "I really didn't mean to make you unhappy." He kisses her neck.

Alice turns and pulls his mouth to hers, letting herself be consumed by the sensation of his warmth.

When Alice wakes, the room has fallen into the darkness of early evening and is cold. She slips out from under Brad's arm and gets out of the bed, pulling on her sweater and socks. The sex was unusually great. She feels relaxed and warm. Almost sort of happy.

As she passes the electric heater, she flicks it on, and walks over to the tall windows facing west. A drizzle outside is turning the streetlights into big glowing dandelions. She hears the cars swishing past, and this sound somehow brings on a new wave of sadness. Her stomach clenches as though roiling with leftover crying. She puts both hands on it to keep it under control and takes a deep breath.

"I'm sorry," Brad says from the bed. "I didn't mean to hurt you. It was nothing. Really."

"But that's all it took," Alice says, staring out through the grimy window-pane. "And I guess that's what makes me the maddest. How little it takes to break me apart like that."

"I was a complete idiot. You can't be all that surprised. I'm a partial idiot most of the time."

Alice smiles.

Brad holds the edge of the blanket up, inviting her back to bed. "Come on, let it go. Forgive me."

Alice turns from the window. "You can't be a complete idiot by yourself," she says, crawling back into the dark warmth of the bed. "You have to have a partner."

Monday the 27th

Elias feels the world trying to change itself. He sits in the quiet corner booth, sipping coffee, and sensing the effort of the air to shed the cold, to rise up buoyed by the fatness of spring.

But it is still too early. Snow could envelop the city in a snap and stifle the glimmering wet life and the tender green throats of overanxious flowers. The withheld urgency, like an engine racing against the parking brake, makes Elias fidgety. Instead of going for his daily swim, he makes a phone call and gets into his car. He heads west on Grand Avenue, taking in a peculiar slice of the city. From Navy Pier, Grand submarines under Michigan Avenue, sneaks through the shadow of the Merchandise Mart, lumbers along the near west industrial belt, across the river, and then gains a little girth and speed for the long trek through the West Side flats.

The Taurus zigs and zags and bounces its chassis over archeological potholes. Past storefront tamale joints, the Area Five police station, past the Radio Flyer factory. Elias imagines Elana streaking down a snowy Boston hill, mittens gripping the Flyer's steering bar. Next Christmas.

He knows he is close when he sees the Village Pump, the neon handle creaking up and down in the gray daylight. Just past Harlem Avenue, he pulls through a gate with soccer balls worked into the wrought iron fencing. Sitting on the bumper of a black El Dorado with smoky windows is Tommaso Falco.

Tommaso is smoking, the hood of his wool parka thrown back to show the sleek, salt-and-pepper hair, back-combed from a rakish widow's peak. He rubs a manicured finger across his thin, pointed moustache.

"I see what you mean," Tommaso says, answering Elias's comment from their earlier phone conversation. "Something in the air."

"You could miss it if you weren't paying attention."

"And I usually don't. So it's good to have you around to help me notice these things. It's a tease, though. We aren't done with snow."

"An early case of spring fever. I needed a break."

"You called the right guy. Italians are good at spring. You know, *la primavera*." He kisses his fingers. "Hey." His eyes brighten. "I brought you some cheese." Tommaso flicks his cigarette into the bushes, pops open the trunk of his car and lifts out squishy cakes of mascarpone, cartons of ricotta, waxy bulbs of provolone, and, with a flourish, five blocks of feta cheese in milky liquid.

Elias laughs. "Goodness, so much."

"What did I say? Lifetime supply."

"How is the feta business anyway?"

"*Molto bene.*"

"And the brie experiment?"

Tommaso waves off the allusion. "Feta is a much better cheese to push. You know how many Greek salads and omelets get sold every day? I guess you would," he laughs. "I'm selling tons of the stuff. Thanks to you, I had to buy another building and hire three people this year. Let me buy you a caffé."

Elias drives back to the diner, still hearing the echoing clack of the bocce balls as they collided in the sawdust. He beat Tommaso two out of three games. For the first time in several weeks, he feels relaxed.

He notices something wrong as he nears the diner. There are too many people inside for the hour. And Luis is out of the kitchen talking to someone. A kid. Luis has a cleaver in his hand. He can hear the voices even before he pushes open the door.

Everyone falls silent as he walks in. He passes through the group of boys, who watch him intently. There are five of them, all in leather jackets and peaked caps. He goes straight to the register and pulls a baseball bat from underneath the counter. It hasn't been touched since it was placed there years ago, but it feels familiar in his hands. He raises the bat waist high and says slowly, "Get out of my diner now."

"We not want no trouble," says the front youth, a slender boy whose cap is stitched with an undecipherable symbol. He removes his empty hands from his pockets and takes a step backwards.

"We just want our friend to come with us," says a boy behind him.

Luis jerks a thumb back at the kitchen and shakes his head.

"I guess you'll have to leave without him," says Elias.

The leader crosses his arms. "We don't have to do nothing."

Elias feels the whoosh of the kitchen swing door opening. Ng comes up behind him.

"I'll go," he says.

"Don't even think about it." Elias puts one arm in front of Ng. "Get back there."

The front door jingles as Florence Finkel sticks her head in uncertainly. She quickly takes in the scene then backs out the door and hurries down the sidewalk, waving her purseless arm and crying for help.

"Shit," mutters one of the youths. They begin to slip quickly and quietly out the front door.

Elias lowers the bat as the last boy fades into the night beyond the diner's window, but doesn't relinquish his tight grip on it, afraid to let his anger slip away from him. Not for a while. Not yet.

April

Saturday the 1st

Tired of waiting, thinks Alphonse, sitting in his car outside the house on Kimbark. No sign of life behind the windows, but it's hard to tell with most of them boarded up. Maybe she's going to blow me off. Wouldn't be the first time. But now I got my hopes up, April Fool on me.

He sips from the thermos bottle. Been here so long, coffee's cold. Give her ten more minutes. He'd really pretty much given up hoping she'd call. Too many days had gone by unchanged. But suddenly, there she was standing in the lot by his delivery truck, looking awful.

"Hey, Pop," she said.

A stack of grocery store fliers slipped from his fingers, a slow cascade. He stood there, frozen by what to say, how to say it. In the end, all he said was, "Well, look who's here."

She looked around, shifting from one foot to the other. "I got your note."

"I was beginning to wonder had the mail let me down."

She laughed. And it sounded wonderful in his ears. She was so skinny, her hair too dry and frizzy. But the smile was there, though she put it away quickly and mumbled, "Can we maybe have lunch sometime, Pop? When you're not busy?"

Alphonse knelt to gather up the spilled fliers. "Sure, baby. You come over to the house and your momma'll cook up a nice big meal." He knew before he said it, but he had to, for Eloise's sake.

She shook her head no. "I can't, Pop, not yet. Just you and me. Okay?"

"All right. Whenever you want."

"Saturday?"

"Okay, that's fine. How about ten o'clock?"

"All right." She looked relieved then, and ready to take off at a run. "See you, Pop."

Alphonse screws the top back on the thermos, trying to remember clearly the last few moments of their meeting. He'd wanted to stop her from going and blurted out her name, kind of loud, and she stopped and looked back, afraid. He didn't have any idea what he wanted to say, just that he wanted her to hold up, to not leave without a touch, a kiss, something hopeful.

At last he thought of what he could say at that moment. "Tony misses you."

Her eyes got small and far away. "I know. I miss him, too." Then she turned and walked away fast, and when she got to the lot entrance, she broke into a run and was gone.

That's ten minutes. Alphonse scans the blank windows again, his heart dropping. Was that something? Did that cardboard panel just flutter? Maybe a door opened somewhere?

He starts the car. Once it gets warm, I have to leave. That's all there is to it. He rubs his hands in front of the heater vents, watching the temperature gauge creep upward.

Suddenly, from around the corner, Giselle appears, bundled in a silvery, quilted jacket. She hurries directly over to the passenger side and slides in.

"Sorry I'm late," she says. She picks up the thermos. "Any more coffee?"

"Had an hour to get cold."

"Maybe your thermos is busted," she replies coyly. Alphonse looks askance at the strange clothes his daughter is wearing. That jacket, stained green corduroys, and black loafers with stacked heels.

"You come from the backyard?" he asks.

"Mm," Giselle murmurs, sipping cold coffee.

Alphonse is suspicious. "Front door busted?"

She makes a face at the coffee. "Can we get going?"

Alphonse clenches his jaw and throws the car into drive.

Sitting in the Cozy Corner, Alphonse watches Giselle pick at her Greek omelet.

"I haven't had much appetite lately. Food sounds good to me until it's right there on the table. Then I feel kind of, I don't know." Her eyes are bloodshot and yellow, her hair rough-looking and clipped into two plastic butterfly barrettes.

Alphonse is still bottled up with things to say. How she looks ill, how she's ruining her health and everybody else's. He goes for the simplest thing he can think of. "That house you staying at, it looks like hell outside—is it clean inside?"

"It's fine." Giselle stabs at the plate with her fork. "People sort of pitch in."

Alph swigs down more coffee and looks out the window. March did not go out like a lamb. A goat, more like. Sky the color of dirty sheets. The thought brings him right back to Giselle, who is silent.

Now's the time, he thinks. Won't get any easier. He watches Giselle eat some toast. The waitress refills his coffee. He pours in some creamer, making the brew an unappealing gray.

Get going, he thinks. Jump in. Go.

He leans back and lets it come out. "What can I do for you, girl? How can I get you to come home?"

She smiles down at the plate, a hard-lipped smile, and her head turns stiffly, as if a big ghost is twisting her head like a bottle cap.

"Your momma and me, we would like you to come home." He's formal, almost down on one knee.

She looks up finally, and her eyes have a not-crying look to them. Things held back drag her eyelids down so she looks almost sleepy. "Pop," she says, "I can't."

"I don't understand, baby. Neither does your momma. Could you just explain…?"

"There's nothing to explain. I'm happy. Things are fine."

"What about this Jimmy? He going to do the right thing?"

"Jimmy's okay, Dad. He takes care of me."

Alphonse stops again, stuck on what he wants to say about Giselle's upkeep as it appears on this morning.

But she has latched onto the subject of Jimmy and begins to talk quickly, with more animation. Jimmy's business dealings. Some investments, or something, a little bit of a hole right now, needing a break.

She leaves the hope hanging in the air. He can hear her voice in his ear, whispering, *Grab it, Daddy, please.*

So this is what the invitation is really all about. He swallows hard and forces himself to wait a minute before he says, "So this boy, he needs some money?"

"Your sister ain't no supermodel." Johnny has Tony pinned down in the yard. Melvin stands by fretting.

"She is too a supermodel. She's in that new Puff Daddy video dancing on a giant Cadillac. You're just too stupid to notice."

"That ain't her." Johnny threatens to smear Tony's face with a handful of mud. "Admit it. Your sister a streetwalking crackhead."

"Get off him," whispers Melvin. "Get off, Johnny."

"Not unless he admits Giselle is a ho."

"I won't," says Tony at the last moment before his mouth is filled with mud.

Melvin pushes Johnny aside and helps Tony stand up. "You okay?"

The mud is cold and gritty. Johnny is laughing. Tony spits and spits. Finally, he gets enough clean saliva in his mouth to say, "My sister is too a supermodel," and then he runs down the street, his jacket flying out behind him.

Monday the 3rd

All Ivan had to do was wait. Ng knew that it was just a matter of time before Ivan would find him away from school, away from the diner and Stimpy's—alone and without a crazy old man or his bitchy girlfriend to get in the way.

Girlfriend—that is a lovely word.

And in a way, it is the unprecedented grace of Leda Villareal that has so radically altered Ng's perspective that he drops his guard. He allows himself to dream in ways he has never done before, dreams both higher and deeper than his heart has ever held. And so this afternoon, window-shopping for gold necklaces in Uptown, he suddenly finds himself on the sidewalk, assailed by blows from all sides. He curls into himself and takes the punishment. It is almost a relief to get to the moment that had been coming since that night at the diner. He gets away light, really—one black eye, a loose tooth, and a cracked rib.

Every day, from three in the afternoon until the ten o'clock closing, Leda Villareal sits at the counter of Stimpy's Strip Shop unaware that she is known in the esoteric circles of comic artists as the queen of the underground scene.

Not because she glorifies the scruffy artists that hang around the shop. She doesn't. And not because her job at Stimpy's has made her an expert on the cutting edge of the medium. She doesn't even read the comics unless she's forgotten to bring along homework or the latest issue of *Glamour*. Leda is renowned just because she is there, everyday, chewing gum behind the curtain of her teased, split-ended, and cheaply highlighted brown curls. And because she is, to everyone but herself, beautiful.

Customers linger near the counter waiting for her to flip back her hair and give them her trademark disdainful look. She thinks their obsession with the flimsy comics and the sums they spend on them ridiculous.

Leda appears in the background of panels in more than a few locally created zines as a character with enormous, heavy-lidded brown eyes, lips big as skateboards, and a pointy chin with a lovely mole on its lower left side. She has never noticed herself in any of these caricatures. And none of the artists has been bold enough to parade their homages before the subject.

She never wonders why she found Ng different. At first, of course, she hadn't. He came, loitered, purchased, stammered, he went. But on the fateful day when he asked to use the bathroom, she had noticed the doodlings on his green canvas backpack. A street preacher. A precise sunflower. A man with wild eyebrows and hair and kind eyes. They were lovely and spare. They were, she realized, more like art.

When Ng walks bleeding into Stimpy's, Leda's expression goes black with anger. She hustles Ng into the stockroom and forces him to sit down.

"I'm going to kill that bastard," she says in a voice tight with rage.

"Why *he* doesn't just kill *me* is the mystery."

"Too messy," Leda suggests, as she puts a rank scrap of towel filled with ice on Ng's swollen cheek. "He can beat you like this every day and the cops won't do nothing."

Ng touches his puffy lip. "The package I flushed was just tobacco."

Leda sits back. "Then what's the problem? He didn't lose nothing."

"Problem is he was testing me, and I flushed it."

There is a distant jingle. A customer.

Leda takes Ng's hand and places it where hers had been, holding the ice pack to his face. She kisses his forehead and then pecks him on the lips. "Be right back."

The thing about a blow to the head, thinks Ng, is how it realigns you with warp speed. One moment you're daydreaming, and the next you're looking at a square of dirty cement. Your x-y axis falls on its ass. Pieces of the world spinning around like shoes in a tumble dryer. Same as a kiss.

He grabs a piece of paper and, leaning on it with one elbow while keeping the icepack in place, Ng begins to sketch. His lips, meanwhile, tingle as though touched with electricity.

Wednesday the 5th

Megan wakes suddenly in the night, running her hand across cool, rumpled sheets. The window is open and a soft breeze swirls in from the street below. An el train rumbles in the distance and a car alarm repeats its repertoire of siren calls. Her brain registers the fact that the other side of the bed is cool. Ellen's gone.

Megan sits up. Christ, she thinks, what now?

She pulls on a bathrobe and walks to the living room and finds Ellen sitting on the couch, legs crossed and bathed in the television's aura, blue like a Hindu goddess. She is abstractedly stroking her cat, Marty, who arches his back and steps in small, mincing circles.

Megan stands in the doorway, a little irritated, and croaks, "What are you doing?"

"Couldn't sleep." Ellen doesn't look up.

"What are you watching?"

"An ancient college basketball game on ESPN. Look at those tiny shorts."

Megan flops down on the couch and watches for a minute. "Those sideburns look almost in style." She nudges Ellen's leg. "What's wrong?"

"Thinking too much." Marty stretches and walks over to Megan's lap. "Dad's going to find out about school soon, and then I'm screwed."

"What can he do? I mean, you're already pretty low. You got nothing to lose."

"He could stop paying my rent. And don't say get a job. I'm going to. I don't have any choice."

Megan watches a skinny guy with long hair bank a shot off the glass. His coach, in a belted plaid jacket, punches the air. "You could move in with me."

"Right. Everything's just peachy."

"I said I'm sorry about tonight. I was just upset about work. I've been working like a total drone lately."

"You were ranting like some I don't know what. Why are you so pissed off at how I spend my time?"

Megan leans forward, reaching for Ellen's hand. "I just don't know how you can wander around all day and do nothing. I'm worried about you. You're drifting."

"I think it bothers you that my day is opaque to you. You can't sit in your office and imagine what I'm doing at any given minute."

"That's not fair. I don't keep a leash on you."

"Then why do I feel like you do?"

"God, I can't win. You only know how to feel suffocated or ignored. I'm tired," Megan groans. She gestures to the room. "And here I am yakking at three in the morning. Oh yeah, I'll be real bright-eyed tomorrow."

"Well, go back to bed. I'm going to channel surf some more."

"Only if you come with me." Megan stands up and holds out a hand. "Come on."

Ellen doesn't budge. "You know, it's horrible when you start yelling. The cat sheds. The plants wither up. And I feel like jumping out the window."

Megan kneels and puts her head in Ellen's lap. "Please, no fighting now. Sleep. Sleep."

One of Ellen's hands hesitates above Megan's head. Finally, she lets it drop down and stroke the tangled hair. Marty jumps onto the coffee table and begins noisily lapping a bowl of melted ice cream.

Ellen sits that way for a long time, listening to the greedy sounds of her cat. Eventually, Megan's body relaxes and her breathing becomes slow and steady.

Why couldn't things be better than they are or worse than they are? Ellen wonders. Then I'd know what to do. And she puts the corner of a pillow in her mouth in case she starts to cry.

Her feelings for Megan are the hardest thing for Ellen to explain when considering her surveillance of Avis the flower girl.

After Megan leaves for work, Ellen watches the film of the St. Pat's parade and other snippets she's captured: Avis walking down Broadway, arranging flowers in the store window, selling them to Mrs. Finkel. The images are dreamy, jumpy, strange.

Oh yeah—she has to remember to call her Alice. The fact that Alice has a real name, is an actual person, that Mrs. Finkel bought flowers straight from the florist's pricked fingers and laid them on the diner counter, is enough to give Ellen a case of the sweats.

Even worse, this camera is supposed to be her tool for a short film of some kind, a ticket back into school. And all she's doing is hiding behind it and obsessing.

She suddenly feels loony and pathetic. She packs up the camera, shoves the tiny reels of film in her backpack, and goes out into the day to find something to do.

Despite being on academic suspension, Ellen often finds herself, by ten or eleven in the morning, wandering the halls inside Columbia College. It seems important to keep going through the motions, as though habit can form a kind of path back into the good graces of the dean and her father. Some of her professors, against regulations, allow her to audit their classes. She even looks forward to her film theory class, because the professor treats her like a continuing student, assigning her papers on Godard and Buñuel and grading them sternly.

She likes to see her friends, but she won't answer their questions about what she's doing. She steers the conversation to gossip and movies and TV. When pressed, she alludes vaguely to making a film on her own. Everyone looks at her with sympathy and disbelief.

On the way to the school today she formulated a plan. She needs to find a way into the editing suite. Without her student status, she has no equipment and can't do anything with her film. Anything she shoots is useless without some way to cut it. The editing suite is locked when not in use, which is rarely. She'll need a key, or a huge favor. She can't ask her friends to risk suspension to get her in. But she can do something much simpler, and much worse.

And the opportunity presents itself in the student lounge when her friend Trudy goes to buy a cup of coffee and leaves her backpack on the table. It does not even look suspicious for Ellen to take the ring of keys from the outside pocket and slip one key off and return the rest. A few seconds is all it takes. She sits waiting for Trudy, feeling like she is going to lose her breakfast in one big existential urp. Like that guy in *Clockers* who kept puking blood, she is rotten inside.

As soon as Trudy returns, Ellen makes an excuse and runs down the stairs and out to the broad Michigan Avenue sidewalk. The spring sky is blue as water and the trees in Grant Park are flaunting their new leaves. And with nowhere to go, she heads for the el and a ride up to the other place where her days disappear, Sophia's Diner. Near Alice. She opens her hand. The key is there, glinting.

Friday the 7th

Robin has the phone jammed against his shoulder, his trembling hands pressed against the cool window. His clammy palms exude a thin, ghostly tracing against the glass. "Come on come on come on," he is chanting under his breath while classical music buzzes in his ear. At last, Nathan comes on the line.

"What's wrong?"

"Did you know we're out of gin?"

"You called me out of a meeting. For which, I should add, thanks."

"Yes, yes," Robin snaps. "But it's martini day and we're out of gin. Don't you think that's an emergency?"

"Are you all right? You don't sound good."

"I'm just very, very thirsty. I'm going on a booze run."

"I still don't understand why you called me."

Robin gives a shrieky laugh. "Well, *someone* has to pick up the dinner I'm going to be too fucking drunk to cook."

"Couldn't this wait?"

"I feel like having pizza. Ask me if my mother's dying."

"What? Jesus, Robin, are you telling me—is your mother dying?"

"Well, how the hell should I know? She can't tell me, and no one else will. Bye for now."

"Wait, Robin, what the hell—"

"See you at home, love, ta-ta."

Robin puts the receiver down. On his way out, he tapes a postcard to the front door. I might as well let him read it, he thinks. Easier than trying to explain it all.

Nathan's back spasms as he looks at the postcard picture of the Alamo. The hand-colored south Texas sky is a brittle azure, and the bullet-riddled stucco of the old fort itself is washed into a smooth, inoffensive beige. Remember, says the postcard in Old West-style letters across the bottom.

So that's why all the dramatics, thinks Nathan. Any contact from Robin's father is cause to head for the bunker. These rare communications, always tersely inscribed on postcards, unleash in Robin an uncontrollable fission of anger, pain, and loss.

He opens the door and sets the pizza box down on the hall table. Nathan peels the card from the door and flips it over. There it is, in the dense, vertical scribble of Mr. Schaefer.

Why does he have to do this? Nathan thinks to himself, grimly.

Thought you should know your mom has lost what mind she had left. No need to write or call more. She's got tubes in everywhere and no sense of day or night. That's about it. Sherman.

And then he notices the apartment is quiet. He calls out, walking down the hallway. There is no answer, but he sees Robin, spread out on the couch, wearing the red silk kimono he bought at the flea market last spring.

"Honey, are you okay?"

Robin waves a hand listlessly. "Can't hear you. I'm in Bombay right now. Via Tanqueray and points east."

"Kimonos aren't really the thing in Bombay this year. I'm sorry about your father's card."

"Sherman," Robin sneers, sitting up. "Sherman is only the big, fat trunk of the rotten tree. It's the withered fruit of the tree that is so upsetting."

"What do you mean?"

"I think you'd better mix up two doubles. A quadruple. Janie is what I mean. Dear sweet sister Janie."

Nathan walks over to the bar and begins measuring the gin into a large shaker. "What happened?"

"I called to find out what's happening. You know she's joined that church?"

"Yes." Nathan skewers three olives apiece on plastic swords.

"Well this church of holy loving, it seems, has taught my devoted sister the true nature of the sin I'm in. She won't speak to me now."

Nathan brings the brimming drinks gingerly to the table. "I'm so sorry." He sits and embraces Robin's red silk shoulders.

Robin sniffs and lets his head fall against Nathan's chest. "I can't even blame Dad for this. He hates the Pentecostals more than anyone. Almost anyone."

Nathan feels the teardrops patting onto his stomach. The warm wetness begins to tickle him. "Sherman can take some of the blame. For making Janie so miserable she has to find solace in such strange places."

Robin shakes his head. He sits up and slurps from the rim of the martini glass.

On a sudden inspiration, Nathan retrieves the postcard from where he dropped it on the hall table. Standing before Robin, he rips the Alamo in half. Robin gasps, and then leans back to watch as the card is torn into quarters, eighths, and sixteenths. Nathan drops the pieces into a large ceramic ashtray and lights them with a long fireplace match. The flames circle the edges of the pile, slightly blue in tint, sending up thin strings of black smoke.

He turns to Robin and says, "It's the least we can do."

Robin holds up his martini glass. "Here's to dear old Sherman. No, wait. Here's to Mom."

"Hear, hear," says Nathan quietly, raising his glass to meet Robin's with the tiniest clink.

Monday the 10th

It occurs to Elias in the middle of his laps in the YMCA pool that he can no longer rely on the mandatory togetherness of holidays, or on the conscience of his daughter, to provide him with opportunities to see his precious Elana.

As he turns his head for air, a voice says, *There is no one to do this but you.*

It is a powerful, basso voice which, although he knows better, he would have to describe as his idea of god's voice.

The sudden command, and Elias's immediate realization of its truth, startles him so that he stops in midstroke and hovers in the water, circling his arms and legs. To suddenly feel in command of something before which you had felt powerless. He barely notices the latex caps of other swimmers bobbing past on either side. His heart is pounding.

"Hey! You okay?" shouts the lifeguard.

Elias waves, and paddles slowly back to his towel. Before he knows it, he is at the diner staring at the telephone beside the cash register. What appeal, he wonders, can he make so that Sophia will understand the spirit that moves him? His resolve, so firm on his way back from the gym, evaporates. His daughter is a puzzle, or rather a tangle of puzzles. After a couple of hours, his brooding becomes apparent to everyone.

"What's wrong?" asks Luis. "You look miserable."

"I was thinking of going to see my granddaughter. For Easter. I just need to ask Sophia if it's all right."

"*Abuelito* don't have to ask, he is always welcome."

"I don't know," says Elias, looking back at the phone. "She probably won't want me to mess up her arrangements."

"That what you worry about?" laughs Luis. "Today she say no, tomorrow she say yes. No big deal. You probably going to see your *niéta* very soon."

The pick-up bell dings violently. Luis looks over to see the waitress waving her order pad and squinting.

"Hello, Luis? Denver omelet, remember?" She snaps her gum sarcastically.

Luis rolls his eyes. As he turns back to the grill, he points at the phone and silently mouths, "Call."

Elias grabs the receiver and quickly dials Sophia's office before he can think. He picks his way through several layers of the automated phone system before he finally earns the peaceful string serenade reserved for those on hold for upper-level managers. His palm begins to sweat on the receiver.

After an entire morning spent poring over the transcript of a focus group on the granola cereal for which she is the product manager, Sophia feels the familiar pain creep up her spine to the back of her skull. With her presentation on the raisin-versus-chopped-dates question less than four hours away, here she is on the road to Migraine City. Unbelievable.

The intercom buzzes. "It's your father on line two."

She rolls her eyes and picks up the phone, simultaneously yanking open the drawer where she keeps her pills, extra nylons, and a few of her brand's granola bars. "Hello."

"Hello, Sophia? It's your father." He tries to put happiness and lightness into his voice.

"Yes, Dad, hi." She grabs the bottle of ibuprofen and pours three into her palm. "What's up?"

"Is this a bad time?"

"I'm preparing this presentation, and I've got a migraine coming on, so I guess you could say." She tilts her head back and swallows the tablets dry.

"I just called to ask if I could visit you for Easter weekend. I know you had some trouble getting free—"

"Well, we normally spend Easter with Jonathan's family. It might be awkward. I mean, his parents hardly know you."

Elias persists, even as he feels the idea slipping beyond his grasp. "I know it's short notice. If it's too much trouble."

"Oh, Pop. I just can't think right now. Maybe later, okay? Call me tonight. I've got to go."

She starts to put the phone down, but Elias breaks in, "I can stay at a hotel. I don't want to be a problem."

His plaintive tone stops her. "I'm sorry, Dad, I'm really sorry. I haven't really been listening. Please, let me get through today. Then we can talk about a visit. Really, a nice long one."

"Okay, I understand." He tries to prevent the disappointment from shading his voice. "Sophia, are you all right?"

His solicitude angers her. Why does she have to feel guilty? "I'm fine. Call me tonight, okay? I've got to go now. I'm sorry. Bye." She puts the phone down and looks at the transcript again. It makes no sense at all.

Friday the 14th

The Friday crossword absorbs Florence for more than an hour. As she fills in the last clue—French composer—she suddenly perceives how she has changed since Arnie's death. As she finishes the loop of the *e* in Satie, she realizes that this is the first time she has completed a puzzle without a thought of Arnie over her shoulder, barking out the answers faster than she can write them. It is shocking to think this thought: Arnie is dead, but she is continuing to live.

Somehow her days are no longer full of holes, but full of, well, her life. A bowl of greenish early peaches sits on the dining room table, and next to it, a disappointing watercolor, only her third or fourth. A vase full of flowers, bought yesterday from Alice at Urbs in Horto, sits on the hall table.

She stands up and walks over to the window. The world below seems peaceful and orderly, cars and the small people below making slow, determined progress. She cranks open a shutter. A breeze carries in the distant sounds of horns, diesel engines, seagulls. A police boat cruises beyond the breakwaters of Belmont Harbor, where a few long-weekend sailors are setting out in their boats.

She is full of guilty joy.

Not feeling quite ready to go home after dinner at Sophia's Diner, Florence walks toward the shops at the corner of Clark and Diversey. Maybe she'll buy some seaweed body scrub and take a long bath tonight. As she nears the corner, she hears the scratchy, drawling voice of the corner preacher. After slowing for a moment, she walks deliberately forward.

"I'm saying God is the great junkman. That's right. Junk Man. And that ain't no blasphemy. You know why I say that? Salvage. Salvage, people. We little specks of flesh and bone, with our egos, our prideful cities, our arrogance of machinery and stock market, we are the junk that litters his blue-green jewel of the earth. Now, sir, I ain't saying you a bunch of carrot peels and crumpled newspapers. You more like something broke, like an old Frigidaire with no compressor, just sitting on somebody's porch, making no ice, chilling no soda pop, doing nobody no bit of good."

Florence stands directly before the gesticulating evangelist. He is beyond thin, like the edge of something unseen, just emerging.

"But it ain't all bad news, brothersister. That's where God the junkman come in. 'Cause you can be fixed. Some of us already riding on down to the fixit shop on God's little junk cart. Flag him down, brothersister. You are the salvage. Just needing a little salvation.

"Salvation, now that's a suitcase of a word. Open it up, brothersisters. Unpack salvation and find salvage bound to elevation. Or find saved with elation. Or find salve and ovation matched up like two socks that each of us will wear on our heavenly journey."

Florence notices a black fedora with an oily crown upturned at the preacher's feet. She takes a five-dollar bill out of her change purse and holds it crumpled in her fist.

"So don't wait, brothersisters, the millennium is upon us. Jump on the back of God's pickup with the spacious cargo bed. Hang on to those two-by-fours nailed across the sides."

Florence drops the money in the preacher's hat and starts to walk home. She walks slowly, not quite ready to let go of his stream of chatter.

"Hang on, brothersister, and he'll take you on down where skinny dogs howl at the yard rats. Where hubcaps nailed across the fences shine like the armor of Saint George. Down to where every lost thing finds its missing part, gets found by who needs it. Where every last object finds its one true final home."

It's a shock to come home and find Arnie waiting with the mail. Or rather, within the mail. After sifting through the usual bills and solicitations, Florence comes across an invitation to a members-only reception at the Art Institute. As if summoned, Arnie appears, as full of umbrage and gentle irony as ever, mocking the affectation of Florence's membership in the Institute.

"What do you need that crowd for?" he barks. "Friday's bridge night!"

Shaking, Florence slits open the envelope and snaps open the folded, creamy card.

Arnie sniffs. "Aw, look at that. Millennial Dadaism: Anarchy and Evolution. You know what that is, don't you? Madonnas made of rice cakes! Tapioca sputniks. Count me out."

She quickly fills in the RSVP and seals the reply envelope.

"Well, if it's important to you, dear," Arnie says, and disappears with a poof.

"Sure, vamoose just when I'm about to take a bath," Florence says to the air. "Just when I need someone to loofah my back."

Tuesday the 18th

When Jimmy finally got tired of the weepy, puking Giselle, he insisted that she go to the free clinic to see a doctor about her bad stomach and sleeplessness. Even dropped a twenty on her for whatever medicine she might need. Because he really wanted her to shape up or get the hell out. It was an ultimatum.

The clinic is in an old storefront on Woodlawn Avenue. Giselle gives her name and sits on a molded plastic chair filling in forms on a clipboard. A history of diseases. Medicines. Parents.

She can't help feeling now that any money Jimmy gives her is indirectly from her father. His loan got Jimmy out of hock to Scout, and Jimmy hasn't repaid the loan yet.

As though to taunt her, Jimmy makes a show of flashing his roll of bills for Giselle.

"Y'old man need his money? I can pay him back now." Jimmy peels a few bills off the roll and holds them out to her.

"Don't give me those. I haven't talked to him since we got the money. Just send it to him."

Jimmy smiles and folds the money back into his roll. "Just say the word, I'll pay him back with interest."

Even so, Giselle feels that she put herself in even deeper debt to Alphonse by asking for his help. He is the worst sort of debtor because he will never mention the loan, but she will feel his not asking as a constant echo of his voice saying, *I'm here, baby, I ain't worried about no loan, don't you worry.*

Diabetes? No. A family history of high blood pressure? Yes.

It seems even leaving home won't get you free of your parents.

Peeking in the schoolroom door, Eloise is startled to see Tony sitting against the wall, looking at the ground. The left shoulder of his shirt is torn and there is a piece of grass in his hair. Tony looks up and Eloise can see a shiny spot under his left eye.

"You okay, baby?" She hurries toward him, but is intercepted by a young woman in a bright sweater and round black glasses.

"Mrs. Duchossois?" says the teacher.

"Yes. What happened to Tony?"

"I'm Helen Summers, Tony's teacher. Tony's fine. The school nurse already examined him. Tony, will you excuse us?"

Tony slinks out of his seat and into the hallway. Eloise hears him slide his butt down the wall and onto the floor.

"Now, what is this about, please?" Eloise crosses her arms. This young teacher does not fill her with confidence. "Who is it hurt my Tony?"

"Fights are commonplace here, Eloise. We don't call parents every time or we'd do nothing but hold parent conferences. I called you for two reasons.

One, Tony is an exceptional boy. A good student, articulate and polite. Two, this is not the first incident of this kind. In fact, it's become almost regular in the past two months."

"And what happened today?"

"Tony attacked a boy bigger than himself."

"He *attacked* someone? Tony?" Eloise laughs. "I'm sorry, but that's pure craziness. That other boy has sold you all a story."

"The fight started when the other boy apparently said something derogatory about Tony's sister."

Eloise stiffens. She shields her eyes as if against the afternoon light sloping in the high, horizontal windows. "Then that other boy started it, right? Tony was provoked."

The teacher pauses. "Eloise, I think I know Tony well enough to say that you don't want him fighting, no matter who starts it."

"That is true." Eloise picks up a red pen and twiddles it. "Do you know what they're saying about Giselle?"

The teacher shakes her head. "No. But it seems to hurt Tony very much."

"I'll have a talk with Tony tonight. There won't be any more fights."

"It would surprise me very much if there were."

"Thank you. You've been more than kind."

"Feel free to come in anytime you'd like to talk."

Eloise smiles grimly. "You better mean that, Miz Summers. I might just take you up on it."

Giselle looks at the white smoke surging in the glass tube.

"Benhoffel," she says. "Lutnivic." She giggles and draws on the pipe again, feeling the tingle race to the edges of her skin.

She knew before the doctor said a word. She knew by the tenderness of her breasts, by the smell of her urine in the cup, by the way the doctor entered the room with his eyes closely reading the papers on the clipboard.

"Ms. Stevens," he'd said, using the phony name she put on the forms. "You probably already know you are pregnant."

She'd shrugged. He was a young doctor, busy and tired looking. His ponytail and earring made her distrust him. But she knew that he was right.

"Have you received any information about prenatal care?"

What the hell. Fuck it, fuck everything. Her head is becoming thin and shell-like. Transparent.

"One thing I must caution you about is the use of drugs. As you know, even simple compounds like alcohol, caffeine, and nicotine should be eliminated from your diet until the baby is weaned."

Giselle looked at the eye chart on the wall across from the examination table, making strange words out of the letters. BENHOFL. LUTNVC.

"I think a drug test would be advisable."

Giselle had jumped down from the table.

"It's only for medical purposes, so we know what we're dealing with, Ms. Stevens."

"Little man," says Giselle, peering through the translucent lighter. "Get off my ass, little man."

"Daddy's home!" Jimmy opens to door to the bedroom. When he sees Giselle sprawled out and dilated in the haze of smoke, his eyes grow small and fierce.

"Did I say it was candy time, baby?" He walks toward the bed with his arm up. "Did I?"

Thursday the 20th

The sure sign that things are really going to get bad is that they get a little better for a while. Making up with Brad after the "Saint Paddy's Day Massacre," as Alice calls it, was fine for a couple of days, but after that night they slept together infrequently. At work, Brad was calm and even polite, almost like Alice was another customer. Everything's fine, Alice kept thinking to herself, over and over. And then two days ago, standing in her kitchen, he broke it off.

"I think I need some time off. From us. It's the pressure of the Fusebox gig," he said. "I've got a lot riding on it. More than anyone maybe."

Alice stood with a ladle in her hand, not saying anything.

"So, we'll see after the gig. We'll talk then."

Pasta water foamed out of the pot, onto the stove.

"I guess I'd better go," Brad said. And he left.

Bam. Just like that.

The linguine is still in the pot, dried into a hard translucent lump.

Brad had never recovered from the shock of finding Lori's hand on his leg at the Rainbo Club. Well, the shock of liking it so very, very much. He'd been tied up in knots ever since. Making this break with Alice was the first thing that had given him a little peace of mind. But it still wasn't easy.

"We didn't break up," he says to Shanklin, who is the first to show up for rehearsal. "It's more like we eased up on the gas."

"Right," Shanklin says. "Whatever. Is Lori going to be here?"

"I don't know." Brad tries not to flinch. "Is that a problem?"

"Not for me. But are you kidding?"

Brad knows Lori isn't coming today. It had been decided as he crawled out of her bed this morning.

He likes waking up in Lori's bed, amid the perfumed blankets, in the spacious Old Town rowhouse her parents had bought for her. All the warm wood and gauzy curtains over the French doors. Little pots of marigolds in the flower box. And a toilet you can walk to naked, and without a key.

With Lori's connections, he thought, the band would get a record deal and he'd be out of that rehearsal space for good.

"I guess I should be scarce for the next few days," Lori said, pinching Brad's ass as he bent over for his underwear. "Except at night, of course."

Brad felt Lori's eyes on him as he dressed. She stretched and groaned luxuriantly. "This is just about perfect, don't you think?"

Brad's memory flashed up a picture of Alice in his bed, not that long ago, post-coitally happy and stretching. "Sure, it will be," he said, stomach turning sourly. "I mean it is."

Alice is on the phone with Molly for the fourth time today, trying to re-explain Brad's behavior in a way that makes sense. And leaves room for salvation.

"It's been okay, you know. He's been nice about splitting shifts at work. And rehearsal's been okay, right?"

"Uh-huh," murmurs Molly.

"But I can't help feeling there's still something going on with Lori. That's probably just my nerves, right? I mean he would tell me if—"

Molly has been sitting quietly, making reassuring noises until she finally snaps, "Maybe your feelings are right."

"What do you mean?" Alice looks at the phone with shock.

"I mean, Alice, this sort of behavior doesn't need any kind of complex explanation."

"So he is trying to leave me? Is that what you're saying?"

"Alice, I'm just saying, did you ever think maybe Brad hasn't got the *cojones* for commitment? I mean, can't you see that he's not ready to settle?"

"Settle?" Alice laughs, relieved. "Oh, I'm not ready to settle either! That's not the issue."

"Well, do you realize that the opposite of settling is moving on?"

"Oh right," Alice bristles. "As if there are only two options."

"All right," Molly sighs. "And what are the other ones?"

"We sound like shit," Shanklin says flatly.

Everyone in the band secretly feels Brad and Alice's separation is a bad omen for the Lather Rinse Repeat debut at the Fusebox. That, on top of the bad rehearsals and poor publicity and Chipper's losing a whole carton of fliers that were supposed to go all over the near west side, and now it's too late to do anything about it except whine and point fingers, which everyone has been doing with greater energy as the show approaches.

Predictably, rehearsal is going badly.

Brad acts as gung-ho as ever. "It's not that bad. We can do this. It's what we all want, right?"

Everyone looks around uncomfortably, feeling how sad it is that something you've wanted for so long can finally arrive at such a time and in such as way that it loses all of the luster you had imagined it would have.

"Let's take a few minutes and then run through the set one last time." Frustrated, Brad grabs the plunger with the key attached and storms down the hall to his toilet.

Alice sits on the couch, feeling naked that everyone knows about her and Brad. I can't even talk to Molly, she thinks, and that leaves who? She feels a poke in the arm. She turns to see Chipper's drumstick, and Chipper's arm, and Chipper's smirking face. It is a less egregious smirk than usual.

"You all right?" he says, sitting down.

"I wish I hadn't come. But the show. Like, ta-da."

"Yeah, the freaking show."

"Our big break."

"Sure, sure. Even if we have to kill each other to make it."

Alice's hair falls in front of her face, and she leaves it there for camouflage.

"Hey," he says. "You know, I don't want to be accused of. I mean, I know it's a little early to say, but. You wanna have a drink? I mean, sometime?"

"I thought you were dating Lori."

"So did I." He laughs, hard and without much mirth. "Until recently."

"So it's contagious," Alice mumbles.

"Yeah, and I think we know who's infected."

Alice stands up. "You know, Chip, thanks, but I don't need this right now."

"I'm sorry." He slaps his head as a clumsy mea culpa. "But think about the drink, you know, when you're ready to."

"Breath-holding would not be advisable."

"Ouch," says Chipper.

At least Brad has agreed not to work the same shifts as Alice for now. Or he decided on his own, depending on whose version you believe. Anyway, it's peaceful in the shop, and Alice can work it alone except during the a.m. and p.m. rushes. Mrs. Irwin, the owner, will be happier with fewer hours to pay for anyway. Molly has come around and is even helping Alice out, as if in silent apology for the cold reality she'd delivered over the phone earlier in the day. She buses tables and makes coffees when Alice gets busy in flowers.

The door jingles and in walks the odd redhead from the diner. Glasses askew on her pale nose.

"Hi," she says. It's almost a whisper. "I'd like." She swallows. "Some flowers? Please?"

"Okay." Alice feels tense for some reason. "What would you like?"

"I don't know. Whatever you think is good."

While Alice makes an arrangement, the redhead walks around, peering into flower buckets, looking at the fliers pasted to the windows. She stops in front of the Fusebox flier on which Alice has scribbled, "Come See Us! Great Show!!!"

Alice often feels that being given free rein to choose someone's flowers is a test of how she feels about the customer. Some of them, it is true, get better flowers than others. It's kind of a law of nature. Watching the redhead poke around the shop, Alice feels like making a pretty good but not great arrangement.

"Is this you?" asks the redhead, pointing at the Fusebox flier.

"Oh, yeah. Our band." Alice blushes. "It's our first big gig." She lays the paper-wrapped flowers on the counter.

"Wow. That's great. Good luck." The girl lifts the bouquet, and her face breaks into a radiant smile. "These are beautiful! Now I really feel like it's spring. Thank you." Her enthusiasm is so genuine that Alice feels guilty for skimping on the bouquet.

As the redhead pays, she says, "I'm Ellen. Would it be okay if I came to see your band?"

"Hey, buy a ticket, take your chance," Alice says, and then laughs.

Ellen jingles out the door, waving.

"That was cute," Alice giggles. "*Can I come to your show?*"

"I've never seen anyone so nervous," says Molly. "I think she has a crush on you."

"Oh, please," Alice says.

"You just said she was cute!"

"But that's—I just saw her up close for this first time. That's all."

"First Chipper hits on you, and now this chick. I'm going to call you the Morton Salt girl. When it rains," Molly says.

"You just shut up," Alice says, with a funny half-smile. "Brad and I aren't over yet."

"Brad or no Brad, your life is most definitely going on."

Saturday the 22nd

How he got here, on the damp sidewalk outside his daughter's house in Beacon Hill, is hard for Elias to explain. After closing the diner Friday night, he went home as usual, drank some coffee as usual, and did some laundry as usual. The loneliness rang in his ears the way it always did in the early morning hours. He was neither more nor less happy than normal. But he was thinking about Easter, about family ties and how thin and attenuated they had become. He even stood by the phone thinking about calling his daughter to say that no matter the objections, he was coming to see Elana. Consider it dropping in for a chat. A cup of tea. He didn't want a fuss, a big dinner, special accommodations. He merely wanted, in that moment, to see the face of someone familiar, that was all, to see from a distance a side view of a nose, the line of a cheekbone, the back of a tousled head. He wanted to hear someone moving in another room, wanted someone to know where he was and what he was doing, even if he were only snoring in an armchair. He needed so little—so little he didn't know how to ask for it.

So he didn't call.

And yet early in the morning he was on a plane. He lands, hails a taxi, gives an address. And then what? There is no next thing. For all the days he has carried the map of his actions in his head, every hour known and expected, he traveled into a Boston that is as blank before him as sleep or death.

The taxi leaves him across the street from his daughter's family, standing on uneven slabs of pavement. The morning is gray and chilly, the smell of earth and leaf mold clinging to the still air. It is quiet in the densely crowded neighborhood, several houses still dark. Across the street, there is light in two windows of his daughter's house, but no movement.

Now what? To knock on the door seems absurd. He imagines himself standing on the porch, streaming with the needy loneliness that seems to be leaking now from every pore. He wants in, but not by selling himself into their pity. He wants to be *wanted* in. Maybe Elana will see him through a window and come dashing out filled with joy. Then he will go inside, wrap his chilled hands around a cup of coffee, and kiss his daughter's cheek.

He rubs his hands together. He hasn't brought anything, no overnight bag or gifts.

How long will they sleep?

A runner approaches, jogging up the hill wearing a stocking hat and silvery tights. Elias is suddenly uncomfortable. Standing in the middle of the block like this, he must appear sinister or confused. The man jogs past, giving Elias a curious sideways glance. He continues down the block, looks once over his shoulder, and crosses the street and runs back on the other side.

He pulls up across the street, right in front of Sophia's house. "Can I help you?" he calls, continuing to jog in place. "Are you lost?"

"No," Elias says. "No. I'm waiting for someone."

"Maybe I know them," the man says. "I live just down the block."

"No, really, I'm fine," Elias says, looking up at the windows, knowing how ridiculous this scene will appear should someone peek outside at just this moment. "They'll be along any moment. Thank you."

"OK," the man says. He turns and jogs away, more slowly than he came. He looks back twice more, trying to judge what Elias is really doing, before he finally disappears around a corner.

I can't stay here anymore, Elias thinks. He'll call the police eventually. You can't stand around in a nice neighborhood for no good reason. He crosses the street. The short walkway to the front stoop halts him. The house, two narrow stories of red brick colonial, seems to leap from the squat holly bushes. Elias is newly struck by how fine the house is. It reeks of old wealth, everything trim and clean, painted, pruned, and swept with a profuse attention. He thinks of his bungalow in Chicago and feels how small and worn it is. Maybe he should feel happier for Sophia instead of frustrated by the occasional missed holiday. She has so much here and he offers so little.

The porch light flicks on and, without thinking, Elias scuttles to the alley beside the house. Maybe Jonathan's coming out to get the paper. Should he walk up to him now, nonchalantly? Or give up this charade and go home, pretend nothing ever happened? While still debating his next action, Elias hears a door creak open and slam shut. Footsteps scuffling through leaves. A small child's sing-song voice. He moves beside the low wooden fence around the back yard. And there is Elana, lost inside her nonsense song, dragging a doll through neat piles of leaves lined up against the back fence. Her tiny figure, black curls, and chubby legs, dressed for the holiday in a peach pinafore and white stockings, combine to mesmerize him. Tears come into his eyes. He could not think of a more accurate expression of what he feels than to say that it is a blow to the chest. A mighty fist swung with force smack in the center of his ribcage. He fights for breath, worried that he is about to blubber.

"Child?" He calls softly. "Elana dear?"

She turns and takes a few quick steps toward the house. And then her eyes brighten. "Grampa!"

She flies over to him, reaching up her small, soft hands, one still holding tight to the doll. He reaches down and lifts her up into his embrace. The smell of her hair, the chilled gooseflesh over the warmth of her cheeks. She is real, an amazing, profound piece of the world.

"The Easter bunny is going to hide eggs tomorrow," Elana whispers into his ear. "Don't scare him away."

"I won't." Elias sets her back down, on the other side of the fence. "I can't stay long. Don't tell your mommy I was here. I have to go home now. I just wanted to see you for a moment."

"Are you being secret?" Elana asks, eyes wide with suspense.

"Yes. I'll come again soon and bring you a toy, but today is secret."

"We're going to have chocolate eggs but first we have to eat our lunch," Elana says.

"Elana? Come inside before you get all dirty." It is Sophia's voice. Elias feels ludicrously exposed. He has turned the impulsive visit into something sinister, created spaces without names between him and his daughter. Why is he such a fool?

"Grampa has to go, but next time I'll come with a nice toy, very nice. Okay?"

"Okay."

He puts a finger to his lips. Elana does the same in reply.

"Elana!" Sophia calls again. "Right this minute."

Elias waves for her to go. Elana runs into the house.

The plane ride back is eternal. The plane is soaring into the oncoming night over the Ohio River Valley when he remembers his promise. Next time? There can be no next time. And he says a prayer that Sophia never finds out about his secret visit. It would be no fun to explain it. Even if he could.

Sunday the 23rd (Easter)

The itch of straw nags Brother Even awake. He rolls stiffly to his side and gets on one knee. His back protests. Sleeping on the floor gets harder every year. He puts his weight on a stack of Modern Classics and rises to his feet, wobbling until his head clears. His feet tingle as the blood flows down to them. He logged extra miles yesterday, passing out his hand-lettered leaflets, Invoke God's Love to Keep Satan at Bay, all over Lakeview. As he stomps the tingle from his feet, his knees respond with a burning stiffness. This is familiar, the pain in his legs from standing all day. He looks at the rumpled burlap bag. Forty days. At last it can be restuffed with the straw and put away until next year.

The front window of Brother Even's two-room West Side apartment looks right down Madison to the ragged canyons of the Loop, where the Easter dawn is glowing pink at the bottom and rising to a washed blue sky overhead.

He puts a kettle on the stove and walks through the large, book-cluttered closet to the bathroom. Unconsciously, he puts a hand over the slight rising of his penis, a frequent morning manifestation. He squats on the toilet and ponders his thin flanks. He groans with effort. His light Lenten diet has robbed him of what little fat he put on over the winter. He tears a corner of paper towel and wipes. He pulls his underwear down from the shower curtain rod. Handwashed nightly with Ivory hand soap, they are discolored but clean. And a little rough from air-drying. Ditto his thin black socks. After lathering up a handful of that Ivory, he scrubs his face and splashes on cold water, sending a cascade of gooseflesh down his back. He fills a

Styrofoam cup and pours cold water on his head, sluicing from his hair the ashes of his sins.

Every Easter Eve, Brother Even writes his sins on a piece of fine white paper. He uses his most careful penmanship and a gold-nibbed fountain pen purchased expressly for this purpose, which spends the rest of the year wrapped in velvet inside a shoebox. He writes clearly, with his best auto-didact calligraphy. God, after all, is this document's one and only reader.

To send his sins via celestial mail, Brother Even sets light to one corner of the paper and lets it burn to ashes in his dry and clean cereal bowl while he kneels and prays for forgiveness. Lastly, he pours the ashes on his head and lies down on burlap and straw to sleep and to await god's reply. He has never, in all his years, been denied absolution by his lord.

His head aches from hunger. He checks his eyes in the mirror. The pupils are clear, the brown irises flecked with gold.

Dressed in his only clothes, a black suit, and his one pair of scuffed, down-at-the-heel oxfords, Brother Even sits down to a breakfast of tea and toast. He prays: Lord this is your blood and your breath. Lord this is your bone and your flesh. Let the spirit rise through these and come into me so that I may read your word upon the face of the world and let it be known. In thy name I eat of you and drink of you amen.

As he eats, he reads from *The Brothers Karamazov*. The margins of the pages are gray with Brother Even's notes. Scraps of paper stick from the top as thick as hair. He turns the pages as quickly as his eyes dart across them, licking his fingers for each turn. He finishes the last of the tea as the sun establishes a firm position above the skyline.

Light slices through the city and into Brother Even's room, pouring down between the stacks of books. Library discards of sports biographies. Used and burnished philosophical readers. Twain. Derrida. Ashbery. Paperbacks curled up like puppy ears. Dickens. Virgil. Carver. Books enough to serve as a room within a room, with which to build furniture, walls, floors, windows.

After cleaning the plate and cup, he reads, very solemnly, twelve pages of *Sonnets to Orpheus*. Amen, he says, as he closes the book.

Lord, thou art truly resident and holy within the word, he says, as he rises and goes out to begin the long wait for the Sunday bus.

His grandma always said that in Tennessee you know God like a favorite uncle who comes to dinner every Sunday. As a child, Brother Even imagined a large, muscular man in a clean white shirt, hair washed and combed, gentle and contrite over whatever lapse he'd experienced in the week since his last Sunday dinner.

In Chicago, the experience of God is more like that beloved relative who has moved to a foreign place and can communicate only by coded telegrams that are as urgent as they are lacking in warmth. Brother Even spends Easter day receiving and translating messages from the far-off god.

"What is this day of God's rejoicing that is newly upon us, brothersister? It is a day in which God will give you the truth through your own mouths. Listen. Say, Easter. Hear the bend and cluck of your own tongue. Ease-stir. Ease and stir. There now, you see that on this day of days God puts Ease upon your souls, blesses you, yes, brothersister, in order to Stir you so that you may realize the greater glory."

The sidewalks are bustling with early churchgoers. Little girls walk carefully in new pastel dresses. Boys mess with the comb-spliced parts in their hair.

"An accident of history, you say? Words bumping into other words, migrating from foreign lands to become misheard, misspelled, and spread like genetic mutations into the fertile ears of the interlocutors?"

A bus driver coming off shift stops and throws a dollar into the hat. Brother Even nods his thanks.

"There are no accidents, brothersister. Despair as your mind comprehends this fact. Then rejoice as your heart understands it more deeply. Glory."

Some folks are grateful for the message. Others not. By day's end, the hat has collected $17.85.

Brother Even breaks his Lenten fast with a chicken burrito. He sits at the counter savoring the first few bites, swelling with thankfulness that the lord permits such beauty on the earth. But halfway through it, the meat sits heavily on his unaccustomed stomach. He walks outside and flings the last pieces of shredded chicken into the alley. He stands and eats the remaining beans and cheese in the tortilla, watching a caved-in tomcat scarf up the savory morsels of chicken.

At dusk, Brother Even rides the bus down to the Museum of Science and Industry. The parking lots are empty. He walks across the pedestrian bridge over Lake Shore Drive to the 57th Street beach. The wind has picked up, carrying a definite edge from the cool far-off center of the lake. At the north end of the beach, he finds his customary rock. It is still there, loose, with a dry hollow behind it, carved out by Brother Even himself over twenty years ago, before his first lake walk.

He sits on the stone and removes his shoes. Into the left shoes he puts his watch and keys. Into the right, his wallet. Both shoes are then stuffed with his rolled socks. He places the shoes and his hat inside the hole and covers it with the stone.

The air has a slightly fishy tinge. The sand is moist and flat, giving underfoot like a rubber mat. Brother Even faces east and closes his eyes. His hands are at his sides, palms forward, fingers curled slightly. He feels the engines of cars racing down the Drive behind him. He steps forward, silently, not praying, emptying his mind of everything but the white star burning in the pure black firmament. As his feet reach the water and sink into the softer lake bottom, his steps grow more labored. The star begins to pulse.

Water sucks at his trouser legs, pushing his body, pulling it out to where he begins to feel buoyant, his feet merely brushing the bottom. When the water is up to his neck, a faint oiliness reaches his nose. He steps abruptly into a sudden depression and drops into the true black and cold water where the lake no longer has any relation to the shore.

He bobs in a middle space, suspended in ear-ringing silence, and the star pulses with more and more brilliance until his mind is filled with its merciful white.

He wakes in the pre-dawn, face up on the sand. His feet eddy gently, pushed by the tiny waves flopping to the shore. The white star's fire is gone, lost behind muddy clouds overhead. He feels his pruny fingertips and smiles.

Delivered for another year. Praise be.

Wednesday the 26th

It seems absurd to be angry to find your lover in bed in the morning. But Megan's angry to find Ellen asleep next to her and once again have no recollection of her coming to bed. And hurt that Ellen wouldn't make sure she knew. Would a snuggle have killed her?

And now the conflicting desires to touch or to move away from Ellen's thin, composed shoulders. Megan compromises. Keeping her body away, she slides her feet over and strokes Ellen's feet with her own. Ellen mumbles and sleeps on.

For several weeks now this has been the pattern. Ellen promises to go out for drinks, come over for dinner, whatever. She cancels, but promises to come over later, and then does so only after Megan has given up waiting and gone to bed.

Megan pulls her feet back. Ellen doesn't stir. Fine. Supposedly, it's the effing film. Ellen insists that she can only edit by night. Which, I'm sorry, is very suspicious. Megan looks at the clock. Six fifty-five. Great. Alarm goes off in five minutes. She rolls over. How refreshing to wake up after a whole night of hating your girlfriend.

The radio pops on. *Our love is a like a ship on the ocean, I mean we're sailing with a cargo full of*— Megan slams the radio to the floor. Ellen bolts up, wild-eyed.

"Oops," says Megan. "Slipped."

"God, I thought a bomb went off." Ellen's red hair is standing on end, like an *Our Gang* sight gag.

"I'll make coffee." Megan rolls out of bed and slips on her robe.

"I feel sick," Ellen moans. She pulls the covers over her head. "I need more sleep."

"When did you come in, anyway?"

"I don't know. Three something." She curls up on her side. "Ugh. I've got that scared-awake nausea."

"You know, between the insomnia and the all-nighters, I feel like I'm sleeping with a big cat that just comes and goes as it pleases."

"I'm sorry," says Ellen. "That was my last nocturnal editing session."

"Oh, really? You finish?"

"No. Not quite." Ellen folds herself back into the covers.

Megan walks to the kitchen, fills the coffeepot with water, and then returns to the bedroom to say, "I feel like a piece of furniture. You come near me, but you don't interact with me. It's like you're proving you're around, keeping some kind of promise, but you're not really around."

From under a pillow, Ellen says, "The less we interact, the less we fight. Much healthier."

Megan gives Ellen the finger through the bathroom wall, then turns on the shower, scalding hot.

Ellen covers her head and tries to fall back to sleep. All she can see is Dean Hollis's head appearing in the doorway of the editing suite.

Four nights a week for the last three weeks Ellen has hunched over this little whirring machine watching the jumpy, gray-toned images rattle past the tiny editing screen. Her armpits pouring with a sour sweat of constant fear. The race to finish something, five minutes, eight minutes of footage before she's busted.

And then the shuffle of feet, a pause, and the door creaks open, Hollis's head poking through like a mutant tentacle probing the air of a strange planet. "Hello?" he squeaks.

Bam. Caught red-handed, parked on a stool with the tiny reels of super eight stacked around her. Two in the morning and the man has nowhere else to be?

"Ellen?" he says. "What are you doing?" His sparse sandy hair is freshly combed forward.

"Um," Ellen says. "This project?"

Hollis's eyes scan the room, taking it all in. "I thought you had to give up your student privileges."

"Well, I've been, you know, in some classes, and—"

"Okay. This is a problem." Hollis crosses his arms in the doorway, outlined by the rather dirty fluorescent light from the corridor.

"Problem," Ellen echoes.

"Ellen, I'm afraid this is trespassing."

Ellen feels tears push hotly at her eyes. "Trespassing?"

"I don't know how you got in, but you can't stay."

Ellen starts pushing reels around, looking for something that will stop this moment from falling completely apart. "But I only have three minutes done."

"I'm sorry," Hollis says. He backs out the door.

Ellen pulls the half-edited section of tape from the machine with fumbling fingers and carefully places the reels in her backpack. Crying all the while. With the backpack in her lap, she sits and cries until she is calm.

That editing machine, she thinks, it's pretty small. I could lift it.

The door creaks open again. "You'd better go," says Hollis.

Ellen wipes her nose with her fingers. "If you don't mind me asking," she sniffs, "why are you here at this time of night?"

He puts his hands in the small of his back and stretches. "I'm sleeping here tonight. Part of a domestic peace accord."

"Not strictly allowed," Ellen admonishes.

"No," Hollis coughs, "not strictly allowed." A pause hangs in the air. "Are you using sound?"

"Silent," says Ellen. "I'm adding v.o. and music after the editing."

Hollis rubs his face and sighs. "An interesting thing about super eight," he says after a pause, "is that with a lot of patience, you can edit it without a moviola. Let me show you." He holds out his hand. Ellen gives him her unfinished reel. Hollis takes it to a light table. He unspools a couple of feet.

"See? You can fabricate a light table at home. Plate glass, two chairs, a lamp. You can also make a sprocket guide with a couple of two-penny nails and a block of pine."

He straightens his back painfully. "It won't be smooth. But if you wanted smooth, you wouldn't be shooting in eight to begin with."

"And how can I edit it if I can't see it?" Ellen whines, just a little put out by Hollis's half-assed solicitude.

"Use the projector, I guess. I didn't say it would be easy. Anyway, that's just until you can re-enroll."

"If ever." Ellen rolls the film back on the spool.

"I'm sorry," Hollis says. "Is there a key I should get from you?"

Ellen hands it to him. "Could you not say anything about this?"

"Who would I tell?" He opens the door and ushers Ellen out. "Good luck," he says.

At around eleven, Ellen wakes up feeling hung-over and oily. She buries her head under a pillow, but there's no getting around it, the day after is here. "Goddamn Hollis," she says.

Now what?

Next to the bed is a cup of coffee. She touches the cup. Cold. And there is a note under the cup.

El, The way I see it, either you spend some real time with me or give up this pretend bullshit intimacy of sleeping here. I need I deserve better than this. —M.

"Well," Ellen says to the note. "Thank you. It's not that I would expect love and understanding."

Ellen pulls her clothes on quickly and stuffs everything she has in Megan's apartment into three shopping bags. At the bottom of Megan's note, she scrawls, *Is this better?*

Ellen dumps the bags in the middle of her apartment and stretches out on the floor, exhausted. Marty comes purring and walks across her back.

Once again, now what? The only thing that occurs to her is the diner. Mrs. F. cheers me up. But she doesn't move. Her arms and legs have lost their will. Her hands and feet ask, *Why do anything?* She hasn't got school, work, art, love, family. There is low, there is the bottom, and below that there is today.

Marty walks around to her face and sniffs at it, meowing.

"Don't mind me," Ellen says. "I'm okay." The cat jumps into the window sill and looks down at Ellen, puzzled.

Ellen lies on the floor, looking at the patterns of dust on the floor fired by the sunlight, until, somehow, the day fades into night. Marty is making his bed for the third time right in the small of her back. His claws work back and forth on her kidneys. Misery has claws, Ellen thinks. Time to get up. Drinking a glass of water in the kitchen, she sees the flier for the Lather Rinse Repeat show. It's tonight. Tonight?

"I don't know," she says to Marty. "This might not be a good time."

The phone call five minutes later decides her. Megan's voice on the machine, full of venom. Words like hate, fuck, and shithead burst out after the beep. The only complete sentence an enraged Megan can spin together is, "And you better figure out just what the fuck you think you're doing."

At which Ellen picks up the receiver and shouts, "I'm seizing the fucking day, all right, goddammit?" before slamming the phone down and pulling the cord from the wall.

The silence is deafening.

"So I go," she says to Marty, who is crouched under the kitchen table, ears laid back for a fight.

Pierced and garishly made-up teens crowd the floor of the Fusebox, shoving elbows. Big boots, bell-bottoms, tiny tees and tanks revealing arm-length tattoos. Everyone has long hair or none. Ellen gets drunk on a series of blackish microbrews. She wanders from room to room in the club, watching and waiting.

The band doesn't go on until almost one. But they do it, finally, with style. Alice/Avis slinking side to side, stroking her guitar dreamily like it is the flank of a big, sleeping cat. Her quote-boyfriend leaning over the microphone does a gentle croak of lyrics which, surprisingly, don't suck.

The refrain pops in and the buzz-cut girl lays a piano line over Alice's harmony, and there is a moment of quite simply riveting beauty.

Ellen is stunned, and flooded with joy. They're really good, Ellen thinks. Alice is wonderful.

Ellen begins dancing, and ends up near the stage. Alice looks down.

Ellen waves. Alice smiles crookedly and then closes her eyes to stay within the music. Ellen dances her way over to the bar.

A wiry little guy with muttonchop sideburns is peddling hand-dyed T-shirts. He holds one up in front of Ellen. It reads, Love Is Bind.

She laughs, "Probably."

He holds up another reading, Love Is Bing.

"I'll take that one," she says.

Alice is twirling with the guitar hung at hip level.

"Bing," Ellen says to herself. "We'll just see about that."

Friday the 28th

It's not a heavy imposition for Leda to get to school a half hour earlier than she used to. The time she spends with Ng is just about the nicest thing she's ever known. Kissing under the bleachers before class is good too, but what she really likes is how open he is. Maybe it sounds stupid, but she does think of him, you know, like a book, with everything there for her to see, to read. There's like one boy in fifty million who has that kind of fearlessness.

She waits, leaning her head against the door of her locker. The empty hallway stinks of polishing compound. "Come on," she whispers.

Leda has an agenda this morning. Instead of crawling under the bleachers for their morning saliva swap, she is going to show Ng a new magazine that arrived at Stimpy's yesterday. One she hopes will convince Ng that cartooning is his destiny.

She pulls it from her backpack. *The City by The Flake.* Cheaply but professionally produced, the zine is a hybrid between the photocopied and stapled do-it-yourself jobs and a low-end mass-market mag. It's on newsprint with a two-color glossy cover. Only thirty-two pages, but the drawings by this guy, the Flake, even she can tell—whoa.

"Hey," says Ng, rounding the corner.

Leda puts the magazine behind her back. "Hey yourself, Mr. Late."

Ng's grin has been growing wider since he saw Leda standing alone in the empty hall like some oasis. "I'm sorry," he laughs. "I brought a note from my mom?" His grin finally peeks out at a full crescent moon of teeth.

"I brought you a surprise," Leda says and then reveals the magazine.

"Holy cow," Ng mumbles, taking the magazine reverently in hand. "This is too cool."

Leda watches happily as Ng flips through the pages. Ng whistles. "This Flake guy, he's a like genius. And he's local?"

"I don't know. He don't hang around the store the way some of them do. Why don't you send him some work?"

A door at the end of the hall crashes open. A sing-song voice calls, "Hello-o-o."

Ng grabs Leda's hand and they run toward the gym.

Five boys push into the hall, each of them slamming the door against the wall as they pass through. "Where you go, friend?" calls Ivan, at the head of the group. "We like talk to you."

Ng stops and turns. Running is pointless. "Don't worry," he says, putting his body in front of Leda. "It's just bullying time."

Ivan claps his hand on Ng's shoulder. Smiling. "Little Too Good, we not see you lately." Ivan's eyes travel up and down Leda's body. "But I see what keep you so busy."

Leda pops her gum and sneers.

"You and me go talk, Too Good. You girlfriend have good company, okay?"

"She has an early class," Ng says, and gives Leda a shove.

"It can wait," Leda says.

"Come on." Ivan tugs Ng toward the stairs.

Ng looks back over his shoulder. Leda is staring down the other boys, snapping her gum in a rapid-fire cadence.

Ivan pushes Ng into his office, the basement-level boy's bathroom. An anemic light drizzles in the high window of thick, pebbled glass. A pool of luminous liquid soap pulses menacingly on the tile floor.

Ivan backs Ng against a sink. "You know Parsley, art teacher, right? You good friend?" He smiles, and Ng can smell his breath, sweet with strawberry gum.

Ng nods. John Parsley is his favorite teacher, and he is Parsley's star pupil. They chat daily, or they had until Ng discovered kissing Leda.

"This Parsley, he kick from school my boy, Eddie Fong. Eddie not do nothing." Ivan's voice grows strident, blade-like. "Parsley file some paper." Ivan leans back against a sink, his posture of power. "Eddie parent still on visa, so Eddie have to go school. You know?"

Ng shrugs. "So? What happens now?"

"We make Parsley change him mind. And you going help us."

"He won't change his mind because I say so."

"Listen, Too Good." Ivan puts a hand on Ng's shoulder. "You fuck us up last time and we don't make you pay so much. This time for real. You know?"

"What do you want me to do?"

"It up to you. Scare him. Give blow job." Ivan laughed at this. "Whatever it take."

"This is ridiculous. I'm not going to do anything to Parsley."

Ivan steps forward until his nose is almost touching Ng's. "You remember last black eye? You want pretty girlfriend with black eye, too? Some empty tooth?"

Ng hears the voices of students starting to flood down the stairs. He says nothing.

"Or maybe she want make a deal with Ivan." The threat, while vague, makes Ng violently queasy.

Ng suddenly feels as though he is looking down on himself from a great height. It is clear from this vantage point that there is nothing near at hand that will help him. No one at all who can advise or save him.

"You have five day," Ivan says. "We keep close eye on you. And on pretty girlfriend."

"Okay," Ng says finally. "I'll figure something out. Don't—"

"Don't what, Little Too Good?"

"Don't do anything. Please."

"Ivan watch you close. When Eddie come back school, you not have more worry."

Ng can't draw anything. He moves from seat to seat around the still-life arrangement, making tentative marks on the paper. Amid the bottles and plastic pears, Parsley has placed a skull borrowed from the biology lab. The eye sockets are terrifying.

At the front of the room, Parsley explains the purpose of the *memento mori* in still life compositions. "Renaissance artists believed art should serve as a reminder of mortality."

"But everybody knows they are going to die," says another student.

"Yes, but knowing it and feeling it are two different things," Parsley replies. "Does anybody here feel keenly the possibility that death may be just around the corner? Hands? Now be honest."

Five hands go up. It takes some effort for Ng to keep his hand down.

"There are always a few," says Parsley. "The sensitive types." Some of the students laugh.

Ng keeps his eyes on his paper. He draws the outline of the skull and sketches two flowers where the eyes should be.

After school, Ng sits on a bus stop bench half a block from the school and, at a distance, watches Parsley walk to his car. It is late, the lot almost empty.

It was hard sending Leda off to Stimpy's by herself, but he couldn't tell her about Ivan and Parsley. She would go nuts if she knew. It wouldn't help.

He watches the tall, angular teacher fold himself into an old blue Honda Civic. Five days, Ng thinks. He imagines a scale with Parsley on one pan and Leda on the other. The scale rocks back and forth. Parsley's car growls and sputters out of the teachers' parking lot. Bad muffler.

Ng feels branded. No one who looks at him will see the real him. What they'll see is a coward, and a fool, who can be bullied by a cretin. If only he didn't care about Leda, he could warn Parsley and take whatever punishment came. But not Leda. He can't make that decision for her.

He pulls the magazine Leda gave him from his book bag. It was so beautiful in the morning. Now it looks ridiculous. Worse, it looks like a joke he was playing on himself. Ng stuffs the magazine in a trashcan and walks home.

May

Wednesday the 3rd

While slicing seven pounds of celery in the kitchen of Qu-Zeen Catering, Robin feels the bottom drop out of his stomach. A moment later, he realizes why. The last day he saw his mother, she was making a soup, potato probably, and trying to chop turnips. The knife kept falling out of her hand, clattering on the counter.

It was spring, like this. Robin sat on the back steps, poking in the wild grasses his father couldn't be bothered to pull. There were wild onions, mint, dandelions, strawberries. The windows were open and he could hear his mother struggling. It wasn't unusual. Since the accident, she'd become erratic in her movements. When she caressed his head, her hand would tremble noticeably.

Robin walked in with a handful of mint, the strong sharp flavor in his mouth from the few leaves he'd nibbled. His mother had begun hammering the sharp edge of the knife against the sink. Blood on the floor, blood on her hand. Were there sparks, he wondered, once she had chipped through the porcelain to the cast iron? He seems to remember sparks.

She was panting and trying to contain her fury. When she saw Robin, she screamed, "Get out of here! Get away from the knives!"

Robin stood, knees shaking.

The knife fell to the floor and stuck point first in the linoleum. His mother turned on the cold water and washed the blood away, saying nothing.

What had he done next? What had happened to the mint? He simply can't remember. A few days later his father drove her to a new hospital, a sanitarium.

"Knock knock," says Robin at the edge of Nathan's cubicle.

Nathan turns and says into the phone, "Listen, Maddy, can I call you back?" He hangs up quickly.

"Maddy?" asks Robin.

"Never mind. What, why are you here?" Nathan pushes a pile of print-outs out of a chair and motions Robin to sit.

"Can't we go out somewhere? Get some lunch?"

Nathan takes off his glasses and rubs the red spots on the bridge of his nose. "Is there something wrong?"

"Why? I just though I'd pop in and see my lover."

Nathan hisses, "Robin, this is a cubicle." He motions to the low, portable walls.

"How about a walk, then. Coffee in the sculpture garden?"

"All right, just a minute." Nathan shuffles a few papers and then stands up.

"Can we walk through the knights in shining armor?"

"The Gunsaulus Hall is out of the way."

"Please? Pretty please with sugar on top?"

The museum is quiet, and their footsteps echo loudly. Robin pauses in front of the flintlock pistols. "Wouldn't I love a derringer some days at the market," he whispers. "You're charging what for radicchio? Pow!"

"Come on," says Nathan. "I don't have long."

"Wait." Robin tugs him over to another case. "This is what I really wanted to see."

The case holds walking sticks with daggers hidden inside, and other items which ingeniously combine benign utility with the capacity to maim. A silver flask with a spring-loaded knife on the side. An ivory fan with a very small pistol in the handle. Opera glasses with brass knuckles folded underneath.

"For some reason, I find these immensely beautiful," Robin sighs.

"Obviously, they speak to your desire for revenge."

"Or how I long to be an opera bully. Why were you talking to Maddy?"

"I thought we were going to talk about you."

"I'm sure we'll end up there, anyway."

As they walk past the admissions desk, Nathan waves to the docents. "I just suggested to her that Uncle Peter might be happier in a hotel," he says to Robin.

"You bastard. The specter of coming out is just too much." Robin pushes through the revolving door. Outside, the air is mild. Art students and tourists sprawl on the broad steps that lead down to Michigan Avenue.

"Robin, he's a *priest,* for crying out loud. He's not the best person in the family to come out to."

"The best person in your mind would be like a person as close to me as possible but straight and your brother."

"Maybe. What's so wrong with that?"

"You can't manage this away. Uncle Peter won't like it, probably, and maybe your family won't either, so then what?"

"Anyway, it's moot. I gave in." Nathan sits down and leans against one of the giant fluted columns. The stone is cool against his suddenly sweaty back. "Father Peter Reagan will be our responsibility for god knows how long starting in two weeks."

"Hoo-ha." Robin slides down next to Nathan, sighing. "For some reason, that doesn't cheer me up much."

Nathan scoots over to put a little distance between his leg and Robin's. "So why did you come down here?"

He shivers. "I had another vision. It was awful."

"Maybe you should stop cooking. It seems to be an emotionally volatile act for you."

"It also happens to be my livelihood. Speaking of which, I should get back to work."

Nathan touches Robin's leg discreetly. "Are you okay?"

Robin smiles. "I'm better. Thanks. See you tonight."

Nathan tries to read a book while Robin paces the living room with the cordless phone, growing more and more agitated. It's too bad Janie is the only one left he can talk to. Since her conversion and re-baptism in the Living Church of Christ's Personal Word, she's barely willing to talk to Robin, and never about the family. If only there were someone else.

"What happened to you, Janie? Why are you like this?" Robin whines. "Fine! It was all a dream, it never happened, and I'm a regular red-blooded American male and you're okay and our family is the picture of health. Wake up, Janie! Just wake the hell up, okay?"

As Robin's voice rises in pitch, Nathan tries humming to drown out the imminent hysteria. Finally, he has to intervene. For Robin's sake and everyone else's.

He begins signaling, "Stop," in the middle of Robin's tirade, and pleading with his eyes for Robin to calm down and be more forgiving. Robin turns to avoid seeing Nathan's pantomime, and Nathan keeps pursuing him, so that they end up pivoting like boxers, with Robin guarding and Nathan looking for the entry punch.

"So all of the sudden, Dad thinks you're Florence Nightingale," Robin snaps. "Let's not forget who nursed Mom for ten years while you played *Dukes of Hazzard* with Bobby Hutchinson!"

Suddenly, Robin stands still, and slowly puts the phone on the table. "She hung up."

"Are you surprised? Why are you so merciless? She suffered, too."

Robin looks shell-shocked, his chest rising and falling as if he'd been running.

"I'm sorry," says Nathan, and puts out a hand.

"Don't, please." Robin leans against the wall and looks out the window. The yellow daffodils in the window box look blown and papery, like used tissues.

Nathan moves up behind him. "Why did you call her? You always get upset, and we fight."

Robin leans back against Nathan's chest. "I don't know…I don't know. My family is just…"

Nathan puts his chin on Robin's shoulder. They stand that way for a moment, just breathing.

Saturday the 6th

Florence regards Les Potamkin's backside with a keen eye as he stretches to replace her storm windows with screens for the summer. A playful study in shapes and blocks of color.

"One more," says Potamkin over his shoulder, and leans through the window to wipe a thumbprint from the edge of the frame. Over and beyond his head the sky is a pearly blue that seems to intensify as it falls into the lake.

"How'd you go so long without screens? Everybody else changed theirs out in March."

His back is a strong, rounded square of navy blue. His haunches a khaki ovoid full of infoldings and layers.

"Oh, you know us old ladies. We're always cold."

Dare I, she wonders, paint in the delicate white sliver between his tee shirt and pants? And the shadowy cleft between the belt loops that implies the beginning of his—

"That should do it." Potamkin stands and tugs his shirt over his hard, round belly. "And you don't seem old to me."

"Oh, please." Florence blushes. "I know I am, and it's fine with me."

"I just mean. You seem brighter, lately." Potamkin's eyes wander around the apartment nervously. "You've come through some bad times, is all."

"True. Rough patches."

After an awkward pause, Potamkin notices a set of framed watercolors stacked in the foyer. "Hello," he says, relieved to have something to put his hand to. "You want me to hang those?"

"Oh, well…yes, I guess so. I was thinking of putting them in the hall there." She shows Potamkin the space she cleared the week before, re-arranging several photos of her and Arnie and putting some of the less attractive pictures away.

"These here are some very nice paintings," Potamkin says around a mouthful of nails. "Where'd you get them?"

She allows herself a small prideful smile. "Actually, Les, I painted them myself."

Potamkin does a doubletake and quickly checks the signature of *Still Life with Jumping Labrador.*

"So you did," he says with admiration. Then he furrows his brows. "You shouldn't surprise a fellow with nails in his mouth. Could cause a perforated framalax."

"Oh my, no," says Florence, laughing. "Sounds serious."

"Putting it mildly." Potamkin hammers three evenly spaced nails in the off-white walls. There is a faint smile on his broad, stubbly face.

Anxious about her clothes for the Art Institute reception later that night, Florence calls Louise.

"It's my first time out, really, since…"

"Are you sure you're ready?" Louise grunts as she bends over to scrub the bathtub, which she told Florence has been turned into an algae farm by

Jimbo's constant showering. "Going unattended to an event like that? Are you sure?"

Standing in her walk-in closet, Florence throws up her hands. "Goodness gracious, Louise, I don't know if I'm ready. It just seems like it's time."

Florence hears scrubbing but no reply from Louise. At last, she says, "I guess I'll just wear the navy jumpsuit you and Jim gave me."

A few more seconds of furious scrubbing before Louise says at last, "Don't you dare wear that to the museum party. Arnie will spin in his grave."

Florence laughs. "I'm sure Arnie would appreciate your steering me away from a fashion disaster. So think May, artsy reception, and widow with taste."

"I'd go sleeveless down here," Louise muses. "Do women of a certain age show their arms up there?"

Summer is arriving at last, and you can feel the full force of it east of Lake Shore Drive, where white sails slice across the water, bikers race past joggers and walkers, and volleyball players in fluorescent spandex shorts kick up sprays of sand.

Florence leans into the cab's back seat and closes her eyes to let the warm breeze flow over her. The rhythms of salsa and rap music wash past her window from passing cars. Her armpits are sweaty. Good thing she opted for dress shields under her long-sleeved, light-green, scoop-necked dress, hemmed tastefully below mid-calf.

"I don't like how that Potamkin ogles you," says Arnie, appearing beside her.

"Good heavens, Arnie, don't be ridiculous." She smiles, suddenly calmed to have Arnie near.

Arnie sniffs. "Just watch out for these guys tonight. They think going to this schmancy-type party means they can hit all over beautiful women like you."

"Oh, Arnie."

"If Donny Rasmussen is there, keep your hand on your purse and watch your behind."

"I will."

"I don't think I like this going alone. You couldn't get a date? What about that Greek? He's a decent type."

"Arnie, I want to go alone," whispers Florence, aware of the cab driver's eyes in the rearview mirror.

Arnie holds up his hands. "Word of warning. Just go easy on the hooch, all right?"

"I'll be fine." Florence feels the heat of anger in her face, which brings with it a kind of déjà vu.

"All right, all right," Arnie pouts. "Oh revere, mon cherry." The vinyl seat beside her is suddenly very empty.

Florence sits, discomfited, fiddling with the clasp of her handbag. Arnie was always such a sweet rat when he got worried about her. All too soon the cab pulls off of the Drive and swings around to the Art Institute's Columbus Avenue entrance. Two long scarlet banners reading "Millennial Dadaism" and "Anarchy and Evolution" hang across the white stone front. Florence passes between them and follows the signs to the Founder's Reception.

Oh boy, thinks Florence. Here we go. She swims into the din of the hall, walking a little nervously past tuxedos and sleek evening gowns. She wanders down the buffet, which must be a hundred yards long. The food displays test Florence's rather dusty knowledge of dadaism. A platter of sliced veggies is arrayed in the shape of Duchamp's *Nude Descending a Staircase.* Florence takes a few pieces of yellow bell pepper from the nude's left foot and a scoop of blue cheese dressing from a bowl that does not seem to signify anything.

She wanders down the table past ice sculptures in the shape of urinals and bicycle wheels. A large portrait of a female's head appears to be made of giant matchsticks, which turn out to be jicama and radishes.

There is a snow shovel hanging over the bar. She picks up a cocktail napkin that reads "Zimzam zanzibar zim zalla zam."

The young, peroxide-blonde bartender arches one multipierced eyebrow at Florence. "What can I get you?"

Florence hesitates. That Arnie, trying to spook her. "I'll have a dry martini with olives, please." *Take that, Arnie.*

She takes the martini by its brimming rim. Florence lowers her lips over the clear liquid. The perfume of the gin trickles up her nostrils. She feels a little dizzy as she quietly slurps the ice-cold liquid into her mouth. A strange numbing heat passes her tongue and down her throat to her stomach. She is filled, for a second time that evening, with a sense of déjà vu.

She motions the bartender close. "If I ask for another drink, just give me a martini glass filled with water and a lemon twist." Arnie's old party ploy: look like a bon vivant but stay sharp.

"Sure thing," says the bartender with a wink.

In the morning, Florence feels smothered by the sun. She is on top of the bedspread, still in her party dress. Her shoes are on the pillow next to her. "Oh my god," she groans. "At my age?"

She remembers getting a martini. Then she walked into the crowd and got lost in the galleries. The only thing she remembers clearly is a cup lined with fur. Did I drink from that?

She stands and walks to the bathroom. Her head is pounding. It sounds like that Dada napkin. Zimzam zimzam zimzam.

"I knew that kid would overserve you," Arnie says from his perch on the toilet. "How'd you get home, anyway?"

Did one martini do this? She gropes for details. How *did* she get home?

The booming gets louder and the light in the bathroom burns whiter than white.

Monday the 8th

The five-thirty alarm wakes Ng to a deep, blue-black dawn crazy with birdsongs. Grackles call to each other over some piece of bread or spilled pork rinds. Starlings chitter, and a cardinal inserts its rising peep amid the new, lime green leaves of the maple tree that tops out just below the Pran-Markowitz's living-room window. The cacophony makes the apartment feel open to the outside world, like a lean-to.

Ng lays on his pillow watching the birdsongs punctuate the air above his head. It's not like he was sleeping, anyway. His brain hasn't paused for a minute since Ivan backed him into this corner. Like that guy in *A Clockwork Orange* with his eyes pinned open, unable to stop the stream of terrible images pouring in. He's been avoiding everyone—Leda, his mother, Elias. Everything now is ashes.

He has walked through this a million times already. Talk to Parsley, try to reason with him, beg him even. But he knows that, in the end, Parsley will approach this as a matter of principle and lead Ng to a confrontation with Ivan. But confrontation brings Leda into it. No, the best outcome is a fast retraction by Parsley. Then Ivan will go away like a fat dog, quiet after feeding, licking his scabby forepaws in contentment.

So how to get Parsley to change his mind? Ng decided that the quickest and, perhaps, less painful way to wound Parsley is to take away one thing, something so close to him that the shock of it will make the teacher realize that the stakes are higher than he thought they were.

Ng is shocked by his own plan. Where did he learn to think this way? From Ivan? Or was he born with such cruel logic latent in his bones? He asks himself the central silent question that's been the private focus of his whole life: was his father like this? The questions pass through Ng with a chill and nauseate him.

He rises in the dark and pulls on his clothes. Into his backpack he puts two cans of spray paint bought before the Cook County ban on anything that could be used for graffiti. He had used half of the paint refinishing some used furniture Soo bought at a yard sale. Red for the spindle-backed chairs in the kitchen. Green for the bookshelves in Ng's room. He rattles the cans, and the ball bearings inside respond with a sticky clacking.

Is it right to hurt Parsley and protect him from something perhaps worse? Can he justify this for Leda? For Parsley? Ng puts the cold cans against his forehead and takes a deep breath.

Nothing to do now but act and hope for the best.

John Parsley walks out of his Ravenswood three-flat with a mostly light heart. The high morning sun of early May signals that the school year's endgames will now begin in earnest. Seniors will be perpetually absent-minded. Juniors will start to act like they own the place. The semester-long projects will be presented, and there are a couple that he is more than usually excited to see completed.

He fumbles for his keys, balancing his lunch sack, briefcase, and dry cleaning, so he is already at the car door before he sees the ragged scratches down the faded blue paint on the driver's side: "FiX You MisTAkE."

"What the—" he says. Walking around the car, he finds another message on the passenger side: "WACtH OuT." The door panel is not just scratched, it is gouged, the metal creased under the scarred paint.

Trembling, he drives to school, hyper-aware that other drivers are staring at his car and wondering what sort of trouble he is in, what sort of person he is. He parks on a side street a block from the school and walks the rest of the way. No point in advertising this handiwork in the faculty lot.

As he walks through the halls, he debates what his next move should be. When he sees the words sprayed on the blackboards in his classroom, he turns and heads to the principal's office.

For some reason, Leda kindles a hope that, with the new school week, Ng will be himself again. She spent the weekend worried out of her mind. Of course, she didn't let Ng know. You never let the boy know he can affect you. Still, as she walks to school, she gives in to the anticipation and breaks into an almost full run when the school rises into her line of sight.

But Ng's late. Which is odd because he never used to be, and only serves to confirm her sense of things gone wrong. She waits at their spot. She pops a new stick of Doublemint in her mouth because Ng says he likes the way it makes her taste.

Students are beginning to drift inside. Leda checks her watch. They won't have time to crawl under the bleachers now, anyway. A janitor props open the outside doors. The rich and green spring air wafts in, breathing a little hope into Leda's growing sense of unease. Something feels out of whack today. Hard to say what, but there is a bustle somewhere. She tries to keep her mind from thinking about Ivan and his recent threats to Ng.

Just then Ng rounds the corner with Ivan at his side. Ivan is talking excitedly. He gives Ng a comradely shove. Ng keeps walking, hands in pockets. Ivan slaps Ng on the back, and, laughing, winks at Leda as they walk up.

"You looking too fine, Leda," Ivan says.

"Look elsewhere," she snaps, reaching for Ng's arm. He allows her to pull him to her side.

Ivan looks very pleased. "Nice couple you make. Very nice. We go out some time, old buddies."

Leda looks at Ng for an explanation, but he keeps his eyes lowered, as though waiting for something to happen, or to pass over.

"I sure Eddie want thank you anyway. All you help."

Leda turns and pulls Ng with her down the hall to the gym.

"Bye-bye," Ivan calls after them.

Leda slams open the doors and then hauls the passive Ng to the top of the bleachers and sits him down.

"What is going on?" she demands, her voice rising in frustration.

Ng shrugs. "Ivan's just got this bug up his ass. He'll leave us alone now."

"Why? What happened?"

Ng sits, staring out at the dully shining wood of the basketball court.

"What happened?" Leda tugs at the sleeve of his jacket. "What did you do? Tell me."

Ng takes a breath and shudders. He turns and looks at Leda and then looks away. "I can't."

Leda's mouth falls open. She starts to say something, but pauses and then says only, "Shit," and kicks her backpack down three tiers of bleachers. "What is going on, Ng?"

Ng watches the backpack's strange, lumbering descent. "It's nothing," he says quietly. "Please just let it go."

"You know I'll find out," she says.

Ng watches her haunches move as she steps awkwardly down the bleachers and retrieves her backpack and walks out of the gym without looking back.

Ng fights his desire to skip art class. He knows he can't, it's too obvious. So he files in with the rest of the students, who fall quiet when they see Parsley sitting on his stool, watching them with a cold, furious look, while a janitor behind him finishes scrubbing the blackboards. A few barely legible smears of green and red paint remain. A piercing smell of turpentine floods the room.

Parsley is watching his students try to read the ghosted residue of the graffiti. It doesn't take long for them to decipher *queer, cocksuker,* and *flammer* before they look away quickly, embarrassed.

"Asshole can't even spell," Ng hears someone whisper.

When everyone is seated and quiet, Parsley sends the janitor from the room. He shuts the door and then sits again on his stool. He is shaking. "I am, as the moron who wrote this has figured out, a fag."

The word pierces the dead quiet of the room. Students stare at their notebooks.

"That means I can be targeted and attacked whenever someone feels like it." He turns and looks at the scarred blackboards. "I think you all know how this feels." He turns back to face the room. "You've all been called names based on your race, your weight, your religion?"

No one says anything. Ng can see a few students around him nod.

"I think I know what caused this. But the purpose, the deeper sickness expressed here, I don't really understand it myself. I'd like you to spend the rest of the period responding to this hate crime. Do whatever you like. I have to speak to the cops."

At the mention of the police, Ng feels lightheaded and as though he is falling, watching the classroom recede through a window.

Parsley leaves the room, and slowly the students begin to speak in hushed voices. Ng's table-mate says, "Man, I know you are like Parsley's friend. You must want to kick some ass."

"I'd like to," says Ng. "If I knew whose ass to kick."

He rolls a pencil in his fingers. He'd like to draw something for Parsley, and express empathy and hope. But the pencil feels inert in his fingers, dead, like a stick picked up from the ground, good only for a brief life as kindling.

Wednesday the 10th

Jimmy is a morning man. Morning is a good time for him, he explains, because all the booze and stuff can make his action a little slow at night. But when he reaches for Giselle this morning, she pushes him away and pukes over the side of the bed into a trashcan she keeps there.

"Oh man, that is nasty," says Jimmy derisively.

Giselle wipes her mouth on the back of her hand. "Could you get me some water?"

"Shit." Jimmy leaves the room for a moment and returns with a half glass of warm, flat RC Cola. "This was in the hall."

Giselle sips from the glass, grateful for the sweetness to mask the acidic taste in her mouth.

Jimmy sprawls out on the bed, rubbing his hands cross his chest and belly. "So what the fuck is going on? What the doctor say?" He jiggles his balls with his left hand.

"Nothing," Giselle mumbles.

"If you didn't go, I want my goddamn money back. That wasn't no gift."

"I went."

"Well he had to say something. You got a virus? Or TB?" Jimmy shivers. "Please tell me it ain't TB."

"I'm—" Giselle cocks her head toward the window. Someone has taped a ragged piece of screen over a hole in the lower pane of the window. A fly is bouncing against the mesh.

"Come on, you're what?" He's only half-listening, fishing inside the pockets of yesterday's trousers for his lighter.

She feels like she's playing blind man's bluff at the edge of a cliff, or the top of a building. The next step could be into nothing. She turns back to Jimmy. "I'm pregnant."

He looks at her. "Pregnant." He looks away. He looks back. He lights a cigarette and stares into space. "I *thought* you was getting awful fat."

"I was afraid to tell you."

"You damn well better be afraid if you think I'm gonna bail your ass out of this."

"Bail me out?"

"Pay the doctor to fix it, or whatever. Maybe you even want the damn thing." He makes a dismissive gesture at Giselle's stomach. "They always do."

"Who does?"

"The damn mothers." Jimmy throws a sarcastic accent on the last word.

"What do you know about what mothers want?"

"Because of the three damn kids I got by three damn mommas."

Giselle does not miss the tone of pride in his voice. "You never told me that."

He makes a casual gesture. "Two girls in Joliet and a boy over on Cottage Grove. Kenneth Dwayne." Giselle's comical expression of disbelief almost makes him laugh.

"Do you ever see them?"

"What for?" He chuckles. "So they mommas can bitch me out?"

Giselle stands up. She's about four months along, and the curve of her stomach is definitive. She covers it with her hands. "Well you won't ever see this one either."

"Good," Jimmy says with a bitter laugh. "Then I won't have to see you get all fat and shit." He falls back onto the bed, laughing. "Damn, and you didn't even say nothing."

"Anyone with half a brain would have known."

"Anyone with half a brain wouldn't keep smoking shit. Even I know that."

Giselle says nothing.

"None of my children was born crackheads."

"How would you know?"

"Oh, Jimmy knows. He knows, all right."

"I'll need some help, Jimmy."

"No way, momma, this bank is closed. Go on back to your family. That's what they all do."

Alphonse is muttering to himself as he loads the route boxes into the back of his truck, so he doesn't hear anyone approaching until he feels the tap on his shoulder. He turns to see Giselle standing there, a look on her face so bereft that it takes his breath away.

"Lord Jesus have mercy," he says, and pulls her to his chest.

She immediately breaks into sobs. Alphonse feels an overwhelming sadness tighten his chest and throat as he holds his shivering girl. "S'okay baby, s'okay, nobody gonna hurt you, s'all right, you safe here."

After she gathers herself, Giselle pulls back, wiping her eyes with the back of her hand.

Alphonse's eyes are stinging, too. He rubs the bridge of his nose. "What's wrong, baby? What's wrong?"

"Nothing. But I'm...I'm... preg—" The last syllable is silent, barely a puff of breath.

Alphonse sits heavily on the truck's bumper. His head begins to shake back and forth. "Lord lord lord."

"I don't know where to go, Daddy."

Alphonse cups his face in his hands. He can smell the inks and the brown scent of paper on his fingers. For a moment he simply breathes.

"Daddy?"

Alphonse rises to his feet. He leads Giselle into the back of the truck. "You wait here a minute. You'll have to ride uptown with me, and we'll figure out what to do."

"Dad, I can't come home. Not now. Not like this."

"Shush, I'll be right back."

She sits on a pile of mailbags and closes her eyes, too tired to really care where her father takes her now.

Alphonse thumbs thirty-five cents into the pay phone beside the Coke machine in the lounge. He hears two rings before a sleepy voice says, "Hello?"

"Hey Buddy, it's Alph. I wake you?"

"Well I'll be damned, Alph. Long time. You just caught me between shifts. What's going on with you?"

"I need a favor."

Buddy coughs. "Is it, um, serious as you sound?"

"Someone's been messing with my daughter."

"Okay." Buddy soaks in Alphonse's tone. "You want this person off the streets, right?"

"Yeah. He's a dealer, name Jimmy White. Or James. Drives a ragtop LeBaron. Stays at this place on Kimbark around 75th."

"Whoa, slow down," says Buddy." Is this an emergency?"

"I guess not, she's outta there. But I'd like him to think about what he done."

Alph walks back to the truck. Giselle is asleep on a bunch of canvas bags in a patch of sun, bare feet tucked under her rump, looking like his little girl for the first time since forever. He sighs. The chance to do something real and fatherly for her. Another chance to do things right. Maybe Eloise will see it that way, too.

Saturday the 13th

It's almost like Brad timed the growth of his hair to reach ideal ponytail length just as Lather Rinse Repeat made a modest but no less mind-boggling leap into a kind of semi-fame. He looks the part of a lead singer now, with his sallow cheeks, slightly bent nose, and now a dishwater-blond ponytail hanging down.

"Is it me, or is he getting better looking?" Alice asks sotto voce.

"Fame seems to agree with him," Molly says.

"The bastard."

Brad is wearing his new rock star jeans, so tight you have to wonder how he gets his rather big feet through the legs of them. He holds up a small magazine. "Get this, a comic book even reviewed last week's show. Says our hooks are fresher than Fulton Street fish." He looks suddenly puzzled. "That *is* a compliment, right?"

"What else?" asks Alice.

"He thinks you and Molly are 'the sandwich meats that Wonder Bread was invented for.'" Brad flashes briefly on the fact he can't see Alice's beauty anymore. It's like he's gone color-blind. To Alice's colors.

"I'm Spam and you're olive loaf," Alice says to Molly.

"Who is this reviewer?" Molly laughs. She has taped to her refrigerator door the Overnight section review by a *Trib* stringer that called their show "ethereal," singling Molly out as "a musical genie poofed out of a Chivas bottle." She has imagined getting this reviewer in bed. Celebrity is a strange thing.

Brad looks at the magazine cover. "It's a pen name, The Flake." He shrugs. "Nobody."

"A nobody with excessively good taste," Chipper adds.

Everyone is a little giddy after their fourth show in two weeks, three of them at the Fusebox, where they are the de facto house band of the moment, a step that almost guarantees a record contract ASAP.

Shanklin punches the door open. "Rello Reorge!"

Molly and Alice and Chipper look at one another.

"Hey, Astro?" says Brad.

"I'm plundering cartoons today," Shanklin explains.

Shanklin's latest obsession is inventing slang and trying to disseminate it throughout the city. His dream is to see Sammy Sosa use one of his freshly minted slang words on a nationally broadcast Cubs post-game interview. He even practices the Dominican accent. *I feel very scooby today, Bob. The ball look bluto big. My swing is very bullwinkle since All-Star break.*

Alice says, "That makes Brad Mr. Spacely, right?" Her defensive and clinging hope to reconcile with Brad has turned over the last two weeks into pique and then into outright anger that she damps down whenever it threatens to erupt.

"No," says Shanklin solemnly. "He's totally Cogswell."

Lori pushes the door open. "Hey! How're Chicago's favorite popsters?" She sends a discreet wink Brad's way, tossing her glossy brunette Sassoon bob. Her assumption of the manager's role without there being any discussion among the rest of the band has everyone but Brad more than a little uncomfortable. Chipper has used the term carpetbagger.

Carpet-bugger, Alice thinks.

"I have been all over the city today. Whew!" Lori fans herself with a manila folder and flops down on Brad's bed a little too familiarly. "You guys are the buzz. Lather Rinse Repeat is on everybody's lips."

Alice notices how Lori sprawls on Brad's bed like she knows the bounce of it on her knees. But the idea remains far away, twinkling like a banner on a distant shore she is in no hurry to reach.

Lori's long legs seem to Brad to flow like little rivers between her mini-skirt and the dusty concrete floor. She's wearing the black high-top Chuck Taylors he bought for her, his first gift, and which he finds unspeakably sexy. His neck is hot.

"Hannabarbootie," whispers Shanklin to Chipper. "Betty Rubble with a rack."

"Shut up," Chipper nudges back.

"I heard that," says Alice.

"I've talked to Delray and the Fusebox and put together a list of possible gigs for the next six weeks, including—" She pauses here for effect. "The Memorial Day show in Grant Park!"

"Headlining?" gawps Brad.

"Oh, right," says Molly. "And Poi Dog opens for *us*."

Lori shakes her head, smiling in a way that could be mistaken for patronizing. "No-o-o, you eager beavers! We're second on the bill, after Robbie Fulks and before Wilco."

Chipper whistles like a bomb falling. "Holy crap."

"Scooby-doo," says Shanklin. "Are we ready for that?"

"Hell yes!" Brad shouts. "Have you read the reviews? We kick total ass."

Lori smiles patiently.

Chipper whacks a drumstick against one of the I-beams that rise up through the loft. "We've been playing the same set for three weeks. It's time to work up some new tunes."

"Well, you've got time."

"Two weeks doesn't seem like a lot of time," says Alice.

Lori narrows her eyes. "It's way more time than you need if you're ready to make music a priority."

Everyone has started to edge toward to bed, and now they give in and crowd around Lori, who has fanned her papers out on the bed like a kid with the Sunday comics, propped on her elbows and kicking her feet up with pleasure.

Only Alice sits back from the semi-frenzy, watching Lori's black sneakers rise and fall in alternating arcs, like a double metronome.

"A month of Fridays at the Fusebox," Lori is saying, "and they'll raise your fee twenty-five percent starting this week."

Suddenly Alice's head is bobbing in time with Lori's right leg as her eyes lock onto the exposed right ankle, which is encircled with a green Celtic braid tattoo. It's fresh, the skin around it a little red and raw-looking. The tattoo Brad wanted her to get.

And Alice is washed ashore under that waving pennant that reads, *Hello!*, and gets at once all of the bad news she had hoped to avoid. She sits, everything forming and building inside, while the rest of the band jostles around the bed looking at the future Lori is drawing up for them. She's going to blow, finally. It's Krakatoa time. The skies above the earth will be dark with the ash of lava, summers will be cool, and the coming winter longer than any in living memory. She bolts from the room, the pent-up tears boiling in her cheeks.

Chipper looks up. "Allie?"

Everyone turns to see the door slam shut. Then everyone turns to look at Brad. Except Lori, who says, "Is there a doctor in the house?"

"I think you'd better let us start practicing," says Shanklin to Lori.

"I was just going. I have some other appointments." She gathers her papers and gives Brad a peck on the cheek before sashaying out the door. Everyone begins to silently set up their instruments.

Chipper is shaking his head. "I think the timing of all of this is really bad."

Brad cranks up his amp, filling the room with a brief blast of white noise.

Molly covers her ears and shouts, "Hey, Brad! Maybe you should try playing a solo with the point on your head!"

The late afternoon sun suddenly drops the angle of its rays under the Cinzano umbrella, bathing the beer garden in honeyed light and making the drinks sweat puddles onto the black metal top of the café table.

Lori sits with her head back, letting the sun warm her face. Her feet are in Brad's lap, and he is rubbing his thumbs hard into her arches.

Lori stretches sexily. "God that feels good. Your calluses are like pumice."

Brad is trying not to be as sexually aroused as he is. It doesn't seem right, his semi-erection, since he has to say something critical about Lori's display at the loft.

"I think Alice is bent out of shape."

"Oh well." Lori sips her gin and tonic. "You couldn't protect her forever."

"It wouldn't be a big deal," Brad stammers, "but with the band and everything—it's delicate right now."

"Everybody else seems pretty happy."

"I just think we need Alice, is all." The waiter sets a new beer in front of him. Brad takes a grateful swallow.

"All you need is you, is what I hear."

"What?" Brad halts in mid-swallow.

"I've been hearing from people that matter that you have the look."

People who matter? Brad places the bottle softly back on the table. A trickle of sweat breaks free of his hairline and speeds down his temple.

"You're ready for a bigger market. You could drop the band, go solo to New York or L.A. and land on your feet."

New York? Solo? He takes a gulp of beer. "Somebody said this to you?"

"Yeah, the Miasma Records A&R guy, for one. I'm just passing this along. Think it over."

Brad is suddenly aware that his mind's eye has opened onto this kind of vast plain where a million lights twinkle—his future.

"But we've got those shows. Grant Park. Memorial Day."

"When opportunity knocks."

"But I don't even write most of the songs."

"It's only an idea. You don't have to do anything about it. But if you did—well, I've been thinking about moving to New York myself." She drains her glass, the ice cubes clinking against her incisors. "Two's company."

The shape of the lights is resolving out of the darkness, and Brad now sees buildings, massive and towering, and tiny, trickling veins of car-filled streets. He is falling toward the hubbub, the light rising around him and filling his eyes.

"I'll think about it," he says.

Lori turns her face to the sun and closes her eyes, smiling.

Tuesday the 16th

The space occupied by Tyler Kovacs far exceeds that required by his physical mass, which is itself considerable. His former varsity linebacker beefiness—combined with the slicked-back Ditka haircut and thick neck, which cut very effectively against the power-broker aura he cultivates—makes Tyler a hugeness that fills Ellen's entire living room.

Ellen finds it hard to be near him and keeps changing seats, backing away in stages.

"It's like Darwin, the law of survival. You've got to be tough." His voice is so mild, so reasonable. Ellen realizes this is the Tyler his employees and colleagues see. "We've made things too easy for you." He sits almost primly on the futon, not quite relaxing against the back of it, but his face is composed, empathetic. "It's our fault, your mother's and mine. I realize—"

"I don't remember anything being easy." Ellen has backed over to an open window, lessening her sense of claustrophobia.

"I'm just saying. It's time you got a job. Full-time, real money, enough to cover rent, food."

"Full-time? Dad, I can't…" Ellen kicks the cat away from her father's legs.

Tyler rubs his eyes. "I just mean we don't feel right paying your way, now you're out of school." His winking Rolex is the size of a dessert plate.

"I knew this was coming." Ellen is starting to hyperventilate, her head becoming light as a balloon. "But I need time to finish my—"

Tyler interrupts, eager to say it all before he loses momentum. "I got you a job. Starting now. Waitressing."

Ellen shakes her dizzy head and plucks a small fluff of cat hair from the window screen. She feels about ten years old, when her father abruptly yanked her out of a gymnastics camp where she failed to conquer her fear of the balance beam and ended up hiding in a dressing room locker.

"It's a new restaurant on Halsted. A friend of mine runs it. She'd be glad to take you on."

Ellen is clutching a pillow, hunched over it. She puffs her cheeks with air and exhales it in a drawn-out poof.

"The place is very hot. Two-hour waits, good tips."

Still nothing, rocking ever so slightly forward on the balls of her feet. Ellen remembers the feeling of the cramped, airless locker, the sound of adults pounding on the flimsy door. There were stickers inside the door. Round, yellow smileys.

Tyler watches his daughter close up on him and feels the moment of generosity slipping away. Like her mother, the girl always focuses on the negative. Drives him nuts.

"Don't worry about experience. She knows you're a rookie, that you want to get back to school and everything."

"Great," mutters Ellen, thinking, she already knows I'm a failure. She rocks another moment then stands up, quickly. "Fine. Whatever. I'll start today."

Tyler reaches out a comforting hand. "Listen, don't get yourself all worked up. It won't be so bad."

"Sure, college dropout cocktail waitressing. It's where kids today want to be." She knows her father really hates her sarcasm.

"Okay, Miss Priss, sulk all you want. Won't change the facts." Tyler's hackles rise at the ungrateful response, but he maintains his placid composure. He wants gratitude, even if it comes with the goddamn tears. "Rent is due in two weeks. Do you know how you're going to pay it?" His still brown eyes bore into hers, a technique that has broken the spirit of veteran negotiators. Men with beady eyes and beadier minds.

"I'll pay the rent," she snaps back. And then suddenly she feels weak, lost. Her shoulders drop. "Out of my lovely tips, I guess."

Tyler smiles. "That's my girl. Just go down to the restaurant as soon as you can." He puts up a hand and inhales sharply. "No rush. Tomorrow's... eh...eh...*fine.*" He sneezes the last word into a quickly flourished hankie. "Goddamn cat."

Ellen picks up Marty and kisses his moist nose, trying not to smile.

Tyler's departure leaves a loud vacuum behind. The pull cord for the windowblinds twists idly in the afterdraft. Marty trots up with his sparkle ball and drops it at Ellen's feet. She picks it up and twirls it in the sunlight, making the bits of metallic confetti inside flicker and jump.

Just last week she began helping Alice O'Leary with the afternoon rush at Urbs. It happened like a cosmic inevitability. Stopping by a few days after her band played the Fusebox to say, "Wow great show," and finding the Rara Avis of her heart sitting despondent, her boyfriend apparently AWOL or something.

"I can't get a real job now," she says to Marty, whose bright yellow eyes are still tracking the abstract movements of the hand holding the beloved sparkle ball. "Alice needs me."

She throws the ball into the bedroom. Marty scampers after it. His rear end, slow making the turn, whacks a chair leg going through. She hears the ball ricocheting manically, then drumming against the floorboards until the cat paws it to a stop.

Thursday the 18th

While by no means fastidious, Robin is fanatical about the organized frenzy of nook-and-cranny apartment cleaning that precedes a houseguest. The arrival of Uncle Father Peter, as Robin refers to him, has generated even more frenzy than usual.

He rises early the morning of the Uncle Father's arrival to scrub the bathroom and secret away all tubes of ointment, lubricants, boxes of condoms and such. He pulls on yellow rubber gloves with a loud snap. For all his bluster about Nathan's closeted behavior, Robin can be pretty uptight about meeting family. It's tough playing the role of mate that comes along with the coming out.

Nathan sticks his head in the doorway. "Where do I put this?" he asks, holding out a box of vanilla-flavored lubricant.

"Linen closet?" says Robin. He dumps a blizzard of scouring powder into the toilet bowl.

"I think it's too big."

"Well then, under the bed. He won't be snooping there." Robin brandishes the toilet brush. "Will he?"

Bringing a priest into their lovenest is, upon cooler reflection, probably a really very bad idea. But Robin has demanded this and will sleep in the bed his big mouth has made.

He kneels in front of the toilet, thrusting the brush as though it were a sword into the gullet of someone keenly disliked.

"Everything, and I mean everything, will be perfect," he assures Nathan as he jams the bristles into his father's gob. "Don't sweat it."

The sticky and pinched edge of the roast beef sandwich Peter Reagan pulls from the triangular plastic Amtrak package is strangely reminiscent of the communion offering served at the Baptist church in Dallas he visited last year. Pieces of white bread scissored into tiny rectangles, grape juice. It was the last Trans-Denominational Fellowship mission he ever agreed to undertake for his diocese. He shivers. That gleaming salesman minister. Those women inside their cones of hair.

Seniority has its privileges. His new bishop, a Cuban, still with an accent and the smell of those fried bananas, bent over backwards to grant his request for a sabbatical.

"I say, give one of those Baptists a month in my parish," Peter grumbles to the sleepy overnight steward. "Let him minister to those Portuguese. He'll learn what tough duty is." Father Peter's parish in Portland, Maine is heavy on Portuguese. He finds them, though fanatically Catholic, to be a bit rough for his taste.

"Portuguese are bad?" the steward awakens enough to ask.

"Got so I couldn't do confession anymore. Stabbings in the neck. Gang rapes." He shudders. "Abortions by self-taught quacks. Molested children."

The steward yawns. "I think it's bad those girls can't go to real docs no more to deal with their, you know."

Father Peter sniffs, "It is not for us to say," and takes his packaged sandwich and hot tea back to his seat.

"I know what I've been putting up with," he mutters.

After rounding the bottom of Lake Michigan, the train chugs up the South Side, slowly being swallowed into a city that seems to rise up around the tracks like an engulfing predator. Peter shakes his head at the rusted, beaten-down wastelands. When he was here as a freshly minted seminarian, this was a land of promise and challenge. People who needed help, good people without fair opportunity. Now, he sees how every good intention has failed. Illegible graffiti on the shattered walls of derelict buildings mark the land as some place outside of god.

The hard, black glass skyscrapers loom over the flatland like bullies. His heart races.

There he is, the erstwhile Father: thinning white hair, round ruddy cheeks, small, piercing brown eyes set under eyebrows like overgrown hedges. Sitting stiffly beside the largest rolling suitcase Nathan's ever seen. The father is looking rather morbidly around the large central room, the high ceiling and ancient terrazzo floor resounding with the deafening footsteps of rush hour commuters racing for outbound trains. When he catches sight of Nathan walking toward him, his round, pasty face takes on a look that blends formal greeting with anticipatory disappointment.

"Nathan, my boy." He extends a plump, pale hand. "Good to see you."

Nathan reaches the priest's hand, is gripped by it, and pulled into a big, back-slapping hug. The black wool suit is rather musty from the train ride.

"Hey, Uncle Pete." Nathan smiles nervously.

"What's wrong, lad?" Peter smiles broadly. "Worried about having a crotchety old priest in your house for a few weeks?"

Nathan shakes his head vigorously, brushing all thoughts of doubt and fear from his mind so that he can't be caught thinking them.

"Well, don't you worry. I'm a model houseguest. Or so I've been told."

"I'm only worried about being a model host."

"Nonsense," bellows Peter, grabbing the handle of the suitcase. "You come from a good family that knows how to treat people. How is everyone, anyway?"

Nathan leads Peter to the cab ranks, passing along his meager family news.

"We don't have to take a cab, you know," says Peter. "The train is fine for me. When I was a young man in these parts I rode the train like it was my limo service."

Nathan insists on the cab, and soon they are in the flow of afternoon traffic that teems beside the lake. Peter is somewhat subdued during the ride, appearing to memorize the cabby's name and license number.

"Are all your cabbies…?" he whispers, circling a finger around his head to indicate the driver's turban.

Nathan shrugs the questions off, and glances up to see the driver's eyes in the rearview mirror watching Peter's pantomime. Nathan shrinks down into his seat.

"Goodness gracious, I smell some delicious Italian cooking," says Peter as they approach the apartment door.

"Robin's a gourmet cook," Nathan says.

"Is she now?" says Peter.

"He," says Nathan.

At that moment the door swings open to reveal Robin, flushed from his exertions over the stove, apron askew over a scoop-necked, tight maroon velour top, hair sticking up in places, and on his face a broad and artificial grin.

"Hello Uncle Father!" Robin shouts gaily.

Peter takes a step back into the hall. "Hello," he says, through lips stretched very thin.

Nathan enters first, drawing Peter and Peter's suitcase behind. As he passes, he gives Robin a questioning look.

"Your timing couldn't be more perfect," Robin bubbles "I just took the duck out of the oven have a seat we've got red wine open and of course other drinks if you want them you can have a drink Father can't you?"

Peter backs into the living room, nodding and gesturing into the torrent of Robin's words, until he almost trips over the couch.

"Well then," Nathan claps his hands together. "If you'd like to clean up, Uncle, I'll fix us something to drink."

Peter shuffles off to the bathroom, looking at Robin over his shoulder.

"Nice top," says Nathan, as the door clicks behind Peter. "A Scare-The-Priest original?"

Peter eats heartily, although he says little. As he tears off a piece of bread, he says casually, "I could sleep on the couch, boys. I don't want to kick Robin out of his room."

Sounds of stifled gags from Nathan. The one thing, out of all the agonized planning, unthought of.

"No problem," says Robin, handing the butter to Peter. "I like the couch. It's nubbly."

"Very well, then," says Peter. "Is this butter salted?"

"I'm not going to survive this," Nathan moans. "I'm not kidding, I feel sick." He tucks the edge of a contour sheet under the couch cushion.

"Of course you will." Robin rubs his back. "The man is a saint. I can feel it. Forgiveness flows like honey from his fingertips. Hand me that pillow."

"He's writing a letter to my mother right now."

Robin gives him a look of, as if. "I'm sure people in Maine are preparing a petition for his sainthood."

"I will be outed, damned, excised from the will and excommunicated in one fell swoop." Nathan slumps down on the couch and puts his head in his hands.

"Acolytes will flock to worship the relics of Saint Peter. His finger bone, or a tooth or something. You'll see."

Robin pushes Nathan flat on the couch and stares into his eyes. "Your problem is you're just too negative."

Nathan squeezes his eyes closed. "My problem is stupidity. And, at this moment, a lack of vodka."

Wednesday the 24th

Larry, the jowly and unwashed guy who has the shift before Leda's at Stimpy's Strip Shop, is royally pissed. When Leda comes in, he pushes the chair back from the counter with an anguished screech of overtaxed ball bearings.

"Thank god," he sighs dramatically. "I almost had to call Sol." Larry pretends to be on a first-name basis with the store owner they have each seen but once—when they were hired. The bulge of neck below Larry's chin is red and sweaty. His eyeglasses are opaque with fingerprints. He redundantly adds, "Do you know what time it is?"

Like most of the other guys who work part-time at Stimpy's, Larry's really a cartoonist and hates working in what he calls retail. His drawing name is Larry O. Larry, which he makes everyone call him, but his real name, Leda knows from seeing his paychecks, is James B. Draxten.

"So big deal, I'm fifteen minutes late." Leda allows her teased hair to cover her look of hatred for Larry O. Larry.

"Yeah, big deal if I'm supposed to be somewhere five minutes ago and now you've made me late." Larry makes a show of zipping up his backpack and slinging it over one meaty shoulder.

The two customers in the shop gently edge toward the back of the store, keeping their heads down in their magazines.

Leda kind of likes Larry, really, since he's never asked her out and pretends to hate her with the furious, self-protective style of a third-grader.

"You know, I should say something. Fifteen minutes is what you get docked if I say something."

"Try and make a sentence without the word 'I' in it," Leda says.

"You bug me," Larry O. Larry snaps back, and surges out door in a huff made comic by the tinkling of the little bell on the door's pneumatic hinge.

Leda settles into the chair, which is still kind of grossly warm from Larry's fat ass. Her mood darkens.

Since a couple of weeks ago, she has been showing up late and reluctantly for her shift at Stimpy's. Sitting in the shop makes her feel really alone despite the steady stream of male customers who sneak glances at her as they pretend to read the magazines. It's not like this bothers her, but she wants to say, I have a boyfriend, you know. And she imagines them, the customers, saying back, Well, where is he, this guy? And she gets even madder. If asked this pointed question, she would very much like to spit back, Good question. Instead, she sits frowning at the air.

And the fact Ng doesn't sit with her anymore, hunched over drawings or saying things about the customers quietly in funny voices, makes her shift a lot worse than it was before. Why things can't go back to a pre-Ng state, no better no worse, occupies a lot of her thoughts. I mean I was better off before I knew him, she often thinks. Don't they say ignorance is like bliss or something? That phrase is stuck in her brain like Muzak these days, as though her head is an elevator to nowhere.

Each one of the peeking customers thinks that Leda's glower is a signal of her particular hatred of him alone, a strain of solipsism especially strong in cartoonists. They fidget between the shelves like spooked animals.

Leda realizes that she has no way to explain to Ng how much his extended sulk has upset her. She makes a list of what could be making him sad. His never-around mom. His nowhere father. The thing with Ivan. The vandalism on his teacher. Maybe something with her, Leda. But what? No, she rejects that idea. No way he doesn't see how good she is for him.

But still work is better than going home most days. Being the oldest of seven with her mother pregnant again. Sharing a bed with her two next-oldest sisters, Alma and Alicia. Eating beans and tortillas and rice until her eyes pop. She would kill right now for one of Ng's weird curried fish burritos.

It's ironic how being around comic books makes Leda even sadder. It's like being afraid of clowns, which her sister Alma is. Totally the wrong response. But what can you do? She looks at the covers of *X-Men* and *Eightball* and she thinks, What a wasted-effort bunch of crap.

And what's also funny is that this feeling doesn't make her any less keen on her plan to snap Ng out of his pout or whatever it is. She's going to help Ng get his own comics published.

Parsley's shadow moves silently behind the frosted glass of the classroom door. Ng taps gently and pushes it open.

"Hi, Ng," Parsley says, aligning a stack of papers. Ng can see the fat red strokes of Parsley's pen on the papers. Comments, encouragement, and applause. Unlike most art teachers, Parsley makes his classes write quite a bit about their projects, their ideas. This practice causes no end of complaints from the students, most of whom take art as a pass-fail no-brainer.

It's like his little joke that, instead of a smiley face, Parsley likes to draw a peace sign on papers he likes.

"Have a seat." Parsley motions to the chair beside his desk. He calls it his guest chair, but the class feels this is one of those teacher euphemisms, like when they call the class troublemakers "Gentlemen," as in, "One more remark and you Gentlemen will be having a chat with the principal."

"I have your project here." Parsley pulls out Ng's canvas, narrow and wide, divided into four squares, like a newspaper comic strip. On it he has painted four caricatures: Soo, Leda, Elias, and Ng himself. The last panel was supposed to be Parsley, but Ng had chickened out after the Event.

"I like the concept, Ng, and you know I think you have real talent. But—" Parsley holds the painting out and takes another look at it, puzzled. "It seems that you just lost focus. Intensity. The first three aren't bad, but the self-portrait is a bit tentative. I thought maybe we could talk about what went wrong and use it to learn from."

Ng shifts in the chair, his high tops scratching back and forth on the linoleum. "I heard today you quit."

Parsley doesn't look at Ng, but keeps turning the painting, as if inspecting the brushwork. "I didn't quit, exactly. It was suggested that a transfer might be a good idea."

"It was suggested?"

"Mm-yes."

"Where will you go?"

"Not decided yet. I probably won't know until August when they reassign the unattached teachers."

"Isn't there any chance you could maybe stay?" Ng tries to make his voice express something he doesn't feel he has the right to say.

Parsley smiles. "Things took kind of a lousy turn here. It's better for everyone, better for you, too, if you get a new teacher in. A fresh start all around." Parsley hands Ng the canvas. "Now, let's try and figure out what this needs."

Ng stares at the blobs of color. He can't remember being responsible for them.

"Was the sketchy effect intentional? Were you making a point that I missed?" Parsley asks, and waits for Ng to say something. A believer in the Socratic method, he loves the long pause as a teaching tool.

All Ng can think is how the airy ping of the cheap rubber basketball on the asphalt court outside is like one of those heart monitors on a hospital show.

"I don't know," Ng says at last, struggling to play diligent student. "I think...I guess I couldn't see what I was looking at anymore."

Friday the 26th

In the spirit of the great adventurers, Lori decided to conquer Brad simply because he was there. If pressed for a reason, she would, of course, mention his dark blue eyes, long dark-blond hair, tight ass, and on-stage charisma. John Cusack with nicer lips, she would say. But really, it wasn't to sample these pleasures that she dumped Chipper and zeroed in on Brad. It was just something to do.

For his part, Brad reacted perfectly, dropping Alice like a hot potato and quitting the job where he worked with her. The ultimate test of Lori's control over Brad was the New York idea. She was gratified at how hard he bit on the slightest suggestion. Lori could feel the reel start to heat up and smoke as the line played out and Brad dove deeper and deeper into unmapped waters.

It's not like she's lying to him. She really has thought about moving. Why not?

"Of course, I'll join you there," she insists. "But you'll have people from the labels taking care of you in the meantime. I'll be out in a month or two."

"Shouldn't I just wait, then?"

Lori considers the suggestion. How dedicated is he? Make him sweat. "You can wait if you want. But the buzz is out there, the iron is hot, red hot."

"All right," Brad says, uncertain. "I guess it's time. I feel ready." He sighs.

"You should tell the rest of them now. It's kinder."

"To be cruel," he adds.

As Alice bends over the sidewalk tables to finish the wiping-down part of closing Urbs in Horto, she looks across the street at the diner. She wishes Ellen would come by today. It isn't a specific arrangement or anything, but Alice has gotten used to having her help, and her wry jokes lighten the atmosphere.

It's really no fun having to stack the sidewalk tables and chairs and chain them all with the heavy iron-link chain by yourself. It's a two-person job. She pulls the accordion grating across the windows and locks it. Brad used to turn the task into a show, balancing chairs on one finger and flipping them in the air.

She remembers what Ellen said about Brad yesterday. "He's the kind of guy they would show the face of in the audience of the old *Saturday Night Live,* and flash up a caption like 'God's gift to himself.'" Every time she thinks about it, she laughs.

It's hot work. Alice draws the long, smoke-colored shades and sits in the darkened café drinking glass after glass of water. The sounds of the street seem very far away, and the store fills with a silence like that of a well, or some other place very deep and still where the movements of the roots of plants are the only measure of time.

She is going to be late for rehearsal. But she can't move. It was never this quiet with Brad around. A longing for him washes over her.

Suddenly she stands up. Why not, she says aloud. She pulls together a delicate bouquet of asphodel and buttercups, with a long stem of hollyhock for drama. On one of the little gift cards, she writes, *Dear Brad, The espresso machine misses you.* And signs it: *U. in H.*

Not knowing how to break the news, Brad just blurts it out before Alice and Molly arrive at the loft. Maybe it's the faint hope of male empathy that makes him say to Shanklin and Chipper, "Guys, I think I've decided to, I mean that, I have to go to New York."

No one says anything at first.

Then Shanklin, apparently working something out in his mind, slowly says, "Do you mean you should? Or the band should?"

"I meant. No. I guess." Brad's cocks to one side, then the other. "I meant just me."

Chipper throws a drumstick at him.

"Hey! Come on!" Brad ducks, covering his head. The drumstick slaps against the wall and spins under the ratty couch, where Shanklin sits looking stunned.

"You are such a—" Chipper looks around for something. "I can't think of the best word right now. Asshole!" He picks up a coffee mug and hurls it against an I-beam.

"Goddammit, Chip, fucking stop it or get out."

"*Me* stop it? You fuck us all up the backside, and you tell me to stop?" He kicks a large chunk of the mug into a far corner.

Shanklin is sitting very still, hands on knees, staring straight ahead, like a Mormon missionary riding the big-city subway for the first time. He's let his sparse facial hair evolve into a blondish weedy beard that appears to be growing out of a crack along his jawline.

"Now? You want to leave now?" Chipper is saying, pacing around the large room. The windows are cranked open and a heavy breeze fumbles in bearing odors of diesel exhaust and garlic.

"There never would be a good time," Brad protests. "We get a contract, I can't leave." He starts picking up pieces of the coffee mug. "We make a record, I can't leave. We have to tour, I can't leave. Why is now so bad?"

"Are you fucking kidding? Because we're *breaking through*, man."

Shanklin sits dumbstruck.

"You guys will be fine without me. Alice and Molly write all the best songs anyway." Brad realizes that the shattered mug is the one he stole from a diner in Oak Park after he and Alice had toured the Frank Lloyd Wright studio. Alice loved the shape of it.

"*Brady Bunch,*" Shanklin says. "The matador suit."

"It's Lori, right?" Chipper fumes. "She's telling you the sun shines out of your ass alone. This is classic ego combustion."

"Look, it's my decision. My risk to take."

"And your decision to fuck everyone else."

"What's going on?" Alice is standing in the door with Molly just behind her.

"Oh, nothing," Chipper shouts, "just David Lee Asshole going solo on us."

Alice flinches and hides the bouquet behind her back.

"Greg Bradied. We've been Greg Bradied," Shanklin keeps saying.

Molly steadies Alice and, reaching around, takes the trembling bouquet from her hand and drops it behind her in the hall.

"Solo?" is all Alice can say.

"Well," Brad says. He saw the flowers. He knows why Molly dropped them in the hall. Suddenly he wants to backpedal, apologize to Alice, fix everything the way it was.

"Oh yeah," Chipper raves in Brad's face. "Mr. Big time. New York, caviar, snort coke with Donald Trump. Root for the Knicks. The whole nine yards!"

"Swimming pools, movie stars," mumbles Shanklin.

"You better back off," Brad says. "Just back off."

"I'm going now," says Shanklin, standing. Brad and Chipper watch him walk very deliberately to the door.

"Wait," says Brad. "We can still practice until I leave. Work on some new material. I don't want to leave you guys high and dry."

Shanklin keeps walking. Alice hears him shuffle to avoid stepping on the flowers, but land on them anyway with a light, crisp sound. He mutters a curse.

"Except for me, everything else can stay the same. Keep the loft even, for rehearsals."

"Like fuck we will," says Alice, waking from her trance. "I won't fucking set foot in here again."

"No one will," says Molly. "We're going to seal it up like a tomb. The tomb of the unknown ego."

She pulls Alice out of the apartment and the door shuts behind them. Brad listens to their footsteps echoing down the steps.

Chipper fishes the thrown drumstick out from under the couch and slips it into his back pocket with its mate. He opens the door and takes what feels like one final look back at Brad, standing across the room with a stunned look on his face

"What I really don't get," he says, "is you had the best thing. You had Alice."

And then he closes the door.

Tuesday the 30th

Florence moves deliberately, as though under a watchful eye. Still in her peppermint-striped bathrobe, she shuffles around the apartment getting ready to go out. It is early yet, the sky over the lake a candy pink. An old jelly jar filled with water, a tray of little paint pots, and a pad of watercolor paper go into the big quilted bag. She pours another cup of coffee and spreads a dab of marmalade across her wheat toast. She feels watched, even though Arnie hasn't made one of his sudden appearances since the night of the Art Institute party. She eats quickly and changes into jeans and a sweatshirt. Arnie had warned her never to become one of the old women who wear track suits all the time. Even with appliqués. It's still pajamas, he would say. She finishes putting her things into the bag and goes down into the fresh, unused early-summer air. After crossing under the Drive, Florence begins looking for a place to set up. The search takes her all the way to the lake. At the edge of Belmont Harbor, she sets down her bag and opens the canvas seat of her walking-stick chair. She erects the easel and dips her brush into the jar of water. Then, with the pad of paper open on her lap, she waits.

Arnie's re-disappearance didn't bother her at first, but she has begun to feel that it is a sign of disapproval. Which is not like Arnie, who enjoyed almost more than anything else the act of voicing criticisms. But then again, was he really there before, in the apartment, in the cab? Joggers and bicyclists huff or whizz behind her back every now and then. Rush hour traffic generates a wall of sound, which seals her and the lake off from the rest of the world. A gull falls from the sky, landing heavily on a bag of cheese puffs. It lifts the bag with its beak and shakes it madly to no avail. She finds, suddenly, something to paint in the day. It begins with a stringy, chafed-looking cloud rounding the north edge of the city. She dips her brush into the paint and touches it to the paper. From there, the rest of the world unfolds and descends and, for forty minutes or so, makes perfect sense. And then, as she finishes the quick tableau, everything is dissolving. The curling wake of a powerboat splits the broad, blue glass of the water. The hard summer sunlight is slowly washing the color from everything. She drops the brush into the water jar and sits back, dazed.

When she returns to her apartment, Alphonse is in the lobby, and on a sudden impulse, she asks him to wait a moment.

"I've been meaning to give you something." She fishes into her bag and pulls out the watercolor. "I'd like you to have this."

Alphonse takes the paper gently in two fingers. "This is really fine, Mrs. F. Did you paint it yourself?"

Florence nods.

"I couldn't," Alph shakes his head. "I'll lose it or muss it up."

"You'd darn well better take it, mister, if you've got any Southern manners left."

Alphonse snaps himself upright, smiling, and says, "I am much obliged to you, ma'am, for this token of your esteem."

Florence laughs.

"Eloise gonna like this a whole lot. I know it'll be in the dining room for sure, by the antique chifforobe her momma gave us for our wedding." He lays the painting carefully on top of the mail cart.

"Perfect," Florence smiles. "I couldn't ask for a better gallery to hang in."

She wakes with a start from her nap. There is nothing in the room but the dusty light of late afternoon. A curtain billows open with breeze.

"I never criticized you that much," says Arnie. "Not behind your back, anyway." He is sitting beside her, a panatela in his teeth.

"Thank goodness for little graces," Florence says, and falls back asleep, smiling.

June

Saturday the 3rd

The Templeton used to be a nice hotel, you can see by the lobby's scratched-up marble floor and butt-shined velveteen couches. Now it's a retrofitted SRO, each room set up with a hot plate and a rank upholstered armchair. It feels as much like a prison cell as any place Giselle's been in her life. Even the television remote—which does not, by the way, work—is screwed to the bedside table. The room, carpeted in a soiled burnt-orange shag, smells really bad. And it gets worse with the hot weather. Giselle sits at the one window, watching traffic. She lights another cigarette, the next-to-last one in her last pack. She still doesn't really think she has to quit. Smoking is a way of hanging on to the idea that the pregnancy might just go away. But her father has laid down the law in this one regard. Anyway, she has come to realize that it's too late to get rid of the damn thing. She looks down at her stomach. Her belly button is on the verge of popping out and her stomach is taut and bright, with a dark line running right down the middle. She's past the sickness, but the heat makes her want to faint. The room is smothering in the hot afternoon, with only a table fan swiveling its face to keep her from completely suffocating. She smoothes the sheet on the love seat. An old sheet from her childhood bed, almost transparent now, ghosted with small yellow flowers. She had Alphonse bring cloths to cover all of the sitting surfaces. The room looks like it's in storage, draped everywhere in old sheets.

Almost noon, almost time for her father to arrive with his daily delivery of food, magazines, and nicotine patches. She has come to welcome his visits, and not just the way a prisoner in solitary looks forward to a tray of wormy food. No, the time they've spent together has reminded Giselle of her father's warmth and empathy, the two things she needs most right now. Not once has he betrayed anger or laid on a guilt trip about…well, about any of it—Jimmy, the drugs, the baby. She can see that he tries to see only what she was before, what he wants her to be. And she should feel more grateful, but when he comes today she's telling him it's time for her to move out.

"That's wonderful," he'll say. "We're ready for you to come home."

Home? Giselle tries that thought. Tony and Eloise are on the porch with open arms. Her mother has a rigid smile on her face, a fake welcome that will quickly give way to questions and accusations. That old pattern, the arguments and tensions that made the house on Kimbark more bearable than her parents' house. And yet, somewhere under her inability to tolerate her mother, Giselle knows there is love. But is that home? Maybe it's easier to stay put, even in this dump.

Jimmy pulls into the hot parking lot of a shopping center with the top down on the LeBaron. He gropes around on the floor of the car and pulls up the grimy envelope with the CelUSA logo. He reads, "Dear Mr. White, CelUSA has selected you, blah blah. Frequent cel phone users. New product test group. Drawing for sports tickets, Harley Davidson, grand prize trip to Bermuda. The South Center Shopping mall at 85th and—"

He looks around the parking lot. A bunch of other men are heading for the little empty storefront between Dollars R Cra-Zee and Harold's Fried Chicken. Jimmy looks at the neon chef chasing the neon rooster with a neon hatchet. Mmm—after this little drawing, he's going for some fried chicken slathered in hot sauce. A white guy appears in the store window to put up a banner that says, Welcome CelUSA Guests. Jimmy jumps out of the car and hurries over. The door is surrounded by a metal-detection gate. Jimmy walks through, but the guy behind him beeps and has to empty his pockets and get the wand.

"What's that about?"

"Just a precaution," says the guy at the door. He scans Jimmy's letter. "Thanks for coming, Mr. White." He gives a shit-eating, white guy smile.

"You know," says Jimmy, "this better not be one of them scams."

"Oh yeah?" says the guy. He touches his moustache, dark brown and precisely trimmed above his lip. "Like what?"

"You gonna make me hand over a hundred bucks or something to get this free trip or whatever."

The man laughs. "It's nothing like that, honest. It's just plain old market research." The man smiles again, even bigger this time. "Just have a seat."

Jimmy takes a seat near the back of the room. If I win this trip, I'll take Giselle with me. Patch things up. After the baby, he reminds himself. Her folks will take care of that.

A heavily muscled black man walks to the front of the room. He is wearing a blazing white polo shirt with a funny insignia. He looks like a Bears linebacker, and Jimmy is wondering which one he could be when the man turns on a microphone and says, "Good afternoon, everyone. I'd like to thank you all for coming today."

"Sure," says one guy. "Just give me that hog and I'll be riding home."

Everybody laughs, even the guy at the mike.

"Sorry we couldn't bring the Harley in today, pal. But I need to make a couple of announcements about today's activities." He pauses to make sure everyone is paying attention. "First, you should know that all those men at the back and on the sides here are police officers."

Jimmy's neck turns ice-cold. He looks over his shoulder and, sure enough, every one of those guys has a shoulder holster and vest on.

"Oh fuck me," shouts one guy, clutching his head.

"Now, now, hold on," says the emcee, holding up his hand. "The second thing, which you may have already guessed, is you're all under arrest."

Immediately, a skinny guy in a red stocking cap tries to dive low between two cops by a side exit. They grab his legs, slam him against the wall, and cuff him in a matter of seconds.

"This entrapment!" the cuffed man is shouting against the wall.

"You have the right to remain silent," says the emcee. "Anything you say can and will be used against you."

There is a general uproar. Jimmy pulls out his phone and hits the speed dial for the house on Kimbark. Just as it rings, the phone is pulled from his hand.

"Just a minute, buddy," says one of the cops. "You don't get that call till later." He folds the phone and drops it into a brown envelope that has "White, J." written on the outside.

Names are called. Arrestees go forward and offer the contents of their pockets.

Jimmy feels a tap on his shoulder. "See, it wasn't a scam," says the cop who was at the door. "You get a free trip after all."

Monday the 5th

Alice anticipates Ellen's arrival at Urbs in Horto by preparing her favorite drink—an iced latte with a shot of Italian vanilla syrup. Since she first ventured over from the diner, Ellen has become a regular, and Alice has come to appreciate her as sweet, funny company. The timing of their new friendship is perfect for Alice, what with so many gaps in her life left by Brad's imminent departure. Wait. She checks her calendar. It's today. He leaves today. She can't help it. The tears burst forth. Thank god it's a slow morning in the store. She puts her head down on a table and cries.

Ellen's eyes register a deep and automatic sympathy when she finds Alice still sniffling and jamming a long spoon into the watery coffee drink.

"Brad's leaving today," Alice says, by way of answering the unasked question.

"I'm sorry."

"No, I'm over it. I am."

Ellen sits down next to her. "It was a shitty thing he did." She pushes aside a mound of moist napkins.

"I wish I could be madder at him instead of just sad."

"There are stages," Ellen says, "and I should know."

"I know, denial, anger, yada yada."

"Yeah, but you're led to believe there's some kind of light at the end of the tunnel. In my experience, the stages just keep repeating."

"Thanks, that's comforting."

"Well, they won't repeat so much with him in New York."

"I hope not." Alice wipes her eyes one more time and squeezes Ellen's hand. "Thanks."

Ellen squeezes back gently, afraid to break the spell of the touch.

Instead of assembling at the loft—the fate of which is part of their meeting's agenda—the now leaderless Lather Rinse Repeat collects at a new River West biker bar. The locale is Molly's choice—everyone in the band knows her soft spot for black leather.

Chipper is disappointed in his food. "It isn't greasy spoon enough," he opines, holding up a paprika-flecked french fry.

"Always the search for the authentic," Molly says.

Shanklin leans forward to peer at Alice's face. "Hey, your nose ring. What happened?"

Chipper and Molly turn, too, and inspect her.

Alice leans away from them, wanting to disappear.

"Aren't you afraid the hole will close up?" Chipper says.

She touches the nostril in question. "I'm hoping it will."

This shuts everyone up for a moment.

"Let's talk straight, here," Alice says. "What does everyone want to do?"

"Bag it," Chipper says.

"Keep going," Molly says at the same instant.

Shanklin looks at everyone else and keeps silent.

Then they all turn to look at Alice.

"What? Am I the deciding vote here? I don't want that. We have to all want to stay together for this to work."

"I think it's a waste of time," Chipper insists.

"What do we lose by trying?" Shanklin says. "It's not a vote, I'm just asking."

"We lose the chance to go onto other things," Chipper says. "Brad was the front man, the band's face. We're like a headless horseman now."

"Remember that old joke from grade school?" Molly grins. "Want to lose ten pounds of ugly fat? Cut off your head!"

"Maybe if we take a break," Alice offers. "Maybe we can try again after some time off."

"That's the worst thing," Molly says. "We have to buckle down. We still have gigs that are our responsibility, our opportunity."

"What's better, the heart or the head?" Shanklin asks softly.

"What?" Chipper snaps, irritated.

"Alice writes the songs, mostly," Shanklin says. "I never thought Brad was as important as the songs."

Chipper turns to look at Alice, silently conceding Shanklin's point. Molly and Shanklin turn also. Six eyes staring at her, measuring her willingness to tackle the unknown.

"Christ," she says. "Okay."

Walking home, Ellen feels almost bouncy from Alice's hand-squeeze. It was the most intimate moment she'd experienced in weeks. She barely notices the familiar-looking, burnt orange Sirocco with a bullet hole in the windshield. She is already past it before she thinks, What the heck? As she turns, Megan is getting out of the car.

"Hey," Megan says.

Ellen pauses warily. And then, as she gets a better look at Megan's hollowed and darkened eyes: "Oh my god, are you okay?"

Megan bites her lip and shakes her head. "I almost died today." She begins to sag against the car.

Ellen rushes over and embraces Megan, who simply stands there, doing nothing. After a moment, she pulls herself loose and eases away from Ellen, whose eyes scan her at furious wondering speed. The layers of anger have peeled away between them, leaving a Megan who Ellen recognizes as a woman she has loved, madly at times, distantly at others, and recently not at all. It is a rebirth that pretty much changes the rotation of Ellen's world.

"Can we go in?" Megan asks. Her voice is husky from crying. "I know it's not really kosher, but I need to talk to someone."

Ellen grabs Megan's hand. "Of course you can. Is that?" she hesitates, pointing at the windshield. "Don't tell me that's a bullet hole?"

Megan nods. "Jesus, Ellie, it was so horrible." She stops and hugs herself.

"What happened?"

"It was a drive-by. I was out on a call down in Humboldt Park. Came out of nowhere."

"Come in," Ellen pulls her arm.

"I hate to have this be from pity. But I need you."

"It's not, Megs." Ellen caresses the haggard face. "Come on."

Megan allows herself to be drawn inside, her steps slow and doubtful. Ellen pulls a few strands of Megan's black curly hair toward the light. Something in there sparkles. "Is that glass?"

∞

Brad heaves his duffel bag onto the pavement beside the eastbound bus. He looks back into the station where Lori sits, jiggling her leg and smoking in a very impatient fashion. Not quite the send-off he'd been hoping for. He gestures to her, and she makes a big show of getting up from the bench and walking out to him.

She's more than a little galled that he's taking the bus instead of flying or at least taking the train. She wrinkles her nose. "This place stinks."

"I couldn't afford anything else," Brad shrugs.

"I can't believe you're going to spend like two days on that thing with these people."

Brad laughs this off. "By the time you get to New York, I'll be decontaminated, I promise." He tries to pull her to him, but she stiffens.

"Hey, remember, you're not doing this because of me." She holds the cigarette up in the air, as though it were fragile. "This is your career."

"I know."

"Well, when you say things like that, it makes me feel like you're going to be just waiting there, like a dog."

Brad feels the anger surge up in his face. "All I mean is how great it will be when you get there. Am I allowed to look forward to being with you again?"

Lori looks at him, or appears to, through her dark, dark sunglasses. "Oh, Bradford. Hang on to that passion. It will knock them dead."

The sight of Megan's hair fanned out wet and shampoo-sweet on the pillow makes Ellen break out in shivers.

"What?" mumbles Megan.

"Nothing, love," whispers Ellen, scooting down to spoon. "I'm just glad you came here. That's all."

"Shocking," says Megan softly, with her last wakeful breath of the day.

Ellen buries her face in the soft, damp tangles of Megan's hair. Shocking, she thinks, as she too begins to drift toward sleep. Yet more evidence that love truly is bind.

Thursday, June 8

As a priest, Father Peter Reagan is reluctant to admit even to himself his most certain emotion: he detests Robin. It is an instinctual emotion, gut-level. He cannot even put into words what it is about Robin he finds so appalling. He sublimates his unworthy feelings in the journal-cum-diatribe he scribbles on a nightly basis: *The man is all surface. He seems to have no ambition, no desire to start a family. His cooking is exactly what you would expect—full of butter and salt, a cuisine of indulgence, prescriptive of an early, chest-clutching death.* This is as close as Peter comes to expressing his true feelings.

And, at the edge of Peter's perception is the flickering knowledge that Robin's attentions to Nathan suggest an affection too unhealthy to contemplate. There is a level at which he recognizes Robin and who he is, what he is, of course—for decades he's heard all manner of confessions, after all, and certainly among his priestly brethren (especially back at the seminary) he's known his share of men who shared many of the qualities that are so obvious, so *flagrant* in Robin. But Peter's means of dealing with these men, and whatever it is they might do with each other, has always been to keep it at a stolid, unquestioning, emphatic arm's length.

It is a wonder, he thinks, that Nathan keeps Robin as a roommate.

Peter keeps himself away from the common rooms, and makes polite excuses to leave the dinner table early.

There is something eternal and haunting about Uncle Father Peter, Robin thinks. More than a guest, Peter is the sudden expression of a latent insanity in his relationship with Nathan. Like the crazy attic wife in *Jane Eyre,* Peter has burst into their lives and unmasked a basic falsehood in their relationship. Both of them still as mice with their heads tilted toward Peter's door, alert for a bump or scream. It's nuts. After three weeks, it feels like Peter has always lived in the spare bedroom. The bedroom from which Robin pretends to have been banished to the sofa. The sofa he covers with rumpled sheets and beside which he sets a book, the bookmark moved carefully forward eight to ten pages nightly. A queer diorama. Robin finds this deception no great discomfort, but rather a whimsical exercise. It is the only part of the visit he enjoys. For if ever there was someone who, after three weeks in one household, could manage to avoid finding a niche in the prevailing routine, it is Peter. The self-proclaimed model houseguest has managed to throw everything into confusion and keep it there—a feat almost beyond comprehension to Nathan, to whom order is a symbol of prosperity and survival.

Peter pleads allergy to almost everything Robin makes. At the same time, leftovers are disappearing from the fridge at a fantastic rate. Robin holds up a terrine of beef, which Peter refused, claiming gelatin allergy. The plate, which yesterday held a full half of Saran-wrapped terrine, now contains only a brownish lump marred by numerous gouges.

"He's eating it with his hands," Robin says, exasperated. "He's plunging his face into it for a midnight snack." A revelation dawns on Robin's face. "He's bulimic!"

"Or he's feeding the neighborhood dogs," says Nathan, absorbed in shoving candy into the pockets of a large, multi-pouched apron.

Robin turns pale. "That's it. He's feeding my dinners to mongrels in the alley."

"I'm not saying he does, the thought just occurred to me."

"That's *it*. From now on, he gets cereal and fish sticks. Ovaltine and toast. Tea and beans."

"Maybe that's a good idea."

"Put a toaster oven in the bedroom and let him cook his own."

"Come on, he won't be here much longer."

"Oh, won't he? You know something I don't?"

"No," Nathan admits. "But he can't stay forever."

Robin crosses himself and whispers, *"Dios mio,"* raising his eyes to heaven. "Are you ready yet?"

Nathan fumbles with the apron bib, which reads *Eat with Pride.* "When does the parade start?"

"In less than an hour. Be sure to put on sunscreen." He touches Nathan's cheek. "Gotta protect that milky-blue skin of yours."

"Where are you boys off to?" Peter is standing on the balcony, measuring the weather before venturing on his, as he calls them, peregrinations.

"A picnic," Nathan and Robin chorus.

"It's an office thing," adds Nathan.

"Looks like…" Peter leans over the railing, "…there's some kind of a street fair over there aways."

"Yes, well we're not going there," Nathan says quickly.

"No," adds Robin, "we're going out to a squeaky clean suburb to play Wiffle ball and put mustard on grilled meat."

"Right," Nathan says. "Right."

Peter, unhappy with Robin's glib air, senses a diversion. He narrows his eyes. "Well, it's a fine day for a walk."

"We should get going," Nathan says, and they beat a hasty exit, leaving Peter with a redoubled sense of the feeling that's been with him since arrived, uncomfortable without a clear sense of why.

Heat washes up from the pavement in waves. Nathan feels woozy and damp as he walks beside the float for Qu-Zeen, the catering company where Robin works, wearing an apron and tossing foil-wrapped French bon-bons to the shouting, waving crowd. The route of the Gay Pride parade is an advertisement for suntan oil and Lycra shorts. A sea of sweet-smelling, sun-pricked flesh. It is Robin's favorite day of the year, bar none. The float speakers blast out Edith Piaf, and then Dean Martin's syrupy *That's Amore.*

Every few blocks, Robin bursts out of a fake meringue made of felt and cotton balls. The banner on his chest matches the side of the float: Qu-Zeen for a Day. He holds up a megaphone and recites: "Gay or straight, bone china or blue plate; breakfast, lunch, or dinner; getting fat, getting thinner—you lick the spoon, we'll box what's left. Call us to cater: 773-GAYCHEF!"

There is a throaty roar of men at the roadside whenever Robin appears. After one performance, a large, artificially tanned man in a pink polo shirt lunges for Robin, shouting, "I wanna ice your cupcake!" Nathan dings him with a bonbon. The man falls backward into the crowd, clutching his eye.

"Oops," Nathan says, "sorry." And marches blithely onward.

They return home sunburned and giggly. "My hero," Robin keeps saying, with mock limpid eyes. The door swings open to reveal Father Peter sitting in front of the TV, smoking a large cigar.

Robin wrinkles his nose. "God, it smells like the US Steel plant in here."

"Hello, boys," says Peter. "What a day I've had."

"Us too. Whew!" Robin says, collapsing on the couch. He is scarlet from sun, and at the scoop neck of his tanktop, a diagonal strip of paler skin is visible.

"Did you enjoy yourselves?"

"I guess so," says Nathan. "It was fine. How about you?"

"It seemed everywhere I went today, I ran into some street fair or parade, so I meandered south until I found this store full of women smoking cigars. They gave me this one." He looks at the label. "It seems to be very nice."

"I stink," Robin says. "I'm going to take a shower."

"Me, too." Nathan catches himself. "Um, I mean, after you."

"You won't believe what I saw coming back here. A man with another man on a leash. Like a dog."

"Really," says Nathan. "You don't see that everyday."

"Had a collar on, and was almost entirely naked. The man on the leash."

"Mm." Nathan looks away to avoid seeing Robin, who, behind Peter's back, is pulling off his shirt in a mock striptease.

"Wouldn't see that in my parish. Say this for the Portuguese," Peter continues, "they know how to take care of people like that."

Robin makes a stabbing motion at Peter's back before pulling down his shorts and jumping into the bathroom with a flash of pale white haunch.

"Strong family values, the Portuguese." Peter pulls deeply at the cigar. The smoke envelops his head like a blue-black veil. "Violent, but god-fearing."

Tuesday the 13th

With a sigh, Ng flips open his sketchbook, applies a sharpened pencil point, and presses down. He pulls the lead down the paper without any idea where it is going. He watches it describe a sweeping line that could become a comet's tail, a breast, or nothing more than what it is, a nothingness, the shadow of emptiness. He lifts the pencil. Drawing used to be about making a world. But now he can't see any world that makes sense. There is nothing and no reason to draw. And what gives him the right, anyway? He snaps the pencil shaft. Not angrily, but with resignation, like, Okay, I give up. So there's no reason to keep all these cups full of pencils, the notepads, and what of the stacked milk crates holding his comic book library?

He gets a large garbage bag from the kitchen and shakes it open. He begins to pull drawings from the walls and shove them in the bag. Thumbtacks click on the floor. There is one pencil drawing of Leda. He hesitates a moment, then crumples it and tosses it away. His mind is a blank space. All of these things mean nothing. A little paper. Clutter. In go the pencils, watercolor palettes, and brushes. He spends a long time scraping globs of blue poster putty off the walls with his fingernails. He is sweating now, the box fan in the window stirring a warm, humid breeze. One by one, he stacks the milk crates filled with comics in the hall. He doesn't even consider taking them to Stimpy's. That would mean thinking about Leda or, worse, seeing her. He stands in the center of the bare, dusty floor. A ball of sweat gathers on the tip of his nose, and then falls to the floor with an audible plunk. The room is sad, lifeless. The paint is spotted with little holes from the tacks and oily spots from the putty. He finds an old, lumpy roller and a can of paint in the basement and begins to cover everything with a thick, clean coat of white.

Another shirt ruined: Amundsen's Brake World in script with two brake pads squeezing a sixteen-inch softball. Except that she didn't ink the screen properly and the ball ended up mottled like a cantaloupe. Her work has been slipping for weeks. Benny had to eat a whole shipment of bowling shirts on which Soo misspelled the team's name, The Parkers, as The Porkers. It didn't seem like such a big mistake.

"You going pay for these shirt!" Benny shrieked. His cigarette had bounced like a bug's antenna as he ranted, flinging the ruined lime-green shirts here and there.

The ceiling fans silently whip the air, creating thick moist currents. As she mixes a new batch of ink, Soo finds her thoughts drifting back to Ng's ongoing silence and sadness. It must be that Mexican girl. Shamelessly kissing on the couch in her own living room. She flattens a shirt on the frame. Clearly Ng has lost himself in something like love, or the teenage equivalent, and it's a short jump from there to heartache and grief. She feels a sadness that is like falling into a deep well and never hitting bottom.

There, the softball is nicely round, with stitching and everything.

Ng just hides now, like a bear in the winter, staying in the apartment, moving from room to room. He needs something to do.

Elias's latest waitress sits in a corner booth smoking in a manifestly aggressive fashion. The dinner rush was obviously not her idea of fun—not that it was really that busy. She keeps the cigarette near her face at all times, puffing hard and steadily, lighting a second one from the butt of the first.

She pointedly ignores the couple that just finished sharing a slice of strawberry-rhubarb pie. The man at the table begins tapping his spoon steadily against his water glass, until the woman puts her hand on his, and frowns. Elias apologetically takes their check to the register and brings their change. The waitress continues staring out the window at the setting sun reflected by the windows of the café across the street. The café's safety grate chops the reflected light into little diamonds that splay across the diner's back wall.

Elias considers reprimanding her, but decides it isn't worth it. She'll probably stop showing up for work some day soon, with the usual lack of notice. He pours himself an iced coffee, his recent summer menu innovation. Tan coffee splashes gaily down the sides of the plastic tank all day long. Only a half-dozen people have gone for it so far. He pushes open the front door and stands in the descending light. There are bicyclists and rollerbladers everywhere. A line extends outside the door of the ice cream shop down the street. And a man is carrying a little girl on his hip. The little girl looks like Elana. Of course.

The iced coffee is symptomatic of the diner's slumping business. Why this is, Elias can't figure. Diners all over the city, no different than his, some in worse locations, many with much worse food, have survived for years. Decades. He's tried adding more salads and vegetarian items, and encourages BYOB while his application for a liquor license continues to languish in City Hall.

He thinks about his secret Easter visit, and how Elana looked—the pink cheeks and dark eyes filled with a surging, pure energy. He wants to brush up against that force again, he needs to feel that zing in his fingertips the way maybe junkies need their drugs. He feels old now, and powerless. Things are in decay—his old house, the diner. His life is slipping away. But when he thinks of Elana, he tries to hold on to the image of her dancing in the wet leaf-piles of that April morning, and use it to fire a sense of purpose and power that he seems to have, somewhere along the way, lost.

It's like a fever, the need to get rid of all this stuff, these things that lie about who he is now. Speckled with white paint, Ng begins dragging everything down to the Dumpsters behind the building. The bags of wadded drawings fly up and in, light as balloons, further convincing Ng that he is throwing out nothing of consequence. As he slams down the lid, he feels an internal spasm shaking his ribs. He runs back upstairs to start on the comics.

He wants to shake all his skin off, like a snake. But then, what would he be left with? No more Mom, no more Leda, no more drawing, no Ivan, no Parsley. No Ng.

There must be a thousand dollars' worth of stuff. Books by local guys he'd spied on at the Myopic Café, hunched over coffee, drawing on napkins and picking their ears with nerdy detachment. One crate holds the mags and zines that were the most special. A first edition of *Eightball*. The issue of *Superman* where he died. A little zine called *Dandy Drorings* that had come out only once and had the best "Spy vs. Spy" parody ever. And under them, issue #2 of *The City by The Flake*. Where did that come from? He searches his memory. He remembers then how Leda pushed it across the cafeteria table to him, her eyes trying not to betray the sadness for which he was responsible. He'd grabbed it and shoved it in his backpack without looking. It was almost the last time he'd seen her. He opens the magazine slowly. The Flake's drawings are really good. He's shown walking all over the city, a nondescript guy with bad posture and glasses witnessing the normal crazy stuff that is really what the city is all about, the commonplace oddness and casual beauty that Ng recognizes as the world he used to inhabit. Is that Leda staring out of the window of the shop called Trilby's? Ng's throat knots up like the neck of a garbage bag.

"You got too much time on your hand." Soo is in the doorway, wearing the last softball shirt she had ruined that day before Benny had kicked her out, yelling, "Go home you get sleep or food—don't come back crazy as you leave, okay?"

"Maybe," Ng says.

"You need job."

There is something odd about his mother's face. Is it in her eyes? The shirt's V-neck is dropped to show her hard, delineated collarbone. She is one bony woman.

Ng makes a face. "You still have a job?" He's pointing at the smeared shirt.

Soo makes a vague but determined gesture. "You come work with me tomorrow. Benny need someone else to design shirt."

"I can see that. And someone else to make them."

Soo crosses her arms and a crooked grin, small but unmistakable, turns up a corner of her mouth. "If you have job and start being happy, I make shirt better. Okay?"

"Okay." Ng snaps a salute to his mother's uncharacteristic decisiveness. He feels a little light-headed, as though a heavy helmet has been pulled off his head. "You're the boss."

Thursday the 15th

There is a pigeon, fat and cooing, on the ledge of the breakfast nook window. Florence pushes the screen aside and drops tiny pieces of torn wheat toast onto the ledge.

"Look at him go," Florence says into the phone wedged between her shoulder and ear.

"You sound, I don't know, happy, Flo," says Louise. Behind her is the sticky, whoopee-cushion sound of Jimbo blowing his nose.

Florence sighs, "It's hard sometimes, not having Arnie around to take care of me the way Jimbo takes care of you."

"The way I take care of him, you mean. Ha ha."

"But I guess you're right, I am happy."

Another pigeon has flown down and is swiveling his head, pointing each eye in turn at the spot where his colleague was selfishly gobbling crumbs a few seconds earlier. He fluffs his feathers in disappointment.

"I'm glad. Arnie would have wanted that," Louise says, but sounds unhappy saying it.

"He's keeping an eye on me, that's for sure." Florence tears off another buttery bit of toast and drops it through the screen.

"Of course he is, dear," Louise says in a consoling voice before ringing off.

What Florence imagines when she thinks about her life, aside from the specific burned-in memories, are the stretches of days where life took on a particular rhythm. The months after Arnie's death have, in Florence's mind, a specific flavor that belongs to no single day, but to the additive momentum of each second, pushed forward by the tension wound into the clock that ran until it expired and was replaced by a new one, with a melancholy tick, in a seamless exchange.

Wings batter the window in haste.

It's about time to start painting. She glances around the room at all the paintings finished and in progress. Alphonse and his mailbag. The high white vees of gulls over the sailboats. One of Arnie's hats on a chair. Les Potamkin said yesterday he'd have to put up some more walls to accommodate them all.

She rises to get some more coffee, thinking she'd like to paint Elias in front of his diner. Holding Elana on her next visit, maybe. As she stands, Florence has a brief sensation, both familiar and strange, passing through her straight down from head to toe, leaving her just a little shaken.

And it happens just like that; as she pours milk into her coffee, her left hand disappears. Poof, the carton drops to floor, spattering liquid across the tile. And then, as some lights behind her left shoulder flare and go dark, her left leg and foot are painlessly amputated. She falls into the puddle of milk.

Arnie's face is close enough that she can smell the cigar on his breath. She tries to wrinkle her nose, but her face feels swollen and stiff.

"I'm sorry, honey. I couldn't stop it." He lays a hand on her forehead, indistinct and cold. "Like Job I feel. I didn't even feel so bad about dying. Somehow, that I understood. But this?"

"What this?" Florence wants to ask. Her mouth is too full of tongue for breath. Her eyes grow wide. She begins to pant.

"Now, now," says Arnie. "Just lie still a minute. Don't go rushing off half-cocked."

Florence turns her searching eyes toward him. Half of her vision seems to rock with a clock-like, rhythmic ticking.

"There's this former doctor I play pool with on Wednesdays. He says it's like a little balloon of blood pops in your brain. It's painless."

She has a wild, shrieking sob trapped in her throat. Fear has clutched her stomach and lungs. She feels a wet spot on her dress. Too warm to be milk.

"I can't exactly call 911 for you," Arnie says, squatting on his haunches in a way his arthritic knees hadn't allowed for years. "Let's see if we can get you up."

An arm passes behind her, and Florence feels herself being raised gently to an awkward standing position.

"I'll get you to the lobby, and someone else can take it from there. I think your mailman pal is due soon. That is, if he decides to finish his rounds," Arnie snorts with his unique flavor of amused derision.

The corridor is silent but for the scuffing of their shoes on the carpet. Florence is vaguely aware of her smell, which is not pleasant. A patch of her gray curls stiffens as the milk dries.

"I feel really bad about this, Flo," Arnie says again. "With everything going so good, too."

The elevator drops her silently down to whatever awaits.

The night train from Kansas City hit a siding outside of Marseilles and didn't come in this morning, so the bag is pretty light today, making Alphonse one happy guy in blue shorts and black socks. The birds they do sing, the sun it do shine. Mrs. Finkel is hovering like a ghost when Alphonse walks into the lobby. He doesn't recognize her at first, a listing specter with a crazy eye set in half a face of fallen dough.

"Awww?" she says, pitifully. Her arms reach out for him.

"Goddamn," he whispers, dropping his mail and rushing over. Whatever was holding her up gives way, and she collapses into him. Her skin feels clammy, and she smells of urine.

"Dog dough," she mouths, drunkenly. "Ah knee."

"Good lord, good lord," Alphonse mutters. He steps this way and that, looking for a phone. Finding none, he carries Florence out to the truck and places her across several mailbags. He rams the truck into gear and reverses rapidly down the street.

"You'll be all right, Miz F.," he says. "Don't worry." He pats her leg as he swerves down the street with one hand, gunning the engine to a shrill whine. "We'll fix you up, I promise." It's like his mouth just works and these meaningless phrases come out. Can she really be fixed? He is doubtful. She looks like a beached fish, mouthing at the unfriendly air until her time runs out. He pulls up beside the coffee shop. Alice sees Alphonse lifting Florence out of the truck and she runs outside.

"Oh my god, what happened?"

"She was standing in the lobby like this. Call an ambulance, quick."

Alice runs inside and calls. Alphonse stands, holding Mrs. Finkel in his arms, until Alice can pull two of the little café tables together and he can lay her down.

"I'm going to get Mr. Kanakes," Alice says. "Wait here." She bounds across the street.

Alphonse doesn't ask why, or say, "Now, where would I be going, girl?" He just stands, holding Florence's clenched left hand, petting it like a little kitten.

"I don't know if you can hear me," he says softly, "but I hope that husband of yours is watching to make sure you'll be all right."

Alphonse is surprised that her right hand moves to give him a meaning-ful, reassuring touch. And it seems to him that the good side of her face finds a way to give him a sort of smile before she closes her eyes to wait.

Wednesday the 21st

By the longest day of the year, summer is in full flower. The mornings break early and hot, sunlight muzzy through a haze of late dewfall. Grown-ups sit dopey-eyed at the edges of their beds, fussy and ill-rested, annoyed by the racket of the window unit or worn out from twisting in damp sheets, reaching for the breezes of the box fan.

But not Tony Duchossois. Tony wakes full of plans, dressing himself quickly and without prompting from his mother in order to have a few minutes in the dew-soaked yard to tend his fort of little green soldiers. Since he can't be home alone, he crams as much event as he can into the evenings and mornings. Bombs, landmines, hand grenades take out the regiment. Hard green bodies fly from the explosions. Snipers pop up in unexpected locations with lethal results.

"Tony?" Eloise cries from the kitchen window. "Come eat something."

Tony walks inside, finishing the skirmish in his head. He pours a bowl of Froot Loops, then sits watching cartoons while his parents bustle past without a word to him or to each other. Just about as long as he can remember, there has been a lot of whispering in the house. When Giselle left, Momma cried behind the door in the bedroom, and that was it. But it's been quieter than usual lately and it's lasted longer than usual, too. His parents wander from room to room without even saying, "More coffee?" or, "What's for dinner tonight?" Today, he has left all of the orange loops in the bowl. They bob on the surface of the milk like a flotilla of life preservers. He feels invisible, like Casper the Friendly Ghost. Summer's like that anyway, a kind of invisibility for little boys. Without the structure of school, you can spend entire days creating yourself in the image of a Green Beret, a point guard, Batman, a fireman. You don't have to be a little boy again until September comes, and fourth grade.

"Say boy, you be good today." Tony feels his father's broad, warm hand on his head, giving his scalp a rough, playful scrub.

"I will," Tony says.

"Play some catch tonight, all right?" Alphonse tugs the bill of his official post office cap.

"Sure!" Tony says. His eyes brighten. He scoops the remaining cereal into his mouth.

"Before dinner. I'll come get you from Auntie Germaine's."

Tony's eyes drop. A trickle of milk escapes the corner of his overfilled mouth. The cereal has swelled up into squishy worms. He shudders. "Okay."

Alphonse looks at the top of his son's short-cropped head. He rubs it once more and heads out to his car. The front door closes behind him, leaving him with the feeling he has forgotten something. He's had this feeling for days, and suddenly he realizes what it is. He hasn't kissed Eloise goodbye.

It all started the day Alphonse came home after holding that sick old woman and saw her loaded in the ambulance that took her away, and he wondered would he ever see her again. It haunts a man, that sudden kind of thing. So he comes home to talk it over with Eloise. Slumped in a kitchen chair, with a sweating can of Bud between his hands, he is ready to get this off his chest, and let Eloise's talent for empathy cover him over and soothe him. But telling her about it, he can see her eyes cloud over with different worries. She begins to stiffen as he talks and eventually reaches the dreaded hands-on-hips position.

"It's all very fine for you to worry about some old stranger lady," she starts.

"She's no stranger. She gave us that painting." He points to the water-color of Belmont Harbor that sits over the sideboard.

But Eloise would not be softened. "It's no different than one day you have a daughter, and the next she's gone, and you don't know will you ever see her again."

"I guess you right," says Alph, his shoulders rounding against the blows. Please, lord, he thinks, don't let's talk about this any farther.

"That'll be Tony soon," she says, winding her fists in the kitchen towel. "You best not let him get away like Giselle."

"Tony's a good boy," he says.

"So was Giselle at his age. Now we don't even know she may be dead or lying in some gutter somewhere." She turns away and lets her tears drop into the sink.

What he said then was: "Don't cry, baby. She's okay, I know she is."

He meant it to sound like the empty assurance he'd given the stricken Mrs. F. But Eloise heard the tone in his voice, the certainty he wanted her to accept on faith, without having to provide evidence.

But she turns around. "What you mean, you know? What do you know?" Her eyes knife into him.

"It's just a feeling, is all." He fumbles with the beer can.

"Didn't sound like no feeling, mister. If all you got is a feeling, then you best not ought to say you know anything about our daughter." She pushes past him and out of the house.

That was it, then. Every day there's the silent drip of her questions: "What do you know? Where is our daughter?" Her questions in his scrambled eggs, in the car, at church, and, brother, all over the damn bed at night. No answer, no cuddle. You can't hold out on this woman, he thinks. She tears at you like one of those giant drills they use to bore out a coal mountain. Until you got a hole right through you and the truth spills out all over the place.

But not yet. He can withstand the drill a little while longer.

Without any plan in mind, Tony has begun to wander a little farther every day, up to Garfield and east to the park. He likes the late afternoons there, where men come and play softball and sit around coolers drinking cans of beer. The park is washed in a field of thumping, staticky music that pours from the open trunks of cars.

He's supposed to play with the twins all day, but Auntie Germaine won't let them leave the neighborhood. And he's not supposed to go farther than the school, but during the summer, with a whole day out in front of him, the prohibition feels like a leash that he strains as far as he can.

And it's safer anyway since the guys in the King 5s decided to give him safe passage through their territory.

"Hey, little man," they shout. "Where's yo cap?"

Tony feels his head. "What you mean, cap?"

"One of these here." A big boy points exaggeratedly to his baseball hat, turned sideways, marked with a crowned number 5.

"I got a White Sox cap," Tony says.

"Thass all right, little man," says the big boy. He comes over and puts his arm around Tony. "You cool, you all right. Maybe Ronnie let you have one of these super-cool hats like this one right here."

"Really?" Tony looks more closely at the hat. None of his other friends would have one of these.

Ronnie shrugs. "Mebbe, if Ronnie decide he like you."

Tony's eyes say it all: What can I do to make Ronnie like me?

Ronnie smiles at the unasked question.

Giselle's room at the Templeton has the funky invalid smell rooms get when they are never vacant. Giselle herself doesn't smell much better. Withdrawal has punished her body with foul sweats and a scaly pungency to her scalp and feet. But overall the withdrawal hasn't been as bad as she feared. Maybe somehow being pregnant has softened the symptoms. Still, every muscle aches and her waking hours are brief and fruitless. She is still dozing in bed when Alphonse arrives. She sits up cross-legged without a word and pulls her big T-shirt over her growing stomach. It is the gesture of a little girl, and melts Alphonse's heart a bit.

He sits down by the window. "Since you still asleep, I guess you didn't go for that job interview at the Kinko's?"

"No." She rubs her face with the back of one hand. Her cheeks are still swollen with sleep and streaked with red from the sheets.

A box fan hums pointlessly in the window. Alphonse shakes his head.

"Who'd hire me?" She waves a hand at her belly. Every day her stomach is bigger. Sometimes, in the evening, she lays naked on the bed and looks down at the smooth, shiny mound and watches it grow. It moves and trembles with the energy inside. "No one's gonna hire four months of work for six weeks of maternity leave."

The word maternity strikes Alphonse's ears like a gong. There are other problems here besides keeping Giselle's whereabouts secret from Eloise.

He pulls his cap off and slaps his leg with it. "I can't keep paying for this room here. You gonna have to come home."

Giselle jumps off the bed and stomps across the room. "No way, Daddy. Forget it. I'll move out, back to the house on Kimbark."

"Why not? We can make things all right. I know we can."

"I'm not going back and have Momma say this is what she expected. That I would get high and knocked up and just be a damn failure."

Alphonse stays mum, unable to argue the obvious.

"I won't ever go back home, for you or Momma." She pauses. "Or even Tony."

"Your momma don't have no more anger. She'll make things right for us. For you."

Giselle winces. "Ooh, I have to sit down." She eases herself back onto the bed. "My stomach's been all messed up lately. It's all that nasty food I have to eat around here."

Alphonse runs to the sink and wets a handful of paper towels. "What can I do, baby?" He tries to lay the towels on Giselle's forehead.

She knocks his hand away. "Just leave me alone." Even pain has not broken the flow of her anger. "You know, it wasn't so bad with Jimmy. Being disrespected by him isn't as bad as being disrespected by your mother." She sits up and throws the wad of wet paper against the opposite wall, where it sticks for a moment before falling with a thud.

"Jimmy doesn't want any baby, but maybe he'll let me stay at the house until I have it." She slowly rises to her feet and shuffles to the sink. "I think I'll give him a call."

Alphonse sits back down by the window. Sweat is pouring freely from his armpits. "You can't, baby. You can't call Jimmy."

"Why not?" She leans over the counter, hands on hips. Eloise's pose.

He swallows. "Jimmy's in jail."

She turns around. "Say what?"

"He got picked up for something, I heard."

Uh-oh, says a voice in his head.

"You heard? It was that cop friend of yours, wasn't it?" She crosses her arms tightly across her breasts, drawing attention to the girth of her stomach. "You told him to."

"Baby, I didn't do nothing to Jimmy." It is a pointless lie. She already knows the truth.

"I can't believe you," Giselle whispers, meaning several confusing things at once.

Friday the 23rd

Ellen hasn't let herself indulge in Alice since the reappearance of Megan. It makes her feel too screwed up, harboring her secret lust. During the day, she tries to make herself think about things besides Alice, like the film and getting back into school. But it all seems so dried up and stale. Since the post-gunshot tryst reunited them, it's been kind of like, Now what? Ellen has found herself riding the familiar fence between hope that Megan will somehow become the woman Ellen wants to love, and fear of committing herself wholly to that hope. Megan's been walking around shell-shocked, trying to re-establish a sense of a world in which bullets don't fly at her out of nowhere. She's become even more paranoid and needy. Vortex-like.

Ellen gets the definite impression that her good behavior is all that keeps Megan's domineering impulses in check—impulses which have developed a nakedly manipulative edge. "I think you should get a beeper," Megan said while reading the Sunday paper. "There's ads for only five dollars a month. It's so much cheaper than a cell phone."

Ellen stared at her. "What?"

"So I can find you during the day. You know, our schedules are so different."

"Megs, you know what I do all day. I'm either here or at the diner."

"Yeah, but there's all that travel time, and I'm out on calls. I could beep you and meet you for coffee, or whatever. A little quality time."

"I can't see myself carrying a beeper."

"Okay, fine." Megan spread the paper over her face. "I just thought you'd be in favor of a way for us to see each other more often."

Finding no defense for this interpretation, Ellen soon found herself owning a bright pink beeper. Which she has managed to leave at home almost every day since getting it. Megan is growing resentful and accusatory. Megan's work schedule has been keeping them apart so much that Ellen chooses not to think about these things. Something will happen to change everything. And not just because she wants it to, she's learned.

Change is exactly what Ellen feels as Alice says, "Hey, stranger," grinning as Ellen walks into Urbs in Horto.

Ellen feels a blush reach all the way to her fingertips.

Alice puts aside a tray of cups still steaming from the dishwasher and lifts an ironic eyebrow. "You look dressed up for a date."

Ellen laughs defensively and says, "Hey, they're just regular clothes." Ellen is absorbing everything about Alice she has forgotten, and she's forgotten a lot. The way her teeth sit behind those lips.

"I've missed you around here." Alice pulls a strand of hair behind her perfect ear in that way of hers. "It's been freakishly dull." Her blonde hair seems full of light. Ellen can practically feel the movement of Alice's breasts inside the sleeveless blue bowling shirt.

Ellen's skin prickles hot and electric. She more or less falls into a chair. "How are things around here?" she squeaks.

"Brad's been gone a couple of weeks now." Alice pulls her shoulders in and sighs, "I'm getting used to it."

"So, did the band decide to stay together?"

"Yeah, for now. We're going to keep playing and see what happens."

"Let me know if you have any gigs. I'd love to see you play again."

There is a smiling pause. Ellen squirms and feels the backs of her legs sticking to the café chair.

Alice cocks her head. "Do you have time for a cup?"

"Sure," Ellen says hesitantly. There is something weird in the atmosphere, a subsonic disturbance.

Alice gets up to dry out two mugs.

Ellen looks around. She feels like a dog hearing a silent whistle, ears perking up. Oh no, there it is. Her purse is humming. Shit. She reaches in the purse and turns off the beeper.

"What is it?" asks Alice from the coffee bar.

"Can I use your phone?"

"Sure."

Ellen walks back to the office and dials the number on the beeper.

"Hey," Megan says. "That was quick."

"Yeah," Ellen says, tightly. "What is it?"

"Just saying hi to my lover. Where are you?"

"On my way home. I went out for some film supplies."

"Great, I'm in the hood. How about I come by?"

"No, Megs. Um, I still need to buy cat food and—"

Alice is peering over the edge of her cup, trying not to listen. I can't even have a freaking cup of coffee, Ellen thinks.

"Don't be such a squirrel. I'll just lean through the window and grab a kiss." Megan hangs up.

"I have to go," Ellen says to Alice, hanging up quickly. "I'm really sorry. I'll come by again next week." She bolts out the door.

As she waits on the el platform, Ellen feels the pager begin to buzz again. She pulls it from her purse and briefly considers throwing it under the approaching train. Instead she simply drops it into a trash can. Oops.

Sunday the 25th

Florence sits up in her bed, separated from her roommate by a curtain of neutral color, trying to make her left thumb click the buttons on the television remote. Images jump by—talk shows, soaps, baseball games, infomercials, and weather maps filled with spiky balls of sun. She's ashamed to find herself nearly helpless. She tries to follow instructions from the nurses and from her physical therapist and acts on them. She has begun painting left-handed watercolors and squeezing a ball. She gets a sponge bath every third day. But she asks no questions, makes no small talk. One channel is a listing of hospital events. Today there is a motivational speaker. Tomorrow is the SPCA visit. *Hug a Puppy! Pet a Cat!*

She realizes that she has been staring at the screen for several minutes, willing the channel to change. She looks at her thumb lying inert on the channel button. This is what it will be like forever, she thinks. Calling my nerves to action and getting no response. Sorry, we're not home right now. The thought is not funny to her, and she is suddenly fearful of having lost a marble or two.

The sitting room is filled with old people in wheelchairs. Some of them fidget and scowl. Others slump against the armrests, staring into the sky beyond the walls. My people, thinks Florence. She pushes her walker over to a chair and settles in. The woman next to her is muttering to herself. Florence tries not to notice.

"Never any good, these things," the woman mutters. "Always glee clubs and puppies. I ask for bingo and roulette. We get preachers."

Florence coughs delicately.

The woman turns to her. "You and me, we're up for more than naps and kiddy cocktails, right?" She winks.

And the speaker is suddenly in the room. Florence realizes with a shock that it is the shabby corner preacher from the neighborhood.

The preacher takes off his dusty fedora and wipes his face with a hand-kerchief. "Oh we bathing in the light of the lord today," he says, and smiles with equine, yellow teeth.

"Lawd yes," says a woman in the back of the room. Her iron-gray hair is teased out like a dandelion puff.

The man shucks off his jacket and throws it across a chair. Semicircles of sweat mark the armpits and collar of his short-sleeved shirt.

"As I walked here today I thought about God's plan for the drop of water." He begins to pace the front of the room. "Worldly desire is like water. It drop on you out the sky and drown you. Come a big hairy storm full of lightning and hail and raindrops fat as your fist wash you out your house. There goes the bedroom set, there goes the sofa chair, the Persian rug and china plates. A-whirling and a-whirling."

The preacher's delivery is slow and melodious as he paces the front of the room, gesturing out like a deep current trying to pull them in. Florence tries to muster up some resistance to this gently seductive discourse, but finds none.

"Get caught up in that big fat river of what you got to have, and your life is just one hurly-burly trip down that river, bouncing off sharp old rocks. Whirling in the undertow. You gasp for air between the slapping waves, everthing blurring past until you spin out into that calm but endless final delta."

"That's right," says the dandelion-haired woman, waving her aluminum cane in the air. "That river is a a good ride!"

"But say you catch hold a branch. You want to stop and see something small and clear. A butterfly wing. A grandchild's Crayola picture. So you catch hold a branch and heave yourself up on a piece of ground, gasping for air, soaked to the skin and shivering."

Oh my, thinks Florence, finding she has goosebumps, and is shivering in the cold air from the overhead vent.

"God is like the sun come to dry you out on that beach you heave yourself up on. Wring all that desire out your clothes and hair, get you all warm and dry."

"But hey, Preacherman, I cain't live without water!" says the frizzy-haired woman, almost rising from her chair with frustration.

"In bourbon," sniffs the woman next to Florence.

"That's exactly right," says the preacher quietly. "Cleave to your sweat, good woman." He mops his forehead again, and flourishes the kerchief back into his pocket. "Hold precious the rainfall and the dew."

"You got a point, you damn fool?" A voice in the back of the room. "I got dialysis in ten minutes."

"We are water made flesh. We are the river of God," says the preacher. "Now let us pray."

After the preacher has gone, the patients begin shuffling out of the room. The dandelion-haired woman limps by, leaning heavily on her cane. "He's a damn fool. But all the good preachers are fools." Then she laughs gleefully and stamps her good foot.

"I feel a little confused," Florence's seatmate mumbles.

"I just feel old," Florence sighs.

"Same thing," her friend says, and dabs at the corner of one eye with a handkerchief.

Jean, the physical therapist, seemed to take a special liking to Florence, and insisted that they find a way to use her talent for painting in her therapy.

Over Florence's objections. But here she is, every afternoon, looking out of the rehab window, dabbing out wobbly versions of east Lakeview baking in the unflagging heat of late June. One thin plastic tray with powdery pigments was all Jean could muster. After several disastrous attempts to paint on typing paper, Florence begged Elias to bring her a pad of real watercolor paper.

"How are we doing?" Jean is hovering over her shoulder.

"A generous person would say I'm developing a nicely primitive touch. But the pigeon is way out of proportion."

"You're getting better control of the fingers. Your fine motor is really coming along. Your speech is basically back to normal."

"Sometimes I bite my tongue."

"That happens." Jean takes both of Florence's hands. "Squeeze."

Florence squeezes with all her strength.

"That was good," Jean says.

"I was wondering, do you know the name of the speaker we had today?"

"The preacher? I think he's called Brother Even. Why?"

"I've seen him before." Florence swishes her brush in the water glass.

"Was it a good talk today? Follow my finger," Jean says, moving a finger beside Florence's head.

"I guess so. His positions are very extreme."

"That's what he's there for, right? Walking on coals so you don't have to."

"I'm not so sure he thinks I don't have to," Florence sighs, and scrunches the brush down into the sticky pot of blue pigment.

It's mostly at night after the last rounds that Florence prays for Arnie to make another appearance. She doesn't sleep much, and it would be nice to have some company. Come on, she thinks, sending her prayers out into the still hot and exhaling bricks of the nighttime city, Just stop by and tell me how I look. That I still look good for an old, cracked-up broad. She squeezes her eyes shut and listens to the rise and fall of murmurs in the night ward.

Monday the 26th

"I think Petey needs a little help deciding it's time to go," Robin whispers, his lips just barely touching the tender folds inside Nathan's left ear.

"You're tickling me," Nathan hisses. And then giggles.

"We'll just give him a nudge." Robin's fingers find Nathan's waistband. "Remind him of the big, wide world beyond the walls of our little abode."

"Stop!" He tries to push Robin away, but Robin is tickling more determinedly, fingers beginning to work between his ribs. Nathan rolls up like a potato bug, trying to shield his more tender parts. "For god's sake, he's probably lying awake in there, listening."

Robin jabs a little harder. "Promise you'll talk to him or I'll tickle you out into the hall and make a spectacle of you."

"Okay, okay," Nathan gasps. "Christ. I will. Look, it's almost five-thirty."

Robin groans and pushes aside the bedclothes. "I'm so tired of playing musical beds."

Nathan sighs. "I know."

As Robin steps out into the hall, the toilet flushes. There is a sheet of light under the bathroom door. "Jeez," he whispers, and pads quickly down the hall and jumps onto the couch, winding himself into the sheet.

The sound of a running tap is soon followed by a clicking light, a squeaking door, and a cough which strikes Robin as notably self-conscious, he thinks, as he falls into the deep sleep that precedes the imminent sound of the alarm.

As it turns out, Robin's threats are unnecessary. Peter, dressed in his now customary sandals and Bermuda shorts, announces his plans for departure at breakfast.

"I'm afraid, lads, that it is time for me to be pushing on," he declares through a mouthful of English muffin. "I've offered to help out a parish in Durango, Colorado. Lost their priest to rampaging colon cancer and need an interim."

"That's sad," says Nathan. "But nice for you?"

Peter bares his teeth. "Always wanted to get out onto the wide open prairie." The muffin, pliant with butter, tears like something flesh. "Solid folks. Heartland country."

Robin blurts out, "So when will you be going?"

"Getting the train out in a couple of days. The Prairie Schooner Limited. It's an overnight. Durango is springing for a deluxe cabin." Peter thinks of dining car pancakes as the peaks of the Rockies scuttle by in the distance, and his mouth waters. He butters another toasted muffin. "I'm sure you'll be glad to get your room back, Robin."

"I'll just be sorry to see you go," Robin smiles. "Jam?"

Peter walks out in the brazen morning, feeling true peace in his soul for the first time in weeks. It isn't as though I asked god to strike anyone down, but if that Father Albertson in Durango hadn't gotten bum medical advice, I'd be on the phone again this morning still begging for an interim position to get me out of here. The bridge back to Portland isn't exactly burned, but he can't return early—not after the fuss he made. And he couldn't stand to be stuck here with his questionable nephew and the decidedly unfriendly Chicago clerics. You think you've got schoolmates, men of the cloth no less, who'd be glad to host you for a week or two, and what do you get? Excuses and budget complaints.

And then the shirt catches his eye. A pretty young woman, passing with an armful of flowers, whose shirt reads Love Is Bind. Can that be right? There seem to be theological issues there, perhaps good for a state-of-our-country's-youth sermon. Knock it off on the train, set Durango a-jitter over the godless state of our Big Cities. He steps off the curb.

And then, with a brush of loud yellow, he spins, and he's lying awkwardly on the ground, his right foot twisted under the tire of a taxicab.

"What the hell!" he shouts. "Help! I'm a priest! Get help!"

A door slams, and a woman's dark face looms over his, blocking out the glare of the sun.

"I'm hurt," says Peter.

The angry-looking woman begins jabbering in a foreign tongue. Peter squeezes his eyes shut and begins to pray for a large, sensible, white police-man to save him.

Peter has already been set in plaster and moved to a room when Nathan arrives. One of the benefits of priesthood, it appears, is quick service in the E.R. Perhaps it was a mistake to ask Robin to join him at the hospital, but that's what panic does to a man. Robin is not good in emergencies, and on this occasion he feels that the doctor's bad news is unnecessarily severe.

"The leg twisted, probably as he fell, causing a double fracture of the tibia." The doctor, a small dark-haired woman, sits across from them and unwraps a stick of gum. "In addition, there are several broken bones in the foot. It's a rather complex set of fractures." The gum, folded double, enters her mouth. "He'll be on crutches for a good six weeks or more."

"Jesus Christ," moans Robin, giving Nathan a look like, Do something!

"So he can't travel?" Nathan asks, somewhat despairingly.

The doctor laughs. "I should say not."

"It's just that he has this important trip for the diocese," Nathan says quickly. "He'd hate to miss it."

"It's out of the question." The doctor crosses her arms, determined to protect her patient from his family. "Any unnecessary exertion is very much not advised. Maybe in three to four weeks."

"So you'll be keeping him here?" Robin prompts.

"Oh no, he's ready to go home now." The doctor's eyes have begun to show signs of amusement at their distress.

"Oh no," Robin says. "Oh no no no. He can't stay with us."

"Robin!" Nathan says sharply.

"There's no way! I can't do it anymore!"

Other people in the waiting room look toward the raised voices.

"Jesus, Robin, don't do this to me, please?"

"Things are going to change around the house, that's for sure." Robin marches off toward the ranks of candy machines. "I'm through playing Mrs. Cleaver for that jerk."

Nathan looks at the doctor. "Can I get a sedative?"

The doctor shakes her head, still smiling.

Thursday the 29th

It happens in the early morning hours, when Eloise shifts her bottom away from the accidental touch of his hand, that Alphonse reaches a decision. His eyes open onto the window blocked with the box fan pushing a thick breeze. That's it, I ain't sitting on my hands no more. As signal of his determination, he scoots over to the forbidden side of the bed and casually drops a hand onto Eloise's hip. She awakens just enough to shove him away with her elbow. He rolls away, staring into the darkness. The faint song of a cricket vibrates within the blades of the fan. Tomorrow I'm going to bring that girl to her senses and stop all this nonsense.

He is up and dressed before Eloise awakes. She sits up in bed to see him standing at the window, the muscles of his jaw at work on something hard and bitter. She turns for her robe without a word, as she has done for weeks.

"This the last morning I gone walk around this house like a ghost."

She turns and looks at him without sympathy or fear. "You got something to say to me?"

"I ain't screwed up anything I can't fix," he says. "That's all. I aim to do some fixing today."

She slips her arms through the silky sleeves of the robe, flexing her fingers free of the cuffs. Should she melt already, or goad him to the finish? "I hope so," is all she says in the end. "They's a lot to fix."

What Jimmy'd like to do is get hold of Giselle and get her to bail his ass out, but jail ain't such a bad place, really, long as you a man's man. Spend all morning reading the paper, then play some chess, a game he'd learned as a kid messing around on the lakefront and regrets never having spent more time investigating. There are some serious players here in the joint, but no one he thinks he shouldn't be able to beat once he rounds into form. He calls the house on Kimbark and says, "Too bad the food sucks shit, or we could sell tickets like this was some damn resort or something."

He knows, though, after his arraignment, they'll move him from City to County, and then things won't be so soft. So he asks everyone in the house on Kimbark, "How come I ain't seen any you down here with bail money?" But without him, the house is no more useful than a box of broken crayons. A chicken with its head cut off. Too bad Giselle had to go and get knocked up. She had some kind of sense anyway.

"You find Giselle," he orders them. "She'll fix it for me."

"Okay, Jimmy," drawls Lem. "Where she at?"

A vein flashes behind Jimmy's eyes. He starts to spit out a reply, then looks at the guard. A wrong word gets him tossed back into his cell. He swallows. "Now how should I know, Lem? I been in this little thing called *jail.*"

Lem must have done the job, because today he is called down from the rooftop chess tables, right in the middle of a hot streak.

"White! You're paid up," calls the guard.

Jimmy knocks over his own king with a flourish and stands up. "You win. Be seein' y'all around." He waves at a clump of other prisoners who've been watching. "This king gone checkmate hisself a queen tonight."

Alphonse's insistence that he "knows" Giselle is safe is still ringing in Eloise's ears, and, like some kind of virus, it infects her brain with strange and uncharacteristic thoughts. The presence of a secret, an obstinate unknowable fact, makes Eloise think differently about Alphonse, how he is when he's away from home. In her head, this Alphonse has become another person, one who harbors dark and unruly secrets. He is a man like other men, and therefore less than she had hoped for when she married him.

But it's still an accident, more or less, that Eloise begins looking at the coins and paper scraps she pulls from Alphonse's pockets in the laundry room and at the matchbooks on his dresser. You pull up a handful of stuff from the postal shorts pocket and happen to look at a matchbook—who can blame you? If it was a Camel's matches, or from that greasy spoon he eats lunch at, no big thing. But The Templeton? She flips the book in her fingers. It is new and still smells of printing varnish. Fresh from a big glass bowl in a lobby full of round, velvet divans and polished brass. In her mind a numbered door closes with a Do Not Disturb sign swinging on the knob. She feels a rush of dizziness and sits down in the basket of laundry.

The Templeton matchbook boasts a coat of arms blurry as a piece of lint, with an address underneath. This Templeton place can be driven to, the lobby entered, and information demanded. Let all hell break loose. It's on Alphonse's head. Secrets are made to be unwound.

Lem has brought Jimmy's car around to pick him up. Jimmy slides behind the wheel, sighing happily. Jimmy can't say anything about how beautiful the sky is, filtering down through the Lake Street el tracks, because it might hint to Lem that he had suffered a tiny little bit from his brief incarceration. So instead he says, "Yessir, next stop beer and pussy."

"So, who paid you out?" Lem asks.

"Giselle, man. Didn't you set it up?"

"Naw, I couldn't find her. How'd she find out?"

Jimmy shrugs as he U-turns the car to head toward King Drive. "All she say was, sorry 'bout this, and have a happy life."

"Why she sorry? She put your ass in jail?" Lem slaps the dashboard, chuckling.

Jimmy snorts at the thought. "All I know is she got me out. Crazy, knocked up…" He abruptly wheels the car up next to a hot dog stand with two picnic tables in front. The thought of a fresh hot dog almost brings tears to his eyes. Suddenly he feels intensely the difference between being outside the jail and inside. But all he says to Lem is, "Mm-mm. Smell those goddamn french fries, Lem. Pussy can wait."

Alphonse looks into every corner of the room, unable to believe that Giselle isn't there. He bites his lip and slaps his hat against his leg a few times.

She didn't go and get a job, did she? He decides to wait. He finds that it's hard to wait in a room with no cable TV and only women's magazines. He completes one of the sex surveys, fibbing a great deal in his answers, and then begins to poke around in Giselle's things. The tiny box fridge has few clues for him. Three cans of Diet Pepsi, a Ding-Dong, a half-brick of Velveeta, margarine, some bread. The pantry is even more meager. Crackers, peanut butter, and on the counter, an empty cocoa box, dry and clean. He sniffs it. Hasn't held cocoa for a long time. He walks over to the window. There is dust in the seams of the box and a strange, chemical smell.

"Hungry, Pop?" Giselle looks furious. Her belly moves before her like an avatar, a new persona.

He tosses the box on the bed. "Where you been? I told you I was coming around today."

"I had something to do. Why are you in my stuff?"

"It was out." He waves his hand at the box. "What's the smell in there? It ain't cocoa."

Giselle quickly moves over, scoops up the can, and dumps it in the trash. "It ain't dope, if that's what you're thinking. Just some make-up and stuff you wouldn't know anything about. What do you want, anyway?"

He takes a good look at his daughter. Her hollowed eyes are not those of a healthy pregnant woman. "I'm moving you home today."

Giselle laughs angrily. "So I just walk in looking like this and say, Hey, I'm home! You want to give Momma a heart attack?"

"She's sick to death already because of you."

"Look, after I have the baby, then she'll have to accept it. And me. Then, maybe."

He begins pulling the covers off the bed and rolling them into a ball. "It ain't for discussion. You're coming home."

She grabs the wad of linens and throws it back onto the bed. "I'm staying!"

"Dammit, girl, I'm telling you—"

"What in the world is going on?" says a third voice.

They turn to see Eloise, enlarged by anger, filling the doorway in her nursing whites. Eloise takes in the scene, and the sight of her daughter, angry, hollow-cheeked, pregnant. Anger is pushed aside by a confusion of new ideas and then by misery-tinged practicality. The transition is lightning-quick and complete.

"Come here, baby," she holds out her hands to Giselle, who covers her face and then bursts into tears.

"Why did you tell her?" Giselle whispers to her father.

"I didn't—" Alphonse stands, a pillow dangling from one fist.

Eloise enfolds Giselle in her arms. "Finish packing her up," she says to Alphonse. She takes a step backwards for stability as she struggles to hold onto her daughter, who is twitching with sobs.

Alphonse looks around the room, then drops the pillow. "There ain't nothing here she needs. Let's go."

The evening air is soft. The women are still in the kitchen, talking and talking. Eloise sent him and Tony outside right after dinner. She will deal with him, he knows, after she's done setting Giselle straight.

They'd played catch until it was too dark and still the women keep going, making sense of his messes and their own hardheaded mistakes. Alphonse, in a lawn chair, folds Tony's baseball mitt around a ball and straps it with a few rubber bands.

"See, this is how you shape it."

Tony is fidgety. "Can I go in and talk to Giselle some more?"

"She and your momma need a little more time. We'll go in shortly, put you to bed."

"But I have to tell Giselle about school and about Ronnie and—"

"Who's Ronnie?" Alphonse asks.

"Just a friend of mine," Tony says, smothering the reply in his chest.

Alphonse turns a book of matches in his fingers: The Templeton. He shakes his head ruefully, taking another sip of bourbon. Someday I got to tell Tony: Any man who a woman washes his pants don't control his own pockets.

July

Tuesday the 4th (Independence Day)

Elias fights off a descending sadness as he enters the hospital. The rehab ward is decorated with bunting and tiny flags. Several of the nurses have tied their soft white shoes with red and blue laces. But the business of the minute and of the day goes on as if nothing else mattered. Ashen-faced patients lie in a hundred beds, receiving their meals through a hundred needles. Sponge baths, linen changes, urine measurements. Those on solid food, however, enjoy a festive gelatin. He finds Florence in the sunroom dabbing paint on a piece of paper. The brush sits awkwardly in the fingers of her left hand. He leans over and sees what appears to be an image of flowers as seen under water. "So now you're Salvador Dali?"

"Why, Elias. My goodness!" She turns, and with paint-tinted fingers, reaches out to grab his sleeve. "What are you doing here? I thought you were going to have a picnic for Elana."

Elias leans down to embrace her. "They didn't show. The usual story."

"I'm sorry."

"I'm used to it." He forces a smile back into his eyes. "You look good, Florence."

"What I look like is a nice old teapot someone broke and glued back together." She laughs.

"I'm glad to see you painting again."

"I'm trying to do fireworks. Something simple for the crooked left hand."

174

"I brought you some treats," Elias says, holding out the foil-covered dishes. "I have a lot of food. Might as well share it."

"We'd better eat in my room so these *old folks* don't get jealous." She grabs her aluminum walker and drags it along as she moves down the hall. "I don't really need this anymore, but I can't seem to give it up."

She eases herself into a chair and Elias removes the foil, uncovering chicken, grilled corn, pickles, and rolls.

"Oh, Elias, look at the chicken—it's beautiful!" She takes a worshipful bite of a drumstick. Her eyes close and a smile breaks across her face. "My stomach is yours forever."

"You seem…back to normal, Flo. When will they let you leave?" He nibbles a piece of corn.

"Soon, or so they say. But I'm going to have to make arrangements for some help around the house. I still get tired a lot."

"I'm at your service."

"Yes, dear, I know. And thank you. But I'm afraid there may be no stopping Louise, my sister-in-law. She's quite set on coming up to nurse me."

"That's very kind of her."

Florence shrugs and licks her fingers. "Louise can be a pill, but it's better than staying here." She lifts the foil from another dish. "I'm ravenous. Did you bring any potato salad?"

The air is cooling, but still thick and heavy. Sweat pours down Nathan's face as he pushes Uncle Peter's wheelchair through the crowded pedestrian tunnel under Lake Shore Drive.

"Excuse me," Peter says to the strolling crowds, parting them like Moses. "Coming through!" He keeps his Hawaiian shirt buttoned all the way up, despite the heat, to look priestlier. His plaster-encased foot bounces before him like the prow of a small, rickety boat.

Nathan navigates the archipelago of blankets on the softball diamonds near the Waveland Beach refreshment hut, secures a southern view of the shoreline for Peter, and locks the wheels in place. Robin saunters up, with the thermos jug swinging from one arm, and a beach blanket draped across the other.

"Damn, you made good time," he pants theatrically. "I just couldn't keep up. Whew!"

"Wheelchairs always get the right of way."

"Especially when the guy in it helps people out of the way with his cane," Robin mutters.

Robin spreads out on the blanket a few feet away from Peter and rolls over to whisper to the cross-legged Nathan. "I've been thinking. In a way, it makes sense that Papa Pete is a master of passive aggression," he says. "Priests aren't allowed to be *actively* aggressive, unless they're one of those revolutionary priests in Guatemala or wherever."

Nathan whispers back, "I can't believe I have to push him all the way back later."

"Everything about him is hard to believe."

Peter whips off his straw hat and begins fanning himself manically.

"Come on, Robin. It's not so bad." Nathan rolls onto his back and looks up at the powder-blue sky. "See how nice the day is?"

"Nice as being wrapped in a boiled horse blanket."

"You needed to get out anyway, after talking to Janie. Otherwise, you'd stay in and wind yourself into a ball."

Robin says nothing, but pours a cocktail from the thermos into a paper cup and throws it back in one gulp.

"You never said why she called."

"It's nothing, just—" He pours another. "My mother's worse."

Nathan touches his arm. "Bad?"

Robin shrugs. "On the scale of bad, it's worse." He holds out the cup. "Socktail?"

"Nathan?" Peter waves from the wheelchair. "Nathan, there's a bee over here. Do you mind? I'm deathly allergic."

Eloise doles out her famous cole slaw and potato salad without any of the joy she wants to feel while celebrating a holiday with all her family together for the first time in so long.

"Hey, beautiful," says Donald, Alphonse's second cousin. "Why you looking so blue?"

"I'm exhausted, Donny." Eloise waves her serving spoon. "Firecrackers been cracking all over the neighborhood day and night since the weekend." She rubs her temples. All along the streets for weeks before and after the Fourth you smell saltpeter from the firecrackers. A bitter smell. The crackers don't go off with the surprising, happy pop of her youth, but in long snaggling cascades, whole sheets of explosives at once tearing through your sleep like a skirmish on a string.

"I hear you," Donald says around a mouthful of potato salad. "Is that chess pie?"

"Not only that, Alphonse caught Tony with a pocketful of cherry bombs and grounded him for the week. That why he cain't play no frisbee or softball with his cousins."

"Don't fret your pretty face. He just acting out."

"Acting out better stop right here, or he's got himself a whole lot of trouble."

"Damn good tater salad, Eloise. You give my Vonda a cooking lesson anyday."

"Just be glad they's somebody willing to cook for your fool self," Eloise laughs. "Now get along."

The sight of Giselle off by herself on a blanket, staring at the lake, hands folded across her belly, turns Eloise's frustration a notch higher. No one has said a word about you-know-what. And that, to Eloise, is worse than gossip.

Alphonse comes up behind and slips an arm around her waist. "Hey, sugar, you okay?" The Big Fight is still fresh enough that he is grateful for the right to put his cheek against hers and just breathe in her scent.

"No." She leans forward, resting her weight on her arms. "I'd just as soon leave now."

"Why, baby? We haven't played ball yet or had the fireworks."

"I've had enough, is all. I'm tired." She scoops up a giant blob of slaw and lets it plop back into the bowl. "Our children are falling away from us, and I can't take it."

"Things are better now, El."

"Are they, Alph? How come I feel even worse, like I'm on some big rollercoaster and the pins holding it together keep working themselves loose?"

"We got Giselle back."

"Sometimes I'm not sure we did. I'm not sure she's there to be got."

In their not-so-triumphant return to the performing stage, the new Lather Rinse Repeat struggle through a thirty-minute set to lackluster applause and then wander through the food stands at the Taste of Edgewater street festival, trying to put a brave face on things.

"Well, you can't lose a front man and bounce back like nothing happened," says Chipper. "This chicken kebab, by the way, is great."

"It'll come around," says Molly urgently. "You know we're good. We just have to get over our old sound and find out what our new one is."

Shanklin, fully aware that his debut performance as lead singer is his last, pushes three stuffed grape leaves into his mouth and says nothing. He wads up the greasy paper plate and throws it in the general direction of the el tracks.

"Hey, it's okay," Alice says, putting a hand on his arm. "Molly's right. We just need to make some adjustments."

"You weren't the one up there strangling our best songs," he mumbles.

"He's got you there, Alice," Molly says.

"Guys?" Chipper gasps. "Isn't that Lori over by the bandstand?"

They all turn in time to see their former manager squeezing the tight, black jeans-clad ass of a guy sporting a retro Glam Rock shag hairdo. He strokes the neck of his guitar suggestively.

"I'll be damned," says Molly. "Looks like she's now banging an Artist-Formerly-Known-as-Prince impersonator."

Alice turns away. "Thought she'd be in New York by now."

The guy jumps onto the stage and yells into the mike, "Hello, Edgewater! We're Tarp! Are you ready to rock?" A brief sample of cartoon chase music is drowned in a flood of guitar feedback and a lung-shaking drum roll.

"Jesus, that guy's even got a fake English accent!" Chipper throws his hands in the air. "And we *opened* for them!"

Before he even reaches the block where Leda's family lives, Ng catches the sound of faint, tinny mariachi trumpets. And shortly thereafter, the scent of spicy seared meat reaches him. His mouth waters.

He hesitates in front of the building. Children dart around the corner and dive into the bushes. The volume of chatter and laughter, trapped between the tall brick buildings, sounds as dense and Babylonian as a stadium or carnival. It seems impossible that he could enter that place.

"Hey, what are you doing down there?"

Ng looks up to see Leda's face, surrounded by dark, fallen curls, leaning out of a second story window. "Hey," he says.

"I'll be right down." She pops back inside. A door slams, feet trundle down the stairs, and Leda bursts through the door, cradling a two-liter bottle of grape soda. "Mom sent me upstairs for some more pop." She rocks the bottle like a baby.

"I'm so thirsty I could drink the whole thing."

"I'd like to see that. It's so warm, the foam would probably shoot out your nose."

Ng laughs. "Hi, Mrs. Villanueva? I don't usually shoot purple foam through my nostrils like this, but—"

Leda looks at the ground. "It's good to see you. I wondered if you'd come."

"Well," he shrugs. "Here I am." He fumbles in his back pocket. "I brought sparklers."

Leda breaks into a smile of such joy that Ng wants desperately to kiss her. But then what?

A little girl flushes an even smaller boy from the bushes and chases him around the building, shrieking.

Leda takes Ng's arm. "Come on, they're going to do the piñata in a minute. Maybe Poppy will let you take a swing."

"Really?"

"Sure. We won't even blindfold you."

"Because I can't see anything anyway, right?" He rolls his eyes.

Leda tugs him along. "I get your candy if you break it."

Ng stumbles forward, propelled by her force, into the swelter of voices, music, food, and laughter. In the alley, children scatter from a sizzling fuse. He takes a deep breath.

Friday the 7th

Brad lies on his back watching rain smear down the tiny window of his apartment. The bedclothes are sour. The dirty soup cans piled in the trash and the empty, grease-tinted cabinets of the kitchenette are an accusation of ineptitude and folly.

"When I say The Window," he tells Lori over the phone, "I mean the *only* window. I feel like a frog some kid trapped in a shoe box. Makes my crappy old loft look like a goddamn palace."

Lori clucks her tongue to minimize his frustration. "It's only for a while. You'll be moving into the Chelsea by Christmas."

"So *that's* why I'm leaving everything in boxes."

Lori misses or ignores the sarcasm. "That's the spirit." She is humming and, judging from the tiny glass clicks, painting her nails.

He gets up and begins to pace the few steps from wall to wall. "And summer here is the worst. It's like you get no sun, only this gross radiating heat from the pavement."

"Uh-huh."

"If it weren't for the music business here, it would be one of those places that you can't figure out why anybody lives there. Like the Gobi Desert, or Indiana."

"Listen," she says sharply, "I've got to go."

"Why?" He stops abruptly, gesturing in supplication at a ripped Spinal Tap poster left by the former tenant. "What's wrong?"

Lori sighs. "You're ranting, Brad. I can't help it. Be a man and just deal with it."

He feels gut-punched. "I'm sorry. Jeez, I'm sorry."

"Call me when you're more positive, okay?"

He hears the faint wind of her blowing on her nails.

"Wait, wait. I *am* positive. I'm just a little, you know, lonely. I miss you."

"Ugh! You know, don't start laying a guilt trip on me." Her voice rises in tenor. "You made the decision to go. It's your shit, not mine. I'm not making you sit around moping."

Brad considers this as a brown, disk-shaped roach traverses the opposite wall on a diagonal to the closet door, where it disappears. "I'm not moping. I've been doing open mikes and stuff. I called that Freeman guy you told me about."

"And?"

"And he's in London until the end of the month. And his secretary, I must say, was a real bitch to me."

"What about Slalom Records or the guy at the Knitting Factory?"

"Well, you never gave me their names or anything."

"Oh Christ, Brad, I did, too. We talked about which songs to put on the demo tapes for each one."

Brad stops, testing his memory for seams through which something this large could have slipped. "We did?" he says at last. "I don't remember that."

"Okay, I don't have time for this. I'll send you another list. I really have to go."

"Wait, Lori. Is there, I mean, are you any closer to making the, um, the big move?" He tries to give this last phrase a jocular, ironically self-conscious tone, but fails.

"I'm working on it. Don't ask me every time we talk, okay?"

"Okay."

"Now go write a song. I'll call you tomorrow."

"Okay. Well. Bye," he says softly into a dead phone.

The shop window frames the sun into a rhomboid of shining heat in the middle of the café floor. Mostly the patrons avoid it, but Molly is sunbathing in it, stretched across two chairs, sunglasses on, skirt pulled up to show her shapely, pale, and hairy legs.

"Why don't you bring down the shades?" Molly asks.

"Then it's too dark."

"Lesser of two evils?"

"I'm saving the desperate measures for August. You know, if Mrs. Irwin came in and saw you like that, she'd bust a gut."

"How often does she come in?"

"About once every three months."

"So there you go. I say beach party time. Throw some sand down, get out the beach towels, and you've got instant Bahamas."

"Come Mr. Tally man, tally me espresso," Alice mumbles, stacking bags of bulk coffee beans.

Molly sits up. "Okay, I've been patient enough. Have you talked to Brad lately? Has he seen the error of his ways? Does he want to come back to the band? Or to you?"

"No," Alice snaps. "And anyway, I don't want to be Brad's personal cable channel. All Brad all the time."

"I understand. But it does affect us, you know."

"I can't believe you would even consider having him back."

"It would make some things easier is all. Not everything, but at least the band."

"Not for me. Brad is nobody, no how."

"Gotcha. *Persona non grata.* Can we still play the songs you and he wrote together?"

"Sure. But you should know I'm changing all the choruses to 'Fuck you Brad, fuck you Brad, fuck you Brad.'"

Molly falls off her chair laughing, and Alice follows, slumping against the table and then down to the floor. The mailman walks in, looks at them, puts the mail on the table, and leaves without a word.

The girls begin laughing all over again and finish in an awkward silence, which Alice suddenly breaks with the non sequitur, "I mean, what has Lori got that I haven't?"

"The heart of a killer?"

"Besides that."

"Eva Braun's body and Hitler's brain?"

"Brad always wanted me to get a tattoo. Celtic braid on the ankle, a rose on my tit. Maybe now's the time."

"A spite tattoo? You know what that is. A rash moment and a lifetime of regret."

Alice gives her a sidelong look. "I'm going. You coming or not?"

"Keeping Brad's place for rehearsal was Old Shanky's best idea ever, eh wot?" Chipper spins on his drumming stool, tapping the cymbals as he swings past.

Shanklin is sprawled on the lone couch. "It's okay since we painted it." He picks a blob of white interior latex off the upholstery. "It was nice of the landlord to reduce the rent once I pointed out a few code violations."

"This heat is moider," Molly groans.

Alice draws back the mismatched sheets that serve as drapes and fluffs her T-shirt at the opened window. "I'd still like to have it fumigated."

"Does that take care of ghosts?" Shanklin asks.

"Maybe Alice is right. I've been thinking, maybe we should have a kind of ceremony. An exorcism."

"There is, methinks, a moral here," Chipper begins.

Alice cuts him off: "I don't want to hear it."

Shanklin bolts up from the couch, staring at Alice. He points at her. "What's that on your side?"

"Is that a tattoo?" Chipper says excitedly. "Let me see!" He scrambles from behind his drum kit and hunkers at Alice's side, monkey-like. "Ooh, a butterfly!" He touches it with a tentative finger.

"Ow," Alice says. "Careful, it's new."

"Hey, Papillon, where do you carry your ATM card?" Shanklin says.

"I'm getting mixed messages." Chipper lingers over Alice's midriff. "On one hand you have the tattoo Brad wanted, and on the other we're talking exorcism?"

"A spite tattoo," Molly adds. "I warned her."

"You know, fuck you guys," Alice says, tugging her shirt down. "This has nothing to do with Brad."

Molly flops on the couch, crossing her arms. "Well, we still have to get over him as a band."

"Let's do Molly's exorcism!" Shanklin grabs his bass and twangs it. "Out, damn Brad!" Chipper begins banging on the snare. "Voodoo!" he yodels. Voo-doo!" He settles into an eccentric tempo, which Shanklin overlays with a wandering rhythm on the bass.

"Come on!" Chipper shouts.

The women reluctantly join in, Molly banging out chords on the piano, and Alice adding ironic wa-wa notes with the guitar. Before long, none of them are thinking of anything but the emerging song.

Monday the 10th

After another blistering weekend of pushing Uncle Father Peter down the lakefront, Robin felt he deserved a treat, and the Randolph Street market at the cool hour of six a.m. feels deliciously illicit, like sneaking into a florist's shop at night. Despite his state of worry over his mother's condition, Robin is surprised to find himself whistling a tangled medley of Abba songs as he packs several shopping bags with butter lettuce, napa cabbage, sugar peas, mustard greens, peaches, and aromatic bunches of rosemary, cilantro, basil, and parsley.

On Sunday afternoon, he had very nearly pushed the priest in front of a Broadway bus just to stop his incessant chatter. His morbid fear of cabs, his discovery of television as a barometer of moral decline. How the *TV Guide* is a roadmap of how we've lost our way. And Nathan hasn't even got the time to listen to Robin's theory of how Uncle Peter needs tough love to get him off his fatherly duff and onto his—surely, by now—quite thoroughly mended ankle.

He rummages in the vegetable crates like a child in a toy store. This is where life has meaning. The sharp smell of a tomato's skin, the delicate give of a cantaloupe's navel—these are sometimes the only tiny threads that keep him tethered to the ground. That, and paying wholesale or better.

"What do you call this?" Robin barks at a vendor, holding up a tomato riddled with worm holes.

"I call that," says the man, with a squint, "a half-price tomato." He wipes his hands on a towel jammed in his belt, and begins throwing crates of red cabbages across the rot-slicked floor.

"The crate's full of these," Robin insists, pushing the wormy fruit under the man's nose. "Just smell it!"

The man jerks back, looks up at Robin, and says, "Then why don't you take the whole friggin' batch and get out of here."

"Sure," Robin says. He makes a dramatic show of throwing the tomato toward a trash bin, in which, to his surprise, it lands with an echoey boom. "Won't be enough decent ones to make a salad."

The man straightens. His neck is already creased with dirt at this early hour. "Free," he says. "Take 'em and go."

"And what do I get for doing you this favor?"

The man glares at Robin, shifts his morning cigar into the other cheek, and goes back to slinging cabbages. Robin smiles and lifts the crate and his other purchases and loads them into the trunk of the cab he has commandeered for this excursion.

"Victory," he says to the driver. "I'm not quite ready for work. Let's detour through Lincoln Park."

The hours after Nathan and his odd roommate have left for work are delicious. Peter settles himself in front of the TV with a mug of tea and the remote control. One hundred and twenty-five channels of the dismal world funneled down to him for inspection and judgment. He can't tear his eyes away. First, he flips between the major network morning shows to get as much weather news as possible. He loves weathermen, so bluff and competent. The paths of change meticulously mapped and explained. It is comforting, like a cup of tea just so.

Then he watches the reruns of Sister Angelica on the religious channel. He snorts at her fat-old-lady platitudes. Nuns like her would have been the butt of so many jokes back in his Portland parish. She is using her homespun and barely canonical theology to explain the failure of the latest peace talks in the Balkans. Her naïveté is appalling. Get a life, Sister!

The faces on the TV are his congregation, and he is fierce with them.

And then the main event: talk shows, with their pageant of warped humanity. The stories pile up, one by one, each fat with biblical depravity. Women who want to marry their stepsons. Former fat girls who want revenge. Would your boyfriend make a sexy woman? Preteens have sex at recess. Women who unknowingly marry gay men. Women who knowingly marry gay men.

He grows increasingly knotted and hypertense, twisting his napkin into a thin paper screw. The most amazing thing, what ultimately gets his goat, is not the behaviors but the endless explanations. *I left my wife cause she let herself go and get fat. It don't matter Lucinda's my wife's sister cause I love her. I di'n't tell him I's a stripper cause I's afraid he'd leave me.* Coming forward to display their sicknesses, explaining away venality, wanting a good enough reason to earn them absolution. This, he thinks, is where religion has left the American soul high and dry. What we need is more abject guilt and the penalties of the confessional.

He squirms as his breakfast sausage backs up on him. He quickly flicks the remote over to Andy Griffith for a little relief. In the middle of a Barney Fife pratfall, the phone rings.

"Hello? No he's not, can I take a message? Oh dear."

There may be nothing more capable of generating irritation in Robin at this very moment than the sight of Padre Peter waiting in the foyer with an exaggerated look of worry on his face.

"My boy, I'm so sorry—"

Robin brushes past him and dumps the crate of spoiled tomatoes on the hall table. "What," he sighs.

Father Peter shuffles closer with his cane, and an exaggerated look of pain. "A message, some hospital in Texas?"

Robin's face turns ghostly white.

"I couldn't reach you or Nathan all day. I was so upset I couldn't rest."

Robin takes the message from the priest's hand and scans it with a numb look.

"They wouldn't say what it was, but I knew it must be serious."

"Long distance calls aren't always serious. Could be my sister having some warped Pentecostal bastard offspring."

Peter stiffens. "Don't let your anger speak for you, son."

Robin laughs with his lips curled back rigidly. "If my anger spoke more often, there'd be fewer sanctimonious padres in this part of town."

Peter's face stiffens into its professional caring demeanor. "After six decades or so, you learn a few things." Peter stands within arm's reach of Robin, but leaves his hands at his sides. "If you'd like to talk."

Robin twists away and walks over to the glass patio door. "Look, not right now, Padre. I'm not Catholic, god is dead, and I don't feel so good myself." He places his hands on the glass, fingers splayed, and lowers his forehead between them.

"I guess you'll want to make your call now." Peter shuffles back a few steps. "Please, go ahead and use your room for privacy, if you like. I hope it's nothing serious."

"Yeah, okay, Padre." Robin walks down the hall to his and Nathan's room and slams the door behind him.

Peter looks at the door for a moment, looks at the couch, at the kitchen, and then goes into the guest room—which is apparently not Robin's after all—and softly closes the door.

After winding his way through several unhelpful operators and nurses, Robin finally gets through to his mother's hospital room. As he listens to the ring purring so many hundreds of miles away, he realizes that he doesn't know what will happen when and if the receiver is lifted. He tenses his muscles to drop the phone back in the cradle, but then a voice faintly buzzes in the plastic earpiece.

"Hello? Janie?"

"Who is this?" She sounds sleepy. "Robin?"

He is sitting on the edge of the bed, arms wrapped around his mid-section, suddenly freezing in the middle of July. "What happened? Is Mom okay?"

"How did you get this number?"

"I had a message from the hospital."

"Oh, that was a mistake. There's nothing you need to worry about. Mom's—she's okay."

"Wait a minute, what's going on? Can I speak to Mom?"

"She's sleeping. I'll tell her you called. I'd better go now."

"Why is she in the hospital? Can I speak to a doctor?"

"You know what, this really isn't a good time right now, Robbie."

He kicks his shoes off. Suddenly, he feels trapped inside his clothes. "I can get a flight down in the morning."

"I'm sure the message was upsetting, but everything's fine. She'll be released real soon."

"But what is it?"

"Just a little flu or something is all. Really, Robbie, I have to go."

"But Janie—"

"No, okay?" Janie hisses, keeping her voice at bedside levels. "Everything's under control. No need to panic, she's *fine*."

And then there follows a few seconds of dead silence before the dial tone breaks in. He flings the phone against the wall where it dings almost comically as its plastic shell breaks into several pieces that thud harmlessly onto the carpeted floor.

The silent moment returns and expands, absorbing into itself all the enveloping sounds of the city—airplanes, the vast, roaring highways, the telephone ring, a playground. He falls onto the bed and screams into the pillow, screams out every ounce of breath, wrenching it out with his stomach and lungs until the sound of his own voice, twisted into a howl, is ambient, sourceless, unreal. Until the goose down filling seems to have absorbed all of his body's breath and is exhaling it gently back in his face.

Thursday the 13th

The one thing that Danny Markowitz's friends would never guess about him is the amount of time he spends sitting in his rust-laced white Impala drinking quarts of beer and watching the comings and goings of Ng and Soo: his first family. He twists the top off another fat, sweaty bottle and the little pish sound the bottle makes remind him that his bladder is just about to burst. In a few minutes he'll have to drive over to the McDonald's and buy a small bag of fries so they'll let him use the bathroom. He tilts his head and lets the stinging, sharp liquid fill his throat. When he eases his head back to level, the bottle is a third empty.

He's done this emotional stake-out off and on for the last ten years. More lately. He never tells his second wife Stacey where he goes. She accepts these absences as part of the price of loving a man. In a way, she is even reassured by his unexplained disappearances; for Danny to be conspicuously mindful of her feelings would make her believe he was hiding something. And it gives her something to complain about while she has her hair done. A kind of double bonus.

Streetlights begin to pop on with an insectile buzz. It's to the point that Danny no longer asks himself what he's waiting for. It's just something he does, like bowling. Except that lately, he's felt more purposeful about maybe making contact, saying something to his son. Being a father for once, if only for a half hour. But can a father's first words to his son in ten years be advice?

It was the car vandalism. The boy's ashamed stoop as he darted to the car, the sad aura of his actions somehow communicated his disgust with the act. It wasn't in his will to do that, it was clear. A freak accident that Danny even saw it, having fallen asleep in the car the night before, and following Ng to school that one and only time. It was fate, Danny knew, a fact he had been miserably chewing over through the intervening weeks. It could piss a guy off, the way fate throws stuff in your way like that. Story of my life, he thinks.

That's it. Time to hit Mickey D's. He tosses the empty bottle into the backseat, along with a half-dozen others, a red Craftsman toolbox, and five-inch-deep layer of *Sun-Times* folded back to the box scores.

Like a triple helping of sugary breakfast cereal, the Fourth of July party with Leda's family gave Ng a breathless, jittery high before he crashed hard into the post-party depression. Sometimes in the intervening days he'd tried to put a name on the feeling. It was the same indeterminate hollowness that's haunted him ever since he defaced the car and Mr. Parsley announced his transfer. The vitality, the genuineness of Leda's family had lifted him up and then left him wondering just where he fit into the world. He had betrayed people and ideas precious to him, and looks back on that afternoon party as an undeserved happiness. And then he woke the next day terrified of the stretch of hours before him. Only his mother's sharp voice roused him to dress, eat and work. She pushes ahead, rain or shine, and her energy draws him forward like a leash. It does not seem possible that school will return in six weeks. That world is blown utterly to pieces, isn't it? He secretly unplugs the phone at night, not even sure what he's trying to avoid.

In Uptown you get used to walking in a scrambled field of random noise, so Soo barely turns her head at the bleat of a car horn. But the instant she does, a weariness floods her muscles. She walks over to the car.

"Hey," says Danny. "Got a minute?"

"I very tired," Soo says. She shifts her weight onto her left hip, and waits.

"It's important."

Soo reluctantly opens the car door and slides onto the vinyl bench seat. She looks disapprovingly at the mess. Soo never has told Ng how she'll be walking home, bone-tired after ten hours at the shop, and there's Danny, irregular as a blue moon, sitting in his smoke-filled car, usually drunk. The first time, it was winter, about five years after he'd slunk away, leaving her with their four-month-old baby son. She noticed the car out of the corner of her eye. A white Impala sitting in a smear of yellow streetlight, dusted with snow, a giant, broken icicle hanging from the chromed bumper, smoke threading around the edges of the driver's window.

That was the last time he touched her, in the cluttered, dirty backseat, on a sliding stack of newspapers. Danny with his beer breath and wet, soft-lipped kisses that he thinks prove what a romantic he is. Her toes had streaked the cold, foggy window. And then he was gone again, fishtailing down the street, a broken taillight the last sign of him for months. Since that time the car has gotten more rusty and Danny has gotten chubbier. Little else has changed.

Despite all that, Soo has never entirely been able to settle on blaming Danny for her unhappiness. True, he gets the brunt of her blame. But now and then, like today, when she's been hunched over a worktable for ten straight hours, he just seems to be one mechanism of a punishment meted out by something larger, more powerful and dispassionate.

"I saw," Danny stutters. "I mean, I have this feeling that—" He squeezes the steering wheel with both hands, the knuckles whitening. "Is there something wrong with Ng?"

Soo raises an eyebrow. "He pretty much okay," she says cautiously.

"It's just. I saw him the other day. He looked, I don't know, unhappy."

"He seventeen. No boy happy then."

"I don't know. I think it was more than that."

"You want to start be father? Now?" Soo's expression is caught between amusement and exasperation.

"I don't know." Danny cranks the window up and then down again. "Maybe."

"He need father, Danny. I always say that."

"Hmmm." The actions that have suddenly become necessary cause Danny to take a long pull on his beer. "Remember the last time you were in this car?" He puts a hand on Soo's shoulder and slowly slides it to touch the back of her neck.

She shrugs him off. "You want that, go home to you wife," she snaps.

"Soo, honey, that's not how it is." Danny's eyes get a hurt look in them. "I'm just with Stacey for right now." He leans forward and urgently whispers, "I never loved her like I do you."

Soo peeks furtively at Danny's lovely forehead. The broad, square space with deep character lines. The way the forelock, combed with wildroot, falls down, bending toward his eyebrows. "Why you don't talk to Ng?" She opens her door. "He the one who need you."

"I can't," Danny says. He moves away and puts both hands back on the steering wheel. "I can't."

"Maybe you need push." Soo steps out into the street.

Danny looks at her. Soo has never been one to force emotional issues. "No, I don't."

Soo leans down and gives Danny a long look that takes in the car, the trash, his gut-stretched T-shirt, the empty beer bottles. "Yes," she says at last. "You do."

The knock on the door bounces between the bare white walls of Ng's room, waking him from a brief nap induced by trying to read Kierkegaard's *Fear and Trembling*. Two paragraphs and he's out like a light.

"Yeah," Ng says without budging from his recumbent trance.

"You eat dinner?" Soo says through the door.

"Not hungry."

There is a pause. "I have something tell you."

He can tell she is speaking right into the tiny space between the door and the jamb. "Not right now, Mom, okay?" He tries to make his tone apologetic, but it comes out irritated. And he is too fatigued to revise it once it is uttered.

"Maybe you right," Soo says after a moment.

He hears her feet shuffle down the hall. He imagines a ghost of himself that rises from the bed, catches her in the hall, and says, Yes, I want to hear it. Whatever it is. Clean the bathroom, get a haircut, anything. Just tell me something that suddenly makes every last bit of me get up and go out there right now.

Then he hears the soft bump of her bedroom door shutting for the night.

Tuesday the 18th

Florence wakes with the first light as usual, when the nurses begin early rounds with their pills and water, their quick-read thermometers, and their cool, pulse-taking fingertips. After so many weeks spent shuffling between the same set of flavorless hospital rooms, the prospect of going home looms almost as terrifying as one of those South American treks to, as Arnie called it, Macho Pacho. Arnie. His sudden appearances appear to be over, whatever they were. Did he decide I was beyond help? Or is he waiting outside the hospital? The thought blends in her stomach, a combination of happiness and dread. She pulls on the pantsuit that Elias brought from her house last week. The fabric feels rough as canvas against her skin. When she stands up, the sleeves seem to devour her hands. It has been such a long time since she last wore this. Let's see, I was potting flowers on the patio. Arnie was lugging that sack of potting soil from the elevator when he got a twinge in his shoulder. That was three or for weeks before he…. Have I gotten so much smaller?

She rolls up her sleeves. The daisy stitched on the left breast looks enormous and depressingly out of fashion. She sits on the toilet, overwhelmed by despair. She touches her hair. It is softer and whiter now. And the face, well, there's nothing much to do about it. She tries to look in her wobbly left eye. She smiles a practice smile at herself. Normal? Arnie would say that normal is you, and abnormal is other people. So I'm normal, she whispers to the mirror. And today's smile doesn't look all that bad.

Elias arrives talking a blue streak—about the drought in the South, the return of the Cubs' injured ace pitcher, and what does she want for her first dinner as a free woman—as he bundles up her few personal items, and then he wheels her into the elevator. He turns her around to face the doors closing on the faces of the nurses waving and calling out their best wishes. The elevator lurches and descends.

"Once you get out in the heat," Elias says, "you'll wish you were back here."

"Oh no," Florence smiles, feeling her sadness lift. "Just thaw me out like an old roast, and I'll be fine."

The elevator shudders to a stop and the doors slide open to reveal a symphonic blast of sunshine.

"Here we go," Elias says, and pushes the wheelchair over the threshold.

Florence sits with her hands in her lap, watching the passing buildings and the trees with rapt interest. Elias steals a glance at her every now and then as he guides the car through the crowded, narrow streets of Lincoln Park. Getting her out of the hospital is a greater relief than he expected. Like a knot has loosened inside.

Suddenly she speaks, her voice soft, amused. "You know what I find so strange? That I don't have any idea what time it is. Or what day."

"It's Tuesday, about one-fifteen."

She's shaking her head. "I'm not sure I can explain. I used to carry this picture of my life in my head, like a game board. Like Parcheesi, say. And I could always see where I was on it. There was sometimes a gap between where I was on the board and where I thought I was supposed to be, but mostly I just moved along, hop hop hop. Happy as a bird."

"Mmm," Elias murmurs, waiting.

"After Arnie died, the board changed, or got cloudy, and I couldn't tell where I was supposed to be on it anymore. I think that's part of what I was fighting, when I was depressed. It was scary, like vertigo, like falling, sort of."

"I see."

"Now I can't see the board at all. I can't even remember what it looked like. Who am I supposed to be now? What am I supposed to be looking forward to? What's behind me to look at?"

Elias turns the car down a street lined with mossy graystones and ancient oak trees. The car's a/c makes the air taste metallic. He has some idea of what Florence means, but no idea of what to say in reply.

"It's July 18 in the year 2000. So what?" She shrugs. "What's that mean? A two with three zeroes." She returns to looking out the window, humming tunelessly, softly.

"Does it make you sad?" Elias asks at last.

She thinks about it, looking at the green bars fencing the playground of a schoolyard where a young girl, playing tag, slips between the bars like a sprite. "No. Not sad, really. Something else."

∞

The apartment has a funny, abandoned smell. Funky. Even though Potamkin kept the plants watered and threw out the dead and decayed food in the fridge. On the kitchen table sits a potted begonia on which is tied a note: *Welcome back! Regards, Potamkin.*

Florence lowers herself onto the couch. "Goodness, I don't know what to do first."

"Here, maybe we should hang up some of your left-handed paintings." Elias holds up one in which the shallow perspective make it appear as though a giant pigeon is hatching an egg in the middle of Lake Shore Drive.

"Oh my Lord, it's awful," Florence cries.

"If you don't want it, I'd like to put it in the restaurant."

"You'll scare all your customers away."

"K-nock, k-nock," says a voice at the door. "Anybody home?"

"Goodness me, is it you, Louise? Already?"

"Here I am, you poor thing!" The door swings open, and Louise pauses before them to drop her two remarkably large suitcases in the foyer. She has thickened since the funeral, and grown browner. Almost an unnatural shade, like purse leather. Her dyed black hair and magenta tracksuit create the impression of a television image with tint and hue control gone haywire.

She sheds her jacket. "I never expected it to be hot as Tampa up here!" And she swoops down upon Florence with beefy forearms and coos unintelligibly.

Florence looks over Louise's head and gives Elias a look of desperate appeal.

"Big Jim and I see this so often," Louise says plaintively. "Husband dies and the wife just falls apart until she follows him."

Florence pats Louise's head, mouthing, "Help!" to Elias.

Elias coughs and says, "Let me take your bags to the guest room."

Louise rises, pulling invisible strands of hair away from her face. "You must be Elias. I've heard so much about you."

He smiles back and says nothing.

Louise claps her palms together. "I should freshen up and then get down to business."

"Business?" asks Florence.

"Why, you, dear. Getting you back on your feet."

Elias begins dragging the suitcases down the hall.

"But I am on my feet," Florence protests mildly.

"Of course you are dear. Positive thinking is really so important. That's what we'll be around here. Positive positive positive!"

Thursday the 20th

Giselle drags her fork through the cold syrup, enchanted by the tiny, parallel wakes of the tines. Food has become nothing more than a playground for long-repressed childhood habits. Making mashed potato forts, or faces out of peas and carrots. Anything but eat.

Eloise sips her coffee and stares back at the mangled but defiantly uneaten waffles. Giselle is thin, everywhere but the belly. Eyes lost inside dark hollows. She sighs deeply. "You got to eat, baby."

"Mom, please." Giselle rolls her eyes. "One more bite, I'm going to blow up like a big fat something."

"You hardly eat nothing at all."

"I ate the bacon." She flips the cantaloupe slice on its curved edge, jams her fork in the middle like a mast, and sails it around the syrup pond.

"We'll see what the doctor says."

"I told you, I'm not going to the doctor. I went already."

There is a faint bell-like chime of the plate being scraped by the fork.

"Listen here, I'm your momma and a registered nurse, so don't you try and tell me about prenatal care."

The cantaloupe boat runs aground and beaches on a shoal of mashed waffle.

Giselle stares at her plate. "Baby's coming whether I want it or not. It doesn't even need me anymore. I could get hit by a bus and the baby'd come out fine."

"Hush up that talk!" Eloise snaps. "That baby's coming, all right. And you best want it."

Giselle pushes her plate away. "It doesn't matter what I want. I'm nothing but a walking suitcase for this—thing."

Eloise tries to hide her shock. Her hand is tight on the handle of the coffee cup. "You that baby's momma," she says firmly. "Ain't nobody more important in the world right now for that little child than you."

"That's just the problem, Momma. That's the main problem."

Eloise stares at her and then says, "We going to fix things so it ain't a problem, ain't we?" She stands and smoothes the front of her crisp white nurse's uniform. "I'm going to wake up Tony." And she walks stiffly out of the room.

Tony finally rises from bed after Eloise's third visit to nudge him and after Alphonse has flipped on the lights and barked, "Up and at 'em, boy!"

He rubs his eyes. It's past eight o'clock. Not late enough. Ronnie says he never gets up before noon.

Alphonse sticks his head around the doorway. "Well, look who's up."

"Uh," says Tony, rubbing his eyes.

"You gone pick up them soldiers out the yard? I don't want to run 'em over with the lawnmower."

Feeling drowsy and besieged, Tony thinks of the little soldiers. The stories they embody are so childish. The infantry has laid in place so long, grass has grown up between their stiff green legs. "I don't care," he says.

Alphonse stiffens. "I care," he says with steel in his voice. "I don't want them sprayed all over my yard. Get them up. Today."

The father and son regard each other in this new relation that has suddenly developed.

"Your momma's got waffles in the oven for you. You don't hurry, they'll be crackers." Alphonse retreats. His hands feel empty of something, and he looks to see if maybe he's dropped his coffee cup or keys.

The summers of Alphonse's childhood were a time for midday naps and general sloth. As he drives into the lot, he sees the heat already beginning to shimmer off the asphalt. He remembers how back in Baton Rouge everyone would escape inside summer afternoons, to lay on the porch and drink iced tea. Up here people don't respect the heat. Not even after all those people died during the '95 heatwave. They respect the winter but not the summer. As if every four years or so they didn't have heat and humidity bad as any bayou hamlet. Heat advisory my ass. Get yourself in the shade with a paper fan and some iced tea, save a lot of lives.

He sneaks up behind Elvin and gives him a slap on the side of the head. "Gone be another hot one."

Elvin turns a grim eye. "You're bright-eyed and bushy-tailed. You get up on the right side of the bed for once?"

"Only bad side of the bed is the outside," Alphonse grins.

"Then things are better at home?"

"Good as they get, I suppose."

"Eloise finally give up being mad at you?"

"Maybe. She's all worried about Giselle now."

"Well, it's a good sign if she's speaking to you again."

But as Alphonse turns away, he feels pained by the gap between the simplicity of the picture he has just painted for Elvin and the way things really are at home. He flips through his package slips and moving notices. There is a re-start order for Mrs. Finkel. Holy moly, hadn't thought of her in a alligator's age. He scribbles, *Welcome Back Mrs. F!,* on a scrap of paper, slips it onto the huge stack of undelivered mail, and wraps it all with a fat rubber band. Something to look forward to on the route today.

And then he remembers Eloise last night talking on the phone with her sister Belle back down in Louisiana. How her end of the conversation was all, "I don't know, I just don't know," over and over again. She will hug and kiss at night, but he can tell she's looking past him, over his shoulder to somewhere else. Something's cooking in that brain of hers. This half-forgiveness is some crummy limbo.

Monday the 24th

Ellen's first strike for freedom was pretending to lose the pager. Megan suspected the loss had been no accident, but accepted the fact that it was a losing battle to keep track of Ellen, whatever she was doing with her days. The second strike was hanging out at Urbs during Alice's slow times. It's a daily thing now, and it's all Ellen lives for. She packs a beach bag with her camera (because you never know), suntan oil, a copy of *Anna Karenina,* and a packet of carefully folded work clothes. Then she gives Marty a kiss on his wet nose and starts walking to the el.

The day is hot as a bitch in heat, as her father would say. Ellen's ribs are slick with sweat, so that her arms slide against her sexily. What is it people have against heat? She raises her face to the sunlight and opens her mouth as if to catch a few soft rays on her tongue.

Megan glares angrily at the arrow made of yellow lights blinking at her through the shimmer of heat as her car creeps toward it so slowly it feels like some form of madness. And Megan feels just that close to insane anyway, unable to get out of her mind the image of Ellen laughing with that girl in the café. And the black and white film images of that same girl's face, moving in the crowd of the St. Pat's parade like a drifting balloon. She watched every reel of film when Ellen was out of the apartment one day, unable to stop herself even though she knew it was as bad as reading a diary. She watched, nauseous, as Ellen's camera followed that other face hungrily, caressing it from a distance. With these thoughts comes a return of nausea. Oh god, Megan swallows. It's the price of jealousy to be proven right, she knows that. Sometimes she wishes she could leave things be, but the suspicions prove as unmanageable as the lousy things her snooping turns up.

A booming car rolls by, the bass notes rattling the windows. She continues to sit quietly, trying to let her anxiety dissolve. And then it slips into her mind: What is Ellen doing now? She knows, because so many other days, she has been right behind her, moving in her blind spots, swallowing up her footsteps like a kind of vacuum cleaner. Her stomach folds in on itself. The distance between them feels like a continent. She could race across those miles and still never know what exists in this moment. The anger surges up in her, and she feels like crying.

She looks ahead and sees no end to the line of car roofs that look like bright tiles emerging from a glazing oven. As they creep closer to the actual point where the lanes merge, the cars around her press ever more tightly together like fish being herded into a trawling net. She tries to swallow the panic rising in her throat. The hell with this. Megan wheels onto the shoulder, her tires popping up gravel and bits of glass as she guns toward the exit ramp.

Ellen takes her camera down into the buttercup. A bee's pointy behind jiggles inside the yellow chamber. She pulls back as the bee stumbles out, weighted with pollen, and woozily flies across the rooftop.

"Don't get stung," Alice says sleepily from under her sunbonnet.

"The dangers of wildlife photography."

"The dangers of urban photography, you mean. You can get stung, stumble around, and fall off the roof."

"Worried I'll ruin your awning?"

Alice laughs and rolls onto her stomach. "What time is it?"

Ellen looks at Alice's sun-kissed thighs and the slice of roundish buttock winking in the sun with a bit of coconut oil. She can almost feel how slippy. That bit of dimpled flesh and how it would feel between her teeth.

"Hey." Alice kicks the reddish soles of her feet. "You there?"

"I'm here." Ellen tries to shake herself out of the daydream, but it won't let go. It's like she's a dog in that experiment. Some kind of bell has rung and she can't stop the reaction. She wants Alice, now. She feels naked, as though the lust is outside of her, covering her skin like coarse hair. "I should really go," she stammers. "I've got laundry and stuff."

"Just like that?"

"Sorry. I lost track of the time." Ellen's palms are tingling as she gathers her things. The smell of Alice's suntan oil is in her nose. She can't see anything. She stumbles for the stairs and is gone.

Alice stares at the space where Ellen had been only moments ago. What the hell was that? The afternoon is lost now, interrupted. The echo of Ellen's voice is in her ears, softly, softly saying, *I didn't want to go, but I had to.* It wasn't spoken, but Alice heard the regret. She tries to push it out of her mind.

Pausing on the sidewalk to catch her breath, Ellen sees a figure dart out of view at the end of the block. Not that she can even recognize anyone from that distance, but the furtiveness of the movement is eloquent. She walks to the end of the building and turns into the alley. There Megan stands, halfway down, behind a trash bin. Not hiding, just standing and glaring with teary eyes at Ellen, who remains at her end of the alley, saying nothing. They stand there, silently looking at one another, tormenting the air between them, until Ellen breaks down, hiding her face in her hands. Why does her life have to suck so bad? Alice up there, Megan down here, and no place for Ellen. She is wasting her life trying to follow paths that just won't ever be smooth. She decides to apologize to Megan, try to patch things up. But when she raises her eyes, the alley is empty.

Wednesday the 26th

Jimmy spends every night of his early freedom talking loudly and trying to dance with all the women in Shug's Haven. But mostly making the point to everyone who will listen that jail time is no big shit.

"Look, you get another hot phone number like you buy gum from a machine," he explains to the back of a man's slightly damp Hawaiian shirt. "Everthing just like I left it, cause everbody do what's right. They know Jimmy's coming back, and he on the case."

The people around him remain absorbed in playing pool and flirting. He points at his empty bottle of malt liquor, and the bartender brings him another. He takes a long pull at the bottle. "Oh yes," he hisses, sifting a belch between his teeth. "Like pussy in a can." A woman with hair that looks like a futuristic aircraft turns a disapproving eye on him, and Jimmy spits back, "S'matter, woman? Fraid you gone lose your fran-chise?" She turns and gives him an eyeful of her drum-tight Daisy Dukes. He laughs and lolls his tongue wolfishly, feeling like his old self again.

But at the house on Kimbark, nothing at all seems the same. In his absence, it has become a filthy, stinking wreck. Rat turds in the closets. A powerful reek of something human, yet alien and disturbing.

Jimmy walks through the house in a state of mild disbelief that the place could have gotten any worse than he left it. But there it is. Summer always makes it stink worse, and swells up the wood so the doors and windows have to be hammered open. Which probably explains the broken panes. Someone cracked the toilet, so it is not only brown with rust, but has to be flushed with a pail of tap water. The whores hanging around the sweltering bedrooms are bonier than he remembers, with voices like steel wool on slate. Inside the stovetop he hears the skittering sound of a hoard of roaches. They have become predatory now and casually emerge from their headquarters in daylight, thumb-sized and aggressive. Worst of all, from both an ego and a business point of view, the drugs he is getting now are so adulterated they're barely illegal.

"More like to get diabetes from this coke than high!" he shouts at Lem. "The jay's just goddamn crabgrass. Them bennies is almost sugar pills with a little aspirin throwed in."

It is all, in his mind, destroyed. He is now officially farther down on the food chain than he ever cared to be, but he is going to get it all back. Don't you bet against him unless you plan on losing.

Summer to Eloise has always been the hardest season, ever since she was a child walking the blackberry fields outside of Baton Rouge, fingertips black with juice, the basket at her side bending her over like an old tree. Summer was field work and mosquitoes and sunburn fevers and snakes coming out on the roads at night to get run over, striping the pavement with their twitchy desire to strike even as they died. Of course, evenings at least had cold fried chicken, pitchers of sweet tea, and games of tag with visiting cousins in the long grass, near the swamp edge where daddy would go frog-gigging, his flashlight sweeping across the long, sloping yard out of the fuggy marsh air. Summer has no such consolations now, down in south Chicago. It is only louder, smellier, angrier than the other seasons. And anyway with your family shambling around like a beggar in rags, what is there to cheer oneself up? She feels the idea singing more loudly inside her. *Home. Get back home.*

Tony is in his age of being a wiseass now, staying out past dinnertime with no excuses when he comes in the door.

"Nuthin,'" he says to every question that he doesn't want to answer, or, "I don't know."

"Don't you *nuthin'* me," she has tried. But he does, still. And it nags at her mothering conscience: What is going on with him?

Everyday she looks at Giselle slumped on the couch behind her round, growing belly, and she can think of no way to work everything out. She has bent down and worked through and under so many kinds of badness. Getting Giselle back home was supposed to be a cure for one suffering, but has brought on just another, more perplexing, more pressing.

"You just feeling shame," Alphonse says this morning.

"And what if I am?" she snaps. "The Lord give us shame for a very good reason. Keep us from waving our sin around like everthing's fine."

"But you got to work through things, honey," he says, laying a hand on her back. "Things like children take some time to work themselves out."

"Or to work themselves into big trouble." She settles a little under his touch, but continues to shake her head with worry. "We just got Giselle back. What's to keep the same thing from happening with Tony?"

"We are," Alphonse says firmly. "We going to keep him safe."

"I don't know," Eloise says. "I feel like the city gone outsmart us ever which way."

"If any outsmarting going to get done," Alphonse says, "I'll be the one does it."

Wasn't hard to find out where they lived. Jimmy steers the LeBaron down Cottage Grove and curses to find himself without a gun. One of the house whores, one with a crush on Lem, if you can believe that, told Lem how she heard Giselle's old daddy had outfoxed Jimmy. Squashed him like a bug, she said, putting an ugly emphasis on the last word. Jimmy hangs his left arm out the window, menacingly, as though, were he to catch sight of Alphonse right then, he would run him over, or somehow do him harm.

Lem rides holding the seat cushion with both hands. "Didn't mean to upset you, man," he says. "Sareena told me not to tell you, and now she probably be pissed I told her secret."

"Ain't no permanent secrets, Lem. Shit slips out and goes wherever it want to go." Jimmy passes a van on the right and cuts it off, responding to their angry horn with an upraised finger.

He drives past the Duchossois house, turns the corner and pulls up a block over. He turns off the engine and sits in silence, letting impotence boil into rage. Lem reaches over and turns on the radio. Jimmy slaps his hand. "You got a fucking death wish?"

"No," says Lem, rubbing his fingers. "I just…what you gone do?"

"I'm planning my plan. I got to make a survey." He gets out and walks down the alley that runs behind the house.

The garage is askew and scribbled over completely with graffiti. There is a large padlock on the door. Like that's going to keep anything safe. He sees Giselle's father in the yard, picking a bunch of little plastic soldiers out of the grass and throwing them into a box. The old man is stumbling and slow. I could take him now, he thinks. Wouldn't know a thing. His hands clench on air. He looks for something to hold, to swing, or throw. A pile of bricks beside the trash cans. Jimmy grabs one and heaves it in a single, slow motion. A searing pain cuts into the muscle of his shoulder. He watches the brick sail in a wobbly arc and thump almost silently into the ground three feet in front of the feeble old man.

"Damn!" Jimmy mutters, grabbing his shoulder.

Alphonse turns, confused. "What the hell?"

Jimmy sprints down the alley, his shoes skittering on dirt and pebbles, his good arm windmilling for balance.

Alphonse runs to the gate in time to see the young man lose his footing on the bad pavement and fall as he turns the corner. He sees the young man's face, and, figuring who it must be, shouts, "You ever come back around here, I'll shoot your sorry ass!"

Jimmy hurtles into the car, stepping on Lem's hand, and shrieking, "Get the goddamn hell out the way!" He winces, fumbling with the key, and drives off with a screech, still looking in the rearview mirror.

"What happened?" shouts Lem, looking around for Jimmy's pursuer.

"He like to shot me, crazy ass nigger," Jimmy growls, fishtailing into cross traffic. "I'm have to come back strong next time. Come back serious strong."

When Alphonse tells Eloise about Jimmy, her way is clear. She calls the family together to make an announcement.

Tony squirms on the couch. It feels very official. "This about vacation?"

"No vacation this year, baby. But there will be a trip. Your Daddy and I discussed some things tonight, and there needs to be a clean start around here for that little baby." She points at Giselle's stomach. "And for the rest of us."

"What's that mean?" Giselle says. "A clean start."

"You and me," she says to Giselle, "we're leaving. I can't take care a you and that baby in this place."

"What?"

"You heard me. This weekend. We taking the bus to Louisiana. Stay with Auntie Belle till your baby comes."

"Momma, girls don't go away to have babies any more. That's like *Gone with the Wind* or something."

Giselle looks at her, and Eloise sees that behind her eyes there is no idea of the future. There is no place, no person, no readiness to nurture. Confirming Eloise's determination to act.

"Do I have to go?" Tony whines. The image of his summer being taken away, his chance to make the King 5s and get his hat, strikes him as cruel. "I don't want to go down there. I didn't do nothing wrong."

"*Anything*," Eloise corrects him. "I know you didn't do anything, baby. If you want to stay—" She looks at Alphonse, who shrugs. "I guess it's all right."

Giselle reaches across her brother for the remote control and turns on the shopping network. "Whatever, Momma." She settles back, arms folded defiantly. "I don't have the energy to fight your crazy old country ideas."

Saturday the 29th

It seems obvious now, but Brad hadn't expected to miss Lake Michigan. Cooler by the lake is one of those expressions that Chicagoans hear so often it becomes meaningless. But at this moment, hanging out the window of his humid, roachy apartment, he'd kill for one of those cool Canadian zephyrs, fresh off a five-hundred mile trip over water, to whip up his block of B Street and caress ten degrees off the overheated surface of his face.

That's just like Chicago, to take a little thing like a body of water and make such good use of it. The city of bold opportunism. Take advantage of what's there. Don't waste valuable time asking why, just use it. In Manhattan, by contrast, people can take very little solace in being surrounded by more water than all the Great Lakes put together. In the Midwest you bake in the direct glare of the sun; here you roast within heat reflected and intensified by surrounding brick and cement and asphalt. It's a giant concrete roasting pan.

The light of the sun, below the building tops for some time now, has almost drained away. Almost time for the early set at Bar Quito. He picks up the phone, and then puts it down again. Calling Lori is like a drug addiction. Doing it to feel better, but feeling worse afterward. She'll bitch about my lack of motivation. It will be better once she moves out here, he continually insists, to friends, to family, to himself. But he can't ask anymore. She can't stand his complaints.

"I lack bold opportunism," he says to the pigeon pecking at a few Doritos crumbs on the window ledge. "I didn't make good use of what I had. The city, the lake." His brain just barely forms the third missed opportunity: Alice.

He remembers Alice at the dog beach near Belmont Harbor. The ends of her hair stringy and wet as she struggled to wrench a slobbery tennis ball out of a labrador's mouth. The T-shirt draped darkly against her ribs. He shakes his head to rid himself of the image. Lori, remember? He flops onto the bed and strums a chord. Cooler by the Alice? Could be a song there. These days, when he thinks of song titles, he immediately drives them away, as though his touch would debase them. Somehow, with all this time on his hands to write songs, nothing. Chorus fragments, ditties. He has bridges without anything to connect. He throws the guitar down on the bed, where it hums sadly. His tunes sound suspiciously like jingles for underperforming car dealerships.

He emerges into the night-blue air of Washington Heights. Why is it that every bar with a decent open mike is some skank-hole in a neighborhood distinctly unfriendly to lone gringos carrying guitar cases? It's like, if you survive the walk from the subway, you deserve to get onstage.

Full of blue-collar Ecuadorians the other six nights of the week, Bar Quito plays incongruous host to one of the most prestigious open sets around. He enters the bar and there are familiar faces, though no one pays him particular attention. Why does he feel so Second City? Who was the last good group from New York—the Ramones? The Talking Heads? But there's something so hideous about the spotlight and the faces who want, really, to hate you, although they might pretend, even to themselves, that they are there to be first to hear the latest true and pure voice. It's more like a stock car race. Half rooting for someone and half waiting for the horror of the crack-up.

After a half-dozen sets of the usual lame crap, Brad goes up into the warm, weak light that washes everyone's face into a single, fuzzy wall of white. And he sings a song he wrote after leaving Chicago. As he sings, he senses the crowd slipping away. The worst thing is that he's just this close to having them in the palm of his hand. When he walks onstage, he has the look, the walk, the presence. The people are ready to be wowed. But when the songs fail to go anywhere, when the snappy bridges connect nothing especially smart or new, he metamorphoses into another wannabe, a never-was. He feels the change take place, just as sure as if he were a Hollywood special effect, stooping, becoming thicker, hairier, revealing the unevolved strummer within. The urgent copycat.

And though he'd promised himself not to do this, for a second number he picks a song Alice wrote for him, feeling a little guilty about it. And the crowd returns for a moment and gives him a round of polite applause. He tries to smile, but all of the muscles in his face seem to be pulling away from the bones.

Brad answers the phone in his sleep. "Hey." He squints at the clock. Three-thirty a.m.

"Hey, sleepyhead, guess what!" Lori's voice is sharp with high-register glee.

Brad clenches up. What could it be? She finally quit her job? She broke her lease? She's rented a U-Haul? She's on her way? She's calling from an Ohio rest stop? Or maybe nothing. Like the time she found a missing earring and called to gloat like it was a gift from a prestigious foundation. "Whatever it is, it must be good," he says at last.

"I just got offered the greatest job," she says, the words rushing out.

"This guy who knows Brad Wood is starting a label, and he wants me to be the PR director, and—"

"Wow," says Brad, as her voice crashes over him. "Are you drunk?"

"A little, from celebrating," she giggles. "Anyway, this guy, Todd, he's already got one of the Smashing Pumpkins talking about a solo project, and he wants me going to all the festivals, and he already wants to sign this band I know called Diacritical Marks, and god, I just can't believe it!"

Brad waits a moment. He listens to her excited panting as she pauses finally for him to respond. "That's great. Really." He untangles his legs from the sheets and leans into the hum of the box fan. "So can you do this from New York?"

"Don't be silly! This is here, it's happening, there's tons to do."

He says nothing, and she goes on talking, telling him about the great opportunity, how it will change everything, and will even be good for him, too, really. Her voice goes on and on without pause, receding to a buzz as his mind goes into some other region, where there are calculations of mistakes, errors, and remembered pratfalls of his youth. The sweat moving through the crease of his earlobe starts to make him crazy. He feels his nerves begin to vibrate with a longing for swift motion, to move violently against something that will make a loud noise.

She is still talking, buzzing and buzzing. He moves to throw the phone against the wall, but stops himself.

"You know what, it's really late."

"Oh." She's offended. "Sorry. I thought you of all people would—"

He places the receiver down gently. He lays back against the hot pillow and listens to an ambulance siren pealing toward uptown. He decides that by the time the siren fades into the general din of nighttime Manhattan, he will be asleep.

And it is almost that way.

August

Thursday the 3rd

"Rise and shine!" Louise yanks open the drapes with a dramatic crack. "Day's wasting!"

Florence pulls a pillow over her face. "Goodness, it's a shock how you do that," she mumbles, her tongue still thick with sleep.

"Big Jim and I greet the morning with a burst of energy. It shows you mean business. Start slow, stay slow. Start quick, stay quick. That's how you do it."

"I always preferred a gentle acceleration up to cruising speed." Florence rubs her face for a moment, and then pulls back the covers and slides her legs over the side of the bed. She takes a deep breath. This is where the struggle with her forgetful muscles begins again.

"Don't you even think about getting out of bed!" Louise snaps. She rushes over and begins pushing Florence back down into the bedclothes.

"But the doctor—"

"I don't care what the doctor said. You can't believe them half the time." Louise comes over to fluff the pillows, but Florence grabs her wrist.

"I have to get up and do things, Louise. Things I have to relearn so I can be prepared to take care of myself when you leave."

Louise seems to overflow the apartment, which is by no means a small one, with her personality. She launches into each day dressed in nylon track-suits in colors so loud they make Florence's teeth hurt. She moves nonstop, cleaning and straightening and planning meals and cleaning again. When Florence scolded her for using a toothbrush to clean the tracks of the balcony door, Louise could not understand what she had done wrong.

"Jimbo loves things to be clean," she rebutted. "It shows I love him."

Florence swings her legs to the floor, and Louise does not move to stop her, but straightens the photos on the nightstand, a hurt expression on her face.

"I would love a glass of orange juice," Florence says.

"Coming right up," Louise says, and charges out of the room.

Florence exhales, already tired.

With Louise around, moments alone are scarce. Louise, of course, would see this as a distinct benefit of her presence. The best part of the day is late morning, when Louise does the shopping and Florence can sit out on the balcony and paint. As soon as the door shuts behind Louise and silence returns to the apartment, Florence settles down at her easel on the balcony, brush in hand.

In a bargain she has cut with herself, she alternates painting with her left and right hands, one small picture each. Today, she uses both on the same picture. The effects she gets from her unsteady left hand sometimes surprise and delight her. It is like a wild card thrown into the mix, sometimes ruining pictures, sometimes adding unexpected and exciting twists.

She pauses, moved by the dark, roiling clouds over the lake. It is not what she would call good light, but it unleashes in her emotions of melancholy and loss. It makes her think of Arnie. She sends her thoughts out to him: It's a good thing, I guess, to know I won't die penniless and friendless. There are plenty of people around, sometimes too many, I think you know who I mean. But dear, on a day like this there is nothing I would rather do than make you a tuna salad sandwich and have you come home for lunch, and cheer me up. Feeling a little embarrassed, she starts painting quickly, testing her poor hand's agility. As she highlights the edge of a cloud with white to simulate the muffled sunlight, the brush slips and a streak of lightning appears in the paint. Almost at the same moment, distant thunder rumbles across the city. She looks up. To the west, clouds have broken apart and stream down the sky as rain.

There is a knock on the door, and Les Potamkin calls, "Hello?"

"Come in, Les," Florence calls back. She pulls her smock tighter, as though caught in a naked moment.

The big man swells through the door. "I thought you might be out here," he says gently. "Wanted to help youse get in before the rain." He pulls up his toolbelt.

"I guess I can't use watercolors in the rain, can I?" She swishes her brush clean and puts it away.

The janitor lifts the easel and carries it lightly into the kitchen. "You're looking very—" He pauses for a word. "Very well."

"Thank you. I feel better every day."

"Where's your friend? Louise?"

"Shopping. It's her favorite thing next to bossing me around." Florence eases her weak arm out of her painting smock.

"Need help with that?" Potamkin asks. He lifts his hands cautiously.

"No, dear, thank you. You've helped enough. You got me inside just in time."

They both look out to the patio, where the first dark spots appear on the cement.

"I'd better check the front awnings," Potamkin says, "in case the wind comes up." He eases himself out the door again, without another word.

The wind carries in a gust of the scent of wet concrete, and throws a handful of large drops against the plate glass. Florence goes to shut the sliding door and pauses, watching how the rain changes everything. What was bright and harsh yesterday now seems occluded, full of hidden sadness.

She pulls a chair up to the door and begins to peel an apple. Another of her therapist's inventive treatments. She is cautious with the paring knife, and turns the apple slowly in her left hand as the streamer of red peel inches its way to the floor.

The air is suddenly rich with apple scent and rain. It may mean nothing, this shower, but then again...

Monday the 7th

Since the heat wave broke, Alice has slept deeply and restfully. Sleeping alone turns out to be incredibly restful. No sweaty skin touching you, no one tossing in the sheets to keep you awake. She lounges in bed, stretching and falling back asleep in a gentle rise and fall of consciousness. She is awakened by the phone's electric burble. She sighs and picks it up.

"Uh, hey." The voice on the other end is hesitant. "It's me."

The voice is unmistakable, but also improbable. "Brad? Wow, hi. I didn't expect—"

"To hear from me, I know."

She can hear the faint hum of a fan in the background and an ambient roar of city noise.

"So," Brad laughs uncomfortably.

For a moment Alice wonders wildly if Brad, perhaps, could be—it's crazy, but you never know—returning? "Where are you? I mean, why are you calling?"

"I just was thinking about you guys the other day. The band."

"Us guys." The flicker of hope is extinguished, and she resents its having risen in the first place.

"And I was wondering how everything was going. You still cranking along? Getting gigs?"

"You mean you have no idea what we've been doing? Doesn't Lori give you all the gossip?"

There is a moment of silence on the line before Brad says, "I'm not really in touch with anyone back there, actually." He swallows and quickly adds, "I've just been you know really busy."

The clumsy cover-up is so apparent that Alice relents. She is aware that her throat is tight and that it won't sound genuine, but she asks anyway. "So, things are going well?"

"Yeah. Well, it's slow. There's a lot of activity in the Big Crapple, so it's hard to get noticed. But I've been working it," he continues, rushing. "Doing open mikes, sending tapes around."

Alice calculates the weeks in her head. "Is your money holding out?"

"It's getting pretty tight," he laughs, with surprising looseness. "Rents here are—wow. It's a favorite subject of mine, don't get me started."

There is a pause. Alice pulls the other, vacant pillow to her lap and holds it against her stomach. "So...why did you call?"

"Well. Hell, I miss you guys. Did you think I wouldn't?"

"No, I guess I didn't."

"Well. I do. Okay?"

"Okay. Whatever. I have to get to work," Alice says. And then adds, "For real, I do."

"Sure, I knew you would. It's okay. I'll talk to you later."

"I don't—" Alice says, but he hangs up before she can finish. "I don't

have your number," she says to the fan in the window, which reflects her
voice as stuttering fragments.

What you're left with, at the end of a relationship, is a part of yourself, the
romantic part, that has no respectable outlet. And then two things happen. There is some atrophy of the romantic impulse, as of an immobilized
limb. But some of that energy gets channeled into other areas—hobbies
become obsessions, small rituals become time-consuming endeavors, and
friendships, especially new ones, often become strangely intense, passing
into a gray area where friendship is no longer an adequate term. More like
the best-friends contracts between children. Brad's call has stirred these
strangled impulses of Alice's into a frenzy of activity, and she finds herself
devoting the morning's slow hours to creating an elaborate flower arrangement for Ellen. She uses one of the nicer vases, picks the flowers she knows
are Ellen's favorites, and immerses herself for a while in composing. She
rings the edge with fuchsia Gerber daisies, tops them with a ring of yellow
anemones, and works upward with ever smaller groups of daisies, lilies, and
tulips, topping it all with three passionflowers. The result is awful, like a
three-headed, Technicolor emu. She dismantles her work and starts again,
less orderly, leaving some spots of softness, caches of frondy ferns, baby's
breath, and shyly hiding fiddleheads. Still dissatisfied, she dismantles again,
and rebuilds in frustration, the resulting concoction having a little chaos to
it. Bunches of dried juniper rest against the soft bell of a tiger lily. Asphodel
huddles beneath a gaggle of the renascent Gerbers. And the whole blinking
mess looks just amazing. She feels like singing.

    The door jingles, and in walks Ellen, looking sullen and without her
usual bag of books, lotions, and tapes for their afternoon tanning session.

    "I can't stay." Ellen drops into a chair.

    "What's wrong?"

    "It's just. Nothing." Ellen slumps further down. "I wish I could stay. It's
all I really want to do."

    "Oh well." Alice brightens. "I'm just glad you stopped by because I have
something for you." She walks over to the flowers, announcing in a deep,
fakey voice, "Yes, because you've been a friend in need, you, Ellen Kovacs,
you have won a fabulous—" and with a game-show assistant's sweep of her
arms, "huge vase of incredible rare and priceless flowers!"

Ellen's face freezes, half in delight, half in something like fear. "God. They're. Well, they're beautiful."

"You like?" Alice claps her hands with glee.

"I mean, god, I can't believe you did this." Ellen laughs nervously. "Wow. It's so big. And everything."

"There's a card, too," Alice half sings, plucking the tiny envelope free and handing it over with a slight bow.

Ellen turns the little paper square in her fingers, looking bemused and frozen. She fingers the flap open and looks at the card. *Friendship is Love without his wings.—Byron.*

Her lips move wordlessly with the phrase, "Without his wings." She looks up. "I can't take this. It's lovely, but I can't."

A look, puzzled and slightly hurt, replaces Alice's smile. She doesn't say anything.

"I can't really explain. It's this other person." She drops her face into her hands. "Oh, I should have told you."

"Hey, it's okay." Alice comes over to her and rubs her back. "I didn't know."

Ellen shakes her head and reaches out to take Alice's hand. "It's so beautiful," she murmurs into Alice's fingers.

Alice ponders, then asks, "Is this other person why you really didn't make it to our last show?"

Ellen nods. "It wasn't car trouble."

Alice straightens and pulls her hand away. "Hey, whatever's going on, it's okay. I'll just use the flowers for display. No big deal."

"She wouldn't understand," Ellen mumbles, wiping at her eyes. "Don't be mad."

"I said no big deal."

"I should get going." Ellen stands, stuffing the note into her pocket. "Can I take one, at least?"

"They're all yours." Alice crosses her arms, all feeling of generosity obliterated.

Ellen draws out one of the fuchsia Gerber daisies. "I know you put these in just for me." Her lip quivers.

"More where that came from," Alice says, suddenly very ready for her new best friend to leave.

"I'm sorry, Al." Ellen backs to the door. "I'm really sorry. I'll see you tomorrow?"

"Sure." Alice lifts the vase into the window. She has her head almost buried in the flowers, busily reordering the area where the daisy had been, when the door jingles closed.

Alice pushes her way out of the train, holding the guitar case before her like a battering ram. "Sorry. Pardon me. Sorry." She bangs it on the turnstile and the hollow body inside chimes. A brief storm, the kind where rain falls through the sunlight like the spray from a waterfall, has left an annoying shimmer on the afternoon. The fight—or whatever it was—with Ellen left her feeling more depressed. Why should the grass vibrate with that green intensity when her life is a big fat nowhere? Practicing with a band that has no future, friendships that take so much work, and not to mention Brad. She feels at this moment like a cartoon character who, having run out of a hollow log smack into the middle of a canyon, looks back at the cliff's edge behind her and turns, for a moment, into a giant lollipop with a wrapper that reads, "Sucker."

And the late, late nights tinkering with fragments of new songs. What a waste of time that is anyway, when you think about it. Pretty worthless. Maybe no one will be at rehearsal. More and more, somebody or other finds an excuse that they can't make it. Chipper has constant meetings with his tenants' association for some kind of drawn-out legal action against their slumlord. Molly's started giving music lessons. Shanklin has a never-ending stream of college friends passing through as they criss-cross the country with their hand-painted cars and shaggy dreams of how somewhere else is better. But that's normal. It's just life creeping up on all sides. When a band loses its meaning, the edges get all soft and porous and eventually it just leaks away.

Why don't we stop kidding ourselves and admit that whether or not we as a band had anything worthwhile to say after Brad, his leaving really ends us, for all intents and purposes. Because even the cartoon character gets wise; even if it means she falls into a canyon like Wile E. Coyote, at least she'll know as she falls what is what.

There's something going on, she can feel it when she opens the door. "What's everybody so happy about?" Alice puts down her guitar case and pushes it away from her with her foot, like a bad dog.

"We're not happy." Chipper balances a drumstick on the tip of his finger. "We can't be. We're serious artists." He says this while grinning like some kind of fool, all right.

"No, really, what's up?"

"Chipper got us a gig for next weekend," Molly emits in an uncharacteristic squeal.

Alice looks at Chipper, who blushes and begins to fake busy, tightening the head of his snare drum. "New snares," he says. "Big cash outlay for the revamped combo."

"It's a charity event at the Empty Bottle, raising money for a musicians-in-the-schools music program. There's a theme, too." Molly pauses. "A kind of memorial to Guyville's glory days."

For this everyone is excited? Alice thinks. "So what, we're doing Liz Phair covers?"

"No way!" says Shanklin. "I'm totally not up for that. We've already agreed that we're doing—" He puts up a box of his thumbs and index fingers like a painter framing a view. "Your new songs."

"It's time we did a set of all new material," says Molly feverishly. "We've been holding ourselves back."

"Guys!" Alice is goosebumped with alarm. "The songs aren't ready. We haven't, you know—"

"We've done everything we can," Shanklin says. "We're ready."

"Of course we're ready, are you kidding?" Chipper raps the snare for emphasis. "We've been acting like Lather minus Brad until now. But that's over. Brad's ancient fucking history now."

"We can't be negative anymore." Molly looks like a woman channeling the voice of a holy roller. "What could be simpler than optimism?"

"So now we're just a band with frontman to be named later?"

"Don't you get it?" Chipper is making chopping motions with his hands. "We're a quartet now, fifty percent of which is babe. We're whole as we are. We rock!"

"You two sashay up front, bewitching people. You know, with your harmonies." Shanklin does a shimmy. "It's a way cooler image than we had before."

"We just didn't see it," says Molly.

"I'm not sure *I* see it." Alice gives a shrug. "But what the hell. If we're going to suck, it might as well be for a good cause."

Wednesday the 9th

The best thing Giselle has to say about finally getting to Baton Rouge is, "At least we're off the damn bus."

But Eloise is already enveloped in the bosomy hug of her sister Belle. Their shrill hellos are like the cries of birds swooping through the clouds of diesel fumes as they swing each other back and forth. Giselle stands amid the luggage frowning like she is trying to explain to the baby inside her that it will forever bear the blame for bringing her to this moment. The long ride and the bad truck-stop food left her queasy and ill-tempered. Not to mention how on the trip her butt started itching like she'd sat on a nest of fire ants.

Eloise, noticing her squirming against the worn down nubs of the bus upholstery, said only, "'Bout time you got those. Part of what being a mother all about."

"Momma, you think living's all about misery."

"May look that way to you, but it's just I don't piss and moan 'cause a little trouble's part of the deal."

"What deal? Life?"

"Life, babies, men, you name it." And Eloise sat back in her seat with her paperback romance novel and smiled to herself.

From the moment Eloise announced they were leaving Chicago, Giselle has felt swept along on a river of her mother's will. And Giselle feels even smaller and more powerless when Belle comes over and drapes her soft, heavy arms on Giselle's neck, cooing, "Oh lord baby doll how are you?" She is thrown back in time to being a little girl among adults.

If only she had something to sneak-smoke in the bathroom, or sniff, or swallow. So she could relax and enjoy this wide, relentless river of maternal Southern caring. But she spent her last money on Jimmy's bail. And not that she could find anything down here in the boonies anyway.

"You look just radiant," says Belle. "And you going to have one beautiful child, too. Is it a boy or girl?" Giselle looks at her mother, and then shrugs.

"Well don't you all know? They can tell, you know, with that ultrasound."

"She ain't had no tests of any kind," Eloise says, almost triumphantly.

"Good lord, how could you go on like that!" Belle cries. "We gone take care of that first thing, get you to my good old doctor, Doctor Mason, get you checked out ever which way."

"I can't tell you how good it is to have another sensible person around for once," Eloise says, her voice rising to a sharp laugh. "It takes more than me to set this girl right."

They push Giselle into the back seat of the dusty Malibu and one of Belle's nephews, a silent, wide-eyed thirteen-year-old named Elmer, heaves the luggage into the trunk. Then Belle steers the slewing car out of the lot and onto the highway. She and Eloise talk excitedly about cooking some of their momma's old dishes. Elmer stares out at the low, swampy fields.

Eloise catalogues the food she is dying to eat. "Fried okra. Fried mush with molasses. Fried catfish and those sweet-onion hush puppies like to make you cry."

Giselle tries to plug her ears against the nauseating names of that fat-old-Southern-woman food. The threat of boredom has never been so real.

"Collard greens with crackling. Sausage gravy."

"We gonna feed that baby, you like it or not," Belle says over her shoulder, laughing.

As the road rises and falls, Giselle starts to grow calm. Nobody here expects anything of her. She isn't Elmer's role model. She isn't the disappointing daughter. She is just another family member to take care of. As this feeling sinks in, Giselle suddenly feels outside of herself, light and peaceful. Maybe it's the smell of the countryside. Maybe it's the forceful caretaking she can no longer struggle against. Well, this does happen all the time. No big thang, when you get a little perspective on it.

Before long, she is asleep and afraid of nothing.

Borrowing the gun had not exactly gone the way Jimmy had hoped. In fact, Shug had laughed when Jimmy suggested that he might need it to do a little business.

Shug had laughed. "The fuck you need a gun for? Just wind up capping your own self with it."

So Jimmy went to his backup plan: sneak around the old man's house and play it by ear. At dusk he makes his way back to the Duchossois' street. He scuttles around to the alley and down along the cockeyed fences. This time, there is a car next to the old man's garage. Jimmy drops behind a swag of honeysuckle vine. He looks for the pile of bricks. Gone.

"Damn," he mutters. But then he sees an aluminum fence post, about the size of his wrist, leaning out into the alley. Gently, Jimmy works it loose until it comes free, dragging a fist-sized clump of concrete out of the ground. He takes a practice swing, minding his still tender shoulder.

Alphonse appears from the garage, reaches into the trunk of the car and hauls out a canvas mailbag. He heaves it into the garage and returns to pull from his car another mailbag and three more trips for plastic mail bins. He gets in the car and drives off. Jimmy watches the car disappear around the corner and then walks warily up to the garage. There is a flimsy padlock on the door. Jimmy measures it and then smashes down with the fence post. The lock flies free. Jimmy heaves the door up and stares with delight at the piles of mailbags, bundles of fliers, and stacked boxes of catalogues and junk mail.

Jimmy stands transfixed. Slowly, a smile spreads across his face. "The Lord helps those who help themselves, don't he?"

The white hum of convenience stores is the sound of danger. They smell like ice cream and detergent, but they taste like metal. Ronnie and Tony hunker behind a Dumpster, pulled around for cover. Ronnie pulls the thin saw blade through the lock bolt four times before it gives way without a sound. Ronnie pulls the door open with a finger and nods his head at the dimly lit stockroom inside. Tony ducks in and runs the weak beam of a flashlight across the stacked boxes. Dolly Madison. Gatorade. Scott tissue. And then box after box of Skoal, Copenhagen, Red Man, Drum, Camels, Winstons, Kools, Salems.

"Let's go, T.," Ronnie whispers. "Get the biggest box you can and come on!"

Tony says nothing, wiggling the light to indicate he understands. A door at the other end of the storage room begins to swing open. Tony pulls a box down and runs blindly toward to exit. The box blocks his vision, and he rams into the wall beside the door and falls backwards.

A raspy voice shouts, "Hey, who's there?"

The box is resting heavily on his face. Tony smells the musty cardboard. A hand grabs his ankle and hauls him out the door. His head raps against the cement loading apron and the sun knifes into his eyes.

"Come on, dammit," Ronnie yells as he sprints toward the car.

Tony scrambles up and follows, leaving behind both the box and the flashlight. The car is already turning in a wide, leaning circle. Ronnie dives headfirst through the driver's side door. Several hands reach out and pull Tony into the back seat. The tires yelp as they swerve toward the street.

"Goddamn, T.," Ronnie shouts. "You the fuckingest worst thief I ever seen."

There is a pop, and the car lurches awkwardly. Tony tries to look back and catches a glimpse of a tall, balding Indian man aiming a shotgun at the car. There is the whumping sound of flopping rubber from the left rear tire.

"He shootin' at us, Ronnie!"

Darol keeps gunning the car, even though the bumper is dragging. All the boys are trying to get under each other, fighting for the lowest point. Tony is slammed in the mouth with an elbow. Another pop and there is a hard spattering against the back of the car. Shards of glass fall on the struggling boys like pieces of candy. Darol stands on the gas pedal, turning left or right at every corner, as though trapped in a maze. Eventually, he pulls to a stop on a residential street. Houses with tiny, immaculate lawns. Everything is impossibly quiet. The boys pile out and stand around, uncertain. Leaf shade dances across their faces.

"Get going, but split up," Ronnie snaps. "Cops'll be looking."

The boys scatter quickly, along every trajectory except back to where they came from.

"I'm sorry," Tony says, watching them go.

"Get lost, boy," Ronnie says over his shoulder as he trots away.

Friday the 11th

It's the dog days. Up on the roof, sun pouring down on her face like melted butter, Alice feels that nothing anywhere is moving. It's like the world's heart has stopped for a space of time, until something comes along to kick it into life again. She has decided not to worry about anything until September. It's like a mental holdover from school days. August is for squeezing the last juice out of summer. So she has stopped wondering when Ellen will come back. Or why Brad hasn't called again. Or why Chipper hasn't yet come through with any contracts for that music festival. There's so much to not worry about these days, that it seems like the right thing to do. Or not do. Instead, she is becoming involved with cocoa butter in a new way. Despite her freckle-prone Celtic skin, she has decided this is the summer of her best tan ever. She slaps another handful of tanning oil on her legs and stomach. The sweet, seductive scent makes her feel as though she's almost hallucinating, no longer flesh but candy or cake. A shining, pink-toe-nailed, butterscotch snack. She feels warm and sexy. The thought of another body—it seems like ancient history. Brad's been gone, what, a month? And before that? She drowsily stretches, groaning. In her mind she sees long white legs shining with oil, a curve of hip. One of those macho-suave Italian underwear models, pouting, shaved and a little feminine. A boy-girl. A girl-boy. Oh god, what am I thinking? Alice sits up suddenly, as though someone else had just snuck a peek at her thoughts.

Whoa. Good thing I didn't daydream like that when she was around.

It has reached the point that there is no excuse so banal or transparent that Ellen won't use it to avoid having to spend the night with Megan. How pleasant to wake alone, without accusatory looks, or the ongoing when-will-I-see-you-next discussion. Even so, the sight of Megan's hair in the loofah gives her an attack of maudlin lovelornness. After all, there's been no one to replace Megan—i.e., Alice. She tries to pluck the hairs free and wash them down the drain. Impossible to get them all. Clean the loofah should have been Hercules' next task.

She towels dry, moving awkwardly to keep her head as still as possible. It seems that stress has different levels of effect. First there is nail biting. Then there is the jaw clenching at night that leaves her with throbbing headaches that even coffee won't cure. And beyond that, at the Mount Everest peak of stress, she hears a wailing woman's voice, keening ceaselessly in her head. A voice of fear and acute distress. The fat lady singing. Wrapped in the moist towel, futile cup of coffee in hand, Ellen sits Indian-style on the bed and sorts through her shoebox of super eight reels. It's been weeks since she looked at what she's been shooting all year. Alice, mostly. Maybe this will give her some way to reconnect with her after the disastrous bouquet event. Not a day goes by she doesn't look at herself in the mirror and say, "What were you thinking, stupid?"

The reels, labeled by date with itty-bitty pieces of masking tape, are out of order. Must have rushed them back in the box with Megan bearing down on me one day. But after she orders them—is one missing? She plops the coffee onto the nightstand, slopping some over the side, and scrambles into the closet. Still on the projector is 3/17/00, stopped halfway through.

Leaving film in the projector is something Ellen would never, ever, under any circumstances, do.

Holy Jesus Christ. It was Megan.

She rewinds the film and watches it through, imagining herself as Megan watching it. She sees the caress of the lens, the lingering image of Alice's distant white face. And she knows irrevocably that she is in love, and that Megan knows she is in love. Holy moly. She is trembling and beginning to cry. She can't go to Urbs today. Maybe never again. Everything is falling to pieces. She can't do this. She feels like a fuse being consumed by a heatless fire.

How long ago? When did Megan see this? Ellen feels a sympathetic nausea for Megan, stunned by what she has seen and not admitting it but grasping to hold onto Ellen, to what they have. Poor Megs. What a bitch I've been to poor sweet Megs. She rolls onto her side and lies there, fetally curled. Why don't I at least understand myself? Oh no, there goes the fat lady again.

Absorbed in arranging rose and iris petals into a Cubs logo, Alice doesn't hear the bell on the door, and the woman is in the shop before she realizes it.

"I'm sorry," she says, jumping up. "Can I help you?"

Without a word, the woman moves past her into the shop. She is not big, but looks strong, athletic. Her curly black hair is pulled back with a comb. The hair around her ears is damp with sweat.

Alice walks over to the counter. "I'm sorry, I was just on break. There's no fresh coffee right now. Or did you want flowers?"

"No," the woman says, her eyes hard with anger. "I was looking for someone." She scans the room, as though there really might be a person hiding behind the pastry case or under a chair.

"There's no one else here."

"I'm a friend of Ellen's," the woman blurts out.

"Oh," Alice smiles and holds out her hand. "Hi, I'm Alice."

A sneer curls the woman's lip. "Alice. Okay, now I have a name to go with who you are."

"What?"

"I'm Megan." Seeing confusion in Alice's face, she persists, "*Megan*. Ellen's Megan?" Then it dawns on her that this name has no meaning for Alice, none at all. "She didn't even tell you about me?"

"I'm sorry? What—"

"Just tell me is Ellen around."

"No, I haven't seen her for days."

"Really. Have a little spat?" Megan's fingers tighten on a used coffee mug until the knuckles glow.

"I don't think it's any—"

"It sure as hell is my business." Megan's voice edges toward a growl. "She's my lover and you stay the fuck away from her."

Alice stares. Her eyes slowly widen with fear and bewilderment.

"Jesus." The woman storms toward the door, and then turns and marches back. "You're not even gay, right?" She laughs sharply.

Alice comes out from behind the counter. "Look, whatever problems you're having with Ellen, it has nothing to do with me."

Megan laughs. "You don't think her wanting to fuck you might be a teensy problem in our relationship?"

"Why don't you just go," Alice says, and points to the door.

The woman collects herself for a moment, then turns to go. At the door, she pauses and searches for something to say, so her erratic behavior will make sense. She starts to say, "You have to understand how much I love Ellen," but she feels tears begin to well in her eyes, and she runs for the safety of her car, muttering to herself under her breath. She drops her head against the steering wheel and stays there a long time, letting the tears roll down her nose and onto her lap.

Alice looks down the street at the car where Megan sits. Could things get any weirder?

Tuesday the 15th

Like a storm front, Robin's fury begins to affect the weather in the apartment even before he arrives. Father Peter wakes from his nap on the couch and stares foggily at the walls. What woke him? He rubs his hands over his face and looks at his watch. Oh yes. Time for Robin. His stomach immediately clenches. This is my torment, he repeats to himself. This is my trial.

He has been living uncomfortably with the knowledge that he has overstayed his welcome by several weeks. Robin alone, just the basic fact of who he his, should have been reason enough for him to want to leave as soon as he could walk under his own power. But for some unfathomable reason he has been unable to rouse himself to the next step. The grand tour he'd dreamed of had fallen flat, ending where it began here in Chicago, and yet he can't really return to Maine. Not yet. So then what?

The door slams open and Robin is suddenly in the apartment, not only in it, but all through it, like the stench of a natural gas leak.

"I just don't *get* the people in this building," Robin snaps, throwing his backpack down the hall. "No one holds the elevator for you. I've got half a mind to go down to Mrs. Hartley's floor and tell her just what an ill-mannered bitch she is." He pauses and arches and eyebrow at the silent priest. "Pardon my French, Padre," he says.

"No doubt she was unaware—" Peter begins.

"Like hell. Ooh!" Robin stomps into the kitchen. "You haven't made any dinner have you? Any tuna waffles? Any spam tetrazzini?"

"I am quite aware that you would prefer I stay out of your kitchen," Peter says, rising wincingly from the couch.

"God save us from your Vienna sausage and cup-a-soup casseroles."

"I was merely trying to help." Peter is suddenly in the doorway of the kitchen, leaning only lightly on his cane. "You could at least appreciate the intention."

"The intention?" Robin laughs. "I seriously doubt you have ever intentionally given a shit about anyone other than yourself."

Peter stands in the doorway a moment, rocking slightly, then turns on his heel and goes to his bedroom.

Whistling "If I Had a Hammer," Robin takes a bag of onions from the pantry, and begins chopping them, his head close to the cutting board until the tears pour from his eyes and his scalp tingles from the pain.

The first thing Nathan sees when he opens the door is Peter standing in the hallway, suitcases at his feet.

"Nathan, I'm glad you're home. I wanted to say goodbye before I go."

"Did I miss something?" Nathan drops his briefcase and folders on the hall table. "Where are you going?"

"The diocese has made arrangements for me."

"But—" Nathan sees Robin sitting at the dining table with a tall glass of what appears to be straight bourbon, looking defiantly at a magazine. His face is red and upset looking. Nathan turns back to Peter. "What happened?"

"It was a mistake to remain here so long. I apologize for the obvious disruption to your…" he pauses, "domestic arrangement."

Robin loudly flips the pages of the magazine.

The door buzzer announces the cab's arrival.

"I don't know what you mean, Uncle Peter," Nathan says.

"God sees through everything at last," Peter says, picking up his bags.

"See through what?" Nathan says. "There's nothing to—"

Peter interrupts. "Would it be too much trouble to help me downstairs with these?" He limps toward the door, leaving one suitcase behind.

Nathan picks up the last bag and opens the door. Peter limps out into the hall.

"Bye Padre, we'll miss you," Robin yodels.

Nathan looks over at him. "Why? When I come back up can you just tell me why?"

Robin flips another page of the magazine. Nathan walks out and the door clicks closed behind him.

Robin holds up his glass, toasts, "God helps those who help themselves," and swallows the last burning remnants of his drink.

Thursday the 17th

The tall fans around the work floor do nothing more than chop the soggy air into chunks to be flung against Ng's face. He imagines the heavy breezes as a slow pelting of soggy tissues. In the overpowering heat, it is a battle to keep from sweating on the tracing paper. The paper itself has absorbed so much moisture it has become thick and raspy against his pen nib.

He can see Soo across the room working at the silkscreen. Her arms move in a regular, practiced motion, sweeping the ink across the screen, replacing each printed shirt with a blank one. Her face betrays no discomfort. A fortitude that leaves him amazed. She can survive anything because she knows that every misery has an end. Summer ends in fall. Work ends in food and rest. He feels weak and selfish.

The sponge coverings to his Discman earphones are soaked. He wrings them out every half-hour; otherwise, Britney sounds like she's singing in a drainpipe filled with socks.

Ng suddenly feels Benny's presence somewhere on the shop floor. A subtle rise in the intensity of the hum of activity as Benny walks the perimeter, a string of red licorice dangling from his lips.

"Good, good," he says to Soo. "Not so bad today like usual." He laughs, showing broad, curved teeth and a tongue coated in red candy.

Benny wears a grimy baseball cap with a logo of the Chicago Federals of the Negro Baseball League on it. From a batch ruined earlier in the summer. The oil from his head has spread out almost to the end of the brim, a permanent soiling of the dark green twill. Spiky bits of hair stick out over the plastic adjustable straps in the back. He pulls off the cap and fans under his shirt. It is one of those square, gauzy shirts, like those worn by dictators in sub-tropical countries. Ng has always thought they look like some kind of institutional undergarment not meant to be worn outside of a nursing home.

Benny saunters over to Ng's worktable. He picks up a few of the sketches and tosses them aside. He takes one and rips it in half.

"No good. Do over."

Ng turns his head only enough to look at Benny askance.

Benny calmly plucks one of the earphones away from Ng's head.

"I tell you I don't like you wear this."

Ng plucks with a straight pin at a balky nib. "I need them to concentrate."

"Money make you concentrate." Benny holds up a piece of paper. "You put towel keep paper dry," he says, tapping a water-wrinkle in the middle of the page. "No good like this."

Ng looks down at his sketch. It reads, Getta Pizza D'Action, with a winged pizza flying over the Sears Tower.

Benny smells like a giant onion, cut and drying sourly in a closed room.

"Benny, it's about three hundred degrees in here." Ng holds out his tee shirt, showing the yoke of sweat-darkened fabric that descends from the neckline. "I can't keep the paper dry."

"It summer, what you want?" Benny slaps him on the back. "Good boy, work very hard. You make mother very happy."

Ng looks at the flying pizza again. He thinks, if I died right now, this would be all that is left of me. The heat is a like a cloth stuffed in his mouth, like a wall at his back. Benny is a few feet away when Ng says, softly, "I quit."

Benny stops in his tracks. "What that?" he says without turning around. "Somebody say something to me?" He looks around the room with theatrical exaggeration before turning back to face Ng. "Hearing not so good. You saying something?"

Ng's heart stops for a moment. Had he really said it out loud? "I said," he stammers. "I said I don't want to work here. Anymore."

"Really?" Benny says, with a menacing smile.

Ng looks across the room and sees Soo's face, looming across the dividing space like a sorrowful apparition. He feels trapped.

"You suck, Benny." Ng's voice is shaking. "This place sucks. You make everybody work in terrible heat and cold for no money."

"No money?" Benny laughs sarcastically. "You been working for free? Very good deal for Benny, yes?"

Soo has drawn nearer. Bright blue ink on her hands. Before she can intercede, Ng blurts, "I'm out of here." He stands, and the cord of the headphones yanks the CD player from the drawing table. It snaps free of the cord and falls to the floor, cracking open.

"Too bad." Benny clucks his tongue. "Those very bad, very cheap, made by people in bad places for bad boss. Cheap, cheap, bad."

The player's batteries roll free with a tiny noise, audible through the hum of the fans. Soo bends to pick them up at the same time Ng stoops for his broken CD player. Their eyes meet across the floor. Ng holds out his hand for the batteries. Soo pauses, and then stands and puts them in her pocket.

"I go, too," she says.

"Oh! Oh!" Benny becomes animated. "Goo-bye, goo-bye!" He grandiosely steps out of their path to the door. "You go to enjoy be so rich, eh? Must be nice so rich to quit job on nice day like this."

Ng stops to say something in reply, but Soo pulls him toward the door. As they pass through the long room, no one looks at them.

A gust of foul air from the sewer grate greets them down on the sidewalk.

"I'm sorry, Mom." Ng looks at the broken machine in his hands. "You don't have to leave, you know."

"You right about Benny," Soo says. "I no like how he treat you."

"He didn't treat you so well, either. But the money."

"Don't you worry. We still eat."

"Now what?" Ng looks for a place to sit, but the sidewalk is crowded and filthy with melted ice cream and gum and the residue of a thousand spilled liquids.

"It's not a nice day," he says. "That's what I wanted to tell Benny. It's a lousy day."

As certainly as if she ordered it, Soo finds the white Impala under the rattling leaves of the oak tree down the street. Danny is asleep, his head lolling back against the headrest.

She raps on the roof.

"What?" Danny says, looking around. When he sees Soo, his face creases into a slow, stiff smile. He rubs his hands vigorously across his eyes and cheeks. "Must have dozed off." Soo crosses her arms and says nothing.

"What? What's up? Are you still pissed off at me?"

"I may need money for this month rent."

"What happened? You lose your job?"

"You got son who needs something. I cannot do alone. Be him father for once."

"I want to, I do. Why else you think I've been—"

"Sit in car not good for anybody. Be man for Ng."

Leaf shadows jumble on the windshield. Amoeba-like.

Danny tries to cover a smile that has crept into his eyes.

"What?" Soo says. "I ask for help and you laugh at me?"

"No, Soo, no, no. I just—" The grin is broad now, and Danny reaches for her arm through the window. "You're still kicking ass and taking names."

Soo jerks her arm away. "What is that mean?"

"Nothing. How much do you need?"

"I don't know. Maybe nothing. But if I do."

"I'll be around."

"Good." She turns to go.

"Hey," he leans out the window. Bashful and eager, like a kid again. "You want to get a bite to eat?"

"I go to a movie." She turns again.

"Wait, I'll drive you," Danny says. "Wait!"

Sunday the 20th

"Lord have mercy, Louise, what is that smell?" Florence appears in the kitchen doorway with an affronted look on her face. Her hair appears to be still in the throes of a vigorous dream.

"It's breakfast," snaps Louise. She holds a tray of carbon-black waffles under the ventilator. Gray smoke curls up into the vent.

"Those are toaster waffles."

"I know that. I was trying something different with them." Louise scrapes the waffles into the trashcan. "Your oven runs way too hot. You better tell that Petosky to get up here and fix it."

Florence sighs. "I'll just have cereal." She walks into the bathroom, lightheaded from waking so quickly. She tries to comb her hair down, but it's fighting back today. She switches the brush to her left hand and finds it snags twice as much. "Shit," she mutters.

"What?" says Louise from the kitchen. "You need help?"

"No, dear, I'm fine." The doctor said there'd be days like this. She holds up her left hand and makes an unconvincing fist. In fact, everyone says that.

The wail of the smoke detector splits the air.

"Oh no!" Louise cries. "The grapefruits!"

There is still a lingering smell of burning when Louise returns from shopping. She parks the wheeled grocery cart and calls out to the patio where Florence paints. "What do you want for lunch?"

"I'm over here," says Florence. The voice comes from the darkened living room. Shades drawn, Florence lying on the couch in the coffin position, hands folded over torso.

"Oh dear, are you all right?" Louise rushes over and kneels by the couch. "Why aren't you painting?" She tries to feel Florence's forehead.

Florence pushes her hand away. "I'm all right. I'm just bored."

"Bored?" Louise says it like a foreign word. "But—"

"Louise. Dear. You know I appreciate everything you've done. But I'm getting to the point, I think, when it might be time for, when I just need a companion really, not a nurse."

Louise crosses her arms. "So I'm the boredom."

"No, I don't mean that." Florence takes Louise's hand. Two cold thin hands together. Fingers dry as paper. "You're family. With Arnie gone, being with family is important."

The chime of the doorbell interrupts them.

"I'll get it," Florence says. "Why don't you make us some lunch."

Louise disappears into the kitchen where she begins to bang cabinet doors with alacrity.

Florence opens the door to find Elias standing with a tall, handsome stranger. Elias holds a lumpy sweater in his arms.

"Hello!" Elias is beaming. The sweater in his arms is wriggling so violently he almost drops it. "I brought you a present." He lowers the bundle, and out of the cardigan stumbles a small puppy. It flounders around Elias's feet, snuffling and whining.

"It's a mutt. A cocker spaniel-dachshund," says the stranger.

"This is my friend, Tommaso Falco."

"Please, call me Tommy."

Please, come in, come in," says Florence. The puppy shambles over to sniff her slippers. "Oh, he's lovely. But I can't keep him, Elias."

"Of course you can. For taking on walks. A little friend around at night."

The puppy's short red coat is glossy. Long ears flopping over its large brown eyes. It still has its round puppy-belly, pink and barely furred. Florence rubs it softly, feeling the warmth of its blood and rapidly beating heart. The dog wiggles on its back, trying simultaneously to lick her hand and to regain its footing.

"I don't know," she says. "Does he have a name?"

"That's for you to decide. And it's a she."

Florence grabs at the dog's snout, and it nips at her fingers. "Tell me about her."

"The mother was my neighbor's dog," says Tommy. "I mentioned the litter to Elias, and he said right away he had a good home for one of them."

The pup licks her hand ravenously. Florence savors its energy, the warmth of its breath. "She's too sweet."

"The mother was named *Dolce*," offers Tommy. "Italian for sweet." He laughs, sweeping back his hair with a fine, manicured hand. "My neighborhood, you know. Elmwood Park eye-talian."

"I'll call her Duchess," Florence says.

"Good!" Elias claps his hands. "It's settled then."

Louise bustles around the apartment, moving a vase two inches to the left, straightening the pleats in the drapes. With Louise, silent fidgeting signals rough weather.

"Good gracious, Louise, what is the matter with you?" Florence is trying to pet the dog, but it keeps chasing her hand to lick it, circling with its wet sniffing nose. Its body is vibrating beneath the short hair like a muscle filled with electricity. A few drops of pee darken the couch cushion.

"Well let's just admit the truth." Louise smoothes down the legs of her slacks. "You'll never move now." She gestures at the puppy.

"Louise...how can I say this?" Florence walks to the window and pulls the curtains aside. "I have never been a helpless woman. Until the stroke. When Arnie was alive, I lived. After he died, I had some trouble, but I made decisions, and I lived with them. Then after the stroke I needed help. But at some point. At some point, once you can—you have to—stop being helpless and start living as a whole person again."

Louise pulls her mouth to one side. "I don't know how to help you."

"Help is help. What is so hard about that?"

"Okay, fine. Stay here in Dirty-ville. But you'd better get some paper down on the floor—unless you want pee city in here."

Wednesday the 23rd

Twins. Since Doctor Mason spoke the word, nothing has been the same. One syllable turns the world upside down. It seemed just irritating to get pregnant. But two of them? Two tiny squirming things? Suddenly Giselle can't see anything around the scrunched-up faces and wide-open pink mouths bawling.

Doctor held that greasy ultrasound paddle to her belly and said, "I'll be damned." And the feeling of foolishness, never to know, and in the eighth month. She is a disappointment to herself. Once more.

One of each. The boy hiding behind the girl in the grainy moonscape of the sonogram. Underweight and fragile. She can feel that to Mason she is something out of the news, a lost soul of the inner city, shriveled up and caring nothing for consequences. His eyes hard behind his old-man glasses.

"I care," she wants to say. "I just don't know exactly how this is done."

She cries on Eloise for about an hour after the doctor's office. She is a daughter again, and terrified. Eloise is careful not to make her feel worse. The family machine simply shifts into high gear, preparing for the day not so far off now. Belle on the phone, collecting clothes, cribs, two of everything. Matching this and that. Socks the size of her thumb.

"I didn't understand," she mumbles into Eloise's shoulder. "How can I do this? This is too much."

"Can't nothing I say prepare you for it, baby." Eloise rubs her back. "Now you got some idea at last."

"I'm going to be another welfare mom. Looking all stooped and wrung out. Dirty barefoot kids."

Eloise grabs her and turns her around to look fiercely in her face. "Not my grandchildren you won't. That's the deal, child. Babies get it all. You might look dried up and broke like a cattail weed in August, but the babies gone be healthy and happy."

"But two of them, Momma?"

"Two or ten. You give whatever it takes."

"What if everything I have isn't enough?"

"You don't even know how much you got. That's what the children show you. That's what you keep on showing me."

"Breakfast ready, boy," Alphonse calls from the kitchen. "I'm giving you two minutes and then I'm stripping the covers off the bed."

Boy could sleep seven days a week.

Tony appears a few moments later, rubbing his eyes. His nightshirt is twisted across his torso, exposing his thin collarbone. "Come on, Daddy. It's early."

"Not that early. And if you want breakfast, you got to have it before I leave for work. Here, sit down and have your cereal. There's toast and juice."

Tony rubs butter on the toast, the knife wobbly in his sleepy grip.

"What you up to today?"

"Nothing. Play with Melvin and Johnny, I guess. They just got Nintendo 2000."

Alphonse looks at his watch. "Damn, I got to go." He swallows his coffee and puts the cup in the sink. "Listen, I'm playing golf with Elvin after work, so I'll be home late, but I'll bring a pizza."

"With sausage *and* pepperoni? Please, Dad?"

He rubs his son's head and kisses it. "All right. Be good today. Tonight we'll call your momma."

After the door slams, Tony stirs his Cheerios around. Be good. He takes his bowl into the living room and turns on the TV. Two men roll on the ground, fighting over a girlfriend. The host, a woman in a purple suit, jumps around them shouting. He's found it more comfortable to stay near home since the day of the robbery. All of the gang had gotten away okay except for Ronnie, who was, he says, minding his own business when a cop confronted him the next day. When Ronnie ran, the cop shot him in the leg. Tony feels bad about that, and a little guilty. But he's decided: he's giving up the gang. It doesn't feel right anymore. And the hat isn't worth it. It's just a hat.

∾

Alphonse sets his ball on the tee and straightens to look out at the lake, smooth and radiant, a color between jade and sapphire that seems to capture and swallow light like velvet.

"What a day." Elvin stretches down to touch his toes.

"Gotta ignore that big fat body of water or my ball gone head straight for it. My ball's magnetized for water."

"Member how you almost killed that woman on the path last time?"

"Never sliced a ball like that before in my life."

"Screamed like a damn banshee. Thought she was gonna climb that fence after you."

"Like I meant to do it." Alphonse huffs and takes a practice swing. Fairway sweeping out and curved like a woman's back. A woman lounging after love-making, cooing and cupping a big green pillow to her head. He misses Eloise.

"'S go, man, let the big dog eat." Elvin is swinging at the grass like a haymower. Whip whip.

Alph puts three weeks of lonely nights into the swing. The ball flies long and straight.

"Nice lie."

"Oh yeah."

"Missed that lake altogether."

"What lake?" Alphonse pulls a pint of Jim Beam out of his bag and takes a swig.

Elvin squints at him. "Never seen that before," he says.

"I'm a bachelor, my friend. Gotta live large while the old lady's gone."

Elvin, shaking his head, settles in for his drive. He takes a slow backswing and unleashes a graceful, bending slice that carries beyond the trees, the course boundaries, and lands somewhere along the shallow edge of the beach. The men watch it disappear in silence.

"Have a pull on this," Alph says, holding out the bottle. "And then take your mulligan."

The south has a funny smell. Like a compost of flowers, sweet, funky, rich. Giselle lies on the porch swing letting the thick, warm air fill her head and lungs. Maybe some floating seeds will waft in behind her eyes and sprout some wildflowers. Maybe kudzu will envelop her. Maybe her children will crawl forth, eyes open, out of nothing more than a pile of vines and flowers, like explorers stumbling into a jungle village. Their mother will be nothing but a folktale, a warning to the wayward girls of the countryside. You heard what happened to the girl who didn't listen to her momma? Well, it was like this.

"You asleep, baby?"

Giselle pulls the *National Geographic* off her face, and winces in the sunlight. The backlit shape of her mother looms over her. "I was."

"Just thought you might want some tea or something."

"I'd rather sleep."

"Why don't you go inside where it's cool?"

Giselle sighs and raises herself to a sitting position. "I'm fine, Momma." The porch swing creaks along every link of its rusty chain.

"Let me take your blood pressure."

"You just did that a couple hours ago."

Belle emerges from the house and settles into a wicker chair. "Hoo, it sure enough a hot one. What you doing?" she says to Elmer.

He looks up from his pocket video game. "Nothing."

Belle shakes her head. "I'd rather be hunting a mess of greens and not finding none than know anything about them video games."

Elmer lowers his head, thumbs working quickly on the controls.

"I think I should take her blood pressure again," Eloise says.

"I'll go get the thing." Belle starts to lift herself from the chair.

"I can't right now," Giselle says quickly. "Elmer was about to show me how to play that game."

The boy's eyes light up. "Okay," he says and moves into the porch swing. "This is Airball 3. It's like basketball, only you can put on a jetpack once you get a thousand points."

Giselle looks at her mother and winks.

Alphonse carefully pencils his par on seventeen into the little box on the scorecard. He peers down the freshly mowed length of the eighteenth fairway. "Long ball for beer?"

"You been outdriving me all day. How about strokes?"

The shadows stretch across the left side of the fairway. The threesome in front of them replaces the flag on the green.

"If you think that'll help."

Elvin slowly cranks the ballwasher. "Listen, Alph. I been meaning to say something this whole round."

"What, like, 'help'?" Alphonse is feeling full of beans by now, on the verge of breaking ninety for the first time in his life.

Elvin smiles weakly. "Actually, it's about work. You know how we've talked about problems on your route."

"Uh-huh." Alphonse fans himself with the scorecard.

"There's been some questions on the bulk mail. I'm going to have to write a report."

"I told you there wouldn't be no more problems like that."

"It's something old, from the winter. Suspicious audit. You know how they are."

"Right. Okay."

"I just wanted to give you fair warning. Make yourself look as clean as you can."

Alphonse rasps the grooves in his driver with a tee.

"This is off the record, Alph. Just tell me so I'm prepared. Is there—or was there—a lot?"

Alphonse wipes his club with the tail of his shirt and stares down the fairway. "Depends on what you call a lot, I guess. Better swing away. I'm thirsty."

Saturday the 26th

Ellen stares at the reels of film, waiting for something to come together in her head. Come on, brain, do something. She rolls the X-acto knife in her fingers, taps it against the can of film cement. They are as lifeless as crackers, those reels.

What gives you the right? Sneer the inscrutable reels. Who do you think you are? John Cassavetes? Jane Campion?

The reels have a point. This film will never be anything. Anything it becomes will not be worth watching and no one will ever watch it so the nothing it has to say will never be heard and thus will never not happen. She puts her head on the table so often there is a dark, greasy mark on the wood.

She imagines an orgy of destruction, snapping the thin films, draping the apartment with dark festoons that from a distance never reveal their infinitesimal light-etched messages. Or taking a needle and scratching out of the film, frame by frame, her face, Alice's face, the faces of everybody she has tried to make into something larger than they are. Blast the pathetic little world she has screwed up.

Her head snaps up. Scratching. Burning. She sees the bubbling celluloid, the bodies twisting, the world turning smoky and then black. That's what the silent images need. They need to speak the voice of longing behind them. The heat, the frustration. What it is like to hunger for someone by peering at the minuscule translucent image of them by the light of a cheap bedside lamp.

She peels loose a few inches of film and holds it to the light. Suddenly, it is speaking. Or rather, it is repeating what she is saying. And goosebumps ride up her arms and into her scalp.

"Speak to me," she mutters. "Speak to me."

Hours later, Ellen, having lost track of time, is still sitting at her worktable amid film scraps, snips of paper, sketches, and sandwich crusts when suddenly she can't sit any longer. She grabs her backpack and flies out the door. She doesn't care where she goes as long as the energy takes her somewhere. Of course, there's only one place she's going to go.

She is still flying on adrenaline when she flings open the café door and sees Alice sprawled on a chair, idly twirling a wilted daisy in her fingers. It takes Ellen's breath for a moment. Alice's arms, suntanned dark caramel yet dappled with fine, sunbleached hairs. The smooth legs, maple brown and sculptural. The white-blonde ponytail.

"Hey!" she says brightly.

"Hi," Alice says without changing her pose.

Ellen walks over and gives Alice a teasing nudge that feels illicit. "You look imported. Like an Australian."

"Sun worshipping will do that to you." Alice gives her a pointed once-over. "You sure didn't hold onto what little tan you had."

"Been working a lot," Ellen says.

"Right. So." Alice takes the clip out of her hair and then re-gathers it into the ponytail. "Met a friend of yours."

"I heard." Ellen shrinks a little, dodging the familiar feeling of damage from one of Megan's hysterical fits. "I'm really sorry about that."

"So you thought after that you'd stay away, is that it?"

"Didn't think you'd want me around."

"I didn't. But every day that passed, I don't know, made me angrier."

"Megan's just like that. Really combative."

Alice begins pulling the petals off the daisy. "Not just Megan. Your staying away was worse. It made me feel horrible, like I'd done something wrong, when I just needed a friend."

"I hated myself every day for not being able to look you in the face. And I hated Megan, too, of course, for making our friendship seem wrong."

"Whatever you got going with Megan doesn't mean we can't be friends, does it?"

Ellen hesitates. "No, of course not."

"But you wouldn't even take the flowers from me."

"Ugh—I felt terrible about that, too."

"If we can't give gifts and hang out then it's not much like being friends, is it?"

"Please, I want to. My thing with Megan is just so—*blech.*"

"Friends can talk about this stuff, you know."

"Yeah. I guess. But to talk about it means talking about so much other stuff. Everything."

"I don't have a problem with that." Alice touches Ellen's hand with a few fingers damp from the daisy's crushed stem. Ellen leans around the table, and Alice leans forward to meet her. They embrace.

"I missed you," Ellen whispers.

"I missed you, too, you dope," says Alice's mouth in her ear.

And within the embrace Ellen feels there is something. And not just her hopeful heart makes it so, but something that maybe doesn't have a specific name or purpose but is there, definitely, nevertheless.

It's just the rush of making up, Alice thinks. That's all.

Making the call was easier than Ellen had imagined. And the cab ride up to Megan's apartment was almost magical—serene and floating on her cushion of peaceful resolve. But now here she is. Really doing it this time. The door feels like concrete against her knuckles, that's how tingly her nerves feel at this moment.

Megan says nothing when the door opens. She is in her cut-off sweatpants and ancient intramural T-shirt, the Kenyon College shield ghostly from so many washings. Her eyes are small and bruised-looking, as though the dark irises have leached into the whites. Megan's hand on the door is swollen and purple, the knuckles barely evident in a lump of puffy lavender flesh.

"God, what happened?" Ellen touches the swollen fingers gently.

"It's nothing." Megan pulls the hand away and sits down in the corner of the couch, pulling her arms and legs in to make herself as small as possible. "Just get whatever you want and go, please."

Ellen spies a ragged hole in the wall beside the bookcase. And another in the bedroom door. Oh, that's why Megan's hands— She starts to feel sick, infected, like she could burst out in hives if she brushes against anything in the room.

"She's not even gay," Megan says.

"It's not about her."

"Oh please. She's pretty and vapid. You'll be very happy once you seduce her."

"Please, Megs. Let's stop, okay?"

"I can't fucking believe you," Megan moans. "I gave you everything." She begins crying into her broken hands, a snot-filled, hiccupping cry.

"I couldn't... It just wasn't—" Dammit, Ellen thinks, why do I have to cry, too?

"Please." Megan lunges for Ellen's arm. "Just lie down with me one last time." Her face in anguish, collapsing into itself as though trying to retreat to a place of safety.

Ellen tries to stand. "No. Absolutely not. I can't. I can't do that."

"Just this one thing. And then. Then you can go." Megan pulls, wincing as she wraps her sprained fingers into Ellen's shirt. And Ellen at last allows her knees finally to give way, and she falls down into Megan's misery, hot and suffocating, salty with tears.

Lying here with Megan's quaking grief was never a place she imagined she would be. Need within contradictory need. Comfort the one you destroy. Was there ever anything more wretched? To stroke the hair and then leave?

They sob together until their throats are raw, and they fall silent. After a while, Ellen pulls herself away, picks up the box of shampoos and soaps, and pulls the door silently open and then closed. She pauses on the sidewalk to fold the box flaps one over the other to keep them closed. She feels her nostrils tighten in the clean, cool night air.

Megan keeps her face in her pillow until the latch clicks. She raises herself to look out the window and watches Ellen walk away, shifting the box from one hip to the other as she crosses the street. The sky has already gone from black to indigo, lighter around the edges, like the inside of a shell. It was over before it ended. And it still can't be over. Endings, beginnings. The artificial ways people try to manage things that extend beyond what they can imagine.

Thursday the 31st

The first day of school, when it's really just the middle of summer, seems like a cruel joke, Ng thinks. How do they expect us to go—*bam*—back to the whole routine just like that? There should be a month of half-days to get us used to school again. Ng moves like a zombie through the strange-familiar smells, aided by the surfacing of faintly remembered movements—spinning a locker combination, the head-bobbing drowsiness of post-lunch chemistry class, peeking around corners to avoid running into people you'd rather not meet.

He passes Parsley's old room. There is a young female teacher in there now, somebody fresh from college, ready to take on anything. If she only knew.

He circles outside the building to get from class to class. It's actually faster than walking through the crowded halls. He drops his backpack and sits on a sun-warmed step. The blonde bricks above him washed almost white by the afternoon sun. The city's Graffiti Blasters trucks have washed all the gang tags away. It will take a while to establish the new gangs and cliques that have formed or evolved over the summer. In a way, when the tags return, it will be like the legend to a map, offering keys to the subtle geographies inside the building. Ivan never tags. His style is more complicated.

"This won't be so much fun in the winter." He looks up to see Leda with her arms full of textbooks. "Are you going to do that forever? Avoid the halls?"

"If I have to."

She sits down next to him. "You can't run from him all year. It's crazy."

Ng stands. "You don't know everything."

Leda tugs on his pant leg to make him sit back down. "Then why don't you just tell me."

"It's too awful." Ng shakes his head.

"I've been pretty damn patient with you." Leda pinches him fiercely on the arm. "*Tell me*. I don't want to see you like this all year long."

Ng sighs. "Me neither. I don't know how to feel better about it."

"Does it have to do with your teacher—Mr. Presley?"

Ng is shocked. "Parsley, yes. How did you know?"

"Oh, Ng, I know everything," she says, grabbing his head and rubbing it fiercely. "Now tell me."

"Okay," Ng says, feeling relieved that he really has no choice but tell the truth. "Here's the whole story."

The version Ng tells Leda is brief and ugly. She avoids his eyes the whole time he talks, staring instead into the sky.

"Oh man," she says when he finishes. "This is pretty awful."

"Yeah, I know." He grabs his backpack and stands up.

"Where are you going?"

"I was going to leave before you had a chance to say what you thought."

"I'm not mad at you," she says. "Sit down."

"Hate me? Loathe me?"

"No. Come back down here so I can hug you."

Within Leda's embrace, Ng wonders is that it? Why did I wait so long to tell her?

"Don't be such an asshole anymore, okay?" Leda whispers. "I can't love you if you do."

Love? Ng thinks. Did she say love?

As Ng was talking, Leda had an idea—Ng could work with her in Stimpy's Strip Shop. And as soon as the idea blossomed, fellow clerk Larry O. Larry was as good as doomed. It is in everyone's interest, she decided, even Larry's, if he makes way for Ng. Larry works only through great condescension. Genius has its own laws, he has said more than once, to cover numerous indiscretions. The dishonesty of his position needs to be made right, she thinks. And Ng needs this.

Larry walks in at seven-thirty-seven. He knows exactly how far he can push the clock without getting docked. It drives Leda crazy. Instead of a greeting, he merely curls a corner of his mouth as he passes the counter heading toward the back of the store. Leda waits a few minutes before following him into the stockroom. Larry is, as she knew he would be, standing over the copier, his jowly face illuminated over and over by a wave of faintly green light.

"We're back to school now."

"Right," Larry sniffs. "And peace will once again reign in the world until three o'clock weekdays."

"But it means I can't work days anymore."

"Too bad." He flips a new original onto the copier glass and jabs at the start button. "We'll really miss you around here."

"Do you think I could switch hours with you, like last year?"

Larry laughs. "Yeah, right. I told Sol last year it was the last time. You knew that."

"But it would really help me out."

"Listen, I don't get up until McDonald's has served its last breakfast burrito. I'm a night owl." He makes a vague intimation of wings with his hands. "In short, not interested."

"I could ask Mr. Slivnick."

"Solly wouldn't do that to me. I'm the old-timer here. He believes deeply, I happen to know, in the privileges of seniority."

"Even though he made it clear that none of his employees were to use his time or equipment for their own comics?"

Larry recoils with mock fear. "Oh my, oh dear. I do believe I'm being given an ultimatum. Blackmail? Is that right?"

Leda sits on the edge of the workbench, her arms crossed. "We just need to be sensitive to each other."

He gasps. "Sensitive? I'm an artist! I've got sensitive where other people have armor plating. I bruise like a peach!"

Leda has seen Larry's autobiographical comic—*Lollipop Man*—lying around the front counter. It's clear that he feels himself to be living a mythic struggle against the forces of ignorance and hypocrisy. His comic self is strong-chinned and yet affably pathetic. Ng called it a fanta-zine.

"I see three alternatives." Leda counts them out on her fingers: "One, you work days. Two, you quit. Three, you convince Mr. Slivnick that we need a third person to handle the stockroom and weekends."

Larry's face slumps a little. "But he pays me extra to handle the stock. I need the money."

"Maybe your comic book requires you to spend more time away from the store."

"I don't see how this benefits you at all."

"I have a friend who needs a little help."

"Oh, your *friend*." Larry twists the last word sardonically. He finishes hand-collating the pages and taps the stack to align them. "Well, now that you mention it, I have been rather swamped with new projects."

Leda shrugs. "Okay. I'll tell him that Ng can start next week." She watches Larry gingerly angle the pages under the stapler. "Even so, you should stop making your zine here. Mr. Slivnick may find out eventually."

"Sol's a sympathetic soul." Larry drives a staple home with a press of his meaty palm. "He understands my special needs as an artist."

Leda purses her impossibly full lips, and Larry gives a silent internal quake at the sight. "We all want the best for you, Larry," she says.

September

Saturday the 2nd

Knowing little about nature, Elias can only guess at the species of cackling bird that is destroying his sleep for the third morning in a row. It's the migrations, he thinks. Looking out his bedroom window through gritty eyeballs, he perceives a murky flutter of small, black shapes against the gray sky. It is like waking to an endless cascade of shattering glass.

The breakfast rush doesn't. Luis stalks around the kitchen without speaking. A dozen customers in three hours. The waitress moves like a zombie, all the time watching Elias from the corner of her eye, a sneer on her lips. He wants to suggest that she use the down time to clean the crusted mouths of the ketchup bottles, but he knows she will say that it can't be down time if there ain't no up time. He has seen the want ads poking out the top of her purse.

Only one customer in the eleven o'clock hour. Outside, the cloudless light and humidity does not brighten the world but castigates it. Only an adolescent sulk could be so profoundly bleak.

Luis comes out to the counter, wiping his hands on a towel. He pours himself a glass of ice water and drinks it down in one gulp. He puts the glass down and flips the towel over his shoulder. "You okay? You look tired."

"Oh, haven't slept well. I have this bird problem in my yard."

"Starlings," says Luis. "Pedro my cousin in Lawndale had them."

"What did he do?"

"I don't know. He looked as shitty as you for a while." Luis laughs, and even the waitress smiles a little. "He scared them away. I think he used a scarecrow. Or was it one of those airhorns."

Elias sighs. "I feel like a scarecrow. Maybe I'll just sit in the tree myself tonight."

Luis nudges him. "That's it. You still got your sense of humor."

The day drags on and Elias longs for a visit from a friend. Anyone. Florence is kept busy helping her helper, Louise. Ellen works all the time. Sophia has stopped calling all together, which is never a good sign. And Ng, he hasn't been by for weeks. Elias realizes he's been staring at the superman drawing that introduced him to Ng. That's it.

A quick look through the phone book and the address is in his pocket.

"I'm running an errand," he says to Luis.

"I'll hold down the fort, boss," says the waitress, as though, who couldn't.

It's a part of town he doesn't know well, streets almost too narrow for two cars to pass, yards dead and trampled-looking. There is an aura of custodial neglect that extends to the flaked paint on the windows and fractures in the masonry, telling tales of drifting foundations and sloppy tuckpointing. He pulls up in front of the building and double-checks the address. Must be it. He cradles the bag of art supplies in his arms as he ascends the steps. As soon as he touches the ringer a head pops out of the second story window. It's Ng.

"Mr. K.?"

"Hello," he calls up. "You got a minute?"

Ng seems to frown. "Be right there."

Elias peeks in the bag. What do you buy an artist? He had gone through the store picking up anything that looked useful—paper, pencils, tempera and oil paints. Elias bobs on his toes and looks around. Down the block, a small Asian woman turns from the white car she has been leaning on and gives him a hard look. To his discomfort, the woman starts to walk toward him. The white car roars into life and tears down the block.

The woman looks fierce. Elias clutches the bag tighter and hopes Ng will hurry down.

"Hello?" the woman says. Her voice is like that of a tropical bird, a piercing nasal tone.

Just then Ng bursts through the door, scowling and tucking in his shirt. He looks at Elias and the woman. "What are you two doing here?"

Elias looks at the woman.

"I him mother," she explains.

"I'm Elias. Pleased to meet you. This is for you," he says, handing Ng the bag.

Ng peers in the bag and his face stiffens into a mask. "I don't draw anymore. All I've been doing all summer is designing T-shirts, and I don't even do that anymore."

"But why?" Elias asks, surprised by the reaction. "You're so talented."

"I threw it all out. The magazines too. You might want to save that drawing I made you. It's a rare thing now."

"He quit T-shirt job," Soo says to Elias. "And me, I quit, too."

"He doesn't need to know that stuff, Mom. He's got his own problems."

Elias looks at the pain in the mother's eyes. "My friends' problems are my own."

"No," Ng says sharply. "They're not. Yours are yours, and mine are mine." He shoves the bag at Elias and turns to start back up the stairs. "I'm sorry, but I can't take this from you. There are things I just can't do anymore, okay? It's just how things are. I'm sorry." He rounds the landing and becomes a series of receding thumps.

Soo touches Elias's arm. "I sorry for Ng be this way. I know you he friend."

"It's okay. Kids are like that sometimes."

"He need father help. But he—" Soo makes a motion with her hands like birds flying. "Big screw up."

"Did you say you and Ng had both quit your jobs?"

"Oh yes," Soo smiles ruefully. "We all big screw up."

It seemed like a good idea when Elias spied the piñatas at the art supply store. Cheap, light, brightly colored. Too bad they aren't noisy, he thinks, holding up the donkey and hearing merely a rustling of its crepe paper fringe. He steps uneasily up the aluminum steps, holding the hollow donkey under one arm. His head is clouded in leaves. He can see the toucan, sombrero, rabbit and bull piñatas watching him from the bottom of the ladder. Pound in a nail and then voilá. Easier than building a scarecrow for those starlings.

"Need a hand?"

He turns with difficulty from his perch, squatting to peer below the smothering leafage. Ng is standing at his fence. Elias starts to say something, but his mouth is full of nails.

"What if you fall and you can't get up?" Ng laughs.

Elias spits out the nails, jumps from the ladder, and runs to the fence. "Come in! Come in!" He pulls Ng through the gate. "I'm so glad you came. I need someone to hand up the piñatas once I get the nail in."

"Wait a minute," Ng interrupts. "First I'd like to—"

"No no," Elias says quickly. "No need."

"But, I'd like to explain."

Elias takes Ng's shoulders and looks the boy squarely in the eyes. "I still have the bag if you want it."

"I guess so." Ng smiles at his feet. He notices the piñatas grouped in the grass. "What are you doing, anyway?"

"It's for the birds."

Ng looks at him blankly.

"See," Elias shakes the donkey. "It's a scarecrow full of candy. Here." He pushes the donkey into Ng's chest. "Let's do this before it gets too dark." He ascends the ladder and disappears into the leaves.

Ng stands with the donkey in his hands, thinking, that's it? Everybody's so damn ready to forgive?

Elias's head reappears. "Let's save the donkey. Maybe we'll break it tonight. A ceremony of no more being stubborn. Okay?" Elias winks and is gone once more.

Monday the 4th (Labor Day)

"Anymore of this heat, I'm going to just about die," Giselle moans from the porch swing. Her stomach is an enormous, shiny sphere. About all she does anymore is rub that mound with cocoa butter and read old magazines and complain about the heat.

"I don't know what it is, but today is enough to kill me."

"Honey it ain't even ten o'clock yet," says Belle, stirring up the layer of sugar from the bottom of her iced tea.

But already the sun is working moisture out of the soil in a steady lurid exhalation. Brittle insects thrum in the fields. For a long time no one speaks, and there is only the creak of the porch swing and the occasional tinkle of melting ice falling into itself in Belle's tea glass.

Giselle shifts uneasily. Her intestines are being forced downward and out of her body by the increasing mass of her babies. It seems a high price to pay. She is suffocating and exploding.

"I can't believe Momma's going to fry chicken today."

"She wants everybody to have a nice family dinner this afternoon. Soon we all gone be too busy with those little ones."

God, does everything in the world have to be about this? Giselle thinks, rubbing her abdomen. She is entirely fed up with inactivity, with being served and pampered as though she deserved some kind of special treatment. You know how I got this way, don't you? She wants to say. You know what their father is, don't you?

She saw in one of Belle's old *National Geographics* an article on ants and how the queen is just this kind of communal womb, a soft, giant freak thing that lies inert in a dirt room, fed and cleaned by worker ants. She felt indignant that god would have made anything function that way. Sacrifice a being to ceaseless procreation. In mere weeks, months, she has moved from wanting nothing at all to wanting more than the motherhood that has been thrust on her. There has to be more than this, she had thought, looking at the grotesque ant queen. Its skin is glossy and vulnerable.

Her mother comes onto the porch with a familiar bottle. "Want some more cocoa butter, love?"

At loose ends, with Leda on a family picnic and Soo out on some kind of mysterious errand, Ng begins to remove the pencils and paints from the bag that Elias gave him and place them in empty soup cans and shoeboxes in his room. Pads of heavy watercolor paper. And professional drafting pens. Elias did a good job. Except for the jars of tempera paints. That's for kindergarten fingerpainters.

It feels almost wrong to break the monastic emptiness of this white space in which he has lived all summer. He opens one of the jars and idly dabbles, mixes water into the tempera, dips in a finger and swabs it across the vellum. The sudden yellow is like a golden knife, or the smell of lemon water, or the mouth of the sun. Then he touches a red thumb to the paper, and the smile breaks out of him. The pleasure spreads sharply up his body, from the soles of his feet into his stomach. He applies another color and another, finally setting in the center a sloppy indigo flower of no particular type, like a cornflower floating on honey. He begins laughing to himself, and panting slightly. He senses an incipient erection. He could lift a car with the sudden adrenaline. He runs down the hall to the living room, spins around and runs back. It's still there, the finger painting, almost pulsing, the colors surging against each other.

The phone rings. It's Leda. "Hey, it's me. I was just wondering if, maybe, are you busy?"

"No, I guess, not really. I was just about to call you."

"Great! Do you want to join us for a picnic at Montrose Harbor?"

"Yes, absolutely." The day ahead leaps into his mind, whole and entire. He can smell the grill, hear the tussling of Leda's siblings. "I'll leave right now."

He is already hanging up when he catches the tinny sound of her voice still in the earpiece.

"Hey! Are you okay? You sound weird."

"I'm okay, yeah, I'm okay. Weird yes maybe, but okay."

He fairly flies down the street.

Peter sinks back into the leather recliner in the rectory lounge. The leather is dry and cracked, but still imparts a degree of sumptuousness that gives him a pleasant tingle. Is that Jerry Lewis Telethon still on? All those kids with muscular something and all I can remember is Jerry Lewis. Hasn't done anything worth watching since his movies went color.

He can hear the ti-pock, ti-pock of the ping-pong table in the next room. Shouts of volleyball players in the side yard. These new priests. The misaligned window air conditioner is dripping into a large Tupperware container.

The other old clerics wander in and out, some of them, like Peter, in undershirts and black trousers. Is it old age or celibacy that keeps them over-dressed in sticky weather, he wonders. Either way you can't enjoy the heat. He finds himself thinking that ugly old Portland, Maine would already be heading into its best season, autumn. In the far corner, Father Algernon has thrown back an entire six of Miller Lite, and Peter shuns him. Such weakness. Why do people think they can get away with almost *anything*?

Rejecting Nathan's invitation to a holiday lunch probably did them both some good. Peter felt braced by the exercise of his moral duty, and Nathan will certainly chew on the import of the, I suppose he'd call it, snub—hopefully to productive ends.

Lewis is humping around the stage like a drunk, his tie strung like a noodle around his flopped-open collar. His retro hairstyle has melted into moppy strings. Everywhere on the stage kids roll in wheelchairs, smiling those eerie incomplete smiles. He suddenly thinks of Robin. Why?

"I feel your pain," Peter mutters, gripping the stock of his aluminum cane. Meaningless phrase.

"It's like a carnival sideshow in a box, don't you think?" calls Robin from the living room. "The poor disabled kids relying on this run-down slapstick comic. I mean, it's horrible, but you can't turn away. It's almost like one of those reality cop shows. Banal, yet titillating in a creepy way. When I was a kid I always wanted to call and pledge like a thousand dollars to make sure they always made a new record total. Isn't that insane?"

Nathan walks through the room holding the phone and looking pensive.

"Oh, stop moping. Be thankful Peter turned you down. Did you really want to spend a free day catering to him? God, would you look at Wayne Newton. Explain how he got so popular. He sings like he just ate a biscuit with nothing to wash it down."

"I guess you're right. But Dad will want to know why I'm not being a proper host."

"Oh pish-posh. Look at the lamps on that Jill St. John. She must be half-plastic by now." He looks at Nathan.

"Come on over, muffin." He pats the couch. "Sit, sit." He wraps his legs around Nathan's waist and pulls him down. "We've got a free day, we're young, healthy, and sober—for now. What say we enjoy the fruits of our hard-won privacy?" His fingers drift across Nathan's lap and his eyes light up. "I'll take that as a yes."

Tony flies through the air, launched from the pool by Alphonse's cupped hands. He laughs and splats awkwardly into the water. The pool is jammed with families. The concrete apron is a patchwork of towels on which people sprawl to get their last sunburn of the year.

Alphonse ducks and resurfaces, shaking the water from his face. "We waited all summer until the last day to do this. Are we crazy?"

Tony doesn't answer. His sides hurt from laughing.

"Next year we gone spend every day like this."

Tony dives into the chlorine-sharp water and shark-attacks his father's legs.

Summer seems to be just starting.

The Taste of Logan Square is a poor relation to the other street festivals that clog the city's neighborhoods throughout the warm months. But it's better than they've gotten lately, so Lather Rinse Repeat take to the stage, trying to be game about it all. Not so long ago they were house band at the Fusebox and scheduled to play Grant Park. Oh, how the mighty.

"Let's do it for Jerry's kids," Chipper says, before rapping his sticks together with the time-honored stadium rock countdown of, "Onetwothreefour."

Maybe it's the evening cool, the liberal beer vendors, the superb Cuban sandwiches, or the mangos-on-a-stick, but by the fifth song, the avenue has acquired a pretty good crowd of dancers. By the seventh song, Alice sees people beyond the trees coming nearer to watch and bob their heads. By the end of the thirty-minute set there is a lusty call for an encore, for which the band supplies three loud covers—the "Road Runner" theme song, "Harborcoat," and "Train in Vain"—and then—holy cow—a second encore for which Alice and Molly do an *a cappella* duet after which there is a stageside scramble of requests for T-shirts, mailing lists, next gigs, and even a couple of autographs.

"Is we is or is we ain't?" shouts Shanklin as he lugs an amp to the van.

"We is!" says Molly, and she and Alice do a moshpit bodyslam out of pure high spirits, causing Alice to see a shower of stars.

Tuesday the 5th

The Easter trip to Boston never left Elias entirely. He savored it in a way that made him feel dangerous. It was risky, wrong, and implicated Elana in a deception—hardly the actions of an honorable grandfather. But still he had, in an entirely uncharacteristic act, gotten what he most wanted: a precious connection to Elana. It left him feeling that maybe there were things he should have done earlier, other unplanned risks he should have taken. It made him want to do it again. So he did.

He could acknowledge the truth of everything he had thought against it, but here he was again, in Boston, unknown to anyone else. What would Sophia say? It wasn't too late to call her. Perhaps another deception is in order. He could pretend to be merely thinking of making the trip…

"Hello, dear."

"Hi Pop. What's up?"

"I was thinking of visiting, coming out today, spur of the moment."

After a pause: "I don't know, Pop. Today's not so good. I thought we were planning for Thanksgiving."

"But I had some free time—"

"We're just so busy. And Elana has a full schedule with piano and swimming..."

That's how it would go. And having that conversation in the baggage claim of Logan Airport—what good would that do? He would have to turn around and go home. No. He looks up the address of Elana's school and hails a cab.

Elias walks up to the playground savoring the fresh balm of the full, flower-scented breeze. He is deep inside the moment, moving forward without thinking about the questions his presence will raise. He hears only the children and the metal screech of swings and carousels. He quickens his pace.

Children galloping in the spring sunshine grab sweaters, stretch away from tags, skip one foot, two feet across chalked patterns on the asphalt. Elias hooks his fingers into the chain link fence and gazes into the wild space where boys in basketball jackets, girls in jumpers and cardigans, smooth towheads and curly dark heads move in apparently random patterns, and collide with musical shrieks of delight.

Elias locates Elana standing in the field of a kickball game. She squats and fumbles in a patch of new dandelions. One solidly kicked ball sails toward her, bounces over her outstretched arms. She runs lightly after it, her legs a blur. Before she reaches it, the center fielder picks the ball up and heaves to the infield, where it bounces against the runner between first and second. Side out.

Elias is transfixed. I will come every day. This will be my hobby. My religion.

The third kicker up is Elana. She runs up and kicks the first ball. Elias watches it sail high over the pitcher's mound. Elana runs and runs like the wind, making it halfway to second base before the shortstop cradles the big ball against his stomach for the out. Elana flounces back to the bench.

Elias catches her eye.

"Grampa!" She runs through the infield, the other kids shouting at her. She runs grinning, until her sweet brown eyes are framed by two diamonds in the wire.

"Grampa! What are you doing here?" Her tone is almost scolding.

"I came to watch you play."

"I'm not winning," she pouts. "They bounce the ball too high for me."

"You did fine, sweetheart. You really kicked that ball."

A whistle rattles through the air.

Elana turns. "I have to go now. I have to get my ride with Mrs. Terry. Do you want to come with me?"

"So soon?" Elias pulls on the fence. The urgency of this desire to extend the moment makes him feel vulnerable, almost frightened. "Maybe there is a game we can play."

"I have to go, Grampa." She steps away. "Come on."

"Elana!" The urge to stop her from going adds an edge to his voice. "Would you like to have Grampa walk you home?"

She looks uncertain. Can't ask her to decide, Elias realizes. She's four years old, for Pete's sake.

"I'll walk you home," he says in the calmest voice he can muster. "We can stop for ice cream."

The girl's torment is manifest in her soft, lucent features. "Mommy said I always should come straight home."

"Okay," he says. "We'll go straight home."

The door is answered by a strange woman in a blue pantsuit, with a pile of dark hair on her head.

"Hello?" she says, opening the door just enough to let Elana inside. "Who are you?" She holds Elana behind her.

"I'm her grandfather," Elias says, with full realization that the scene as it is unfolding and will continue to unfold is going to put him in an unflattering light.

"Her grandfather?" the woman says. "Far as I know, the child only got one grandfather, and you ain't it."

He could not express it, but the full impact of that sentence spreads before Elias's imagination a terrible universe of elisions and erasures. He exists—how could anyone not have heard of him?

"And you are?" he counters.

"I'm the cook, but don't matter who I am."

"Come in, Grampa!" Elana says from behind the cook's ample bottom. "We can play with my Pokémon. Mommy doesn't like it. Do you like it?"

"Wait here," the cook says, shutting the door in Elias's face.

He stands on the porch fighting the urge to flee. No, he has to stay. He belongs. How would it look now if he left? He waits, hugging himself for warmth in the September heat. The house he had seen in April is unchanged.

The yard is still the same: trim, swept, immaculate—only more verdant. The crisp, postage stamp lawn looks as though he could bellyflop into it, sending up cascades of rich, deep green grass as he sinks to the bottom. He notices how the steps are worn in the middle from decades or maybe centuries of wear. There is an intricately woven wicker rocking chair on the porch; how he would love to rock Elana to sleep there. His porch has only a worn-out lawn chair—aluminum with tired nylon straps for a seat. He would not sit in it even alone.

The door flies open. Sophia's angry face confronts him. She pulls him inside without a word and sits him down at the kitchen table. Elana is not there, but Jonathan is. Sophia whirls and, with her hands on her hips, is the very image of her mother in a fit of passion.

"What the hell were you thinking, Dad? Elana's carpool called here in a panic when she didn't show up and Mrs. Garcia is beside herself! She thought you were some kind of molester."

"That's horrible!" Elias says, shocked. "What kind of place is this where a grandfather can't take a whim to walk his grandchild home?"

"From halfway across the country? This is the twenty-first century, Dad. No one hands a kid off to someone they don't know personally."

"I don't know what you were thinking," Jonathan says. "Why wouldn't you call first? It's unprecedented."

Elias notes that Jonathan's anger is muted but dangerous, spoken through thin lips, behind crossed arms.

"It was a crazy impulse. I wanted to see my granddaughter, that's all. I'm sorry for not calling."

Sophia leans against the kitchen counter. Elias is between them, like a suspect on a crime show. And he feels guilty.

"This is, well, it's disturbing really, that you would do this." Sophia shakes her head regarding her father. "Are you all right? Is there something wrong?"

"No, I'm fine. I just jumped on a plane. I can't explain it. I'm sorry you're so upset. But I only wanted to—"

Jonathan snorts.

Suddenly the chemistry of the moment changes. Sophia gives Jonathan a severe look. "Forget it, Dad," she says abruptly. "We were just spooked. I overreacted."

"All right," Jonathan says, in regard to nothing in particular. He brushes invisible crumbs from the front of his cardigan and walks out of the room.

"Let's get some air, Dad." Sophia grabs a bottle of wine and takes Elias into the back yard.

Elana is already outside, hanging motionless in a tire swing that Elias is sure wasn't there at Easter. He gives her a few pushes on the swing and then sits down with Sophia. She hands him a glass of cold white wine.

Sophia sighs. "I wish you hadn't done this, Dad." Her tone is softer, more tired than scolding. "The timing is lousy."

"You're right. I was crazy to do it. But I—" He pauses, wondering how much of the truth either of them is ready to hear. "Greeks need their families around. That's how we are. I try to be strong—"

"The world isn't like that anymore, Dad. Are you going to guilt me over that again?" Sophia takes a large gulp of wine.

Elias is frozen. How can he talk about it? It isn't about guilt or respect, or any of the other words he can think of. It's about how he wants Sophia to want the same things he wants. And since she met Jonathan, the common ground has simply washed away.

Sophia rubs here eyes—lost within soft, dark holes. She watches Elana pushing the swing and trying to climb aboard. "The energy she has. Was I ever like that?"

"Sure, of course. Ran like a squirrel. Everywhere you went, you ran. That's how kids are. Everything is a game."

"I don't remember that. Being that way."

Elias refills her wine glass. She is drinking it like water.

"I know I haven't been there for you, Dad," Sophia says, as though commenting on the weather. "I just don't know how to change that."

The sentence hangs in the air. So that's it, Elias thinks. I will never get what I want. He tries to imagine the world now, without the days and hours shaped by how near he can be to Elana. It won't be easy, he thinks. And what then do I have to live for?

Sophia's face is hard and distant, barricaded against the pain she has just inflicted.

I don't understand, he wants to say. I'll try to forgive. But that, too, sticks in his throat.

Just then, Elana jumps into Elias's lap. She smells musky and sweet with exertion. Sophia doesn't move, lost somewhere in her thoughts.

"Swing Mommy now," Elana says. And when the adults don't move, she understands their hesitation. "It's easy, Mommy. Come on, I'll show you."

Saturday the 9th

Shug's Haven is a weird fucking place in the morning. There's no ladies for one thing, just a bunch of sorry-looking old men fresh off their night shifts. And the place smells sour, like a shirt left in the washer too long. But there is Early Times and 7-Up, in tall glasses, as much as you want. And Jimmy wants a lot. There is not a man in the city suffering as keenly as he is at this moment. Some city department came and closed up the house on Kimbark after one of the stupid women left her kids on the stoop all day. Social workers scooped them up and then all hell came down. Jimmy saw the report on the news—right here at Shug's, as a matter of fact, an Eyewitness News Exclusive report, with some Latina reporter standing right where he would have parked his car in another two hours. He kept well away from the mess until all the official cars had returned to their official garages.

So it could be worse. He has just returned from breaking past the locks the city put on the doors to retrieve his clothes and a Ziploc bag of rock he had stashed under a loose board in the attic.

"God smiling on me since my improper incarceration," he says to the bartender. "Could have had my ass caught up in that home alone shit."

The bartender raises an eyebrow. "That *your* house?"

"Where I stayed." Jimmy tilts the glass until all the ice tumbles down against his bared teeth. He belches. "I'll have me another one of those. Sure tastes good."

The bartender picks up the glass and refills it in a few practiced motions and settles it on a warped cardboard coaster.

Jimmy takes a big swallow. "Yeah, I could have been fucked good, if I was there. Nosy damn neighbors. Or—" Jimmy pauses, considering.

"Can't blame them, really," says the bartender. "With the kids and all."

"Or a nosy fucking postman," Jimmy mumbles.

"What?"

"Got to make a visit," Jimmy says. He throws down a few bills. "Keep the change."

The bartender picks up the bills. When Jimmy tips, you know it's a fucked-up day.

Despite the doctor's orders for bed rest, Giselle insists on moving daily from the bed to some other flat surface, usually the porch. We might as well look at all the green we can, she reasons, before we go back to the city. The slow shuffle out to the porch is all she can manage, holding her stomach out in front like a heavy sack of groceries. She and Elmer lounge away the afternoon while Eloise and Belle keep themselves busy scrubbing down a second-hand crib and washing numerous loads of cloth diapers, blankets, footed jammies and the other baby clothes dropped off over the past two weeks by relatives near and far. Giselle was moved by the generosity and kind wishes of people she had not seen since she was a toddler herself.

Elmer hands her the wallet-size game pad. "I got a triple bonus and five extra minutes for beating the alien zone defense."

"That's level four. You are schooling me, cousin." She applies her thumbs to the buttons, and her game character rises slowly to the floating free-throw line.

Elmer watches her for moment. "Can I ask you something?"

"Sure." She's intently watching her fuel level while going up for the block.

"How come you left home?"

Her thumbs freeze. "That's a long story."

"Momma said you was unhappy."

"That's right enough. Damn." Her player has run out of fuel and dropped back to earth, burning up in the atmosphere. "I thought my parents were too strict."

"Were you sad when you were gone?"

Giselle hands the game back to Elmer. "Yeah. I guess I was a lot of the time."

Elmer's eyes widen. "What's that?" He points at a pool of liquid darkening the scuffed porch planks.

"Did you pee?" he whispers.

"Worse than that," Giselle says. "I think my water just broke."

Like it was laid out for a bonfire, rickety garage full of envelopes, catalogues, canvas bags. A few splashes of charcoal starter, one match is all it takes.

Jimmy watches from down the alley until the smoke starts to come thick. Then he takes a pull on his pint of Early Times and drives slowly, calmly, like any regular person coming home from a regular job, to the pay phone at the Amoco. He is wired, his fingers light and nervy as he punches 9-1-1 on the number pad.

He screeches, "Fire!" and babbles out the address. "Hurry—I think they's a baby in there!"

Jimmy slams the phone down, jumps into the car and pops the clutch, whooping. Hope Lem's got his TV fixed. Or we'll just have to head back to Shug's to watch the news.

Eloise and Belle sit beside Giselle's bed, each one rocking a tiny, wrinkled infant. Where Giselle's face has relaxed in sleep after the trying hours of labor, the tiny faces are clenched, as though clutching the threads of that best, deepest sleep from which they were rudely awakened.

"Mason's a good doctor, even though I couldn't argue him out of the c-section," Eloise says.

"All I know is he got these little ones out safe."

"A few more days and we'll have them among us, causing riots."

"Won't it be lovely?" Belle says.

"Hope she can handle it," Eloise says, running a soft hand across Giselle's brow.

"She'll handle it just like she handled the labor," Belle says. "Holding tight to her momma's hand."

Tuesday the 12th

Ellen hurries to Urbs in Horto, driven by a hunger for more Alice. She travels without seeing, musing only on the ever-expanding cosmos of Alice's beauties. The shy look from under golden bangs. The thoughtful lower-lip bite. The sweep of soft white stomach between a cropped T-shirt and her jeans. Yowza.

As soon as she swings open the café door, it's obvious that something's wrong.

"Hey," Alice says flatly.

"What's wrong?"

Alice holds out a small envelope. "I found this at work this morning. Under the door when I got to work."

"Oh, Christ," Ellen mutters, seeing Megan's handwriting.

"What's her problem?" Alice says. "Does she think you live here?"

"She's just—" Ellen shakes her head. "She wants something I don't think anyone can give her." She opens the envelope and pulls out a folded piece of notepaper covered with small, agitated print.

"You don't have to read it."

"I think I do." Ellen regards the paper nervously. "Do you mind sitting with me while I do?"

"No, of course not." Alice touches her shoulder reassuringly.

Ellen unfolds the paper and begins to read. Her eyes move quickly over the page, to the end and back to the top, absorbing it with a grave unhappy look. At last she looks up, eyes welling with tears.

"Oh, Ellen," Alice whispers. She holds out her arms and Ellen falls into them, every muscle giving into the crushing too-much-ness of it all. She shakes in Alice's arms, her body growing slack and heavy, settling against her shoulder into shoulder, breast to breast, forehead to collarbone. Alice keeps her arms loosely about her friend, touching her every so often and muttering things encouraging but possibly pointless.

After a while, Ellen looks up, her lips luffing with every breath. Her eyes are terrible in her face gone putty soft, without contour.

"Don't cry," is all Alice can say. She presses her lips to Ellen's cheek, and then, light as a petal, to her lips. She takes the hot, mussed head in her hands and regards it.

Their eyes explore each other and, seeing what is there, fall slowly, slowly into it, mouths following. Slightly open, the shock of softness, the pressed moist mouth, and was that tongue? They pull back, dazed.

"Woah," Alice whispers.

Ellen leans forward, searching again for that indistinct sweetness left by Alice's Pepsi. And finds it. Tender, exploratory, kind. And, at some point, it is no longer consolation.

Please don't throw this away as soon as you see the handwriting. I really need to reach you. I'm desperate. I've been watching you. In the middle of the day, when I'm between appointments. In the evening. Maybe you know this already.

Sometimes I go where you've been. Other times, I go where I know you're going, but leave before you get there. I don't know why. Maybe I'm trying to infiltrate your days, spread through them something of myself that will reach you, maybe below your senses. My smell on the breeze, a stray hair on the floor where you step. I watch you and wonder if you ever think about me. There were beautiful things when we loved each other. You may have forgotten. I know I was awful sometimes. I treated you worst when I was trying to love you most. I tried not to be. I'm so sorry. The fact that you continue to live gives me pain. To the point that I almost forget that I am living, too, in a grotesque fashion. To see you leaving a cheap restaurant with somebody else is almost beyond bearable. Those were my evenings, the adventurous hours when the world made sense to me. A beautiful kind of sense. Now I live like a kind of rodent, watching the world of humans from a hiding place. I know who you're with. But I don't care. I'm beyond jealousy now. It makes no difference anymore. I don't care who you sleep with, or how many others, as long as I can be one of them. This is the last time I will bother you. I swear. But couldn't you let me know that it wasn't so easy to cut me out of your life? Please?

Suddenly, Brad awakes to the smell of a woman's hair. The weight of her along the length of his body. A mouth is pressed into the crook of his neck. One arm and one leg thrown across his torso pin him down like a giant staple. Jennifer. Or is it Jeanine?

Oh, he thinks. Right. Without opening his eyes, he replays the previous few hours. His three-song set went okay. He got a fair amount of applause, seeded by this woman's furious clapping. He bought her a drink. She turned back every modest protest. Her aggressive kisses all over his face in the cab. Then into his apartment, and—

He shifts away, hot, and stiff in muscles that hadn't been used in a while. The sex had been like an out-of-body experience. He didn't lose himself in it, the way sex is supposed to be. He actually thought his way through every step. Press, lick, fondle, thrust. It feels like he was bumping into a coffee table all night long. He scratches his head. The woman murmurs in her throat and resettles herself against him. There is a raw smell in the bed, like hamburger.

This is so weird, is all he can think. It isn't me she fell for. Maybe it's a kind of neurotic imprinting. I'm like her father or first boyfriend or something. Because why else would she?

But then there is the sound of an ambulance in the distance, and he thinks, Maybe you fall for the people whose wounds are not yet visible to you. He looks at the woolly light stuck between the blades of the blinds. If that's true, it would explain a lot.

He lies awake thinking of nothing but Alice.

Friday the 15th

Elias leans against the prep table, gnawing on a carrot. "Luis, I don't know what to do anymore. First winter is slow, then spring is slow, then summer is slower. Excuses we make, this and that. But it's not summer anymore, except technically, and things aren't any better."

Luis hums thoughtfully while flipping a short stack and five strips of bacon on the griddle. "This is my thinking. Our food is good." He gives a pancake a showy flip. "It's those coffee places. People like them. They're cozy. They've got fireplaces. Or, like that place across the street, they've got cute girls working there. Businessmen stop in for a cappuccino and a scone, maybe flirt with a hottie, instead of Denver omelet and attitude from a bitchy waitress."

"Please, Luis. I know you don't like her."

"She's stealing tips. If she's too good for this job, she can go get another one." He slaps the spatula on the iron griddle, and it sizzles. "I don't understand that kind of thinking. It's not like you some kind of bad boss." He flips the food onto a plate and tops it with two pieces of toast and an orange slice.

Elias shakes his head. "It's a struggle to keep good ones with the business so slow. I can't entirely blame her."

Luis slaps the order-up bell. "I can."

Elias spends the afternoon reading trade magazines. New food? Re-design? What can he really afford to do to the business with his cash flow dwindling down to nothing? He finds himself staring out the window at Urbs in Horto, and the casual flow of customers. They're diversified with the flowers, but on average, how high can their tabs be, a coffee and a muffin?

He feels a shadow over his shoulder.

"Mr. Kanakes?" The waitress chews his name like the piece of strawberry gum that is as permanent in her mouth as a tongue. It isn't that she gets his name wrong, but she throws the accent in the wrong place. KAN-a-kess. After six weeks, still getting it wrong.

He turns a fatigued eye on her. "Yes?"

"I'm afraid that I won't be able to stay on here."

He gestures for her to sit. "I'm sorry to hear that. When is your last day?"

She looks surprised. "Today. I have another position starting tomorrow."

"That leaves me kind of short."

She fumbles for a reply.

Elias puts up a hand. "Never mind. I understand. Anyway," he says, a small smile breaking slowly on his face. "I think I have someone I can get on short notice."

Elias feels a little quiver of excitement as he hangs up the phone. Maybe a stroke of genius, or maybe not. But having Ng's mother work at the diner will certainly be a positive thing. He'll see Ng more often, and help them through a tight spot. But what if she really isn't any good? Her English is poor, and she seems brusque. But no, he shrugs off the doomsaying. She was so grateful, he knows she'll be a good worker, and things will start to turn around. For them, and for him. For the first time since his return from Boston, he feels a glimmer of good feeling about things.

To celebrate, he pours a glass of retsina and walks through the backyard. He touches the leaves and marvels at the piñata zoo that has kept him starling free. He takes the garden hose and sprays down the swing set. Keep it nice for whenever Elana comes again. That done, he settles into a chair and watches the final black of night settle into the earth. A slight breeze tosses the leaves, bends the tips of the grass. The greens are growing brittle, preparing to go underground.

Sunday the 17th

At last—the first fresh morning, and you can almost allow yourself to hope that bracing autumn is going to wash the city clean of summer's gritty, sultry aftertaste. The bedroom window is open, and Robin wraps himself in a sheet as he enthuses about the quality of the air and the light, as if he had just awakened from a long sleep.

"I can't remember the last Sunday morning like this. Sex, eggs benedict, and more sex." He circles a finger around Nathan's navel. "The first breath of autumn always gives me this rush of like life-force."

"Mmm," Nathan murmurs. "It's like a mint."

"Let's call it Certs Day." Robin rolls on top of his lover. "Happy Certs Day. How should we celebrate?"

"More kissing?" Nathan pecks Robin's lips.

"On Certs Day," Robin says thoughtfully, "it is customary to run like an idiot through the park until you fall down. Then sex, and a bit of shopping. More sex, and then a very nice dinner out. French provincial is the traditional fare."

"This is a more official holiday than I realized."

"Did you already forget last year?" Robin sighs theatrically. "What am I going to do with you?"

"I don't know. More kissing?"

"Is this Nathan?" Robin grins. "Tell me, you funky, horny hunk, what have you done with worried Nathan?"

"He is taking Certs Day off."

Walking through the lobby, on their way to the park, Nathan spies a Fed Ex envelope propped in the corner.

"It's for you," he says to Robin, surprised.

"A Fed Ex? For me? What the hell?"

Nathan scans the invoice. "Must have been delivered yesterday. It's from a mail box place in Texas." He places the slim cardboard in Robin's hands.

Robin rolls his eyes. "Probably some crazy legal document spawned by my father's walking dementia. This ought to be good for a laugh or two." He rips open the mailer and pulls out a single piece of paper. As he reads the brief note, the light falls out of his expression and is replaced by something that strikes fear into Nathan's heart.

"Oh god. Oh god." Robin inhales sharply, folding in on himself, and falls heavily against Nathan. "It's Mom."

Nathan grabs Robin tightly and helps him over to the ornamental marble bench. "What is it?" He shoves aside a stack of junk mail and settles his lover on the cold stone slab. "What happened?"

"She's dead." Robin's voice is barely a breath as he rolls his forehead back and forth on Nathan's shoulder. "She's dead, and the son of a bitch wouldn't even call to tell me." He laughs shrilly. "Can you believe it? An overnight fucking letter. It's a riot."

"Let me see." Nathan grabs the paper and smoothes out the wrinkles where Robin had been clutching it. A plain piece of yellow legal paper, bearing the broad, hasty strokes of a felt tip pen. The cursive letters are rough, akilter. The writing reveals no care taken to phrase the news with delicacy.

R, Your mother died last night. To be cremated. Service Wednesday. No point in your coming down. Dad.

No love. Not even normal tact. He refolds the letter. "I don't know what to say."

"Why does it have to be like this? The only person who ever loved me has to die and I find out from a misplaced overnight letter."

Nathan tries to get Robin back upstairs before he disintegrates into full-blown hysteria.

"Janie didn't even call. No one. Her only son, no one calls."

Nathan gets him into the apartment and onto the couch. Robin moans and flails with brief seizures of anguish. Nathan watches him from a distance wondering what to do. He brings a glass of water, aspirin.

Robin reaches out blindly. "Just hold me."

Nathan takes Robin's sweltering weight into his arms. They sit for well over an hour in this pose.

"What do you want to do?" Nathan asks at last.

"I have to get down there."

"Of course. I'll call the airline."

"Tonight. Before they do anything to her."

"I'll get the earliest available flight."

"But." Robin sits up, wiping tears and a shiny mustache of snot on his sweatshirt. "I have to do something first. I have to go to a church and pray."

Despite his familiarity with Robin's abrupt emotional tangents, Nathan is still taken aback. "Pray? Where?"

"I don't know. Catholic maybe. Something beautiful and perfume-y."

"Okay. I'll go grab some files from work to bring with, and I'll meet you back here in a couple of hours. Then we'll pack and get out of here."

"All right." Robin sniffs with a quavery breath. "I'm so sorry, Nathe."

"Sorry for what?" He says, kissing his lover lightly on the temple.

"For ruining Certs Day. I was loving it so much." And he bursts into a fresh round of sobs.

Janie? Are you there? Please pick up. I just found out. Please? What's going on down there? Just call me, please? I'm catching a plane today, and I'll see you tomorrow.

∞

Father Dominic breaks into Peter's Sunday nap with a tap on the shoulder. Peter starts with a snort. He glances to the television. The baseball game's still on, so he mustn't have slept too long.

"There's someone to see you, Peter."

"Who is it? My nephew?"

Dominic shrugs. "I don't think so."

When Robin walks in, Peter thinks immediately of taking cover, of protecting himself. His second thought is, Why here? He looks around quickly. Who else is around to see this embarrassing creature?

Robin kneels at the side of Peter's armchair. His face is pasty and swollen. "Father." His voice is wispy, pleading. "Father, I need some spiritual help."

"Get up off the floor. Sit here." He pulls Robin up and sits him in the next chair. "This is a rec room, not a confessional."

"Forgive me father. I know I was not—have not been—very welcoming to you."

"What are you doing here?" Peter glances at the television. It's the top of the seventh and the Cubs have a one-run lead. Pirates on first and second with one out.

"My mother just passed away." Robin wipes a sleeve under his nose. "I'm angry and just so sad. Like I've never felt before."

"Then you must turn to your family." Peter notices how the boy's fists are balled up inside his sleeves, clenching them, like a girl with a chill. "They're the only ones who can comfort you."

"That's the thing, Padre—excuse me, Father. We're not on good terms. My father and I."

The runners are pounding around the bases against a background of browning ivy. That's where he should be. Some vacation. What did he really see? The lake. A hospital.

"We haven't spoken in years. Not even yesterday when she died."

Peter controls a reflexive rolling of his eyes. "You must admit that the choices you've made are not easy for everyone to accept."

"But that's what I don't get. Why can't anyone accept me? Why would he, of all people, reject his son? What does that get him? It just seems like the most wrong thing you can do."

His voice is rising, and a few eyes in the room turn their way. Peter intercedes quickly.

"Everyone is, er, precious to the church, Robin. But there are paths of righteousness and other paths that lead to, um, disgrace."

Robin's eyes are filled with desperation. "Paths? I don't even know what that means. Only one person has a choice to break our family apart, and that's my father."

"You can ask yourself, Robin, if you've been the best son you could have been. Given your, well, lifestyle. Did you consider his feelings?"

"It's always been about *his* feelings. But I was just protecting myself against him, don't you see?"

This is getting too deep, too personal. Anxious to bring the discussion to rapid close, Peter reaches out and places his hand on Robin's head. It is hot, humidity flowing up from the curling hair. "The Lord blesses you, and forgives you and carries the soul of your mother into heaven."

Robin falls forward in quiet tears.

The game is tied, and the bases loaded. Another game going to hell once the bullpen takes over. Can't they see they need a southpaw short reliever?

Peter takes his hand away.

"Thank you, Padre." Robin tries to clutch Peter's hand. "Thank you."

"You can only try to repair what has been broken," Peter says quickly. "The Lord be with you. Now, I'm sorry, but I have to go."

"May I, would you mind if I came to see you again?"

Peter watches a ball sail into the stands where there are still shirtless lunatics, even on this brisk day. "I will be returning to my parish very soon."

"I understand. But thank you." Robin shuffles out.

Peter sighs with relief. On the TV, the opposing team's home run ball is tossed back onto the field. Peter smiles. That's a nice touch, he thinks. Take that.

Robin, I just go your message. I think Dad's really hoping you won't come down. Just accept the blessing of her passing, okay? She's at peace. At last. God's will be done. Take care.

The flight attendant leans across Robin's body and gathers the half-dozen mini vodka bottles in her fingers. Nathan stacks the empty plastic cups for her and hands them over with a whispered, "Thanks."

She gives him a sympathetic smile, and then touches the shoulder of the sleeping seatmate.

Robin sighs and settles deeper into the seat. His cheek squelches against Nathan's shoulder, releasing a puff of boozy breath.

Nathan leans up, screws open the ventilation nozzle, and glances at the magazine on his lap. *Southern Living*—little slices of domestic perfection. House porn, Robin calls it. And it is seductive. The order is what gets him, the appearance of rooms peaceful with every item in place.

Outside the lozenge-shaped window, small downstate hamlets appear as splashes of light on the distant ground, as though fluorescent paint had dripped from an oversaturated celestial brush. He looks back at the figures. Robin's hand drops onto his thigh. He closes his eyes and imagines life in one of those little towns with a public square, post office and diner. What would he be in such a place? Straight, probably, in an awkward way, but steadfast. Owner of a gallery selling country hokum, with a cache of fine art in a back room for the dozen connoisseurs in the county. Fried chicken suppers with his squat, blue-eyed kindergarten teacher wife. Or someone like that girl in the flower shop, Alice, but less hip. It would be peaceful. No Robin, of course. But happy?

Wednesday the 20th

Danny Markowitz takes his coffee out to the garage. This is his space, the walls festooned with tools and a bench holding a Folger's can half-full of cigar ashes. He runs the toe of his work boot through the oily spot where, until yesterday, his 1978 Harley Sportster stood. He shakes his head. It was something, that machine.

Stacey sticks her head out the door. Pretty as a picture, as always, eyes done and hair teased, with her blonde bangs combed precisely to just above her plucked eyebrows. He can smell her Windsong perfume over the motor oil and coffee.

"What are you doing out here? Still moping over that thing?"

"No. Just wondering what to do with the extra space."

"I still don't get why you sold it."

What can he say? The bike represented dreams upon which he had rhapsodized endlessly. How he was going to get it running eventually—no, not just running, purring, roaring. Then add on saddlebags, a sidecar and take her on a road trip. To the Grand Canyon. To the Cascades. Mount Rushmore. A dream of wind pouring over their faces and star-lit screwing on sleeping bags in the Sierra Nevadas. And then he up and sells it.

"I had to face reality. It was just gathering dust."

"I'm glad to see it gone. But I still say you should have got more for it."

"Aw, hell. He drove a hard bargain. After all, it never ran for shit."

"It was a classic, Danny. I don't know how many times you told me that. And then you let it go for less than you paid for it."

He is lying badly and he knows it. Stacey is used to not knowing the contours of his interior life, but where money is concerned, she zeroes in on his lies like a fucking guided missile.

"It was mine to do what I wanted," he says, hoping to put an end to the third degree.

"All right," she says, her scarlet lips pressed together like a fresh knife wound. "But I get a say in what we do with the money."

"Sure, of course."

The door closes.

"Smart bitch," he says. You marry what you think is a dumb one and they turn up smart in ways specifically designed to screw with you. Story of my life.

Like an abused cat, Soo is slow to adjust to the atmosphere of Sophia's diner. Elias's behavior unsettles her. He brings her a Coke after the rush, sits and talks with her. He patiently explains the dishes. Tuna melt. Greek omelet. Texas toast. He is friendly and he cares about her son. She keeps finding herself queasy with guilt. Almost fearful. As though someone at the next table she serves will hold up a badge and will tell her it was only a trap.

At the end of every day, he tells her that she has done a good job.

"But I forget to bring toast." She hangs her head, waiting for the rebukes. "And I pour regular coffee to man who ask decaf."

But instead of yelling at her, Elias only laughs. "You'll be fine."

After a few days, she settles on the word respect. That's how he treats her. It is a word she has heard a lot about, but that seems to apply only to other people. But there's the cook, Luis. She overhears him talking to Elias through the service window.

"She won't work out," he said on her first day.

"Why not?"

"It's just the way things are. Asians are bad waitresses. They're just not built for it."

"Luis, this opinion does not speak well of you."

"Greeks own diners, Mexicans work in them. Indians own convenience stores. It's not good or bad. Everybody knows it. Look at the TV shows."

"I don't watch much television."

"Maybe you should."

"Anyway, you can't let TV shows predict everyone's ability."

"It's your business. I just think things are tough enough without taking on another bad waitress."

"I have a good feeling about her, Luis."

Luis seems genuinely affected by this news. He wipes his hands together slowly, and then says, "Why didn't you say so?"

Soo quickly mastered order taking and developed an acceptable if not exactly trend-setting waitress demeanor. Her sincere concern that the customers be happy eventually inflected her pidgin queries—"What you want? May I take order?"—with greater delicacy. Certainly the tables and the condiment bottles had never been cleaner.

After a few days, Luis came to thank her for bringing in better tips. "Not like winning the lottery," he said, smiling, "but an improvement."

Ng is hurrying to Stimpy's when Ivan calls to him from across the school parking lot. Oh shit, Ng thinks. Here we go again.

"Wait up, artist boy." Ivan's voice is brassy. "I want talk to you. A business proposition."

Ng steels himself.

"No, it okay." Ivan laughs and puts and calming hand on Ng's shoulder. "I told you no more problem. This real business. Straight player."

"Okay, what."

Ivan looks around and pulls a piece of paper from his back pocket. It is weird paper, gray, obviously unbleached, and soft—apparently carried for some time, the creases beginning to fray and tear.

Ivan gently smoothes out the paper. "I need artist like you. See, last summer, I was in Saigon with father. I see so many cool thing, but I can draw badly."

Ng can make out a wormy sort of dragon drawn in soft pencil. It seems to be breathing crude flames or crystals or maybe swords.

"It's interesting," he says.

"I make name for gang." He looks at Ng with an eager expression. "Dragon Sword. This going to be our symbol."

Ng says. He glances at his watch. "I have to get to work."

"I need logo," Ivan says quickly. "I pay you. And you be honorary member of gang."

"Ivan, you know I don't want to join."

"No, no, only you be off-limits. We protect you, that all. Friend always if you do this."

"I'll think about it."

"Meet me tonight at the McDonald's." Ivan's eyes are fired with excitement. "I want to get started."

The doorbell rouses Soo from her half-snooze on the couch. She looks at the muted TV, where a talk show host lies on the ground while small dogs jump over him. She looks out the window, and sees only the top of a baseball hat bobbing on the stoop. And then she sees Danny's car parked just down the street. She smiles to herself as she goes down the stairs and opens the door.

"You out of white car," she says matter-of-factly. "Big step."

"Yeah." Danny lowers his face in a supplicating look, and his forelock falls fetchingly across his brow. "Um. Could I? Do you think I could come in?"

"I very tired." Soo covers a slight yawn.

"I came by earlier but you weren't here."

"I was working. I got job."

"Oh." He is taken by surprise at this. "Really? Jeez." He looks around, running his fingers through his hair. "That's why—that's sort of why I came by. I mean, 'cause I thought you still didn't. Have one. A job."

"Ng, too, working at store. We fine now, thank you, okay?" She starts to close the door.

He stops the door with his palm. "Listen. I know I didn't come through right away, but I got a little something together for you, and maybe you should—" He fumbles a roll of bills out of his jeans pocket. "I'd like you to go ahead and have this."

"What this?" She looks at him with a mixture of amusement and detached pity.

"It's just a little fund to keep you going. I'm sure you had bills piling up and stuff, you know, in the last month?"

"Bills getting paid. Don't you worry. Keep money. Buy jewel for Stacey. Big ring."

Danny is flummoxed. He looks at the erupted blossom of money in his palm. He can't keep it. How could he explain three thousand more dollars all of a sudden? Stacey had already sniffed something fishy in the sale price he'd told her. What next? The lottery? Stacey would want to see the ticket. He couldn't spend it. He sold his hog for this roll to help his ex-wife and son. And now his gift is rejected? What the fuck has he done?

Soo says nothing, watching the emotions crossing her ex-husband's face. It is better, she's sure, than anything on the TV.

He looks at Soo astonished that he could be here once more—outflanked by fate and begging Soo for forgiveness. He explores her face for some sign that he can understand, but finds only a kind of obdurate glint, like a quartz fleck in a piece of granite. He'd had a guilty lust for Vietnamese women since his tour of duty, but it was the hard thing in her eyes almost twenty years ago, when he met her while fixing the kitchen plumbing in her parents' apartment—that's what turned him on. It was like seducing a wild animal, a tigress. Tame the thing that resists taming. He fought her with every bit of his charm and virility. They fought tooth and tail, he used to joke with his buddies. Eventually he got the young, lithe, semi-feral creature her on her back, worked his cock inside her, and felt like the king of the goddamn forest. But then he knocked her up. Oh yes. And it was then, round and needy, and with the hardness in her eyes replaced with need, that it—that she—turned on him. Devoured him.

"Come on, the kid's smart. Money for a good college, at least that."

"Offer to him, not to me."

There she goes again, for the jugular. Knowing it's the thing he least wants to do. But oh no, she will not have the last say. He will make a father's mark on his son's life. It is suddenly the most important thing he can think of, the foundation and purpose of all his remaining days, so help him god.

"Maybe I will," he says, and turns his back on the tigress, who, with a satisfied smile, goes back up to her den to rest.

The beer bottle rises and falls in front of Danny's eyes as he watches his estranged son talking with that trash bastard gang punk. Whatever it is, it isn't good. Some kind of threat. Blackmail most like. The two boys lean across the table inside the glowing window of the McDonalds. It's like watching lizards in a terrarium, tiny lives in pantomime, in boxes made to look like real life. Ignorant of the fact that they are watched.

The boys part outside the restaurant. Danny watches them separate and, after a moment's consideration, follows the scrawny gangbanger. The kid hops onto the Broadway bus. Danny follows it for about a mile until the kid alights, crosses Thorndale, and heads a few blocks west into Edgewater, pulling on the handle of every third parked car as he goes. All locked. On a bleak stretch of courtyard buildings, he finally cuts down an alley and disappears through a scarred metal door into the basement of an apparently abandoned building. Danny makes a mental picture of the building's back entrance, the alley, and the surrounding areas. He unscrews the top of another bottle of beer.

"Boy, you just bought yourself a visit from the U.S. Marines."

Thursday the 21st

Robin slept soundly, his head bouncing against the window of their rental car as they powered across rough Arkansas two-lane roads. Poor thing, he was wrung out emotionally. Until they got into the foothills of the Ouachita Mountains. Then he got carsick.

As they sit at a turnout overlooking Lake Hamilton, Nathan is already regretting his insistence on a relaxing detour before they returned to Chicago. But what else was there to do with a day to kill in Texarkana after the fiasco of a funeral service and his father's refusal to allow Robin anywhere near his mother's possessions? Not that there would have been much left after all her years in the nursing home.

Robin splashes water on his face from a water fountain that isn't much more than a rusty pipe. Then he eases himself down into the sunburnt grass and moans.

"It's a beautiful view," Nathan offers.

They haven't spoken much since they arrived in Texarkana. Robin has moved like a zombie since the moment they walked into the funeral home and found no casket. Despite his appeals, his father had gone ahead with the cremation.

Robin never protested. What was the point? His father had nothing to say to him beyond hello. Sherman looked at Nathan with contempt, leavened only by a complete lack of comprehension as to Nathan's role or purpose in his son's life. He did not invite Robin to his house. Janie had no room in hers, as she was sharing a large, dilapidated Victorian with five other members of the Living Church of Christ's Personal Word. He and Robin spent three nights in the Well Come Inn on the side of a two-lane highway. The only amenities were a hot water dispenser affixed to the wall and two Melmac cups with packets of instant coffee and cocoa. Robin drank both cocoas before bed.

Nathan stands up and offers a hand up to Robin. "Let's go. We're almost to Hot Springs."

Robin's face is like a bleached stone in the broken grass.

"It's supposed to be a great old hotel. We can take the hot mineral baths."

"As long as they have a bar."

The service was poorly attended. Robin's father sat alone in the front pew. Robin and Nathan sat two rows behind, and Janie sat across the aisle with a dozen members of her church who rocked and gesticulated in their own private mourning prayers. There was, of course, no casket, or urn. There was, in fact, nothing to represent the deceased except the portrait photograph that Robin had carried from Chicago wrapped in a sweater. Robin asked for some of the ashes to take home.

"You can have them all," his father said.

The metal canister rides in the backseat, wrapped in a quilt Robin bought from a half-blind old woman at a roadside stand.

"You take care now, honey," the old quilt-seller croaked in parting. Robin cried for the next twenty miles.

They reach Hot Springs before noon. It is a rainy day, and the main street sits below a canopy of clouds strung between two fair-sized mountains. A massive WPA hospital looms over the bath houses, most of which are empty, but still maintained on the outside to keep up appearances. People carry giant water jugs to the several water fountains along the street to fill them with the iron-tasting water steaming up from underground.

Robin leans his head to the water gurgling up into a large stone basin. "Shit, it's hot." He wipes his mouth. "Blech. I need some gin to get rid of that taste."

The lobby of the Arlington Hotel exudes a faded elegance. They check in and retire to the lounge, a large empty space with aquamarine velvet settees. A large-screen TV is set on the bandstand, surrounded by a jungle motif mural. The rather small martinis arrive in thick-stemmed glasses. The waitress set a large paper cup of popcorn in front of them. Robin smiles for the first time since their plane landed in Little Rock.

"Mom always wanted to come here. Dad wouldn't come because of the horse racing. Gambling is a no-no."

"This may be impolite to ask, but whatever did your mother see in your father?"

Robin swizzles his olive. "What's to explain? It's an old story. Lovely girl marries an aggressive go-getter, the kind parents like. He's domineering. He beats her down, crushes her dreams. His aggression reveals itself as a twisted, underground kind of misanthropy. He grows moodier and weirder after his wife's accident. His kids turn out to be his worst nightmare. Especially one of them."

"Things must have been okay once, when you were young, at least."

"Sure, everything was fine when we were still sexless, undifferentiated munchkins. But then came the awkward years. I was afraid of everything. It galled him. He once called me, get this, everything he hated in the world."

"Christ. What about Janie?"

"I used to call her Janie the Turtle. She went into a shell when Mom got hurt and stayed in there until those creepy fundamentalists went in with their bibles and got her. Dragged her out. You saw her. Looks like she hasn't seen TV or daylight in twenty years." He holds his empty glass upside down.

Nathan signals for another round. They drink and talk as the lounge grows quieter, darker, more redolent of faded elegance.

Finally, Robin stands up woozily. "I'm an orphan now. There's nothing back there that has anything to do with who I am. Let's just go home."

"Tomorrow. From tomorrow on we'll dedicate ourselves to putting greater distance between Chicago and Texarkana."

"Distance literal and figural," Robin says. He falls back onto the settee.

"Right." Nathan lifts him back to his unsteady feet.

"Metaphyshical," Robin giggles. "Mother-phorical."

Saturday the 23rd

Florence swishes her brush furiously in the water jar. After all the trouble she'd gone to getting the puppy to sleep out on the balcony, all she's got in the center of the canvas is a brown circle representing Duchess curled, nose to tail, on a paisley pillow by the porch railing. She paints another circle and another. Then she switches the brush to her left hand and paints one, slowly, that is a bit collapsed on one end. She crumples the paper and begins again.

The lake is littered with chips of light. She spreads a blue wash across the paper. She imagines how it will look up close tonight, from the deck of the dinner cruise ship. She thinks of this, her third date with Tommy, at his club's annual dinner dance, with more tingly anticipation than she would like to admit. If Louise doesn't drive her completely around the bend first. She flicks a couple of black v's into the sky for distant sea gulls. It makes her feel better.

Louise is still running the vacuum cleaner mercilessly, from one room to the next, pushing chairs and knocking table legs. It is a little payback, Florence knows, for going out with Tommy again tonight. Louise refused to join them, not wanting to be a third wheel. Nothing short of Florence avoiding Tommy would satisfy Louise, though she would never say so.

"Louise, could you finish sweeping later? I'm having trouble concentrating."

She hears the drone recede to a back room. And then a rough gargle as the agitator strangles on the bath mat. The dog sits up with ears cocked.

Florence points the brush at the dog. "If you don't lie back down, I'll paint you playing gin rummy." Duchess tries to give the bristles a conciliatory lick.

A bit later, Louise enters the room, dusting now, something she accomplishes by whipping the feather duster furiously over the vases and knick-knacks collected on the shelves. Pieces of Florence's life with Arnie.

Florence bites her lip nervously. "Louise, if you don't want me to go tonight, I won't."

"It's not that," Louise drops the duster and sits down next to Florence with a long, pent-up sigh. "I suppose I should tell you now. Big Jim called me home. He misses me."

"Oh my." Florence realizes just how unprepared she is for the arrival of this moment she has longed for.

"Come on, Flo." Louise puts an arm around Florence's shoulders. "You don't need me anymore."

"When did he call? Why didn't you say something earlier?"

"Oh, Flo. Let's not kid ourselves. You've been ready for me to leave for some time now. And it's getting harder for me to stay."

"What do you mean?"

"Try to see it from my side. It's hard for me to see you being courted by another man." She cuts off Florence's attempted counter-argument with a raised finger. "Hear me out. My head understands, but my heart is a little slower. A lot slower, maybe. Arnie was my brother, after all, Flo. And together you were like—I don't know—part of the sky. Or a landmark I could drive by and know that the world made sense. Imagining you with someone else, it's..." She pauses and regroups. "Well, that's not what I want. I don't want to stand in the way of your happiness."

Florence forces a breath deep into her lungs. Every fiber of her body has begun locking itself into the familiar stiffness of controlled sadness. The moment throws her right back to sensations she remembers out of foggy days of black dresses and muffled conversations. Church candles by day and tuna casseroles by night. She feels the familiar weight of lonesomeness settling in.

"I'll stay if you want to," Louise says gently. "I just thought we were both ready."

Florence doesn't reply at first, but fluffs the decorative pillow on her lap. She looks outside where the hard, gray buildings wobble inside a lens of tears.

"I'm ready," she says at last. "Ready as I'll ever be."

Tuesday the 26th

Looking down Ellen's torso, twin nipples tower fuzzily in the distance like mountains, and Alice has a recurrence of the dizzy feeling that's been dogging her since the first kiss. It's like a walk on the frigging moon. It went from a kiss to exploring hands to tongues and fingers to the whole enchilada in a little over a day. It's like her first time getting so drunk she blacked out. First the thirst for more and more tequila, then loss of equilibrium, then the soft, unconscious falling. Except that this time she's lost herself in a sudden, enveloping desire for sex. Sex with her friend, with a woman, with Ellen.

Her lips are swollen and rubbery, her tongue tired and worn down from biting, sucking, kissing. Even her skin feels abused and sore from tingling twenty-four hours a day. It's exactly what she imagines the third or fourth day of a bender must be like. Woozy and disoriented. Happily lost. Except.

Whenever they stop kissing, however, she has a perverse inclination to think about all the people she can't tell about this moment. There is, in fact, no one she can tell.

Ellen has a radar for these thoughts. "You're weirding out again."

"No I'm not. I was just thinking."

"'Bout what?" Ellen hands her a bottle of water.

"Chipper wants us to cut a demo."

"Terrific. You guys are so ready." Ellen's hand caresses her pubic bone, causing an instinctual arch in Alice's pelvis. "Mmm. What time is it?"

Alice peers at her watch on the nightstand. "Time to get ready for work."

"For you, maybe. I'd rather this."

"Nice work if you can get it. What are you going to do today?"

"I have this project I've been working on."

"The film?"

"I just call it the project. Not to jinx it."

"How does that jinx it?"

"Things don't work out if you admit that you want them."

Alice rubs her cheek against Ellen's neck. "I don't get it."

"You just can't grab these things too hard or they break."

"Are we going to be like that?"

"How do you mean?"

"Are we something that can't be spoken? Will it hex everything?"

"Hex what?"

Alice leans up on her elbow. "That we're, whatever—together. I mean, is this something for real or a thing you can't grab too hard?"

Ellen nuzzles her. "You can't really be worried about that right now."

"Are you kidding? I can't stop thinking about it—my parents, the band. Everybody's going to freak, I just know it."

"I guess I forgot."

"I'm scared. I didn't expect this at all. I don't even know what it—what you—mean."

"You mean are you a lesbian or just in love with a woman."

"Sort of."

"I predict—" Ellen places a deliberate and wet kiss on Alice's neck. "—that you will eventually realize what a ridiculous distinction that is."

"Great. Philosophy in the bedroom."

"I'm just saying, maybe you should look at it another way. Not that you're stepping out of yourself." Ellen's hands are roving now, in support of the point she is making. "But that you're stepping into yourself. Just give it some time." Ellen begins to slip down the bed.

"Easy for you to say." Alice flops back on the pillow, and says, weakly, "Hey. Hey, I'll be late for work."

Alice arrives at rehearsal early and sits on the windowsill working on the chorus for a new song. Or pretending to work on it, since her brain is about twelve miles away looking over someone's shoulder as she works on her "project".

Molly and Chipper walk in together, arguing. "Don't be so lame, Molly," Chipper is saying as Molly shakes her head vigorously.

"Alice will agree with me," he says. "*She's* serious."

"About what?" Alice asks.

"You'll agree that it's time for us to get into a studio. Can't you just see it? Our sexy photos inside the crystal-clear gem case." He frames his face with his fingers. "A precious, iridescent disc as shiny as our hopes and dreams."

"I agree with the CD part," Alice says. "Of course."

"I think we should wait for Shanklin," Molly says.

Chipper, disappointed that he got no laughs, drops his hands. "He's already on board."

Alice senses something missing in Chipper's pitch. "On board what, exactly?"

"The CD. We've got the material. It's the step we've never taken."

"Tell Alice the rest." Molly stands up and crosses her arms.

"And we know the producers and studios. All we lack is the nut, the kitty, the ante that gets us in the door."

"This is like water torture," Alice says. "What *exactly* are you proposing?"

"Just a couple of jingles. Or a few."

"Jingles?"

"You see? He's gone insane." Molly sits down again—flops really, laughing in a not-amused way.

"Just hear me out, okay?" Chipper says.

"Sure, fine. Sell me on the sell out," Molly snaps. "I'm all ears."

Alice, watching Molly and Chipper go at it, feels she should be taking a position. But somehow can't muster the concern. "Jingles for what?" she asks.

"It's a chain of coffee houses. Caffeine City."

"I've seen that place, over by the Belmont el stop."

"Well it's only the first. They're opening thirty in Chicago next year and they want to do a series of radio ads featuring a local band."

"And they want us?"

"We've got that coffeehouse-girl harmony thing. They like it."

"And how do they know about us?"

"Through me."

"I can tell by the look on your face."

"Okay. You'll find out anyway. Lori met one of the chain managers at a bar and yada yada yada, and she thought we'd be the best fit."

"So she's got her claws in us again."

"It's not like that. Her business is hooking people up. She's *handing* this to us. As a favor."

"Are you fucking her, Chipper?" Molly puts her hand protectively on Alice's arm. "Because if you are..."

"That is entirely beside the point. This is an honest-to-god break. Big *big* money."

Molly groans, "Oh my god, you are! It's just too *sick*."

"I am *not* present-participle *fucking* her. I merely past-tense *fucked* her, okay? It's history."

Alice gets up from the sill. Even with all that's happened, it still makes her feel nauseous. "I'm going to the john." She takes the key and leaves.

Chipper claps his hands to the sides of his head. "It's just business."

"Was the fuck business, too?"

Chipper pulls his cheeks down with his fingers, ghouling his eyes. "This is the brass ring, Mol. Exposure. Money. Don't you know what the music business is all about? Do you think it's just dorking around in this freezing cold room for the hell of it?"

"What I get is you don't care about your fellow band members' feelings."

"Look. I'm sorry. I didn't mean for it to come out this way."

"No Lori. We'll get the money we need some other way." Molly grabs her backpack. "I'm going to check on Alice."

"Well, I'm not going to wait around debating ethics while opportunities slip away." Chipper's voice suddenly sounds pubescent.

"What will you do? Move to New York? Did Lori put itching powder in your jock strap, too?"

Thursday the 28th

Giselle struggles from the car, holding a tiny child in the crook of each arm as though she is balancing something ponderous and unwieldy. Family members crowd the porch and then pour down the steps.

Belle charges the babies at a trot. "Here they is, the little darlings finally coming home!" Her voice rises to a shrill register reserved for occasions of great delight. "Just look at them."

Giselle stands in the eye of the cooing, petting storm, feeling like the handler of some priceless art objects. "They're just babies. You've all seen babies before."

"Not any sweet as this. No, sir. Look at them little toes!"

Second cousins touching the fontanels. Great-aunts petting the thin, soft arms. Giselle wants to yank the babies away from their hands and just sit with them, listening to their breathing, smelling their unaccountable sour-sweet baby smell. It's a kind of peace she has not felt for a good long time.

"The momma's tired. Let's sit her down." Eloise takes her daughter's elbow and leads her to the porch swing.

Someone says, "Look at Grandma getting all bossy," evoking general indulgent laughter.

Giselle still moves heavily, with a noticeable waddle. Making her right at home among the other women in her family. In her mind, though, she is still the skinny, pointy-breasted girl that everyone wants to sleep with. As she lowers her behind into the swing in the middle of the gale of family attention, the disjunction between her life now and a year earlier is almost dizzying.

"Have you settled on names for them?"

Eloise shoots her daughter a glance.

"Yes." Giselle jiggles the pinch-faced bundle in her left arm. "I'm calling her Jimelle after daddy and me. And this little man," she adds, kissing the moist head of the other, "is Evander."

"Oh. Ain't that sweet. Such pretty names."

"Like the daddy should get any credit at all," Eloise sniffs.

"It's not his say, it's mine."

"It's a real pretty name," Belle insists. "They both going to be so beautiful like they momma."

Elmer is at the back of the crowd looking nervous.

Giselle waves him over, sensing a chance to shift attention away from her accidental co-parent. "Come on and sit here. They won't bite."

Elmer seems taller and more lanky than usual as he collapses himself onto the swing.

"Go ahead."

He reaches one long, trembling finger to touch Evander's cheek. The sleeping boy shifts and shudders and relaxes again.

Elmer is full of wonder. "He so *soft*."

"I'll let you hold him later," Giselle whispers.

Elmer's eyes widen in terror, and Giselle laughs, suddenly happy to be in the midst of meddling, fussing family.

At least once a day Alph goes out to look at the ragged square patch where his garage went up in flames. Stupid luck that kids would choose his garage to set fire to. Which had nothing valuable in it aside from a couple of yard tools. But what was least valuable—a bunch of old mail that never would have been anything but incinerator trash in the end, anyway—that's what the fire laid bare like some kind of secret disease he'd been hiding from everyone.

That inspector had come by sifting through the ashes. If only the damn fire department had been slower there wouldn't have been anything worth sifting. As it was, he could see the still-colorful fragments of charred Levenger catalogues and neighborhood circulars. But those could be his, right? He dropped a comment in the inspector's ear about how sorry he was to lose all the papers he'd collected to make some spare change. No one said anything. But there were looks.

"Hey, Dad, you got time to play Nintendo?" Tony hangs out the back door, still in his night shirt.

"Sure, sure. Be right in." Alph kicks a chunk of charred timber. That's the thing—the boy. If something happens, what will he think of his old man? But god wouldn't do that, would he? To a man cleaning up his act? To a new grandfather? With all the worse people in the world, why mess with him?

Looking down into her children's huge, brown eyes, Giselle sees how they seem to pull in everything around them like one of those round supermarket mirrors. Giselle can see herself, and around her head, the bobbing faces of her family, and beyond them, the fields, the trees, the sky. Everything pouring into these tiny, soft eyes. But her face is always at the center. She feels their eyes bore into hers. It makes her feel both enormous and small all at once. She cries often and long for the first few days, but only when no one but her children can see her.

Alphonse gets this weird feeling when he returns to the post office after his round. As soon as he pulls into the lot, it's like people are looking at him sideways. Things are normal—it's probably just nerves makes him feel this way. He puts the undelivered packages in their bins and goes to his locker. Every day he reaches the end of puts him closer to Eloise coming home and everything being all right again. He lifts his T-shirt and rubs Old Spice under each arm. Maybe he'll take Tony to Harold's Chicken tonight.

Elvin taps him on the shoulder. "I need to see you in my office."

And everything Alphonse fears unfolds before him in that moment. Not in every specific, but like a crudely drawn map showing where you start and where you end up, with big, blank spaces in between. He closes his eyes.

"Come on." Elvin puts his hand around Alphonse's arm. "I've done what I can to make this painless as possible."

"Fuck, man." Alph turns to his friend with tears beginning to rise in his eyes. "It was that fucking fire."

"Why'd you do it, Alph? I warned you."

"I just got so tired some days."

"Everybody does, Alph. Doesn't mean you build a bonfire under your own ass."

Alph is shaking his head as they walk toward the glassed-in box where Elvin has his paper-covered metal desk. Two dark-suited men are waiting inside.

"Hurts me as much as it does you," Elvin says. "My ass is in the fire, too."

"I'm sorry," Alph murmurs. He feels the cool trails of the tears on his cheeks.

"There wasn't anything more I could do." Elvin pauses before opening the door. "I couldn't save you."

"I know." Alph blinks and bugs out his eyes to shake off the unmanly desire that is upon him to weep openly, to supplicate himself, to beg for mercy from all those with power over him at this moment—god, the government, his wife and children. He wipes the moisture from his face. "Thanks for trying."

Tony stands in the yard, throwing the baseball up and catching it. He throws it high as he can, and straight, enjoying how it almost disappears against the thin blue evening sky, before racing back, growing larger to slap into his mitt. Wish Dad would hurry up. He's wearing the White Sox cap his dad bought him last summer. He had to let the strap out two notches. Another hat, the one Ronnie gave him, is in the trashcan at the side of the house. Done with that. Ronnie turned out to be just another crazy, unreliable person. Tony wants to make the hat more than garbage. If he could, he'd burn it right now, but his father would be angry.

Aunt Germaine comes across the lawn. Her hands are folded across her stomach. Tony waits for her, holding the ball. Something stiff in her walk.

"Tony, baby." Her hand is cold and soft against his cheek. "Your Daddy ast me to have you eat with us tonight."

"What?" He takes a step back from her. "Why?"

She tries to give him a smile of reassurance. "Oh, he just ran into a little trouble at the office."

"What trouble?"

"Why don't you come on and eat and we'll talk about it later?"

"No. I want to know now."

"It's just. Something happened to some mail and they need to talk to him about it."

He could tell it was only part of the truth. But he didn't know how to ask for the rest. And he was afraid of it.

"Why don't you get your pajamas, too? Because he maybe gone be real late, and you may have to sleep over."

"Just a minute." Tony walks inside the quiet house and stuffs his nightclothes into a plastic grocery bag. He stands for a moment in the quiet house and looks out the window at Aunt Germaine wiping her eyes in the yard. He goes to the back door, lifts the lid of the garbage can, and takes the King 5 hat from underneath the stack of magazines he'd piled on top for camouflage. The hat is slightly damp and smells of coffee grounds. He shakes it for good measure and then puts it in the bag and goes outside to be led away to dinner.

It is many hours before Alph can sit in the shuffling, imperfect quiet of the cell. By chance, he has one to himself. Must be one of the perks of committing a federal offense. Less competition for bed space. Who'd have thought it was federal? He should have known, of course, as a veteran civil servant. But it was so small-time, setting aside a few pieces of mail each week. It was fatigue, is all. "I was just tired," he said to one after another of the somber faces that explained to him just how sorry his immediate fate is to be.

They took away everything, even his shoes.

"Can't have laces," said the fat cop when he asked why.

He begins to wonder what he could do with laces, and comes up with not very much. Maybe he lacks the imagination.

His ass feels tiny and vulnerable on the cot's thin mattress. The springs creak into ever lower registers as he rolls onto his back. It's not nausea, exactly, what he feels. More like his fibers are shaking—bones, muscles, veins. He covers his face again, and then removes his hands quickly. The smell, it's the ink on his fingertips.

He was just tired. He didn't hurt nobody. He used his own kind of scruples on what mail he kept. His only moment of greed maybe was taking those grapefruit. But he more than made that up. Helped that old woman, even a kind of hero.

But so tired. If he could see Tony now, or get some look of understanding love from Eloise, he wouldn't be tired any more, he's sure of it. And now he can do nothing but rest. He curls his knees up and folds his hands under his armpits. There's a breeze from somewhere. Summer's finally broken entirely apart. It's cold. And gently, so as not to create a tell-tale creaking of the springs, he rocks himself to sleep.

October

Wednesday the 4th

Nathan awakens suddenly with the sense that Robin is not beside him. He scans the darkness and finds Robin sitting at the edge of the bed, silhouetted in the dim morning light, motionless, like a piece of wall left standing when the rest has fallen away. Nathan squints through gritty eyeballs at the clock.

Robin senses the movement. "I'm up," he says.

"You don't have to go, you know."

"What can I do, sit home all day watching TV? I can't defend more than two weeks off. They'll fire me."

Nathan wraps an arm around Robin's waist. "Don't worry about that. You don't have to be on anybody's schedule."

Robin says nothing. He sits thinking about the shopping, the cooking, the people he will have to deal with. Might as well climb Everest.

Nathan rolls up onto one elbow. "Honestly, are you sure you're ready?"

"No, of course not. When have I ever been sure? Uncertainty is part of my elusive charm." The fatigued tone of Robin's voice belies the intended humor.

"Just don't kill yourself making something fabulous to assuage your guilt, okay?"

"But lover, that's why I cook," Robin says, disappearing into the bathroom.

Ellen projects the film against the wall of her bedroom. The texture of the paint underneath the images makes them seem ancient, otherworldly, like animated cave paintings. She frowns. The edits are rough—what do you expect working with an X-acto knife on an old pine kitchen table?—but she has to admit that even so, her film exudes a powerful melancholy. She's working on scenes of Alice before they met. She sometimes hugs herself with giggling glee watching the tiny glowing angel on the screen and thinking how much of that image she can now map with her hands.

It needs music, so she re-runs the 90 seconds she has completed with an ad hoc soundtrack of Dvorak's *String Quartet Number Nine in D minor*. The simple scenes swell with grand pathos. She runs the footage again, over *Blue Rondo à la Turk*. The effect is mesmerizing. What do I want to capture, the melancholy of wanting her for so long, or the delirium of finally getting that kiss that I thought would never happen?

Maybe she should add in white-on-black titles, like a silent film? Corny, but if done correctly…. God, how can you choose out of all the world only one thing to express the million billion things you can feel all at once? She rolls back on the bed, exhausted with the possibilities.

Frankly, it's a relief to be busy again after two weeks of hanging around the house, watching too much TV, and napping. Robin's exhaustion surprised even himself. He napped away afternoons until he began to loathe the smell of the couch. At night, he slept little, tossing on sheets hot and scratchy. Nathan apologetically removed himself to the spare bedroom on more than one night, desperate to get a few hours of sleep.

After taking an inventory of the catering kitchen pantry, Robin cabs it down to Randolph Street. They need just about everything. Today will be more shopping than cooking.

The worst thing is Robin feels ugly. He's lost weight, and his hands look positively scrawny. He knows he looks haggard. His hair feels as though he has a terminal case of bed-head. But the idea of staying in one more day makes him feel nauseous. So here he is, bracing himself in the backseat of a cab driven Chicago-style—an emphatic alternation of pressure on the gas and brake pedals.

He tries to focus on the outside. All of the sudden it's become autumn. While he slept, in a sense. Although the summer was brutally hot, he's sorry to see it gone. Won't be another good hot day for another six, seven months.

Suddenly, he reaches up and touches a sealed envelope in his shirt pocket for reassurance. If he lost it now, well, he'd freak.

He does his buying. Plenty of fruit. Mangoes and berries done for the season, but the Michigan apples are in, looking rough and real, not waxed and engineered. And pears—comice, seckel, anjou, bosc. Greens and tomatoes and pattypan squash.

He has the clerk put the box of groceries aside. The cab hasn't returned yet. Maybe now would be a good time. He sits down on an overturned orange crate. The sky is low and scuffling with clouds. The breeze has in it an early taste of the winter's clean, hard bite. He zips up his jacket. But only after he has removed the envelope from his pocket. It is a plain business envelope, sealed. He carefully tears open one end and pours into his hand a pile of coarse, gray ashes.

"Mother," he addresses the ashes. "This is one place I would have shown you, if I could, so you would have understood me and the joy I take in what you taught me about cooking, and about love." He opens his hand and allows the ashes to catch and blow in the breeze. "You were always with me in this place, and now you will be forever." Robin brushes his hands lightly together, folds the envelope, and puts it in the jacket pocket. Looking at the ground, he suddenly notices how soiled and rank it is, with spoiled fruit, cigarette butts, and trampled food wrappers. Perhaps it will rain soon, he thinks. And then prays that it will.

The cab takes Robin up Halsted, past a derelict old bar on Lake Street. He's passed it hundreds of times. But as he glances at the sign outside, it hits him. Stenciled white letters on a rough, black board, it says, FOR THE WAGES OF SIN IS DEATH.

Funny, he thinks, looking at the fine gray film on his palms. Same as the wages of love.

Alice is reveling in the shift of seasons. The autumn flowers that have begun to trickle into the shop have refreshed her sense of play with composition and color. The darker, bruised shades of purple, the reds and deep yellows burnishing toward gold. Maybe now is the time to make another bouquet for Ellen. She begins combining colors and shapes. Nothing too elaborate.

The door jingles and in walks that man. Her mind whirs for a minute to recover his name. Nathan. He is wearing one of the most elegant suits she's ever seen. A fine herringbone in light gray wool. His hair: perfect. His face: perfect.

"Hi," says the perfect mouth.

"Hey." She can tell she is blushing.

"I need something special today." He leans against the counter and sighs. His face relaxes for a moment and reveals the fatigue it carries.

"You look tired. Oh—" she claps her hand to her mouth. "I'm sorry. I shouldn't say that."

Nathan laughs softly. "It's true. I just got back from a funeral. I mean, not just. A few days ago." He rubs his eyes. "Been a long couple of weeks."

"I'm sorry," she says. "Are you all right?" Something about him—the depths of his brown eyes? The sheen of his wind-mussed hair?—makes her want to smooth his brow with her fingers.

"I shouldn't complain. My friend has it worse."

"Robin?"

"As a matter of fact, yes," he says, surprised. "I can't believe you remember."

"From running into you on Belmont that time."

"Long time ago."

"I guess so."

Just then, Nathan moves ever so slightly and his eyes fall in line with hers. There is a momentary shock of looking directly into them. Her stomach yo-yos. And as she looks back at his look, there is, she is almost sure, something in it that she has not seen there before.

He coughs as a way of breaking the glance. "So, I need a kind of somber arrangement. For Robin."

Alice begins pulling together the purple irises that make her think of an old English dowager in mourning. She glances over her shoulder and Nathan's eyes are right there. There it is again, that something in his look. And she reminds herself to keep breathing.

Sunday the 8th

Eloise wakes from a head-achy drowse just in time to see the sign for Cook County pass beyond the gray-tinted bus windows. Her heart sinks. Every milestone along the way home, Eloise has felt sharp stabs of fear. Coming home was supposed to be a relief. But then the phone call from Germaine had come, and they had to rush back to face their lives entirely wrecked, in pieces. As if a twenty-seven-hour bus ride with two month-old babies would not be dreadful enough.

They'd stretched their fellow riders' patience thin as floss, all right. Evander is a crier. His face is most often screwed up into a tiny prune of general unhappiness. Whatever his eyes light upon seems to bring new misery upon him. Only milk and sleep seem to break the cycle of crying fits and recovering from crying fits. His sister Jimelle, on the other hand, has about her a supernatural calm. Her large, liquid eyes absorb the world with an assured readiness. Strangers and family get equal regard. When everything is strange, Eloise thinks, nothing is more strange than anything else. Eloise has seen that look before—Giselle had it—and knows it will slowly fade as the world somehow becomes alien and more terrifying, just the opposite of what you would think. By contrast, Evander's constant perturbation seems quite understandable.

The bus rolls up the Dan Ryan, and Eloise feels her spirits dropping lower and lower. The dirty concreteness of it seems newly horrible to her.

Giselle sleeps with her head against the window, with Evander resting briefly—curled up, mouth open—in her arms. Eloise had seen the wind knocked out of her daughter before, but never as it was at the moment she heard about Alphonse. Seeing a parent fail is a ruinous thing. It takes your childhood away in a moment and replaces it with something that has no exact and comfortable nature. What she prayed for more than anything now was that Giselle would keep her head.

Eloise notices Jimelle looking up at her. She feels as if the infant is asking her for some kind of explanation. And she has none.

Elvin's nose wrinkles instinctively as he enters the old woman's apartment. From experience he knows to expect old people's homes to breathe the squalid odor of fish or cooked cabbage or the pee smell of some old dog kept alive past its days. But there is none of that. A sweet breeze blows in through the open balcony door. He can see past the woman's welcoming smile that the place looks homey and clean. And the dog is a mere puppy. A wiener dog. He is relieved that the dog at least conforms to his expectations.

Mrs. Finkel ushers him inside. "Come in, please. I'm so pleased to meet another friend of Alphonse's."

Elvin steps cautiously. Why do old people make him so nervous? "Alph sure needs all the friends he can get right now."

"He's lucky to work for someone like you." Her sympathy is brisk but sincere. "Tell me again how much for the bail?"

"Seventy-five hundred."

Her skin is almost see-through. He sees the veins living, moving, like aquarium creatures underneath a cover of barely frosted glass.

"I'm glad to help any way I can." She writes out the numbers in cursive and then pulls the check from the book carefully, popping each individual perforation before moving on to the next.

"Now, you tell him for me that I expect to hear from him as soon as he gets settled again."

"I sure will."

"Would you care for something to drink? Tea? Soda?"

"No. I should get down there. Sooner I do, sooner he gets out." Must be money keeps everything so clean and fresh, he thinks. Keeps her well-preserved.

"Is there any chance he'll work for the postal service again?"

"No ma'am. If he pleads his way out of jail time, I'd say he's in line for a new career."

Something is obviously troubling the old girl. Elvin searches for the right phrase to get out the door quick. He knows how old people can spin a story to keep you prisoner for days. And then she puts a hand on his arm. Oh brother, here we go, he thinks.

"I just wonder." She looks at him squarely. "Do you think that's what he wanted all along?"

"What, jail?"

She chuckles at the misunderstanding. "No, no. I mean to say, do you think he wanted to quit but didn't know how?"

Elvin swallows an impolite laugh. After all, she is doing a generous thing. But he can see that what this old lady doesn't understand about Alphonse would fill Lake Michigan.

"Just maybe," she adds with surprising force, "maybe Alphonse has some other dream he's been sitting on all this time."

"Could be," Elvin allows. "He sure didn't dream about delivering mail."

The old lady, he can see, is less than satisfied with that answer.

After school, the King 5s collect at a hot dog place near the el stop. Tony sits quietly attentive as the bigger boys banter back and forth. Ronnie's suddenly the most rock-solid thing in Tony's world. Ronnie does business. He knows the gang codes and how to be strong in ways that are obvious and real. Other boys follow him like a hero. And he seems to want Tony around.

The shop is mostly empty. People come in and out, ordering char-dogs and cheese fries. The odor of old oil and burnt cheese is powerful. The boys sit near the door, where a fine breeze puffs in every so often, challenging the primacy of the ancient fast-food smells.

Darol stands, legs wide apart, rapidly tapping the control buttons of Kung Fu Firestorm III, which emits a barrage of digital cracks, explosions, and roars. He throws body english at the game and emits his own guttural emphasis. It looks like competitive typing. When a timely thorax kick induces a generous geyser of digital crimson blood from his digital opponent, he whoops.

The shop owner brings over an order of fries. He singles out Tony for a once-over. "Hey, little man." He grabs the bill of Tony's cap and tilts it back to get a good look at him. "Why you want to be hanging round with these punks? Huh?"

"Aw, shut up, old man," Darol says.

"He my little bro," Ronnie says, throwing an arm around Tony's neck.

The man's eyes narrow with suspicion. "That right, son?"

Tony nods, but avoids the man's eyes.

"Bunch a punks looking for trouble," the man mutters.

Tony scrunches down against Ronnie's side. Ronnie's windbreaker smells musty and unwashed. It exhales a warm body smell that Tony finds comforting.

"We ain't give you no trouble, awright?" Ronnie says. "Just buying some fry for my little bro." He picks up a couple of fries and stabs them in the direction of Tony's mouth. "Nice family meal."

The old man shakes his head and walks away.

Tony eats the fries, hot and salty, mashed on one end by Ronnie's fingers. And he's a little sorry when Ronnie removes his arm, saying, "Hey, don't eat all the damn fries, little bitch," and, laughing, squirts four packets of ketchup over the fries until they glisten.

Alphonse can't stop hunching his shoulders. Even with Elvin playing that soft jazz radio station, supposed to soothe you. The car windows are down, allowing the rich lake odors to sweep through the car. They are passing the South Shore golf course, giving Alphonse pangs of better days.

Elvin breaks the silence. "You ever wonder about that fire? Maybe not being some accident?"

Alph turns sharply. "What? Why would you say that?"

"Don't know. Just looked funny. From what I heard."

"Nobody said anything like that to me."

"They had other concerns."

"Guess so." Alph falls silent again as they pass two maple trees across the street from each other like a gateway. He sees how they've taken their autumn colors on the outside leaves first, as though the orange, gold and scarlet were rained down on them from the lowering sky. He is humble before every manifestation of god.

"What you think is going to happen to me?"

Elvin drives with the Detroit lean, one arm out the window, only two fingers of the other hand nonchalantly on the wheel.

"Short-term or long-term?"

"Both."

"I've got a buddy who's a lawyer. Says he'll take your case. He already told me you got to plead yourself out."

"Meaning what?"

"Meaning don't go in saying innocent on account of insanity or stupidity or any of that bull. Say you're sorry and take what comes."

"That doesn't sound very—"

Elvin gives him the look that Alphonse has given his own children, meaning, think over what you're about to say.

"Okay," Alph says with a sigh. "And long-term? I need a new career, right?"

Elvin bobs his head casually, as if, well, no shit.

They are heading into the beginnings of sunset now, the sky starting to blush. The houses and streets begin to lose the faded glamour of the old lakeside developments.

Alph feels his shoulders beginning to bunch up on him again. "Could we not go straight to my house? I'm not quite ready to see everyone."

"Let your family see *you*, Alph." Elvin negotiates a turn circling his index finger inside the steering wheel. "You got to be strong for each other now."

The presence of the babies has the effect of a balm on everyone's shattered nerves. Even when Evander cracks open another one of his roof-rattling crying jags, which begins just when Alphonse takes the baby in his arms.

The grandfather jiggles the baby's tiny hand in pointless supplication.

"Gracious." He looks up, his face swimming with a hundred emotions. "Guess he has the good sense to be afraid of me."

Eloise and Giselle close round, embracing grandfather and child.

"There is nothing this family can't survive," Giselle says. "I should know. I've put everyone through enough."

Alphonse begins to rock himself and the child, both of them now crying over how the world has beset them without warning, cause, or sense.

"Speaking of family," Giselle nudges Eloise. "Where's my baby brother?"

Friday the 13th

Not that Elias is a superstitious man, but the first frost of the season falling on Friday the thirteenth feels ominous. Then he challenges his pessimism. What's wrong with winter? It's not as though summer offered any special blessings. Let winter come. But when he walks out to the garage and sees two members of his piñata zoo—the toucan and sombrero—down on the ground and broken among the dry and curled leaves, that's when he thinks it may well signal a long and unpleasant day. No way to tell if it's animal or human mischief. The paper-wrapped candies appear to be untouched. He gathers the pieces into a garbage bag. He looks at the piñatas that remain among the leafless branches. Their tissue paper fur has been bleached by the sun and flattened by the rain. They glimmer with patches of frost. Oh well. It's time to take them down, anyway. His mood is black as he drives to work.

Ivan has proven to be a real pain in the ass about the logo. It's a good thing that Ng has been able to find some pleasure in working on the damn thing. Otherwise, he'd have liked to fire Ivan as a client. But can you fire someone who'd probably send five guys to kick your ass?

They meet at the McDonalds again, after school and Ivan once more regards the design with a critic's eye-squinting and chin-fingering appraisal.

"Can make dragon more fiercer?" Ivan taps his finger on the dragon's snout. "Teeth more like knife?"

"Ivan, this is the fifth version I've done. You keep changing what you want."

"But I like very much!" Ivan insists. "Only small change." He smiles ingratiatingly. It gives Ng a dizziness something like vertigo.

Still, Ivan's eager as a puppy. Whenever they meet, he has some new idea of how he wants to use the image. As though people all over the city are going to want shirts and caps sporting his gang's logo.

Ng glances over his shoulder. He has the strangest feeling that someone is there.

He sketches quickly on top of his artwork. "How about this?"

"Yes, yes!" Ivan says, happily. "That's it, that's final. We make into billboard. Big big over street." His eyes are glazed over with the power of his newfound weapon: advertising.

Seeing Ng with that punk again is the final straw. Danny's seen enough to know that they have reached some kind of truce. But that only serves to increase his fear. What compromise has been struck, or what threats made?

He calls Stacey from a dank bar near the corner of Lawrence and Broadway and tells her that he's in Stony Island drinking with some of the guys from the crew. He knows she can hear the liquor in his voice, so it's pretty convincing.

"Whatever," she says. "Just don't wake me up when you come in."

"Sure, I'll be quiet. You sleep tight now, punkin."

When he hangs up, it is, for a moment, as if Stacey is a part of his life he is putting behind him. As though she and Soo have traded places. And it makes him suddenly angry. But he has to admit, what Stacey doesn't know about his inner life could choke a goddamn whale. The hours he has spent lurking around his first family has become like a stain, spreading out, obscuring his motives, even to himself.

He hasn't planned this moment, exactly, but he's been ready for it, wearing dark colors and carrying a crowbar and club-sized flashlight in the trunk. He waits at the bar until it closes, staring into his glass. Then he drives up to the building he saw the gang kid enter. At this time of night, the streets are as quiet as they ever get. He parks one alley over and, taking the crowbar and flashlight, makes his way to the vacant building. He watches the entrance until he is satisfied that everyone has cleared out. He creeps down to the basement entrance. The door gives ways easily, held closed only by a simple spring lock. He stands, listening for movement before turning on his flashlight and panning it across the room.

What he sees is the furtive banality of adolescence. A couple of mildewed couches salvaged from the alley. Porno mags by the dozen. Empty liquor bottles and the trash of a hundred fast-food meals. He inspects some draw-ings taped to the wall, some kind of dragon emblem that must be the gang's I.D. He kicks through the magazines and garbage. No weapons, nothing interesting. Another door at the back of the room has a more serious lock on it. The wormy wood succumbs with one swing of the crowbar. He is panting now, all nerves and movement.

This room is different, orderly, with a burnt and medicinal stink. There are unmarked buckets of liquid, sterno cans, and cakes of a hard, dark brown substance wrapped in plastic. He cuts into one of the bricks and sniffs it. A fresh surge of adrenaline sends his mind into hyperspace. He is going to set Ng free of these people. He places several open fuel cans on a couch. On top of these he piles magazines and all of the heroin bricks. He moves quickly, instinctively, his mind loosed, freed by booze and a white-hot energy in his blood. With his lighter, he sets a corner of a *Hustler* on fire.

Danny bombs down the Dan Ryan in his Impala with the windows open, slapping the steering wheel in time to ZZ Top as the wind chills the sweat along his hairline. He can't wait to get home and slide into the sheets next to Stacey. Maybe he'll wake her, and they'll make love. And then he will sleep deeply. And dream.

Sunday the 15th

In her newly recovered solitude, Florence realizes that space only makes concrete the more abstract spaces you hold inside. As concrete as the far, smooth side of the king-size bed. Or the green, sagging bottom of the La-Z-Boy recliner. The scroll-backed chair at the dinner table, the one Arnie always complained about. And the guest room, filled so many weeks with Louise's barging presence, now tidy and still as a museum diorama. Florence pauses to reflect on the room's seeming vastness and shoos the dog off the bed. A faint circle of brown hair remains in the dented quilt. She clucks her tongue. Duchess skulks to her water dish.

But Florence isn't sad. And at least her time is full these days, despite the echoing space left by Louise's departure. She'll have time now to rededicate herself to her painting. Having supper at the diner again with Elias. And of course she'll have room to wrestle with the status of her heart. The moment is coming—she can feel it, like a weather system that signals a new season—when her feelings for Tommy Falco will pass from a pleasant distraction to—dare she even think it?—love. That she is flowing into this romance so smoothly amazes her. How could it be so easy, nothing more auspicious than a cloud crossing the county line? No cataclysm. Just a kind of natural order taking hold.

Arnie was a man raised to do business. Every Saturday morning, from seven to eleven, he was at his desk, organizing the next week. It was more important to him than religion, keeping his life on the rails. He was the fully realized twentieth-century American Male. Everything had a place for Arnie. Even romance. So he was romantic, in the sense that he made time for Florence, to dine out, buy her gifts and such, but his feeling for life was more what you would call practical. Saturday afternoon to Sunday night was personal time. The schedule was rigid. Not in a painful way, but in order to keep chaos at bay, to make the most of time, to succeed. Tommy has shown her another way to live. With her senses open, savoring, letting perfume, food, and wine flavor her days. His Mediterranean zest feels natural and right to her, almost like Tommy is an outgrowth of her painting, a fresh look at the world.

What business does a seventy-three-year-old woman have being alive, she asks herself, much less, *alive*?

After she gets the mail from the new mailman, a sulking boy with stringy hair, Florence brightens to see a card from the Duchossois family. It is a thank-you signed by Alphonse and Eloise. It also contains a snapshot of Alphonse looking dazed and grateful holding two tiny babies—his newborn grandchildren, the note says.

That family has its hands full, she thinks. Then she sits down at her desk and takes out her checkbook. You can't take it with you, she smiles to herself. So you might as well use it to give someone a push. She wonders briefly if Arnie will appear to stop her hand, but as if to chide herself for thinking ill of him, she writes a larger figure than the one she had originally intended. So there.

Wednesday the 18th

Chipper has been a complete piss-ant since his plan for funding the Lather demo CD was nixed by the band chicks. He's been making grumbling noises about common vision and artistic control. He makes excuses for missing a couple of rehearsals, like he's some kind of union worker on a sick-out.

"But you're the drummer, remember?" Alice wants to say. "Rhythm, not melody."

Molly wants to summarily kick Chipper out of the band. Shanklin has remained firmly unaligned. Molly and Alice start referring to him as Swiss Mister. But they know that with the usual deep sympathy between members of the rhythm section, plus the girls versus boys coloration of the whole squabble, he would probably split along with Chipper.

At any rate, the sour vibe affects everybody equally. Rehearsals are no fun. To Alice, it's like déjà vu all over again. After everything, to rebound this far after Brad's defection only to fall apart again over an issue orchestrated by Lori? It's almost more than she can stomach.

At least everybody makes it to the rehearsal today. Chipper is smug with cosmic righteousness.

"Have you heard the Caffeine City ads on the radio?" He is fiddling with the wing nuts on his cymbals. Spin on, spin off, spin on, spin off. Alice can tell it's just posturing so he can make everyone listen to him.

"Yeah, I heard them." Alice knows what's coming.

"Sweet airplay. Q101, XRT, the Loop. That could have been us. What would have been so wrong with that?"

"Well, either the fact that we would have had to sing that stupid faux-Ramones ditty, *Gimme Gimme Caffeine*—"

"Or," Molly jumps in, "the fact that you still think with your dick when it comes to Lori."

"That has nothing to—this is *business*," he says. "Fame or failure. We made the decision to stick together. That means doing what it takes to succeed."

"Oy, Machiavelli," Molly says.

Alice finally snaps, "Chip, why has this got you so worked up? There are a jillion similar things we could go after. Why this one?"

He's frozen by the question.

"Anyway," Molly interjects, "Caffeine City has gotten on with their lives. So can we. The problem remains, where do we get the money for the disc?"

"I brought you my idea already. Someone else's turn now," Chipper says, still spinning the wing nut—*on, off, on, off.*

"A bake sale?" Molly says, throwing her hands out like, ta-da.

Chipper drills her with a look. Shanklin quickly turns to a problem with his tuning pegs.

"What? I'm serious. We could have it at Urbs, maybe?"

"Right," Chipper says, "and we earn enough to record a four-track cassette."

"Does it matter so much, Chip? As long as we feel good about what we do?"

"How could you feel good about a bullshit tape over a CD?"

"Whatever we do, no Lori," Alice says. "Period."

Brad's not sure why he chose Molly to call. Who else? Not Alice. And not one of the guys. So Molly it is. He needs to announce his decision immediately, and anyway, he's drunk. Tonight was his final set at Bar Quito, all the musicians buzzing with rumors of an unnamed Elektra exec in the house, and for all of his ten minutes he quite thoroughly sucked. At one point he not only forgot the words to a song he had written in just the last two days, but also had stared at the neck of his guitar like it was some kind of inscrutably interesting wood carving without apparent purpose. He stared into the lights and realized he was lost in every possible sense of the word, physically and morally displaced. But at least Bar Quito has a deep inventory of rye whiskeys, which he now knows—and this piece of knowledge is disproportionately critical to him at this moment—are a great way to figure out how drunk you are because, if they taste good you must be near death from liver damage.

Molly answers the phone in a voice croaky with sleep. Brad starts right in, speaking softly and urgently. It's taken him hours of drinking to come to this reckless point, and he doesn't want to lose the momentum.

"What it is, I've been thinking about why I came here, and why I can't be happy. I think it's that I came here because of a lie. Almost from the beginning I've been here feeling like a dupe. Because someone had a crush on me, because I had a crush on them, I mean, I gave up a life that made sense to come here and suffer. Everything that's happened since then is tainted by that lie. And this whole time, really, I think I've been just waiting for the right time to go back and try to fix things."

"What? You're coming back? Now?" Molly says hoarsely. "I hope you're not expecting *me* to be thrilled. Or Alice either. The world has moved on, Brad. It wasn't waiting for you."

He feels a sense of gratitude for Molly's honesty even as it shreds the barely formed fantasies he'd begun to form in his mind.

"I don't know what I expect."

"Okay, Brad. Whatever."

He hears the phone settle back into its cradle. And despite Molly's reaction, he is flooded with a sense of buoyant relief. He looks around the room, and sees it will take no more than a couple of hours to pack everything.

Saturday the 21st

Weird how you don't always feel as happy as you think you're going to feel when something happens that you thought was going to make you happy. That's as close as Tony can get to why, despite his mother and sister's return, he finds himself staying away from home as much as he can. It's just not a place he wants to be.

Giselle walks around half-asleep, carrying this or that baby. Momma has nervous energy that keeps her running from room to room. But the worst is his father's attempts to pretend that nothing's wrong. His fatherly touch, now full of silent appeals, makes Tony want to squirm away and run outside.

Alphonse pokes his head inside Tony's room. "Play some ball with your old man?"

Tony keeps his eyes on his book. "I got homework."

In past days, his father would have cajoled him outside. But all he says now is, "All right, son. Sorry to bother you."

The days are bright and clear, with a dry, cloudless sky that you can almost see contracting toward winter, like the mouth of a sack being closed up over you.

"Don't make me worry about you, baby." Eloise strokes his head before moving on to fuss with a baby or dinner or laundry.

Tony ducks away, prickled with a sudden rash of sickly goosebumps. He has a million questions about what's going on, but he keeps mum. Anyway, he's got other things going on.

Alphonse eats his meals slowly these days, in part to savor the home cooking that he has missed for so long, but more because shame has settled into his joints and muscles like an arthritis. Almost as though he's relearning all the parts of living. He thinks of Mrs. Finkel after her stroke, crinkled on one side of her face, tilted, having to teach her hand its own business.

Used to be sadness gathered up slowly, like leaves in the gutter. Those rocky places in marriage. The way Giselle moved away from them in little invisible changes, not one big jump. The way Tony is becoming like she was, aloof, secretive. You never see it happening, just look up one day and you can't recognize the world. You can't see yourself when you look at your own eyes in the bathroom mirror. But never have so many problems clumped in one place that a big wind couldn't return things to normal. Like Giselle coming home, ready to live as a part of them again. Eloise back at his side, giving love and support. He looks at his hand holding a forkful of scrambled eggs, and it feels detached, like a strange other being that he has to petition for each bite of breakfast.

Today he starts his community service. Given a list of options, he has chosen to work at a night basketball program run by the park district. The other men there will know he's there by direct order, a criminal. But the boys won't know. He hopes they won't, anyway.

So everything can be ripped apart. He understands something about the world now that he never knew before. He would have respected it more.

His teeth grind the bacon under protest.

Jimelle is at her bottle now. Evander has just been burped and is falling twitchingly asleep in the crib. A moment of quiet.

Giselle's life is a stutter-step cycle of feeding, burping, diapering—a new rhythm obliterating the old regime of day and night. Eloise and Auntie Germaine give her breaks, for which she's grateful, but she knows they don't understand just how little of her schedule they are able to relieve. She often thinks of the babies as like one of those pro wrestling tag teams, combining to pummel her to the mat. With a finger, she lightly sketches a mask on Jimelle's tiny, velvety face. Her daughter sighs—the pitch and tone of a happy animal—and shudders. Her tiny fingers work the air.

There has to be something more, Giselle thinks. She has no idea how to make this work.

She turns at a sound in the bushes near the window. She tries to see through the glass, but the lamplight whitewashes the night. All she sees is herself. And the face that stares back startles her, until she makes it smile back.

Even though he hasn't slept at all, when Tony opens his eyes in the dark, it feels funny—as queasy as waking to a loud noise, but also special, exciting, like the few times he and his father got up in the dark to drive over into Indiana to fish in the dawn light. He dresses, shivering from cold and fear, shoving his legs through the jeans that seem strangely heavy and unyield-ing. Last, he pulls the King 5 hat onto his head. He climbs out his window, stepping carefully between the evergreen bushes and the house. And, just like that, he is outside. He rounds the house to the alley, past the square of burnt concrete and lumber, and breaks into a run, out into the alley, over to meet Ronnie.

Eloise checks the clock. Almost ten. Alph won't be home for a couple of hours. Should she wait up, or catch up on her sleep? He needs everything she can give him now. Finding her asleep he might think she didn't care how it went on his first night of service. When really, that's all she can think about. Please god, make it painless.

Poor Alph. Walking out all hunched and slow like a man made old overnight. His teeth don't even seem to fit his head anymore, like they all the sudden became false ones you can set in a glass of water. She wants to shake him, put him back together, throw a new battery in, and make him go like he used to. He's like an old boy she once saw after he got spider-bit and his muscles kind of seized up on him. Watching him drink a glass of sweet tea could make you crazy with the trembling and the rattling of the ice. She folds back the paper. The Jumble's done, and word search. Now the crossword puzzle. It will take her two hours at least, if she can stay awake.

Darol pulls the car next to the LeBaron convertible so that Ronnie's side is next to the other driver.

"Yo." The man doesn't look over. "You need something?"

"Yeah." Ronnie's voice pitched low.

The man chuckles. "You can't afford nothing."

"Hell I can't. Show me the goods, I'll get the green."

The parking lot runs for several blocks along the lake. The cars parked here and there maintain a careful distance between one another. Tony watches them for a moment, but can't see anything other than shadowy heads moving every so often and cigarette smoke threading from thin spaces at the tops of the windows.

"What you think, Lem? He can't afford no guns."

"Look like he want things he can't afford," says a voice from the other side of the LeBaron.

"I don't see no guns, neither," Ronnie says.

The man tosses a paper bag into Ronnie's lap. "Check it out, my man."

Tony cranes his head to see the gun. Matte black, almost invisible in the darkness. He can almost feel its weight as Ronnie hefts it, inspects the clip, and snaps the trigger a couple of times.

"Who that with you?" says the man. "In the back, he looks familiar."

"I'm not," Tony says, quickly shrinking into the back seat.

Ronnie looks back at Tony. "You know this guy?"

"No," Tony says.

The man is peering into the car and then gives up. "Okay, what you say? Deal?"

Ronnie shrugs. "Awright. We'll take six."

The referee whistles and the biting squeaks of air-soled shoes on the varnished wooden floor remind Alphonse of the calls of exotic birds at the zoo. Things with great, garish-colored, clacking beaks replaced by boys with long, baggy shorts, shiny jackets, baseball hats—a different riot of color.

The high windows are cranked open, to keep the refrigerator-sized radiator in the rafters from overheating the room. The exertions of the boys' bodies lace the air with a penetrating smell.

Alph waves players on and off the court, gesturing like a traffic cop. "Okay, let's rotate the teams now. Let's see some team ball now. Can't everybody dunk on every possession."

Most of the boys have a hard look already, and generally ignore him. But he likes the regulated chaos of the game, the boys' energy. He feels like a father again, with temporary sons whom he has not yet failed.

Monday the 23rd

Leda is determined to change Ng's fortunes. She doesn't care anything about comics, not like the absurd passion of the customers who come to Stimpy's, but Ng has made her interest personal, and she knows more clearly than she knows just about anything else that he is meant to be one of those weird, depressive artists in color print on the store shelves.

It wasn't easy to sneak Ng's drawings out of his room. It took her several visits and lots of misdirection—Can you get me some water? What's that noise? Is that your mom? One by one, she accumulated enough drawings to make a sort of portfolio. She scribbles a note to Mr. Slivnick. He is an elusive person, only coming into the store during business hours once every three or four months. He usually comes in looking just-awakened and unshaved, asks what's selling and when he last gave her a raise. Then he shuffles a few papers on his desk and, about fifteen minutes later and looking quite bewildered, leaves again with a distracted wave.

This has to work, she thinks. Otherwise, Ng might never come back to his old self again.

Hey Mr. S., I thought you'd be interested in seeing this. If you have any thoughts about how my friend could get published in one of those magazines, I'd sure be grateful. Leda.

His shirt is always caught between tucked and untucked. One tail in, one tail out.

She slips the envelope onto Mr. Slivnick's desk where he won't be able to miss it. Here goes nothing. She stops herself. What does that mean, anyway? Here goes everything.

The white Impala crawls through the small, cramped, one-way streets like a rat in a mouse's maze, moving quickly, undeterred by dead ends, oblivious to the narrowing of the walls between which he moves. But there is no cheese in the center of the maze. In this maze, the target is elusive. Ivan is the cheese.

Danny has dropped into combat mode. He has not imagined or planned his actions when he finds the boy. It will happen. As the moment unfolds, his purpose will find its expression. He starts at the high school and works his way out, criss-crossing through alleys, crawling past liquor stores and any loitered-on corners. He gets a lot of angry stares, and stares back angrily. He guns down Granville all the way to the lake, then turns back and roars west, turning up and down streets according to no other plan than his gut. He has a bat, a hunting knife, a crowbar, gloves, and three bottles of beer. He tunes the radio to an oldies station. The worst thing now would be not to find the boy and be left with this electricity in his system. But somehow he knows that it won't come to that.

Ng has been aware that the leaves are coming down every day, but it seems abrupt that the trees are now bare, the craggy black limbs of the oaks inked against the slate sky. The elegant upreach of the elm branches is like a protest, an appeal to keep the winter away. Ng draws supplicant trees on the back of his McDonald's tray mat. And then above them he draws a version of Leda that he keeps seeing in his mind, with hair alive and writhing, almost like that Greek lady with the snakes on her head.

"Hey, my friend." Ivan drops into the molded plastic chair across from Ng. He has been very somber for the last couple of weeks and hasn't asked about the logo. Ng finally asked him to look at a final final sketch, just to get the whole process over with. He's having dreams about the stupid dragon. Enough already.

Ivan flicks a nail at the scribbled mat. "Working hard?"

"Just doodling." Ng pulls his dragon sketch out of his portfolio. "Here it is, my best effort."

Ivan looks at it briefly. "This very best. Very good. Thank you much. How much I say to pay you?"

Ng is unsettled by Ivan's abstract demeanor. "Don't worry about it. We're trading favors."

Ivan gives him a fierce look. "No favors. Make contract, keep contract."

"Whatever you think it's worth, then."

Ivan crosses his arms. "You think I not know business? Good logo not cheap. Five hundred."

"Five hundred?" Ng laughs and grabs the edge of the table to keep himself in his seat. "Five? Hundred?" he repeats. He looks down and sees his thumb in a spill of old ketchup.

"Sure," Ivan says, looking tired. He produces a thin billfold and, with discreet, practiced motions, counts out five Ben Franklins.

"Jesus," Ng says, his mind racing to capture what five hundred dollars means, exactly. The bills settle weightlessly into his palm, like the merest feathers.

"I going now," Ivan says abruptly. "Much business." He returns the artwork to the portfolio. "Bring to school tomorrow, I not want to carry tonight."

"Sure, okay." Ng is pleasantly fogged in a shock of sudden opportunity. His fingers close over the bills and their crispness, the reality of their paper, gives him a shiver of excitement.

Ivan makes himself steer clear of the old basement on his way up to the new place. He feels drawn back to look for answers. But he knows better. The fire wasn't an accident, he is sure. He can't exactly ask the fire inspector. It's just a gut feeling. It's getting dark early now. He zips up his jacket, feeling the hard shape of the knife inside the lining.

The upper floors had collapsed into the basement. The building was reduced to four ragged walls, the remaining windows blown out and smeared with black like a woman's eyes after crying. He'd walked past it the next day, looking for the building he remembered. When he realized what he was looking at, he scrambled into the still-warm ruins, stumbling over charred beams and fractured mortar. Down where their stuff would have been, it was still hot to the touch, and he juggled stinging bits of melted plastic in his fingers, wondering if some powerful chemical process could salvage any of the hash.

He came to his senses later. And then the rage began to build.

He walks with his head down, thinking, thinking about his enemies. Somebody better take credit, so he can get busy with his revenge. Why would nobody take credit, to enjoy his temporary victory? He checks the handles of a few cars. One is unlocked, but offers nothing worth stealing. He pockets a chewed-up Bic pen out of habit.

They had relocated their den quickly. Plenty of boarded-up buildings to choose from in this part of Uptown—the renovations haven't reached every last block yet. But the clean, sand-blasted apartments are within shouting distance, and Ivan knows the police will be cruising the area more often, now that bright new SUVs are parked on these streets, and soon he'll have to take his business to another part of town.

"Don't move, punk."

Ivan feels the blunt pressure of something cold and hard against his neck.

"Didn't get the message yet, huh?" The breath on his neck is boozy, and the voice it carries is a white man's voice, deep and low.

"What message? Who? What you want?"

A jab with the gun. "I saw you giving money to that kid. What does it take to get you to back off?"

"What money? You crazy." Ivan tries to see what kind of gun the man has.

"Keep still. Hands where I can see them."

Ivan freezes.

"Stay away from that boy is all I want. Go fuck with kids in some other part of town."

"What kid? I no fucking with any kid."

"Ng," the man says. "Stay away from Ng."

Ivan glimpses the end of the gun—and sees it is merely a length of pipe. He whirls then, reaching for his knife. But he'd zipped it in, dammit, and in the time it took to reach into the pocket, the man swings the pipe down on Ivan's wrist, sending the boy lurching back in pain as something in the small network of bones cracks and sends up his arm a flare of pain.

Through his wincing eyes he sees the man—large, with greasy black hair falling in his face. Eyes large and wild.

"I know what to do," the man says. "If I have to."

"Get the fuck away you crazy," Ivan says.

"Call the police," the man says. "Go ahead."

Ivan turns and, clutching his arm, hurries away from the crazy man. The curses and vengeful things he wants to say are still forming in his mind. He hears the pipe ring against the pavement where the man has tossed it. He keeps going.

Only later does he realize that it is Ng—evil, deceptive Ng—who has brought this pain on him. And his rage, like sunlight passing through a lens, collects itself on this one tiny point, and begins to burn.

Thursday the 26th

Ellen is determined that finishing her film will somehow change things for the better. It will convince her parents that she's serious, she hopes, and maybe buy her some leniency from the college. She's developed this idea of getting back into the program in the spring, having blown right past the fall application period.

And these ideas find fuel because, really, the film is coming along well. Of course, that depends on when you ask her. She works on it a few hours every day, and in that time she usually runs the full range of emotions from bliss to despair. It is time, she decides, to embrace the risk. Was anything worthwhile ever created without a leap of faith? It's almost a cliché now, about independent films getting made on maxed-out credit cards. But do people understand the heedless passion it takes to put every dollar, even future ones, at risk? You make your own safety only by rejecting how others define it for you.

She makes a list of personal heroes: The Lumière Brothers, Chabrol, Akerman, Svankmajer, Linklater, Varda, the Coens, the Keatons (Buster and Diane), Scorsese (of course), Greenaway, Techiné, Anders, Cronenberg, Soderbergh. She takes pride in leaving off the list nearly every Boring White Male they studied in school. Spielberg my butt. Fassbinder can stick it. Truffaut—don't get me started.

It's almost a guilty pleasure, toying with the sequences, manipulating the frames by hand. It's more a film than a visible, moving object. She begins to write a polemic describing how her film should be viewed. She cries, alone in her apartment, sometimes, at what she has made. Which always brings Marty to rub against her with plaintive concern.

She feels stranded at times, and crazy.

She scribbles "Sundance 2002 or Bust!" on the erasable memo board on her refrigerator.

Of course, it's Ellen's savings that are going quickly bust, especially the way she's showering gifts on Alice. It's hard not to, she explains when Alice protests her latest present—a cream-colored Irish cable-knit sweater.

"Everything I see means something to me about how I feel for you."

Alice pulls the sweater over her head, then flips her blonde hair free—a beautiful movement.

"You're writing country songs now?" she laughs.

"You have my permission to use it if you want."

"Maybe I will, maybe I won't." Her lower lips extends itself like a young strawberry.

When Alice teases like that, it means, kiss me.

So Ellen does. Until they become self-conscious about being in the café. Alice has this theatrical way of coughing that signals, okay, return to Normal Behavior. Kissing girls, to Alice, is still Not Normal.

"So what happened to your friend?" Alice plucks idly at the sweater. "Megan?"

Every time this comes up, Ellen feels like a criminal. "I don't know. We haven't talked."

"But you will, right? I mean, people don't just disappear like that."

"Sometimes they do."

"She seemed pretty stubborn about getting you back."

Ellen shrugs. "She'll maybe call someday. We were friends for a pretty long time. Would that bother you?"

"No. Of course you should still be friends." What other answer is there? Alice wonders.

They link fingers and begin stirring their coffees intently, looking for a way to dispel the moment of discomfort when a relationship begins to look rather small in the light of time.

Which is when, like a bull stumbling through a break in a fence line, Ellen's father walks into the café.

"Dad?" Ellen stares in disbelief.

Tyler stares back. "Ellen?"

Alice looks at them both, and slides her fingers away from Ellen's. It kind of tickles, like a handful of water trickling away.

Even though she didn't really want to leave, Ellen allows Tyler to give her a ride home. His car is more cluttered than an office, with a memo pad stuck to the windshield, a cel phone with speaker attached to the sun visor, a notebook computer in the backseat, folders, binders, insulated coffee mugs, a battery-powered razor, an ashtray full of cigarette butts.

Tyler pats her leg. "Well, I'm glad I bumped into you."

"And why does this make you glad?"

Tyler runs a finger inside his collar. "Well. I understand you never took that job I set up for you."

"I didn't have time." Beyond the strip of park land at Wilson Avenue, the lake is the color of ashes. A burned-out alien landscape, the ashes rain-stirred into a heavy, granular putty.

"No time? What are you living on? Do you have a plan?"

"I sold a few things. My TV. And I plan to keep working on the film as much as I can."

Tyler raises one beefy palm. "Hey, whoa. Are we still talking about that film course? I thought you had decided—"

"I hadn't decided anything. I just had to stop taking classes for a while."

"But what does that lead to? We thought, your mother and I, that working for a while, being on your own—"

Ellen hits the power window button, and the air rushes in, rich with brown, sere smells.

"You asked me my plan, Dad, that's my plan."

"Here we are," Tyler says, pulling the car up in front of her apartment. "Will you please reconsider that job? You'll eventually run out of things to sell."

"I'm not ready to give in yet." Ellen jams her finger on the button that powers the window back up.

"Honey, why don't you let me put some feelers out? I'm sure I could turn up some kind of job you'd like. It's time," he says with gravity, "for you to get serious about your life."

It's like a slap. Ellen stares at her father, trying not to fall to pieces.

"There are different kinds of serious, Dad." She steps out of the car and gives the door a push.

Tyler leans across the passenger seat. "Honey, I don't mean—"

But the well-constructed door muffles whatever it was he didn't mean.

Alice makes a special trip to Rogers Park at Ellen's urgent request. It's way out of her way, and she's a little annoyed. It seems somehow too early in the relationship to be called on for such emotional support.

Ellen buzzes her in, and the apartment door is open. Ellen is wrapped in a knitted afghan on the couch. She looks pretty wrecked, Alice thinks. She settles in at Ellen's feet.

"What is it, El?"

"Dad's on the job warpath again. He said I wasn't *serious* about my life."

"He just meant his kind of serious. You know how parents are. They worry."

"Fuck him, you know? Just fuck him for saying that."

"Oh, Ellen. I think it's kind of sweet how they worry about you. It's all they have to express their love with."

Ellen gives her a disgusted look. "You don't understand." Her disappointment is tangible.

Alice says nothing. It isn't that she has no empathy, but that she can only find it on the most general level, as one can feel pain seeing a family stand outside their burning house on the TV news. This kind of generalized empathy is possible to do, Alice has found, just walking down the street, if you look at a person and imagine their hardships, the ones you can be 99 percent sure they've had to go through, or are going through at that moment. Birth, death, money troubles, funerals, hateful bosses. It can break your heart.

Ellen wants more than that, deserves more. But Alice is left wandering in that broad field of imagination, never able to get closer to the richly contextualized pain that Ellen is suffering, and they both want to drop the moment, as though it has become a totem of how tenuous their attachment really is.

Alice checks her watch. "Shit, I have to go. We're meeting with a producer tonight about the demo."

Ellen looks out the window. "Okay. Have a good time."

"Look, I'm sorry. I'll call you later. Okay?"

Ellen only moves her shoulders in reply. Alice leans over and kisses her forehead. Ellen touches her cheek briefly, sadly.

∞

After sulking her way through a pint of chocolate ice cream, Ellen rouses herself from the couch and puts all of her film and editing equipment in the bedroom closet and closes the door. Just for now. Everything that is about Life Meaning has to be put out of eyesight for tonight. She nukes a bag of popcorn and sits down to watch some stupid old Van Johnson movie.

The phone rings. She leaps for the receiver, absolutely certain it's Alice calling to smooth over the rough parting.

"Hello?" Ellen keeps her voice muted, not to seem overly eager.

"Hey, stranger."

Ellen is momentarily breathless.

"It's me," Megan says.

"I know," Ellen stammers.

"Are you—I wasn't sure—is it okay to call?"

"Yes, I guess, I don't know, what do you want?"

"I don't want anything," Megan flares. "I just called. I don't know why I called."

"I'm sorry, I didn't mean—"

"I was just sitting here thinking about you. It seems like such a long time since—"

"I know," Ellen interjects. She is surprised by her own enthusiasm.

"I hate not getting to talk to you at all."

"Yeah, I've been missing it, too." And it's actually true, she realizes as she says it. The comfort of someone familiar with the rocky places of your life, not having to work so damn hard to make yourself understood, to beg for empathy in just the right ways.

"Would you like to, maybe, get lunch sometime? Or coffee?"

"Sure, maybe," Ellen says. "I would. Yes."

Tuesday the 31st (Halloween)

It's like a march of the zombies out there, all the figures in the dark meandering slowly house to house, the roaming lights, voices drifting, the cloaked, inhuman shapes emerging with shrill cries at every door.

Alphonse stands on the porch, savoring the activity. "The trick-or-treating ain't good like in our day. You can't eat anything people make by hand no more. There goes all that sweet divinity. The real good caramel apples. Popcorn balls that taste good and buttery. Praline squares."

"Mmm," agrees Eloise.

"Now all the candy got to look like something. Saw a kid the other day with a cel phone full of Red Hots. Saw a pager full of sour candy." He shakes his head. "Guess they all want to look like dealers."

"Not Tony," Eloise says.

The unspoken question within the assertion hangs in the air.

Tony emerges from his room and puts on his corduroy jacket.

"Hey, son, ready to go?" Alphonse takes a good look at Tony's costume. He looks again, and keeps looking, until he realizes his son is dressed in normal, everyday clothes.

"Ain't we going out? Trick or treating?"

"Naw," Tony says. "I'm too old for that."

"We did it last year."

Tony looks at him as if to say that was a long, long time ago.

"Let him be," Eloise says softly.

"I got to meet some guys, anyway."

"You're not going out. All the crazies are out."

"It's not safe," Eloise adds.

"We're just going to see a bonfire in the park," Tony lies. "By the DuSable Museum," he adds, hoping to add a benign air to his fib.

"That doesn't sound safe," Alphonse begins.

Eloise nudges him. "Okay, sweetie. Just be home by eight-thirty."

"But it's already seven!"

"Don't talk back to your mother."

"Okay, then, bye." Tony pulls his cap on and goes out into the dark.

Alphonse watches him go, and tries to quell his feelings of uneasiness as his son is swallowed by the ominous shapes abroad in the night.

Ng has his face so close to Nestor's that the little boy begins to giggle.

"Hold still," Ng says. "You'll make me mess up."

"The brush tickles," Nestor says.

Leda grips her little brother's arms. "You don't want to look like a girl, do you?"

"No!" Nestor shouts.

"Then be still."

Ng braces his hand on the child's thin shoulder.

"Nestor makes a beautiful cat," Leda says.

"I don't want to be a cat," he moans. "I want to be Spider-Man."

"But Flaco is already Spider-Man."

"So?"

"Look in the mirror, Nestor, and then tell me if you want to change it," Ng says.

The little boy runs off to the bathroom.

"I love you for doing this," Leda says. She drops into Ng's lap and presses a fat kiss on his cheek. He can feel the lipstick adhering to his skin.

"They're good kids," he says.

"No, I mean, I love you," she says in his ear. His skin prickles all over.

"I don't want ever to be without you," she whispers.

Ng is enveloped in a warm fog. He hugs her tightly, unable to say anything.

Nestor races back into the room.

"I'm not a cat, I'm a tiger!" He roars shrilly, making claws of his fingers.

Alice has never before seen a place so teeming with women. Not even Lilith Fair seemed quite so self-consciously un-male. Oh, there are guys, here and there, but so swishy that Alice feels butch by comparison. Only about half of the guests are in costume. At least, Alice thinks the shave-headed women dressed like lumberjacks are not in costume—at least not any costume other than their everyday one. Femme or butch are not even terms she wants to think in. It was easier, wasn't it, being a simple, heterosexual woman? Has she just traded problems?

Most of the guests are within ten yards of the fire burning in a big, open kettle. Others linger in the garage, which has been turned into a kind of mad scientist's laboratory, with glowing and oozing and twitching and flowing things. Yards of rope are stretched from the fire escape to the garage in the form of a giant spider web. Alice feels an involuntary shiver.

"Are you butch?" she asks Ellen. "Or am I?"

Ellen laughs. "I don't know. Neither?"

"Don't you have to be one or the other?"

"No! Why do you say that?"

"Well, look at everyone here. I don't know where we fit."

A Melissa Etheridge song is wailing grandly from speakers propped in the apartment windows.

"We fit right where we are. We're originals."

Ellen pulls her over to the apple-bobbing tub. "Wanna?"

They plunge their heads into the cold water and, between the apples, bump noses, lips, and finally come up biting a red delicious between them.

Alice feels someone push roughly at her shoulder. She turns to see a large, tassle-topped carrot stagger drunkenly away from her.

"Excuse you," the carrot mutters.

Ellen has the apple still clenched in her teeth, like a roast pig, and all the giddiness of the moment has drained out of her face. Water drips from her short-cropped bangs.

"What's wrong?" Alice says, pulling strands of wet hair behind her ears.

Ellen pries the apple off her teeth and inspects the two semi-circular bites in its glossy skin. "That was Megan."

"Great," Alice says.

"Treat?" Ellen says, handing Alice the apple.

"I'd like to go home, I think."

Michelle Shocked sings, *anchored down in Anchorage.*

"If you want to."

A drop of water dangles from Alice's sweet nose. "What was so great about her that you stayed together for so long?"

"She wasn't always like that," Ellen says. "It's complicated."

"Yeah. Always is."

Nathan argues that Halloween is redundant this year. There's enough macabre in their daily lives, frankly, with that urn of Robin's mother's ashes looking down on them everyday. He's pretty certain that Robin's been taking bits of the ashes and dropping them around the city. He's peeked inside, and the level of matter in the urn appears to be dropping. But he can't bring himself to ask. Robin wouldn't—gulp—be cooking with them, would he?

He'd been afraid Robin was going to set up some kind of séance or something. So a quiet evening is fine.

"Momma loved Halloween," Robin sighs. His martini has a garnish of candy corn on a toothpick. "I wish kids trick or treated more in high-rises."

All he's gotten to do is hand out about a dozen orange and white popcorn balls to kids who live in the building and for whom the extent of Devil's Night's is a foray between the third and tenth floors.

"She made me the most darling costumes."

"What was your favorite?"

Robin smiles at the memory and nibbles a vodka-softened candy kernel. "Well, we had an understanding. If I didn't throw a tantrum to be Sleeping Beauty or Cinderella, she would make me something kind of swashbuckle-y, gallant but fey—you know, pirate captain, musketeer, Zorro—so I could still feel light and pretty, but Dad wouldn't really get it."

"So she was supportive like that when you were young?"

"Mothers and sons sometimes have these understandings outside of the father's, you know, range, I think. I know I'm not the only one who was, shall we say, abetted by a sympathetic mom."

Nathan shakes his head. "I can't imagine that."

"Well, sweetheart, you never let your mother see behind your mask. Halloween's over in a few hours. Maybe you ought to think about taking it off."

Nathan drains his drink and inspects the ice cubes intently.

Robin sits up on his knees. "It's perfect! You could call your parents up and ask them to guess what you're wearing for Halloween."

"All right, I get it. Enough."

"And then," Robin says, orchestrating the scene in the air between them with his fingers, "you say, 'I'm dressed like a heterosexual man! But—'" Robin holds a finger in the air, holding the drama for a beat. "'I'm taking off the costume starting now.' What do you think?" Robin bounces down to the floor at Nathan's feet. "Give everybody a treat this year. No more tricks."

"Why are you so hung up on me coming out?"

Robin's grin falls. "Why do you think, stupid? Did goblins steal your brain?"

Florence takes Duchess for an extra-long walk, enjoying the bustle on the streets. The little dog is sporting a new tartan sweater, and Florence has a large rubber bat pinned to her shoulder.

When she comes around the corner, she is both surprised and not surprised to see the preacher, Brother Even, standing on the corner, talking as usual to the air. But his tone is different this time. She pauses. Duchess sits and turns both huge brown eyes back to look at her. Brother Even's voice comes sharply through the bracing air.

"My little secret, you know, is that this is my second favorite holiday. No, it truly is, sisterbrothers. Not for the candy, nice as that is, but for the wargames we stage tonight between good and evil. The morality play sublimated in the costumed shenanigans that all us good people get up to for one night."

A child walks by, eyes full of wary wonder, and Brother Even hands him a chocolate coin wrapped in gold foil.

"For obvious reasons it overshadows the day for which it was once merely doormat—All Hallow's Day. Angels and devils walk the sidewalks, up to the doors, and strike deals in good, Old Testament fashion. Maybe candy is all the grace that's given, eggs and shaving cream all the hell, but aren't we playing angel, just a little bit, brothersisters?"

"You, good woman, there, with the little shivering dog. They also serve who sit and wait. That may be from a different war, but that makes it no less true, brothersisters."

He walks over and hands Florence another golden chocolate coin.

"Consider it sweet communion, sister." And he fades back through the pools of dark between the streetlights, back to his corner.

She unwraps the candy right there and pops it in her mouth.

"Let's go home Duchy," she says, tugging on the dog's leash. "That's enough treats for one night."

November

Friday the 3rd

Robin gets to work early to minimize his contact with other people. It's when the prep work gets done—soup stocks begun, fishes de-boned, ducks and other fowl dressed. The catering kitchen is eerie this early, the long stainless steel counters gleaming with cloudy brightness, all the instruments hanging as though waiting for animation. The colors remind him of the silver Moroccan pill case in his jacket, his new sacramental tote for bits of his mother's ashes. He checks his watch. Maybe today he can take her to the Oldenberg bat sculpture after lunchtime.

Robin drops a roughly carved chunk of smoked pork butt into a vat of fresh lima beans. He can taste how the heavy, salty beans, mashed with garlic, will go so slowly down the gullet. The weight of everything in the mouth. It can become a burden, eating. Especially when the world is upside down. He remembers his father's alien and repulsive cooking. Franks and beans so salty it burned the tongue. Bacon that was half-charred, half-raw and translucent rubber. Undercooked chicken, hard gray burgers. The sense memories threaten to overwhelm him. His gag reflex starts to kick in. He runs to the bathroom and throws up into the toilet.

Dearest Nathan, I don't know if you got my phone messages. Your sister had a darling baby girl this morning. I couldn't be happier unless it was maybe your child I could be grandmother to. Please call me, and call your sister. You'll have to visit soon so Phoebe can meet her Uncle Nate. Love, Maddy.

Nathan looks at the picture of the radish-red infant in a pale blue stocking cap. She doesn't look like anything I'd want screaming for my attention at four a.m. Anyway, I've got a baby already. A big one. Still, wouldn't it be nice to have his family take joy in his life, to share something with them again? But that doesn't seem possible with Robin.

Early to be drinking, but only a glass of wine will remove the taste of bile. Robin sits on a stool, making radish rosettes with a large paring knife. He has selected one of the open bottles of wine, left over from last night and reserved for cooking. His father never drank. Can't blame his terrible parenting on booze, like so many others. He's a teetotaler in the great Southern tradition, displacing obnoxious drunkenness with obnoxiously pious sobriety. Which made Robin eager to join the bad crowd of his junior high, drinking square bottles of fortified wines in the woods behind his school.

He drives the knife completely through the rosette. Shit.

Of course, it had a different effect on Janie. Maybe part of why she turned into a bible-thumping, speaking-in-tongues nutcase.

Robin makes a furious cut at the wet radish. It slips from his grasp, and as he grabs it, the knife slices neatly through his palm and into his wrist. He gasps, even though there is no pain yet, and no blood. The knife clatters on the floor. Robin can see into the wound very clearly, for what seems an extended moment of time—the precise cut spreading open, the sides of it not so dark as he'd imagined, somewhere between pink and red, bisected by the white line of a tendon—before blood wells into the gash, across his palm, and begins dripping onto the floor. Moving as though in a dream, Robin grabs a towel and wraps it loosely around the wound.

"I don't think it's that bad," he whispers to the empty room as it wobbles.

He gets up and walks out to the street. A woman glances at him and hurries down the sidewalk. Robin stares at the kitchen towel, dark and heavy with blood.

Not until he is in a cab, clutching his now-throbbing hand, does he allow himself to faint.

"Did you get the pamphlet I left you?" Allen Overcamp's blonde head is peering over Nathan's cubicle wall.

"This one?" Nathan holds up the brochure for an upcoming arts marketing conference in Mexico City. "It's over the holidays. I don't see how I could go."

Allen shrugs. "Holidays for me are the perfect time to grab my passport and run."

Allen Overcamp, head of the Institute's graphics department, is devastatingly bright and stylish. As soon as he and Nathan met they entered an unspoken agreement not to have any romantic notions about one another. But as with all such agreements, it remains present between them as a reminder of what they are nobly resisting.

"You have a point there."

"I'm going," Allen says. "If I can get this place to pay for the airfare, I'll cover the rest. And I'll actually have a holiday over the holidays."

"What a concept," Nathan sighs. "I'll be in one of two hells. Maybe even two at once."

"Suit yourself," Allen says, disappearing from view. "I just thought you might need the diversion."

Later that night, Nathan pushes the pale blue curtain aside and there sits Robin clutching his bandaged hand.

"I'm sorry," Robin says. His lip is quivering.

"Are you okay?"

Robin shrugs. "I guess."

"What were you doing?"

"I don't know, just making some garnishes."

"The doctor says it's a deep cut, almost into your wrist."

"Well it wasn't *that*, if that's what you're thinking."

'You've been under a lot of stress."

"Can we go home now?"

"The nurse says you're released."

"Listen, Nathe." Robin says this in a voice somewhere between hard and pathetic. "When I want to off myself, it won't be almost. You'll know it."

Nathan's scalp prickles. "I know. No half measures for you."

Monday the 6th

When Ng walks into Stimpy's, Leda doesn't come forward for the usual peck on the cheek. She remains behind the counter and jerks her thumb at the back room, flashing him a warning with her eyebrows.

"I'm sorry," she mouths as he walks through the curtain to the stock room.

What have I done? Ng wonders. Is Larry waiting back there to bust his chops over some clerk-ish error? He pans quickly through his actions of the last few days. He hasn't been very focused on work, it's true. Plenty of opportunity for mistakes. He is surprised to see there, sitting at the boss's desk, a guy who isn't Larry O. Larry. He gulps.

The guy has his chin in his palm, looking gloomily at some papers on his desk. Ng has a terrific view of the man's bald spot and the stringy hair combed over it with insufficient vanity. He is slow to sense Ng's presence, and when he does, he leaps to his feet, scattering the papers on the desk.

"Hey, you must be Ng. I'm glad to meet you. I'm Sol Slivnick." He sticks out his hand.

"Oh, Mr. Slivnick." Ng wraps his hand around Mr. Slivnick's and finds so little resistance that he recoils, afraid of crushing the man's fingers.

Slivnick regards him with nervous eagerness, his eyes watery and curious above his long, pale cheeks. "Call me Sol, please. I'm sorry we haven't met before. I don't come in often." He runs his thumb across his bangs to keep them directed more or less toward his left eyebrow.

"That's okay. The place kind of runs itself."

"With Leda here it does," Sol says. He sits back down and directs Ng to a chair stacked with returns.

Ng moves the stack and sits. "Is there something you wanted to see me about? If there's a problem—"

Sol laughs. "No! No problem. The reverse." He jiggles his eyebrows meaningfully.

"The opposite of a problem?"

"I wanted to tell you that your work is really good. Very good." Sol taps some papers on his desk.

Ng sees that the papers that Sol was inspecting are his drawings. But how?

"I'm working on an issue now, and if you have something ready, I'd like to put you in."

"Issue? I'm sorry," Ng says. "You lost me."

"Oh, I forgot. I also publish a magazine, under a pen name." He riffles through his various boxes—In, Out, Filing, More Filing, Invoices, Outvoices, Pending, Overdue, Urgent, Super Urgent. "Ah, here we go." He hands Ng a copy of *The City by The Flake,* the special Urban Beautification issue in which all of the comics proposed new ways to extend the mayor's mania for urban enhancements, such as adding ivy to the *outside* of Wrigley Field, or creating a float-in theater on the Chicago River by projecting movies onto the smooth glass exteriors of riverside office buildings.

"The production values are pretty lame," Sol says apologetically, "but a few of the artists are really talented."

Ng is staring at the paper. "This is yours?"

"Well, yes. Something I started doing a few months ago. It's become the hobby that ate my life."

"But I *love* this book. It's like everything I want to be as an artist."

"Well, that's high praise," Sol giggles at a girlish pitch.

Ng hesitates. "But I thought you were against employees bringing their art to work. That's what Larry told me."

"Well, yes. That is what I told Larry. But, well, Larry is a nice guy, you know, but he's really, you know, a terrible artist." Sol sucks in his lips and blows them out again. "It was kind of a special Larry-only rule."

"He doesn't know you're the Flake?"

Sol shakes his head. "It would just make trouble. And you and me, we'll keep this our little agreement. It's better for Larry this way."

"Okay. I won't say anything to him."

Sol looks at him expectantly. He laces and unlaces his fingers. "Well? Are you interested in maybe putting something in the next issue?"

"Absolutely. I don't know what to say. Yes."

"Okay, then." Sol looks around. "I've already been here too long. I'm getting jumpy. Just leave it on my desk next week, I'll pick it up."

When they emerge together, Leda is biting her thumbnail ferociously.

Sol waves and departs without another word. Before the door closes, Ng notices that the back of Sol's hair looks ruffled as though he just woke up.

Leda pulls Ng behind the counter. "Oh my god," she whispers, seeing the pale and dazed look on Ng's face. "Did he fire you? It's all my fau—"

"No, no," Ng says, feeling woozy. "The reverse."

Ng is not walking beside Leda, he's floating. He circles lampposts and walks backwards. He flaps his arms and does an impression of Lord of the Dance. Nothing his body can do is equal to this amazing rush of adrenaline.

"Maybe this is everything turning around, finally. Ivan's dropped out of sight. I got five hundred bucks from him first. And now this."

Leda is watching him with a half-grin. "I'm stunned," she says. "I had no idea he was the Flake."

"You must have known," Ng says. "You're good that way. You can see things that are hidden."

"Really? You think so?"

"God, I want to tell someone. Mom will be happy, but she won't *understand*." He gives her a wicked look. "Larry would understand."

Leda frowns. "You can't, Ng. It's mean."

"I know." He hops and balances for a moment on top of a fire hydrant before allowing his momentum to carry him over.

"You know," Leda says thoughtfully. "There is someone who would understand."

"Who?" Ng sidesteps a parking meter. "Elias?"

"No. I mean Mr. Parsley."

Ng freezes, and then sits down immediately on the curb. He exhales like a loose balloon giving up the ghost. He clamps his hands between his knees. "You haven't forgiven me for that, have you?"

"No, you moron, it isn't that." Leda throws her arms around his neck, half-hug, half-threat. "You have to ask *him* to forgive you. Then you can be clean about everything. Show him that what he taught you meant something."

"He won't care. He'll just want me to pay for the damage to his car."

"Maybe he will. Then you'll do it."

"It's so long ago," Ng moans. "Can't it just be over?"

"You just said how I can see things that are hidden. I'm telling you I can see this."

Ng rolls on the pavement with a groan. "Ugh. Just when I was feeling so good."

Wednesday the 8th

There's no doubt about it: Alphonse is happy today. Eloise hears him whistling in kitchen while he cleans his golf clubs to put them away for the winter. She's ashamed that her first reaction is a touch of indignation. He's been in too much trouble to be happy. But then she corrects herself. Give the man a moment to feel all right with the world. Trouble ain't done with him yet. Besides that, it's kind of a vacation for Alphonse, as long as he doesn't remember about being in jail or think about the business of applying for a job with a criminal record. He's kept himself busy. He's cleaned up the remains of the old garage and started talking about building the new one himself. Got a book from the hardware store on simple frame structures and started making drawings on notepaper.

Eloise puts down her magazine, perplexed. "What's that you whistling, anyway?"

"'Papa was a Rolling Stone.'" He laughs to admit it out loud.

"Wishful thinking."

Alphonse walks in drying his hands on a kitchen towel. "Can't roll nowhere on probation."

"Can't roll nowhere nohow."

He changes tack. "Maybe a brick patio would be nice, too."

She purses her lips. "Build a garage ain't enough for you."

"We got the bricks to start with," he adds, indicating the pile of burned masonry stacked at the fence line.

"Sure. And while you're at it, don't forget the hot tub."

"Hey, woman, I get my next job, don't be surprised you end up with a Swedish sauna bath, too." Alphonse sings, *"Wherever he laid his hat was his home."*

Ronnie makes Darol drive them all over to the lake, even though Darol complains that no one helps him pay for the gas, ever.

"I'll buy you a damn tankful, bitch," Ronnie says. "Just drive."

It's dusk, and a gusty wind flips mattress-sized slabs of black water onto the concrete pilings. The sky looks rubbed with charcoal.

They pull up next to the convertible LeBaron.

"Let's do this," says the man through his window. "I got someplace to go."

"Lemme see them," Ronnie says.

A box is handed through the window. Ronnie opens it and runs a finger across the contents.

"They just regular pistolas, man. Don't start waving them around now."

"Don't wave them," echoes the man's partner, a shadow on the other side of the car.

"Shit man, I'm your customer, right?" Ronnie says. "I got a right to see."

The man drums his fingers on the steering wheel. "You got to do these things fast. Boom-boom, that's how you do it."

"Awright." Ronnie pulls out an envelope and hands it through the window.

The man opens the flap and fans through the bills. "There, see? That's all I need. I trust you, my friend. I see the green, and I'm good to go."

Ronnie hands the box to Tony in the back seat. "Just making sure you got the right ones."

"I'm a businessman, right? You order, I deliver, C.O.D." The man throws the car in gear. "Play nice with them toys, now." The LeBaron describes a wide arc backwards, wobbles forward, and then straightens as it guns forward. Tony thinks he hears laughter underneath the engine's roar.

"Here." Tony holds the box up for Ronnie to take.

"You keep it," Ronnie says. "Hold onto it for us."

"Why me?"

"Cause you got a house, T. You got lots more places to hide something than any of us do."

Tony has no argument for this. He cradles the box in his lap, as though it were something fragile. It is lighter than he expected, but uneasy to hold, like an egg that wants to break itself.

Giselle looks down on her two children, sleeping, in a rare symmetry, at the same time, wrapped in matching yellow blankets from Aunt Germaine. Her little butter beans, Germaine calls them. Giselle leans back in her rocking chair and puts her feet up. She feels wrung out like an old rag. She touches the bags under her eyes—they feel like tiny water balloons sewn into her skin. It would be nice to go out somewhere, get a little wild. She remembers the warm mumble of bourbon on her tongue, how a shower of bright cold cocaine in her sinuses would make her feel as though her mind had been cleaned like a window, with light pouring through unimpeded.

But she has never forgotten waking up in Jackson Park that morning, shoveling up snow with numb fingers and trying to melt it in her dry mouth. One of these babies will wake up in a few minutes and she'll forget her aches and pains again.

She takes out the envelope from the Circle campus. She started to fill out the application last week, but didn't get past her address before something took her away—a smelly diaper, a puddle of puke. She wrinkles her nose at the mere thought.

It's crazy. How can she go to school with two infants at home? But at the same time, she has to start creating a world in her mind again, a story for herself with some possibilities, rewards, hope. And at the very least, this will make any job application look like a piece of cake. Write an essay? Take the ACT? It's too much. She puts the papers back in the envelope. Evander whimpers, his tiny fists clenched up by his mouth.

"Who you want to fight, big man?" Giselle coos, taking one fist between her thumb and index finger. "You got a chip on your shoulder?" She shakes the tiny fist. Evander suddenly opens one eye, and the grin that spreads across her tiny son's face sends a delicious chill through her body.

"Your momma's going to be something for you," she whispers. "Yes she is. Yes she is."

The windows glow warmly, oozing a diffuse yellow light onto the grass. Tony moves at the edge of the light over to the pile of sooty bricks left over from the garage. His dad saved them for some reason, and with winter coming on, they'll stay there a good long while. He can feel a fine layer of frost melt away from his fingers as he grabs the topmost bricks. They are solid and cold. He sets them carefully on the ground. It's better than bringing the box in the house. Could be anybody's, if someone finds it out here. Shadows move across the windows. If someone should look out and see him. He hunkers down, hoping to make himself another shadow. He hears the muffled voices of his parents from the kitchen. He moves enough bricks to create a hollow in the middle of the pile. He settles the box in the cavity and covers it with a plastic bag. The bricks go back on top, two layers deep. No way to see down inside.

His father's laugh seems to come closer. He freezes. Then the voice recedes. He can feel the oily soot on his fingers. He wipes them on the grass. He sniffs them: still smoky. He'll have to make a dash for the bathroom without being seen. But before he goes in, he sits on the back of the brick pile, looking at the tiny slice of the night world around him. Eroded pavement mixed with ground glass sparkles between his sneakers. Dumpsters lean against each other like listing drunks burping up garbage. The cold air carries only a faint trace of the hot electrical smell that sometimes comes up from the steel plants further south. At his back, he feels the warm shuffle of expectations, of an idea of him that lives within the house, one that looks strange and stupid to him right now, slightly out of breath and sweating, dirty and dangerous, on the edge of the alley that, if you never turned around, could be anywhere.

Friday the 10th

This is going badly. Alice has gone from nonchalant mumblings of trust about Ellen's plan to have dinner with Megan tonight, to saying things like, "Maybe you're just not ready to move on," and, "Maybe I should leave."

In a way, it feels good to have Alice care enough to get upset. But there's the more immediate way in which this is just awful. Alice pulls on her backpack to leave, and Ellen tugs it back off her shoulder.

"Come on, please." Ellen keeps after Alice, trying to catch her, slow her down and make her hear. "Just listen." It's like the emergency brake slipped and Ellen's chasing their relationship as it careens down a steep, winding hill.

"I was listening. I heard you." When she's angry, Alice's face seems to simplify into a few dark, dour lines, like a kabuki mask.

"It's just this one time, to get things on a new footing. So we can be friends—if we can be friends, I mean."

"Do you mean if you can be less than lovers to each other?"

"No—god!—that's like totally the furthest thing. What I mean, I mean, to just close the door on what we were. Is it wrong to want to be friends, to see if that's possible with her?"

"Has that ever in human history really worked?" Alice huffs. "When lovers say let's be friends, it means let's break up. When ex-lovers say let's be friends, it means we could become lovers again."

"Oh, come on." Ellen's voice begins to snap with a little of her own anger now. "Look, I just won't do it if it's so upsetting to you. I'll tell Megan I can't."

"Don't *not* go because of me. Do what you think is right."

And here they are: the stare down. There is no longer any possible outcome untainted by the feeling of having given into the other person's will. They are both losers.

"Well, I did think it was fine until you got all upset," Ellen offers.

"Maybe I just don't understand something about what this is for you."

"This dinner, or this *us*?"

"I meant the dinner, but maybe, you know, both."

At this, they both stare at the walls until their eyes grow fuzzy with untraceable thoughts.

The digital kitchen timer beeps, and Robin sighs as though wounded. He unwraps the elastic bandage from his hand and slowly, painfully, begins manipulating his fingers. Doctor's orders to do this every two hours to keep the tendon from healing short—leaving his two outside fingers curled. Tough to cook with a claw. And talk about unattractive.

Moving slowly in the kitchen, it's taken him all afternoon to make a simple soup and a salad frisée. Some fancy cooking.

He presses his thumb against the pad of his pinkie, and a dull pain sparks a small fire in this middle of his palm. He takes a swig of cooking sherry, grits his teeth, and forces both fingers straight against the butcher-block countertop.

As Megan's car pulls up to the curb, Ellen's mood brightens unexpectedly. She tries to measure it, taste what she's feeling about this. It falls somewhere between obligation and a murky itch of her own that wants scratching. All in all, however, seeing Megan feels like a tentative easing of pressure, like a visit to the doctor when you may get your braces off, or he may tighten them for another season. But will it be worth the argument with Alice?

Sliding into the passenger seat is kind of a sensory dislocation, Twilight Zone-y. Something so familiar, with all the casualness and comfort wrenched out of it.

"Hey," Megan leans forward and their cheeks brush. Was that a merest sensation of lips against her ear? Ellen's nape tingles.

There is an awkward silence. They look away from each other, then look back, alternating in different hues of chagrin.

Megan has a large-eyed, contrite look, like a pet that has been punished. Her wild black hair is pulled back smooth; her drawn and pale face adds light to her hazel eyes. There is a new softness about her gestures, her voice. A wounded, apologetic defiance.

"Before we go anywhere," she says, "I want to apologize officially about Halloween."

"That's okay. I understand."

"Was Alice, you know, upset?" The name catches almost imperceptibly in her throat.

"I think she's more upset about this."

"Meaning dinner?"

"Yeah."

"Jealous?"

"Sure. Wouldn't you be?"

A small smile tweaks Megan's lips. "I know a thing or two about jealousy."

The afternoon is cold, iron gray, without personality. There's nothing that can break Alice out of her funk. Not a triple espresso with four cubes of raw sugar. Not the guilty pleasure of playing her guitar amid the flowers. If she could make a song out of this emotional mess, maybe then. Alice wonders whether it's inclement weather or her own major bad vibe that keeps the shop almost entirely empty all day. She's in the midst of closing—the diamond-pattern grating is already across the windows—when there is a light knock on the window. It's Nathan. She runs to unlock the door.

"You just made it."

"I was hurrying."

His hair, she notices, is wind-fluffed and begging to be smoothed by someone's fingers.

"Is there an emergency?"

"Not really. Well, sort of. I just really needed to stop in here and get some perspective before I get home."

"Glad to be of service." She tries to be casually ironic, but it doesn't quite come off.

"Are you sure?" He leans across the counter and peers into her face with comedic scrutiny. "Do you have any idea how pissed off you looked through the window? Do you mind if I ask what's wrong?"

"Oh, it's just—" She shrugs. "Relationship stuff."

"Your friend, the redhead."

"Ellen. Yeah, she's having dinner with her old girlfriend." Alice laughs suddenly. "It sounds so weird saying that." She blushes. "Ellen's my first, um, female relationship."

"Really?" There is a complex sort of surprise in Nathan's tone. "That must be hard on you."

"It has its moments."

"I'll tell you a secret. This is my first gay relationship, too."

"Wow, you're kidding."

"And it hasn't been all roses."

"I can tell. You look pretty worn out."

"Anticipatory fatigue. There's going to be a nasty scene tonight."

"Would you like—I could make you a coffee or something?"

"You know what." Nathan smacks his lips and nods toward the street. "What I could use is a drink. Would you join me?"

Alice savors the idea for a moment and then smiles. "Okay. That sounds great. Just give me a moment to lock up."

"I'll wait outside." He returns her smile and steps out to the sidewalk.

Don't think about it, she says to herself as she rushes through her closing duties. Don't wonder or worry, not now.

When Alice steps outside, she hands Nathan a rose. "I thought you might need something to take home," she says. "To help smooth things over."

He takes the flower with a smile of mild amazement. "You may never know how unaccustomed I am to such consideration," he says, bowing slightly from the waist.

"It's not considerate," she says, nudging him. "You're buying."

Even though the restaurant's exposed brick walls have the property of doubling or tripling the collected din of the voices around them, nothing really penetrates the cocoon that Ellen and Megan's small table has become. Everything falls away as they approach and retreat, gently fencing, half in opposition, half in cooperation, around their one true subject: themselves.

The hours pass in a series of truncated conversational forays, each one eventually coming to an end in the cul-de-sac of their romantic past, which each of them has reasons for wanting to keep at a distance.

"So, how are you keeping busy?" Megan asks.

"You know, work. I've been making a lot of progress on the film, too."

"Oh," Megan says. For the film means: Alice.

Ellen says nothing for a moment. Then, "How's your work?"

Megan shrugs. "I got a little backlogged." Meaning: I was too wounded to work.

The ordering and dispatching of food offered a passage of neutral topics. But now there are dirty plates around them, sticky and littered with the remains of food inattentively dissected.

Megan breaks first. Stirring the sauce on her plate, she gives Ellen a hooded glance. "El, I know maybe I shouldn't say, but I really, you know, God, I miss you."

Without looking up, Ellen says, "I miss you, too."

She can feel Megan's wounded smirk.

"I do, Megs." She looks up and then examines the wine swirling in her glass. "You know I do. It's not like there wasn't something, you know, kinetic between us."

"Was. There *was*."

"Well, yeah." Ellen sighs, caught between soothing Megan's feelings and getting sucked into some other confession she isn't ready to make. "There was, along with the bad, crazy stuff."

Megan suddenly reaches across the table and grabs Ellen's hand. "El, do you remember that night last winter I came to your apartment?"

Ellen is willing her hand to remain still and noncommittal. "You mean when you snowballed my window?"

"Yeah. That night, I thought, if this doesn't last, it will still have been worth it to be with you even a week or a month or a year."

Ellen stares at their hands, entwined on the tablecloth. Megan's fingers seem to have a separate message to send—more direct, fumbling, and needful.

Megan's whisper is like a tendril of smoke entering her mind. "You were so beautiful. When I saw you naked in the candlelight, you had a halo, you were blue white like an angel."

Ellen tries to remove her hand, whispering, "I think the people at the next table are listening."

"No, please." Megan squeezes her hand, "It almost made me believe in, like, martyrdom, how fanatics throw themselves in front of bulldozers or on grenades or whatever."

Ellen turns her head. Megan tightens her grip, and Ellen's hand remains.

"Everyday I thought, just one more."

"One what?" Ellen's voice is tearful.

"One dinner. One kiss."

Ellen pulls their clutching hands to her mouth and kisses Megan's fingers.

"One anything."

"Nothing goes easy with Robin," Nathan says. "It's all more of the explosion type of thing. Ka-blooey."

"Why?" Then Alice waves the question away. "I'm sorry, it's none of my—"

"No, it's okay." He leans toward her and touches her arm. "Robin lost his job today."

"I'm sorry," Alice says. She rubs his back with a lingering touch. "That's really rough."

"On a lighter note," Nathan turns to her with a fuzzy grin, "we've tried martinis with twists, onions, bleu cheese olives, and anchovy olives. Your favorite?"

"Bleu cheese, definitely. But we haven't tried the jalapeño olives yet."

"I don't think I can." He checks his watch. "It's almost midnight. Oops."

They sit silently facing the end of their evening. And then slowly, like a house with its foundation washed away, Alice tilts toward Nathan's shoulder, more and more, until her cheek rests against his shoulder.

"You better go," she says through a mushed mouth.

"I guess." Nathan sighs and lets his hand drop onto her head. His fingers trail down the back of her head, tickling the hairs, feeling the realness of her.

"I don't seem to be going," he says at last.

"Then maybe you should just kiss me." She looks up at him teasingly. "Just kidding."

"That's too bad," he says slowly, approaching her face, and pressing a perfect, soft kiss on her cheek, just catching the corner of her mouth.

"Mmm," Alice says, and shifts her mouth just that little bit.

Somewhere in Pennsylvania, Brad kind of realizes, wow, he is coming back to Chicago, and is stricken with panic. Why did this seem like a good idea? He glances out the bus window, as if to find a soft spot in the onrushing dark foliage to land if he got up the balls to just jump. But all he sees is his faint reflection, backlit by the muted sleeping lights in the cabin.

When the bus pulls into the eerily lit Pittsburgh bus station at three o'clock, he steps out to stretch his legs. Half a dozen people lie in open-mouthed stupor along a row of black plastic chairs with pay-as-you-go televisions bolted to them. He buys a cup of bitter coffee from a machine and walks around the station. Grates cover the newsstand and cafeteria windows. Cold breezes swipe freely through the interior, carrying a blend of diesel fumes and cooking oil. His hair hurts from where he slept curled against the nubby seatback.

Without thinking too hard about what he's doing, he steps into a pay phone and dials Alice's number.

"Hi," he says to her machine. "Guess who's in Pittsburgh at this time of night. I'm heading back, that's right, tail between my legs. I guess I wanted someone to know. I'll get in touch when I hit town. Sorry," he adds, "for calling so late."

When he boards the bus again, he is wide awake, with caffeine and expectation.

One more anything or one more everything? It happened so fast after the dessert came, was ignored, and then taken away. Megan drove with one hand on Ellen, shifting with her left. They mashed at stoplights until cars behind them blared their horns in anger. The mouth is familiar, the smell is familiar, the motions are familiar, and yet as Ellen feels Megan's mouth moving down her stomach, there is an electric actuality to the moment that renders all thoughts of purpose and intent and rightness a little too academic to ponder. She is known here, neither strange nor confused. Letting go here, now, is familiar, releasing to the fall that becomes a kind of sustaining flight.

Saturday the 11th (A.M.)

Alice's waking: a minor shift in tone from the fragile sleep in which she floats. She moves her head and is awash in a comprehensive throbbing behind her eyes. With her hands to her temples, she presses on her skull to keep the bones from separating and then lies motionless, listening to the air. It's winter, almost. There are no bird sounds at all to narrate the black morning. Just the slow, rhythmic hiss-tink of the radiators. The smell of heat is comforting. Her mouth has been lined with wallpaper paste. Beside her, Nathan sleeps, exhaling deep, gin-sour breaths. You can almost see the cigarette smoke curling up out of his hair. As she pulls up the covers, Alice absorbs a deep inhalation of the thick, sharp smell of man-woman sex. Not what she's used to lately. She smiles. It's like a spadeful of rich, rain-soaked soil. But green, somehow, and peppery. With the merest hint of latex.

Nathan's left eye opens and his pupil finds hers.

"Shit," he mumbles. "What time is it?" His hands move with half-drunken futility at the edge of the strange bed. "My watch?"

"It's a quarter to six."

"Oh, god."

"I know."

"How will I ever—Robin is going to—"

"Yeah. Me too."

"I'm not sure I can move."

"I feel like old china. A cup that's been broken and reglued several times."

"This is, wow, this is probably pretty bad." He sits up and the sheet falls away.

Yes, Alice thinks. A man's torso is a fine thing.

He looks at her with a fractured smile. "Well, what now?"

Alice reaches under the sheet and touches his upper thigh.

Nathan slides away. "Alice. Let's not make this any worse."

"How could it get worse? You mean like let's not double the sin of having sex with me?"

He reaches to embrace her, but she shrugs off his touch. "That's not what I mean." He regards her angry, arm-crossed posture. "Am I the only one who dreads facing the shitstorm that today is going to be? I mean, what about your friend?"

"I called last night from the bar, remember? There was no answer?"

"You don't know what that means. It could be nothing, or just something like this, a moment."

"A fucked-up moment."

"Hey, this was absolutely not all bad." He touches her cheek. "It's just if things were different—"

"I know you're right." She scoots down into the sheets and curls her knees up. "But that doesn't mean I'm not angry about it."

Ellen wakes up about every hour during the night, which seems both endless and fleeting. Megan sleeps like a bear in winter, her feet clasping Ellen's left ankle. Everything's normal, Ellen tells herself. Nothing that hasn't happened a jillion times before.

As dawn comes into the room, Megan turns and throws her arms around Ellen. "I haven't slept that well in weeks."

Ellen tries not to squirm inside the hot, stifling hug.

Megan looks at her face. "What is it?"

"Nothing. I'm just antsy."

Megan's expression is stunned. "Are you joking?"

"Don't please get all worked up. I just have some things to think over."

Megan rolls away and says to the ceiling, "Good, fine, think all you want."

"What are you so pissed off about?"

"I can't believe you would do this to me again."

"Me? Do this to you?" Ellen gives a sharp, affronted laugh.

"You let me in again, and you don't think maybe I thought it meant something?"

"It did mean something."

"But here we are again, no-man's land. I get to wait and worry while you measure everything again so I can find out where I stand."

"You come after me and after me, what am I supposed to do?"

"I come after you because I want you. I've always wanted you. What you're supposed to do is know what the fuck you want so I can get on with my life one way or the other. Shit or get off the pot."

"I prefer fish or cut bait."

"Did you ever think that maybe you made me come after you?"

"How, like I'm dropping breadcrumbs?"

"You don't think it's possible that you push me away with one hand and pull me back with the other? You're going to tell me there's not a grain of truth in that?"

Ellen starts to refute this ridiculous assertion, but stops, her mouth hanging open. Megan is the unstable one, right? Not Ellen. As Megan's accusation begins to settle in, the room and the world outside of it spin in a way that for Ellen is not entirely metaphorical.

Nathan stands in the long carpeted hallway trying to imagine a way to get through this, get past it, without having his life break into a million pieces. There are a thousand ways this could go once he opens the door, and none of them are painless. He looks at the doorknob. There is no buffer, no time to absorb and figure out what is going on. Robin is waiting behind that door. He has no place else to go. He touches the knob and it turns in his hand. The door opens itself, and Robin is there in the doorway, wearing silk boxers and a blanket around his shoulders. His hair is disheveled, his eyes almost fluorescent with blood. He is a dervish. A dervish with a nearly empty Absolut bottle in his hand.

"Well, at least you came back."

Nathan pushes past him. "Please don't turn this into the end of the world, okay?"

"Oh, sorry. I thought it was."

"Just because I stayed out?" Nathan shucks his sport coat off and lets it fall to the floor. "You're just spoiled because I'm always so normal, so stable. I am always there for you. One time I'm less than perfect, and it's a catastrophe."

"Nathan, my mom died, I lost my job and you stayed out all night to have a screw." Vodka splashes in the bottle as Robin gestures. "I guess you're right—it's no big deal."

"A screw? Where do you get that?" Nathan kicks off his shoes and sheds his pants. His clothes are smoky, scratchy, disgusting.

Robin goes to his dresser and pulls on a sweater and a pair of jeans. "Is it cold out?"

Nathan moans and rolls across the bed, nauseated.

"I realize it's been difficult to be with me lately," Robin says, tying the laces on his tennis shoes. "The emotional roller coaster from hell." He drains the last of the vodka from the bottle and wipes his lips. "You've been a good passenger, a trooper. You haven't thrown up once."

Nathan sits up groggily. "What are you saying?"

"You'll be glad to know the ride is over."

"What does that mean?"

"The ups and downs are over."

"Where are you going?"

"I promised to do something special to honor my mother, and today is the day. It's a fresh start."

"I don't get it. Are you flying off the handle?"

"Absolutely not. Quite the reverse. For the first time in a long time, I know exactly what to do." He leans over and gives Nathan a long kiss on the mouth, then pulls back to into Nathan's eyes. His words come slow and clearly enunciated. "I am sorry. It has all been my fault." He turns and leaves.

A few moments later, Nathan hears the front door close. Instead of being alarmed, ready to rush out to stop whatever the hell Robin is up to, Nathan is crushed by a wave of debilitating fatigue. He looks out the window. Gobbets of cloud are breaking loose from the underbelly of the heavy sky. It is a good day for a nap. He grabs two pillows and wraps himself around them. It feels good to close his eyes, rubbing his cheek against the cool, smooth pillow.

From her perch on a kitchen chair, Ellen watches Megan dress. She's paralyzed, unable to say anything—not, "Stay and kiss me," or, "Take your angry shit and go." Or even simply, "Forgive me." She swallows a gulp of tea just to keep her mouth busy. It is punishingly hot. It feels good.

Megan says nothing either. She stands slowly combing out her hair, wet from her pointedly separate shower.

"Can I just ask, how angry are you?"

Megan strokes the brush through her hair several times before answering. "I don't think I'm really angry. Funny, huh?"

The top of Ellen's tongue is scorched to a kind of numbness. "I meant what I said to you last night. I really have missed you, the stuff we had together."

"Don't think I missed the past tense."

"Are you listening? I'm trying to apologize."

"I'm listening. I don't think you ever lied to me. I never lied to you, either. But we ended up juggling a whole lot of incompatible truths."

"So now what?"

"I don't know." She walks over to Ellen and kneels at her feet. "I really don't know. I haven't managed to imagine my life without you in it." Looking up, her face is vulnerable and sweet. "I guess today I start trying."

The tears that have been lurking at the back of Ellen's eyes finally start forward. "Oh, Megs, why does this have to be so hard?"

"I don't know." Megan kisses her fingers. "What doesn't kill you, I guess." She stands abruptly. "I should go."

"Oh god," Ellen moans, and starts to fight back the wilder weeping that is building in her like a wave.

"Bye, love." Megan kisses the top of Ellen's head, turns, and is gone.

Ellen gives in to her sobs. The sudden quiet makes her life feel all the more stupid and misspent. The weird finality of Megan's leaving makes her feel sucked forward into a black, formless space. Like a tornado has simply pulled a wall away from her life.

She jumps up and runs to the closet. She fumbles her camera out of its box and runs to the window. Yes, it's loaded. She leaps onto the couch, heaves the window up, and looks for Megan. There she is, walking to her car. Her shoulders rolled over in pain. She looks back at the building—does she see Ellen?—and then unlocks the car door, opens it, steps in, and disappears. Ellen keeps the camera on the car while it shudders, emits a puff of exhaust, reverses with a flash of white taillights, angles from the curb, and pulls away.

The struggle to remain still, to prevent the camera from transmitting her trembling, constrains Ellen's sobs into a high-pitched ululation, a comical, singsong whine. She is able to keep the orange VW in sight through the leafless trees for almost two blocks, before the brief blink of the left turn signal and a quick twist of the tires removes the last emblem of Megan from her view. She releases the shutter and stares into the darkness.

About an hour after Megan's departure, the world seems so much clearer. I am a total dumbass. Ellen picks up the phone.

Alice, come on, pick up. I know you're mad at me, but you'll have to talk to me eventually. Please? We'll both be miserable until we talk this thing out. I'm coming over, whether you like it or not. I'll make a bonfire of leaves on the sidewalk, I'll chant your name. Let's not make this worse by staying silent. Okay?

But the unasked, unanswered question is, do I tell her? She decides not to decide—it would only slow her down, and she can't stay in the apartment another minute. She grabs her jacket and runs out the door. If it's the right thing to do, I'll do it. Let the moment decide.

There doesn't seem to be anyway to move on from last night. So Alice doesn't even try. After Ellen's message, and Brad's from last night, she decides to unplug the answering machine. It's not helping her get clear about anything.

About the only thing she's sure about is cheese fries. She walks to her favorite corner stand, Devil Dog Deluxe, and gets a greasy paper cup full of fries drenched with cheese sauce. She walks and nibbles the fries, the cheese growing hard in the breezy, brisk air. It is a perfect day for emotional turmoil. Which makes it a little more bearable. But not in any sense pleasant. Part of her wants to call Nathan and talk about what happened. Another part wants to get in Ellen's face and say, "See, that happened because of you. You started the ball rolling by pretending that people can just be friends when they can't."

She passes the athletic field by the high school. The half dozen netless soccer goals look like giant staples shot into the ground.

And then Brad turning up in the middle of everything? Sorry, but who's got time for that?

She realizes that she can't go home—someone is bound to show up there. She doesn't feel like going to the rehearsal loft either. So maybe she'll go to Urbs. She can play with flowers or work on a song if she feels like it. The sense of owing herself a quiet, safe place is strong. She licks the cheese from her fingers, checks her pocket for her CTA pass, and crosses the street toward the el station.

After wiping away a few water rings with a paper napkin, Robin sets the urn of his mother's ashes on the table.

"See, Mother, this is Newport's Café I've been telling you about. Where I met Nathan. I thought we could stop here for some coffee before we head downtown. There's so much I want to show you."

A young waiter with short-cropped hair and sleepy eyes comes over to bring Robin a cup of coffee. He spies the urn, but in best live-and-let-live style betrays no sign that he finds it at all unusual.

"Do you want some breakfast?"

"I'd adore a bran muffin," Robin says. "But nothing for my mother."

"Right," says the waiter. "Do either of you want water?"

"Ha-ha, That's very funny," Robin says. "Ha-ha-ha." He turns back to the urn. "Being here brings back so many memories. We used to come here for coffee before we'd go shopping on the weekends. He was so beautifully shy at first. I'm his first, you know. Yes, it's difficult sometimes. No, I'd had others. My first? Do you remember Chuck McGee, the freckled kid down the block? He had that chin like a pie server. Well, one day he and I—"

The waiter appears again. "More coffee?"

"Yes, and lots of butter for the muffin, thanks. Anyway," he says to the urn, "you were already in the home. I had lots of free time. And one afternoon, we got out back in that grove of trees behind the house and found some girlie magazines that some big kids must have been hiding out there. Anyway, the nakedness, but more the badness of what we were doing, we got all excited, and before you know it, we were showing our little, you know, stiffies. We started going back there everyday, going a little further each time."

Robin closes his eyes. "In a way, you know, that was the best time. There weren't names for the things we were doing. We just did them."

Robin stops to stuff a butter-slathered chunk of muffin in his mouth. "We were hot and heavy for a while, but then Chuck's dad got transferred or something."

He stops and frowns at the urn. "No, Mom, just because there was a copy of *Hustler* involved does not mean I'm really straight." He licks the butter from his fingers. "Let's go. We have a lot to see."

Saturday the 11th (p.m.)

Ellen walks up behind a man standing in front of Alice's front door. He is looking up at the second floor and shouting.

"Hey, come on," he shouts. "Can we at least talk?"

He is unshaven and crazy looking, but is dressed a little too cool to be a homeless veteran or something.

"Problem?" Ellen asks.

"No," the man says without turning around. "She's probably not home."

"Too bad." Ellen walks past him and pushes Alice's buzzer. While she waits, she fluffs the daisies in her grocery store bouquet. It's a small collection of drab flowers, intended to signal the fact that Ellen can't pretend to match Alice's greater class where flowers are concerned. But you can't show up empty-handed.

"If you're looking for Alice, she's not home."

Ellen turns. The man is sitting on his duffel, chin in hand.

"Hey, I think I know you." Ellen moves the bouquet behind her back. "You were with the band, with Lather Rinse Repeat."

"Yeah." He is suspicious.

"Alice's boyfriend."

"Former," he says with a pained smirk. "I'm Brad." He offers his hand without standing.

"Ellen." She reaches to shakes his hand.

"She's probably at the shop. If you don't mind my asking, are those flowers for any special reason?"

"Oh well, yes." Ellen feels an uncharacteristic blush sweep across her face. "They're an apology, sort of."

"Do you, like, work together?"

"Not exactly." She draws the two words out, enriching them with meaning.

Brad catches something in her tone. His eyes widen. "You're not, you know, are you—?" He diagrams a strange figure in the air with his fingers.

"If that means lovers, then, yes."

Brad rolls backwards off the duffel and smacks his head audibly on the concrete.

Ellen is secretly pleased by this reaction. She strolls over and peers down on the face contorted in pain. "Are you okay?"

Brad is holding the back of his head. "I think I just need to rest here a minute." He sighs. "When did this, I mean, how long have you two…?"

"A few weeks."

"Christ. I've been out of touch."

Ellen squats beside him. "I don't see any blood."

"It's all behind my eyes." He rises up to his elbows. "I don't mean to be so, I guess, Republican about it. It's just a shock."

"Well, don't get too used to the idea. I may have screwed it up royally."

"That sounds like an interesting story."

"It's a long one."

"I don't have anywhere to go." He laughs, adding, "I just got back in town this morning, and I don't have a place to sleep tonight."

"Nice plan. Were you counting on Alice?"

"I guess so. But just for the couch, that's all, honest."

Ellen stands and then helps Brad to his feet. "Want to go find her?"

"Might as well." He hoists his bag.

"I think I'll pass. She doesn't want us to walk in together."

"Then you should have first go."

"I have a place to stay, remember?"

"You do have a point there." Brad closes his eyes and opens them very slowly. "This is turning into the weirdest day."

Nathan awakes from his nap in a curious state of calm. There is a deep and comfortable fatigue in his muscles. He resists rising, enjoying instead the silence of the apartment. Rare to have a moment when Robin isn't around. His pleasure results in a twinge of guilt for feeling pleased at Robin's absence. What should he do? Maybe nothing. He argues with himself: if Robin is going to do something dramatic or stupid, it isn't entirely his responsibility to stop him, is it? It would be a kind of tough love to let him go off without chasing him. Chasing after him just encourages this kind of grandstanding gesture. But the wrinkle is that he has, genuinely, done something to encourage drama this time. No getting around that.

He tries to think of what to do, where Robin would be likely to go. He had mentioned his mother—meaning the urn. Okay, what would a distressed person do with a container of his mother's ashes? Where would he dump them?

Oh no. A thousand slivers of ice form in his blood. Oh shit.

Brad can see Alice through the glass, in the back of the shop, hunched over her guitar. He reaches through the security grating and taps one knuckle on the door glass. She looks up, unable to see who it is. He taps again. She comes crankily to the door.

Brad drops the duffel bag at his feet. "I'm back."

With a quizzical look, Alice walks over and, after a moment's hesitation, puts her arms around his neck, and settles against him. "Welcome home," she says into his shirt.

"Wow," he says, "I didn't expect—"

"Me either," Alice says, sniffing.

He looks at her, and she looks at him, and he sees in her face that the tears aren't for his return, specifically. But he is still relieved.

Alice brings him inside, whips up a couple of enormous lattes, and peppers him with questions about how he happened to arrive here, now. He tells her everything—how horrible New York was, how horrible he was in New York, even how Lori never followed—all the way up to meeting Ellen and what she told him.

Alice turns even gloomier at the mention of Ellen.

"It's okay," Brad reassures her. "I'm not, you know, I mean, whatever you need to do is cool."

She avoids his eyes. "Pretty shocking, huh?"

"I don't know. Well, yeah, sure. But is it, I mean, are you happy?"

"That isn't an easy question to answer right now."

"Me, too," he says. "I don't know, but I feel like, whatever happens now, this is the right thing, coming back."

"That's good."

"What I've decided is that the best you can do is whatever feels the most right regardless of any particular outcome."

Alice looks at him, surprised. "You think so?"

Brad looks equally surprised. "I guess so. It just popped out."

Traffic is stopped dead several blocks north of the bridge. I hope this isn't what I think it is, Nathan thinks as his taxi rolls to a stop.

"Too many hotel around here," the driver says. "Makes bad for traffic."

"Is there anything getting through at all?"

"Not I can see."

"Hang on." Nathan opens the door and lifts himself above the car roof. Are those blue lights coming from the bridge? "Oh no," Nathan says. "I can't believe this."

The driver sticks his head out the window. "Dispatcher say bridge closed. Crazy man want to jump."

"Fuck," Nathan mutters under his breath. He fumbles a couple of bills out of his wallet and pushes them through the driver's window. "I'll walk."

"Bridge *closed*!" the driver shouts after him. "No walk, no drive!"

So this is how I have to be punished, Nathan thinks, zig-zagging through the ranks of honking cars. As he gets closer to the bridge, the full nature of the nightmare unfolds before him.

Inside a semi-circle of blue- and black-suited police, is Robin, straddling the guard rail on the east side of the bridge and clutching the urn to his chest. His voice is faintly audible, but Nathan can't make out what he's saying. He edges past the fire truck and the paramedic van, both of them silently spinning their emergency lights. The entire scene flashes like a fallen Christmas tree. He moves toward Robin, trying to make out his stream of talk, which has the appearance of the late night talk show monologue to a captive audience. He detects delicate amusement on the faces of several cops. He tries to climb over the barricade of yellow sawhorses, but a policeman stands in his way.

"Where do you think you're going?"

The sharp leather odor of the police jacket clogs Nathan's throat.

"He's mine," Nathan squeaks.

"Who's what?"

"The guy, the jumper. I'm his roommate."

"Really? So you're—" He flips open a small notepad. "Nathan?" The man's beefy face breaks into an amused grin. "He's making you famous."

Nathan glances at the cop's nameplate: "Officer Blatz, is there anything I can do?"

"Sure, come on, maybe you can keep him from going over. Not that it matters."

Nathan can see two police boats holding positions on either side of the bridge.

Blatz has a firm grip on Nathan's arm. "The chances of his getting hurt are about nil. Course, he could break his neck when he hits the water, but odds are they'll fish him out a little waterlogged but salvageable."

"Thank god."

"He got a history of this stuff?"

"Not like this."

"But crazy?"

"In his way."

"You two have, you know, a spat?"

Nathan looks at the cop. "We're just roommates."

"Right. Whatever. Maybe you ought to let him know that."

Blatz maneuvers through the press of police and rescue workers. "Make way, coming through, got the boyfriend right here."

There are shreds of film everywhere and Ellen in the middle of them, looking at Alice with those small, watery eyes. It's pretty obvious what they're asking, those eyes, but Alice isn't having any of it.

"Thanks for coming. I didn't think you would."

"Me neither." Alice's face is closed up crudely, like the end of a bread sack with a twist tie on it. "I couldn't just let it lie."

"I've been missing you." She stands to hug Alice, who remains motionless, stiff.

"Okay," Ellen backs away. "You're mad. I think I made a mistake last night."

"Maybe," Alice says. "Who knows? Maybe that's what was supposed to happen to slow things down."

"Slow down?" Ellen gulps.

"I think there's some stuff we both need to work out. Before we decide if we want to do this. Commit to something."

"Look, I know it may not seem like it, but I'm committed already. I'm there."

"Maybe you're sure of that now. But taking a break to make sure? Could be a good thing."

"Is this because Brad came back? Are you thinking—?"

"No, it's not Brad, and it's not you, not entirely. It's just the whole mess."

"I don't get it. Is there something else? Something I don't know?"

"Just me," Alice says. "Just me you don't know."

Officer Blatz pushes Nathan forward and Robin's face breaks into a beatific smile.

"Hi, Nathan!" he calls brightly. "Isn't this perfect! We've had such a lovely day. I showed Mother where we met—Newport's, remember? And then we went to the Hancock and looked at the whole city and now here we are, and you show up. Perfect!" He giggles.

"Robin, what are you doing?"

"I'm just sitting here."

"Why don't you sit somewhere else?"

"Like in my patrol car," mutters Officer Blatz.

"I don't think I was going to jump at first. I was just sitting here with the urn, with Mother, talking things over. Then some busybody called the cops, and when they said, 'Don't jump,' I thought, Oh yeah, why not? Maybe that's a good idea."

"Why?"

"Well, I don't know. Just a feeling. You know, with everything that's happened, the next logical thing might be to simply fall a very long way."

"Say something," Blatz says in Nathan's ear. "So we can get out of here by dinner time."

Nathan wracks his brain for some way to stop Robin from doing what his mind is set on. It isn't something he's ever been very successful at. He decides to be blunt.

"What can I say to keep you from going over? Do you want reverse psychology? Do you want me to beg? To apologize? What?"

"The fact that you came here at all is sweet," Robin says. "You've always gone the extra mile for me. And I can repay you by letting you know that it will never be necessary again."

"That's not what I want," Nathan says.

But Robin has disappeared from view. A woman screams, and then several other voices join in the cry.

"He's over," barks a tired voice through a megaphone.

As Nathan runs to the side of the bridge, he hears the distant sounds of splashing and voices and boat motors sputtering.

"Not too far," Blatz says, grabbing Nathan's belt.

Nathan leans over the side and looks down to the soft, flat carpet of gray-green water in which Robin is floating, face down, like a crooked starfish. The urn is briefly visible bobbing a few yards from Robin's left hand, then, coughing forth a large, ashen bubble, it twists and drops from sight, leaving a gray smear in the water.

There seems to be no sound for several seconds as Nathan looks down on the maybe fatally broken body of his lover, trying to summon up some sharp feeling for what is happening. But where he should be feeling fear or anguish, there is only a remote sense of change, a far-off shudder through a padded, unresponsive system.

"Don't sweat it, buddy—they've got him," says Blatz, placing a firm grip on Nathan arm.

In a flash, a diver is beside Robin's body, and pushes him into the arms of someone on board. People swarm around him, and Nathan is left trying to reconstruct in his mind the image his face—the familiar eyes, nose, and lips of his lover—and finds it ultimately impossible to do.

"Come on," says the policeman, with an almost solicitous tone. "I'll take you down to the ambulance."

"If you don't mind," Nathan says, "I'd like to sit here a minute and collect myself." He immediately drops to rest against a massive iron girder.

"Suit yourself," the cop says. "But you'd better get your feet out of the road. Those cabbies are pretty pissed off."

Wednesday the 15th

With the light for outdoor painting gone, Florence has turned to a darker palette of oranges, reds, and greens imbued with the black of almost-nightfall. It matches her melancholy mood. On her left is a mostly blank paper, lightly scored with pencil marks—the beginning of a portrait of Tommy. On the easel now is a sheet of paper that's still entirely blank—what may yet become the face of her departed husband.

It happened like this: as a surprise for Tommy, she was copying a snapshot taken of him on board the cruise ship that was the site of their first real date. But just as she began, a feeling of guilt stole over her: she had never painted Arnie. Oh, she had tried to paint him in the life, but he would never sit still long enough, not without something like sales reports to fiddle with or a stack of magazines to catch up on. Perhaps it would be a sweet, cleansing thing to paint Arnie from memory. So out came the blank sheet of paper. And the effort froze her.

Idly, she fills the brush with ocher, then mashes it into the paper, spinning the splayed bristles. She repeats with burnt orange, viridian, and a color she calls blood lemon, until the paper is riddled with colors. Then with a fat brush she water-washes the field of color blobs, transforming them into vivid wounds, or distant ruined planets.

There is too much weight on everything. What kind of relationship should she have with Tommy? The thought of sharing a night has certainly occurred to both of them, but to actually do it—she feels a shudder that is not merely physical. Once again, and not for the first time, she thinks: Does life never reach the plane where it is a familiar, manageable string of days?

She sighs and crumples the paper. "I'm sorry, Arnie. I don't have it in me today."

Duchess sniffs her way over to the wad of paper, lifts it gingerly in her teeth, and trots over to her pillow to enjoy a long session of shredding and devouring the soggy pulp. Florence sighs and pulls out a fresh sheet and falls once again into a brown study.

The ringing buzzer interrupts her battle with the blank paper. With a sigh, she goes to the intercom. "Yes?"

"Yes ma'am, it's Alphonse Duchossois?"

"What a pleasure. Come right up, Alphonse." She presses the entry button, glad to have a distraction.

In a few moments, Alphonse is in her doorway. He appears smaller, as though risen from a long convalescence.

"Come in, dear. How are you? I hope everyone is well?"

"Tolerable. The twins are a handful."

"How about you? Getting along?"

He follows her to the living room and settles into the couch, looking tired and lean.

"I'm adjusting. They've got me working in a night basketball program for kids at Horner Park."

"Would you like some tea?"

He shakes his head. "I better say this quick 'cause it ain't easy." He swallows. "I came to say how I appreciate this." He pulls a letter from his jacket. "But I can't accept it."

"Oh, Alphonse, please," Florence says. "It's something I want to do."

He presses the letter into Florence's hand. "You've been kind enough already. This is too generous."

"With Giselle going back to school, I'm sure you could use the help. And honestly this is the best thing I could imagine to do with the money."

Alphonse shakes his head. "Eloise and I talked it over. It just don't feel right. No disrespect to you, ma'am."

"Don't you 'ma'am' me, Alphonse. We know each other too well by now. For whatever reason, we have gotten involved in each other's business and I don't want it any other way."

Alphonse looks uncertainly at the walls and the paintings done as part of Florence's rehabilitation. "We hung that one painting you gave me. In our bedroom."

"I'm honored." Florence blushes slightly. "Please, Alphonse. Let's think of someway I can help. Would it be easier if this was just a loan until you get back on your feet?"

"Well that would be a different way of looking at it. It's just for a time."

"Of course it is." Florence touches his hand. "What do you think you'll do?"

He sighs. "Well, helping these kids at Horner—it feels pretty right to me. More right than I expected. I'm going to look for a counselor position and maybe do some coaching. Course, I'll need some other job, too, but it's not so important what."

"I miss you coming by every day."

Alphonse nods and then puts his hands on his knees. "Let me talk with Eloise. I appreciate your hearing me out."

"Why, of course." She hands the letter back to Alphonse. "Just hang onto this for now. I'll keep hoping you can accept this…loan."

"We're obliged," Alphonse says, bowing to kiss her on the cheek. "Much."

Taking Duchess for her afternoon walk, the buoyant mood that followed Alphonse's visit has evaporated. Duchess trots beside her, eyes bright for everything in the world, as if every day is new. But with the sky pressing down on the barren trees, Florence feels that she is scuttling, like a bug under a descending boot. She cannot get the portraits out of her head. What is wrong with her?

"There is nothing that is never with us."

The voice, still about two blocks away, begins to insinuate itself into her thoughts.

"The Oriental sages described birth and death as a temporary phase through which our enduring spirits pass."

Florence allows the dog to continue pulling her along, but there is a hesitation in her step, a backward leaning keeping the leash taut.

"Life, death. They are much the same, sisterbrother, as dreams and wakefulness. But which is which? Other equally ancient religions argue that the world is the hell of biblical prophecy, and at times it is a contention hard to argue."

She approaches nervously, but then with more confidence as a new idea breaks upon her.

"Is aging not a punishment? Is it not cruel to count the passing of days? This the afterlife will spare us. Hell indeed is as eternal as heaven."

She is close enough now to see the shiny patches on his black suit. And the careful mending of the left cuff, and the belt loop loose at one end, hanging below the worn belt.

"But what is the true difference? It must be more than climates, one hot, one cool. Is one state desire and the other state a profound absence of desire? And if so, which is heaven, which is hell?"

The hat at his feet has two bills in it, and a smattering of change. Florence steps up to it.

"Excuse me." She works the handle of her purse hard within her fingers.

"Yes, sister?" His smile bestows upon her a row of large, yellowing, almost equine teeth. "Can I be of service to you?" His non-preaching voice is smooth and calm.

"May I?" she stammers, "May I buy you dinner?"

He cocks his head, appearing to Florence very like a sparrow assessing a bread crumb. He pats his stomach and says, "Why, that is an idea."

"We can step over to that diner, if you don't mind."

"I normally take a fast food dinner home with me, but I heartily welcome the change." He scoops the money into his coat pocket, settles the hat on his head, and follows Florence to the diner, where Elias seats them with a quizzical look.

"You can order whatever you like," she tells the preacher. Out of the corner of her eye she see Duchess press her nose against the window and whimper.

His voice rumbles deeply within his bony frame. "I have always fancied navy bean soup and tuna melt in a sit-down establishment."

After Elias takes their orders, Florence regards the preacher. "I've seen you many times," she says. "You gave me a chocolate coin on Halloween."

He smiles to himself. "I am around throughout the day."

"I have often felt—" She struggles to make sense of her thoughts. "That you have preached specifically to something within me."

"I am not a gypsy," he says seriously. "The word is not telling fortunes."

The waitress, Soo, brings the soup and Brother Even attacks the bowl as soon as it hits the table.

"But what you say," Florence presses, "your sermons, always seem to be something directed at me, at what I'm experiencing in my life. How do you do that?"

With every sip of soup, the preacher extends his lower lip to greet the bowl of the spoon, funneling the broth directly down his wattled throat. "The word is the word, and what we hear is what we need."

"Are you cryptic by intent or by nature?"

"I don't know how to answer that." He tilts the bowl to get at the last of the bean soup. "I guess that means by nature."

"If I asked a direct question, could you give me an answer?"

He regards her with a Mandarin smile in his eyes. "To that I would say, sister, that direct questions are rarely to the point."

"What do you know about the afterlife?"

He chuckles softly. "Sadly, I am not privileged with such an exacting vision."

"It's not that I think you're a messiah or anything," says Florence, suddenly self-conscious. "But you have given these things so much thought. The things you say about life and death. You must, well, I thought you must have some idea."

"I would say," the preacher says slowly, "that you know as much as I do. But you mustn't doubt what you know to really know it."

Florence sighs. "I wanted answers. I'm too old for religious instruction."

The preacher wipes his chin. "Every morning is a call. The call is constant and unrelenting."

Soo slides the hot sandwich in front of the preacher. He lifts his eyes and whispers, "Thank you, Jesus." And then to Florence: "Would it be an imposition to get a side of onion rings?"

Perhaps as a response to the preacher's frustrating abstractions, Florence picks up the brush as soon as she gets home and starts to paint. Just to capture something. If you can't express everything, the whole thing, just capture one small, definable fragment of time, of light, of feeling. Working in browns, cutting some with white, fortifying others with black and red, she draws a cloud of feeling around her, pulls it tight, and, funneling it down into paint, dabs it tenderly to the paper: knuckle and nail, liver spot and cuticle, and the scar, the honeymoon scar where the hook caught him as they fished off the coast of Texas in 1957. Only a hand, perhaps, but as much of a portrait as she can manage. Arnie would understand.

Friday the 17th

It comes as no surprise—since there is no greater fan of *The City by The Flake* than Larry O. Larry—that the arrival of the winter issue is cause for an all-out assault on its pages when he arrives at Stimpy's. Without a word to his coworkers, he grabs the zine out of the box and takes it directly to the tiny bathroom stall where he does his most intensive reading. What *is* a surprise is the roar of outrage that precedes by mere seconds the explosion from the tiny, graffitoed cube—which Ng has likened to an upright coffin—of Larry, scarlet across both vast expanses of jowl, and waving the flimsy zine in the air.

"Are you shitting me?" Larry cries, looking from Ng to Leda and back to the magazine—the last receiving the looks of deepest injury. "You?" He points at Ng. "Got in this magazine?"

Ng shrugs. He can't conceal a smile.

Larry looks at the magazine again. "The Flake doesn't take unsolicited submissions. How did you do it? Can you help me?"

Ng and Leda exchange glances. "It was just a lucky break," Ng says.

"You met the Flake? Is that it? I knew he came in here. There's always those caricatures of Chiquita Banana in it."

"Watch it, Larry," Leda snaps.

"Tell me who he is. Give him some of my work. If he likes your stuff, he'll go nuts when he sees what I'm doing."

"I can't tell you. He's got this thing about staying anonymous."

"No shit, Sherlock. I figured that out. But you could help me out. We're compadres. Slaves in the trade. Kindred, you know, souls."

Ng looks pained. "He has these rules. Special rules about submissions."

Larry holds up a hand to stop the stream of rationalizing. Looking skyward for sympathy, he moans, "Is this really necessary?"

On the whole, Ng thinks later, Larry's loss of composure is one of the most satisfying ancillary benefits of getting in the book. It almost beats the glow of pride in Leda's eyes. But not quite.

∞

The Art Institute smells dusty. Ivan thinks of it now as the museum smell, having been to nearly every one of the boring places in the past few weeks. He waits behind a group of old women chattering and shaking out their umbrellas on the marble floor.

After the fire and the attack by the crazy man, Ivan had dropped out of sight. He sensed danger everywhere, and avoided his usual haunts. So he began spending his days wandering through museums, the only places you can stay all day for only a few dollars.

He pays the entrance fee and receives a blue metal button to pin on his shirt.

A painted urn reminds him of the logo Ng drew for him, which is all that remains of the gang. Ivan takes the paper out of his pocket and looks at it. The golden scales, the pointed claws dripping with poison. The signal of his grand schemes, and the token of his betrayal. Looking at it now is a mingled, pleasure-pain sensation like grinding down on a bad tooth.

Ivan spends hours looking at the weapons—tiny guns, enormous axes, and especially a knife he wishes he could own, with spring-loaded side blades that jut from the main blade. He imagines the terrible wounds it could make if he stuck it into the Marine. Or Ng.

But it is later, as he wanders among the pretty, boring paintings that he suddenly understands what he has to do. He stumbles upon a large, brightly colored painting of a picnic beside a river. A girl is running, from where her parents sit on a blanket, toward a man playing a trumpet. Even though you can't see their faces, everyone looks stupidly happy. He turns away in disgust. But something makes him turn back. He stares at the painting, and through the old-fashioned clothes and the tiny points of color, he begins to see something else. That is where Ng gets his strength. Those people. That is where Ivan will attack. Ivan remembers the old man at the diner wielding a bat. And then the Marine. How are they connected? Sometimes none of it makes sense. He is grasping, and keeps coming back to one thing: the diner.

Fire devours fire.

Ng almost passes Parsley's house because the Honda in front is no longer blue, but re-painted a dark, somber green. The paint job is cheap, bubbled, and obscures the brand logo on the trunk. He winces, trying not to notice whether his insults are still visible, scored into the metal under the new paint.

All Leda had said, when the magazine appeared, was, "Now you should go." They hadn't discussed it further. He knew she was right.

The unpainted pine steps up to the front porch are weathered, spongy and uneven. A few dried marigolds straggle from the window boxes. The windows are dark and dusty on the inside. Ng swallows hard and knocks.

Parsley's face appears briefly in one pane of the door's fan-shaped window, vanishes, then reappears, with an inquisitive arch to the eyebrows, and then wrinkles at the corners of the eyes—which to Ng's point of view could mean, without the rest of the face for context, either pleasure or pain. Then the window is empty again.

There is a pause, and Ng is almost on the point of going back down the steps when the door finally opens, and Mr. Parsley is standing there saying, "I must say, Ng, this is quite a surprise."

"I hope I'm not disturbing you. I didn't call first."

"I'm not really prepared for company, but you can come in if you don't say anything about the mess." He ushers Ng into a dark, close room, the walls of which are covered with paintings and drawings. Ng recognizes some of them from his class, and finds one of his own right above the couch where he sits.

"To what do I owe the pleasure?" Mr. Parsley asks, dropping into a large, overstuffed armchair, the back of which is draped with a lace antimacassar that seems to emerge in rays from his head.

"I've meant to contact you for a long time. But I wasn't sure I should." The teacher looks drawn, ill. His Adam's apple protrudes even more than before.

"What changed your mind? Wait." He sits forward. "Do you want a soda?"

"No, I'm fine. I decided to come by when I got into this magazine." He pulls a copy of *The City by The Flake* from his jacket and hands it to Mr. Parsley.

The teacher flips through the pages, smiling. "I'm very proud of you. I know you'll do well. Are you taking oil painting this year?"

Ng shrinks into the seat cushions. "No, I'm taking some time off."

"Really," Mr. Parsley says, infusing the word with suspicious recognition.

Ng falters. He tries to imagine a quick exit. But he hears Leda's voice in his head saying: *It's why you came here, stupid.* He swallows. "I felt bad about what happened. To you, I mean."

"Oh? Why is that?"

Ng tries to read his old teacher's expression, but the evening shadows seem to deepen every moment, making Mr. Parsley appear even more distant.

"It was unfair. What happened had nothing to do with you personally."

"Really? It felt personal."

"You were just a target for what…for what happened."

Mr. Parsley regards Ng carefully. "I still don't know why this brought you here."

"To apologize," Ng blurts. Every muscle in his body has gone rigid with fear.

"Why should you apologize? Do you have that much guilt?" Mr. Parsley laughs. "I mean, you're not saying it was *you?*"

Ng's face is a mask. "It was a mistake. I didn't have a choice."

Parsley releases a laugh that is more like a gasp. "What? You? How could that happen?" He starts to rise from his chair, then collapses. "I'm…wow."

"Look, I brought some money to pay for the car." Ng places an envelope on the coffee table. "Five hundred dollars."

Parsley stares out the window. He rubs his face. "Seriously, Ng. Does that look like a five hundred dollar paint job?"

Ng can hear the lid of a pot rattling as its contents boil up on the stove.

"I'll take the money, Ng. I don't know what else to do. I forgive you. I don't understand, but I guess I know you're a good kid basically."

"You were the best teacher I ever had."

"Can I ask why you did it?"

"It's a long story."

"It would have been cheaper to refuse to do it."

Ng says nothing.

Parsley stands. "Listen, it's time for me to take my medicine. Can you let yourself out?" Without another word, the teacher disappears into the kitchen.

Ng opens the front door and steps outside. The street appears quite naked. Somehow, all of the leaves have disappeared.

The diner is in a busy neighborhood, lots of whores and drunken frat boys at night, but Ivan knows a thing or two about locks. It's a simple matter, once inside, to fire up the giant grill, stack some boxes of napkins on top, and slip back out again. From down the block, Ivan watches until the first lick of flame appears above the diner's roof. When a window explodes and smoke pours out, he has to tear himself away.

Monday the 20th

Nathan brings the toasted bagel on a plate, with a mug of strong coffee. "Bagel and a shmear," he says cheerfully.

Robin says nothing, staring at the weather map on TV. It's been this way since the Plunge.

A fall from a smidge over one hundred feet can apparently render water momentarily solid, with the equivalent flex of a pine deck extension on your average suburban bungalow. That is, if it's not entered skillfully. Robin did not enter the water skillfully. He struck it, rather, like a moth trying vainly to paddle out of the way of a windshield. He came home from the hospital after a couple of days with a collar brace on his neck, crutches to ease the strain on a badly twisted knee, and a patchwork of bruises on his face and torso, which took the brunt of the impact.

And that's the good news. The bad news is the thousands of dollars in fines, the looming legal fees, and the expensive schedule of frequent psychiatric consultations stretching into the foreseeable future. With only one income and Robin uninsured, Nathan regularly pores over the checkbook, wondering how long they can last before something will have to give.

Nathan spreads some bitter marmalade on the bagel. "It's the kind you like," he says.

Robin's conscious, wakeful silence is worse than a coma. It's like he's opted to be a vegetable. His lacerated tongue had been repaired with seven stitches, but he seems to not have the will to make the swollen muscle work. He sits on the couch, almost motionless, except to sip a mug of tomato soup or click the remote control from talk show to the news and back.

Nathan talks to him about work, weather, sports—whatever bland things he can think of. But all the time he wants to scream, to have a shouting argument about what happened, why, and how can they possibly go on. He lays the plate on the coffee table.

"Are you going to be mad at me forever? Just nod or something, I have to know."

The head remains uncannily still in reply.

∞

The first thing Nathan does at work is check his messages—and there are a ton of them. He's been screening calls in order to manage the deluge of appeals from concerned friends, lawyers, doctors, and well, Alice.

As expected, there's another message from her: "*Hey, it's me again, just checking in. Getting a little worried. I really hope everything is okay. If you get a chance today.*"

Thoughts of Alice conjure up a complex flavor in Nathan's mouth. He has powerful but fuzzy recollections of her body, the taste of her. But those sensations were the force that tore his life apart. He hits the skip button and continues writing phone numbers on individual yellow sticky notes. Nathan attacks his messages for hours, pulling every last annoying sticky note petal off his phone until it looks strangely denuded and small. There is one more call to make. He pulls the number from his wallet and dials.

"Hello?" says a small, drawling voice.

"Hi, Janie, it's Nathan. Robin's friend?"

"Oh. Yes." The already demure voice retracts further in this one word. "I remember you."

"The reason I'm calling is Robin's had an accident—it's not serious, I mean not very—and I was wondering if you would be able to visit him?"

"Is he hurt bad?"

"He's home now, recuperating, but I think it would mean a lot to him if—"

"I don't think I can do that."

"Look, Janie, you're all he has left. Thursday is Thanksgiving. You can come for dinner."

"It's awful short notice."

"I'll pay your way, whatever it takes."

"I'm not sure…I don't know if Robin and I have much left to offer each other."

"Janie, you're the only person I know who can reach him. If nothing else, do it for your mother."

He can hear the echoey sound of her hand covering the receiver.

"Please think it over," he says loudly.

She uncovers the mouthpiece. "I'll think it over. I have to go now."

Nathan's been skirting Alice's flower shop, cutting onto a side street two blocks earlier than normal. Not that he wants to avoid her forever, but there doesn't seem to be anything to say. The problem is, he's running out of clean shirts, and his dry cleaner is perilously close to Urbs in Horto's window. Today he decides to make a dash for a batch of shirts that have been circling the cleaner's motorized rack for two weeks now. Which of course means Alice steps out of a copy shop, right in front of him, carrying an armful of purple fliers.

"Bump," Alice says, and giggles nervously.

"Oh, god, hi," Nathan says. "Ha-ha."

There is an awkward pause in which Nathan considers falling to the ground to avoid the rest of the exchange. In the end, he merely blushes, the sight of which causes Alice's heart to swell painfully. Her eyes betray her attempt to muster a nonchalant expression.

"I'm sorry I didn't call," he stammers. "I've hand my hands full."

"Sure, I understand. I heard, you know, about Robin. How awful."

"Yeah, well."

Alice shifts the stack of fliers in her arms. "Oh, hey." She hands Nathan one off the top. "We're having a bake sale. To fund our first CD." She looks away. "Not that you have to come or anything. But if Robin's feeling better, I do a killer cheesecake."

They stand there, each searching for a comment that will release them or bring them to a place where they can be at ease again.

"Is everything, you know, okay?" Alice says casually.

"I'm just playing nursemaid right now. How about you and your friend?"

"Hiatus," she says simply.

"That sounds nice. A total vacation from everything is what I need."

Alice's eyes droop sadly. "Funny, isn't it—you can pine for love and affection, and then when you get it, too much of it, you crave being alone again."

Nathan opts for a change of subject. "What happened to the diner?"

"Burned a couple nights ago. Isn't that awful? Poor Mr. Kanakes."

"I guess the end of the world really is approaching."

"God, I hope not," Alice laughs ruefully. "If this is how it ends, I'm going to be pretty pissed off."

Coming home to find Robin unmoved from his spot on the couch—same bathrobe, same half-eaten bagel before him—causes Nathan to unravel.

"When did you bathe last?" he says, standing over Robin like an angry schoolmarm. "You don't have to answer. I can smell you. That's it. You're bathing tonight. I don't care where you sleep, you can't smell like that."

Robin looks at him and nods.

Nathan runs a bath and helps Robin undress and lowers him in. The sight of the bruised flanks and Robin's underfed stomach touches him. He ladles water over Robin's hair with his two hands and squirts shampoo into the damp curls. Robin leans his head back and Nathan scrubs the shampoo vigorously. Robin's head begins to loll, and Nathan wonders if he's falling asleep when Robin clears his throat.

"When ah dumped—" Robin says.

"What?" Nathan is startled at the sound of the croaky voice.

"When ah dumped," Robin speaks slowly around his sutured tongue. "Di you dump apter me?"

Nathan's hands continue to scoop and pour water, more and more slowly.

"No," he says at last, his eyes filling with tears. "No, I didn't jump after you."

Robin's hand reaches up and touches Nathan's face. "At's okay. I unnerstan."

"I didn't even consider it." He cradles Robin's wet skull and kisses it. "How's that for love? Can you forgive me?"

Unexpectedly, Robin nods in reply. "Yesh," he slurs. "Cause you got Danie do call."

"What? Janie called? Here? Is she coming for Thanksgiving?"

Robin, trembling, nods, his silence this time perfectly eloquent.

Tuesday the 21st

The world is crazy. Opening the *Sun-Times* these days is like turning a radio on at full volume. Everything is loud, sensational. Just a few days ago, reading about that guy jumping off the Michigan Avenue Bridge, Danny had actually winced, as if in pain, at the attention grab of another self-absorbed fruitcake. Obviously the guy didn't have a real death wish. You want to die, you don't jump into water, you jump into pavement. But hey, he wants it that bad, a guy's entitled to his fifteen minutes.

And today, as he winces through the police blotters and gossip columns, he happens to see, buried inside, a small item about a fire on the north side. One of those things too common to really be news, except there is some probable petty arson. Insurance fraud, most like. And as he places the address on the city map in his mind, he realizes it is the diner where Soo works. His first reaction is to think he should call Soo, make sure she's okay for money, and all that. But then he remembers—the gang punk had been there—didn't Soo tell him that? His blood stops, leaving his hands stiff and cold as though dead.

Elias feels like a cave dweller, entering the windowless, reeking space that was his diner, stepping over melted ceiling tiles and crunching glass—slabs, shards, and dimly sparkling grit—underfoot. Tommy is at his side, holding his arm. Tommy raced over as soon as he heard about the fire and offered Elias every sort of sympathy, outrage, and support. His hair, still wet from his shower, falls into his face.

"Gimme a broom," he jokes. "I'll get this place ship-shape by lunchtime."

"We can't clean up anything until the insurance company has settled the cause of the fire." Elias sighs. "Where to begin, anyway?" He wipes off a bench seat with his handkerchief and sits down.

"I'm going to check out the cold storage," Tommy says, and marches off to the kitchen. "Your cheese may be okay."

Elias looks around at the dark, alien interior of a space in which he's spent, what, two-thirds of his life? He can pick out various things he recognizes—the dishware, the menus—but the whole of it looks strange and even threatening. The odor of smoke within the cold rubble continues to evoke in him a primal sense of fear. The bubbled linoleum appears soft and fathomless as movie quicksand. He sees phantom sparks at the edge of his vision. In stark terms, the damage is light enough—mostly smoke and melted plastic—that the diner could be open again in a matter of days. But it is hard to imagine the place busy again—open, light, and smelling of Luis's hot grill.

That's the hell of a thing like this—it snaps your reality at the roots, and suddenly you're floating in this other place without familiar boundaries, and there's no way back. It's terrifying to Elias how hard it is to reconstruct what there was before, even hours earlier. That's why he keeps the portrait of his wife by the door at home, to keep him in touch with a part of his life that he was pushed from in one flashing moment. But that doesn't work, really. Even he'll admit that the photograph of his wife's face no longer signifies her as a living, breathing person, but has taken its own place in the landscape of his life. It is the picture he would miss if it were suddenly gone, not his wife.

The diner has been the same kind of totem, tended all these years with the love he feels for his absent wife, daughter, and granddaughter. He feels there should be a funeral, or some kind of ceremony to memorialize the loss. He should pour ashes on his head, tear his clothes. But instead there are insurance forms and discussions of money, which signify the diner in terms that grown men can share between themselves, and write into the boxes on forms that describe and capture the event and put it safely to rest.

Out of the swirl of alien sensations emerges a familiar sight: Ng's drawing is still taped to the counter—Elias flying like Superman. The paper is discolored now by smoke and warped by spray from the firehoses. Elias carefully peels it loose and slides it into his overcoat pocket, feeling suddenly better.

As Danny suspected, the punk passes by the diner as though he lives in the area and has to run his daily errands—pick up laundry, buy milk, that sort of thing. He barely pauses, hands in pockets, to survey the damage, just as many other people are doing, surprised by the sudden, violent change in the neighborhood's fabric. Even half a block away, Danny can feel the boy's satisfaction as he passes by.

Danny leaves his car and follows the boy on foot, keeping well behind. He trails him onto the el, riding one car back, watching through the murky windows. They exit at Chicago and State. Still without an idea of what he's going to do, if anything, Danny follows the kid to Michigan Avenue.

Damn, is it that close to Christmas? Danny thinks, eyeing the fluttering candy canes hanging from the streetlights and the Santa Clauses chuckling in display windows across the street.

The kid pauses in front of the Victoria's Secret store, and then crosses the street and into the lobby of the Hancock Building. Danny follows, hoping the kid will go up to the observation deck, where he would be trapped.

Unfortunately, Danny momentarily pins an old woman's handbag in the revolving door, and her angry cry causes the boy to turn around. He sees Danny and takes off running. Danny pushes past the old woman and gives chase.

Surprisingly, the boy isn't very fast. He runs with a young kid's abrupt switches and cutbacks, sliding on the smooth lobby floors. Danny bounces himself off the walls to keep up. The kid bursts back outside, running past a giant rabbit sculpture and down into the sunken courtyard. Danny grabs the rabbit's foot to pivot around the railing and down the clattering, shallow stairs. The boy stumbles at the bottom, sprawling briefly, already up on hands and toes when Danny lands on him, and both man and boy splay, spread-eagled like a single blurred image.

The boy doesn't struggle, but pleads in a high-pitched, hysterical voice. "Why you doing this man? Come on, man, fuck off."

Danny quickly pats the boy down for a weapon. The boy is whimpering, and smells like cigarette smoke and, well, like Boy. Kind of funky, and insufficiently washed.

The round-toed shoes of a cop skid to a stop beside them. A hand pulls Danny to his feet, and Danny pulls the boy up with him.

"What the hell is going on?" the cop says. He is red in the face and blowing hard.

"Well, officer." Danny leans over, hands on his knees, and panting. "This kid attacked my son Ng and burned down a diner where my ex-wife works."

The boy interrupts his squealing protests, and stares at Danny. "You lie. Ng have no father."

"Not always, no," Danny says, feeling dizzy. "But today he does."

Thursday the 23rd (Thanksgiving Day)

Tony wakes feeling that something is not right. He sits up and cocks his head. There is a silence underneath the usual noises of his family that he can't place. He is momentarily frightened by the dream-like sensation of something pressing down, muting the world. He pulls the curtains aside and sees the first snow of the season flocking the trees and grass like fluff sprayed out of a can. At almost the same time, he smells the turkey smells, the onion and sage stuffing smells, and a happiness wells up inside of him that is so natural he doesn't even remark on how long it's been absent. He shuffles out of his bedroom rubbing his eyes, feeling comforted and small and, for the day at least, a child.

"Hey, sleepyhead," says his mother.

"Why is everybody up so early?" He yawns extravagantly, and his ears pop.

"We get up when the babies get up. Your sister's studying for that test, so we got to watch them."

"She studying on Thanksgiving?"

"Test is next week," Alphonse says from the rocking chair where he is bottle-feeding Evander, who grabs and fusses at the nearly empty bottle.

"After you eat something and get dressed, you can help me," Eloise says. "There's potatoes to do, and—"

"Can I see the turkey?"

Eloise opens the oven door, and Tony peers inside at the just barely brown, taut skin of the bird.

"I want to squirt it," he says, grabbing for the bulb of the baster.

"Later," Eloise says, shutting the door. "You letting all the heat out."

"That Tony?" Giselle calls from her room. "Come in here and ask me questions for the test."

"You come out here. I want to eat some Sugar Smacks."

Giselle comes out with her fat *ACT Made Easy* book. "They got questions in here you couldn't answer if you were some kind of Einstein," she sighs.

Tony pours his cereal, humming to himself. Eloise bumps him with her hip, and he bumps back. "Quit it, you'll make me spill the milk."

Giselle looks over at Alphonse, who has a funny look on his face. "What's wrong, Dad? Evander wet on you?"

"Nothing." Alphonse touches the corner of his eye. "Evander's fine. Everybody's fine. Can't a man sit peaceful on a Thanksgiving morning?"

Elias sets the bottle of wine on the table. "I can't tell you how much I appreciate your inviting me to dinner."

"How are the repairs coming?" Ng says. He dunks a potato chip in onion dip and devours it. "Will you be open soon?"

"I have to confess I've been letting the question hang," Elias says ruefully. "I'm not sure it's the best idea. The diner was losing a lot of money."

"I know, Mom told me. But *why* do you think?"

"I thought it was bad service, but hiring your mother fixed that, and we still couldn't break even."

"I tell you why," Soo says from the kitchen.

"I know what you think," Elias interrupts. "Your mother thinks the food is boring. But how should I change it?"

"Not boring," Soo says, entering the room with a towel-covered platter. "Too much like every place." She sets the platter on the table. "This your answer." She pulls away the towel, revealing three large rolls.

"Hey, those are my Mexican spring rolls," Ng exclaims. "I thought you hated those, Mom."

"Not hate," Soo says. "Not my taste, but good for make better restaurant business."

"This is my answer?" Elias picks one up and turns it. "An egg roll?"

"You try, it explain everything."

Ng takes one and dunks it in the pool of green salsa in the middle of the platter. "It's what I made trying to cook Mexican food with the stuff in our kitchen. Call it Mexicanese, or Vietnamexican."

Elias takes a tentative bite. "Luis would have a few choice words to say about this."

Soo takes a bite of her own roll. "Luis happy if we make money."

"I like it." Elias dips the second bite in the salsa. "It's strange, but I like it."

"But Mom," Ng moans, "don't we get real Thanksgiving food?"

"Sure! I make fish soup, beef salad, full menu show Elias."

Ng rolls his eyes. "Couldn't you have done this *tomorrow*?"

Hobbling and hesitant, Robin took charge of the meal over Nathan's protests, setting the table with every serving dish, candlestick, and obscurely intentioned utensil in the house. As he cooks and runs between stove and table and cutting board, he maintains a stream of chatter directed at Janie, who sits quietly at the table with a lukewarm cup of coffee, heavily creamed and sugared—the way she insists she likes it.

Nathan watches her with a kind of awkward fascination. She moves through their apartment with a bearing of impermeability, as though she imagines herself Joan of Arc, walking untouched through a hail of arrows—protected from the perils around her by keeping a firm grip on her sense of personal salvation.

But Robin seems unaware of her remoteness, just happy to have her nearby. His chatter is mostly of childhood happenings—"Remember when you dropped your fishing pole and Dad lowered Mom by her ankles to get it? Remember that Halloween you wanted to be Alice in Wonderland, and you made Mom dye your hair blonde?"—to each of which Janet offers a smile that could be anything from bittersweet pleasure to merely polite.

Nathan, after everything he could do in the kitchen had been done, lounges in front of the TV working his way slowly through a six-pack of microbrew, feeling acutely the outsider.

Slowly the meal emerges—traditional, rich, fatty, and enticing. A ham steams from its burnished skin, the creamed sweet potatoes repose under a blanket of sabayon—Robin couldn't bring himself to do marshmallows—the cranberry relish bejewels a cut-glass bowl. The opulence of the food seems to dress up the moment beyond its meager capacity. Robin calls everyone to the table, as if there were relatives galore spread throughout the apartment.

The three of them take their places. Nathan is feeling a little buzzed.

"Janie, would you say the grace?" Robin takes her hand before she can answer.

"All right." She looks at Nathan and they tentatively clasp hands. Then Robin reaches his other hand across the table, and Nathan places his fingers in the open, scarred palm.

Janie lowers her head and thinks for a moment. "Lord our father in your heaven, bless us on this day for we have suffered a year of trials."

"And then some," Nathan mutters.

Janie briefly opens one eye. "Father, in your wisdom you have given us trials to make us grow in spirit. We have not always met your challenge, but we have struggled to do your work. We have tried to follow your word, even when it isn't especially clear with regard to our duties and obligations."

Nathan opens his eyes and steals a peek at Robin, whose own eyelids are squeezed tightly shut.

"But know that always we try to find our way within the righteous path, and give thanks for your benevolence and love."

She pauses so long at this point, that Nathan and Robin unclasp their hands and sit back, ready to have at the ham, which is exuding cruelly delicious odors.

"And please help all of us to avoid doing more damage," Janie adds softly.

Even without a clear referent, Nathan has to admit she's summed things up pretty neatly.

"And bless this food," Janie finishes quickly. She opens her eyes and briskly moves her napkin to her lap. "Amen."

The restaurant at the Four Seasons is about half-full, mostly older people and out-of-towners. It feels to Florence as though she is in another city, too, one that she hasn't seen before but which evokes a mild case of déjà vu.

"One of the benefits of old age is not having to cook a turkey anymore," she says.

"I'll toast to that," Tommy says, lifting his glass of Chianti. "I always wondered who ate at restaurants on Thanksgiving. Now I know."

"No dishes, no leftovers, and no football."

"Well, maybe a little football later."

"Oh, Arnie always—" Florence stops herself.

"It's okay to talk about him, you know. I don't mind."

"It wasn't anything. As soon as I started to say it, I thought, why interject that? What point is there?"

"You don't have to edit yourself. We've both got memories. They pop up."

"I suppose so. Especially on holidays. But I'm not sad," Florence says earnestly. "I don't want you to think that."

"I know." Tommy reaches for Florence's hand. "I know."

"Everything about this is makeshift," Alice says, as she and Molly place the door across two sawhorses. "We're a makeshift family eating on makeshift furniture."

Molly drops her end with a bang. "Is that a criticism?"

Alice flings one end of the gingham cloth across the table for Molly to grab. "No. I think I like it."

"Ah, home away from home," Chipper says, waltzing in proudly with a covered dish. "Behold the *pièce de résistance* of any Midwestern holiday meal." He whisks the cover away and flourishes a molded ring of red gelatin onto the table.

"Gorgeous," says Molly. "And I am *not* entirely joking."

"Watch it wiggle." Chipper pounds the table and the tangerine slices and pineapple chunks do indeed shimmy inside their translucent medium like eyeless sea creatures. "Cooking isn't so hard," he says.

"Careful," Alice says, "this table is rickety."

"Who's bringing the turkey? Don't tell me it's Shank."

"No turkey for me," Shanklin says, walking in with his arms around a basket of rolls and biscuits and cornbread. "I baked."

"Gimme one, dough-boy," Chipper says, lunging for a biscuit.

Alice unfolds another crepe-paper gobbler and sets it in the middle of the table as a centerpiece. "The turkey's coming," she says.

Chipper bites into the biscuit and then winces. "Butter?"

Shanklin slaps his forehead. "I knew I forgot something. I'll be right back." He lopes out the door.

Molly grunts with frustration as the stack of paper plates refuses to separate. "Why all the mystery about the turkey? Someone *is* bringing a turkey, right?"

"Yes, yes."

"It's that friend of yours—Ellen, right?"

"No!" Alice exclaims.

Molly gasps with exasperation. "Well, who then?"

"Me then," says Brad, standing in the doorway holding an enormous brown bird in a foil pan.

Chipper looks Brad up and down. "I don't know if I have enough appetite for two turkeys," he says drily.

"Now, now," Molly says, but makes no move to welcome Brad.

Chipper drops onto the couch in a posture of abject cynicism. "Is this some kind of Scrooge-and-the-Christmas-goose apology thing? Sorry I was an asshole, have a drumstick?"

Brad sets the turkey down and says, "Bingo."

Shanklin bursts in the door with a tub of margarine. "Holy crap," he says, stopping short. "I don't believe it."

Brad stiffens for another round of abuse.

Shanklin walks over to the table with awe in his eyes. "What a beautiful fucking bird."

Ellen remembers the Thanksgiving dinners of her childhood as crowded, boisterous events, with many layers of activity—women bustled in the kitchen, men lounged in the den, children hid and romped in relatives' houses to amuse themselves—and the sharp yearning to someday join the adult table.

Well, here she is at the adult table. Big whoop. Inter-family squabbles, relocations, and too many divorces have shrunk the dinner to just her own nuclear unit, Ellen and her parents. And Thanksgiving has certainly lost any romantic glow it might ever have had.

"The trouble with you kids—now, wait a minute." Tyler holds up a hand to secure silence. "I don't mean to be critical. But the trouble is that our generation treated you too well."

Ellen leaves her fork standing, for a moment, in her mashed potatoes. "Dad, do we have to?"

"I'm just talking about factual things. You're a perfect emblem of your generation. You don't want to work."

"I don't think generalizing is a healthy way to have a discussion," Carole says, hoping to deflect her husband's train of thought.

"Let me finish. You won't get a job, you can't finish school, and you can't stay in a relationship." He counts these indictments on his fingers, using his vodka gimlet to tick them off. "A job that's handed to you, and you won't take it."

"I still don't understand why you think I'd be like, yippee, I'm a waitress."

He peers into his drink. "Where's the hazelnuts?" he asks.

"I'll get them," says Carole.

"You know I like hazelnuts in my gimlets," he calls after her.

"I can finish things," Ellen mumbles.

"I'm not trying to be hard on you, honey. It just pains me to see you flounder."

"I finished my film."

Carole returns, dropping a handful of nuts into Tyler's drink. "Did you say you made a film?"

"Yes. It's a little crude, but—"

"What ever happened to that guy you were dating? Why didn't you stay together?" Tyler fishes a nut from his drink and munches it. "Steve Dooley or something."

"Dad, that was *years* ago. I was a freshman."

"Well, what happened? Nothing since?"

"No, *not* nothing since."

"Well, I don't see any boys around here."

Carole spoons more stuffing onto her husband's plate. "Tyler, don't be so—"

Ellen sets her fork down. "Dad, don't you think it's odd that I never mention any boys? That I spent so much time with Megan, and now with Alice?"

"I don't know what to think with kids your age. Everybody's got secrets."

"Anybody want coffee?" says Carole quickly. "Ty, coffee? Ellen?"

"Are you saying that you're a—that you have girlfriends?"

"That's right, Dad." Ellen pushes her chair back from the table. "I'm a big fat dyke." She walks out of the room.

Tyler looks at his wife. "Did you know?"

Carole plucks a strand of dark meat from the turkey and gives her momentarily silenced husband a cool look. "I wouldn't say she's fat. If anything, she looks a bit underfed."

Tuesday the 28th

Tony waits until Giselle leaves for her test and Eloise has taken the twins over to Auntie Germaine's. Then he sneaks out while his father is in the bathroom reading the paper. He creeps across the lawn, feeling his breath freeze on his lips. A hard cold set in over the weekend, leaving the persistent Thanksgiving snow over everything like a white stain. For a moment he fears that maybe someone came and took the guns. What would Ronnie say? But no, he had just buried them way deep, two layers down. There is the shoebox. He pries the lid off and wraps the gun in a plastic bag before jamming it in his backpack. The frozen bricks feel light in his fingers and clack together with a brittle resonance.

They give you this paper filled with little, empty eggs and a pencil to fill in certain ones, the right ones, choosing your destiny. I know a thing or two about eggs, Giselle would like to say to the worried-looking blonde girl beside her. Hatched two babies two months ago this day. But these eggs are even scarier, blank, unrevealing but filled, collectively, with her future. Maybe she won't like what hatches out of them.

The room is filled with more tension than Giselle's ever felt in one place before. And she has been in rooms where the conflict of human needs have left people weeping, caused weapons to emerge, evoked blood. But this tension almost has a voice, emerging piecemeal from everyone in the room, and blending in the air into a unified silent lament that registers in the scalp.

The proctor, a round man with a dramatic comb-over of once-red hair and a mouth like the bumper off an old car, writes a few notes on the board. Underlined four times is the phrase, "No talking."

"I have personally confiscated the tests of seventeen students in eight years," he says. "I remember the face of every one. Don't let me remember yours."

The blonde girl whimpers.

Giselle fills in the eggs that spell out her name.

The fear of what this moment represents makes her fingers stiffen. Why is she doing this again? Oh. She puts a photo of the twins on her desk, next to the calculator. Being a mother, the mothering part of it is easy, she's found. When Evander's mouth is open, she feeds him. When Jimelle's mouth is open, she changes her diaper. But being a mother in the way of giving them not life, but a Life—that's what wakes her at night.

She's done everything she can think of to prepare for the next four hours. She worked all the way through three study books, took all the tests. At first, the pain of working through the problems was like waking up after a bad night's sleep, groggy and with the sense of an unnatural weakness behind her eyes. Sleep was a constant threat as fatigue seeped down into her stomach and then into her limbs as she stared at the word problems. "Fill in the missing word or phrase." "Which three-dimensional object does this pattern form?" "Five people share three bedrooms, three are men, two work night shifts, how many are married?" But here she is, number two pencils sharpened. She kisses her fingers and touches the babies' picture.

"You may open your test booklet."

Tony lingers near the wrought iron fence, waiting for Ronnie. It's almost time for the bell and he doesn't want to walk in with the gun still in his backpack. Behind him kids are playing winter kickball, which involves a lot more throwing the ball at base runners than it does kicking. Tony is usually a favorite for winter kickball, being small and quick. He likes nothing better than eluding a wild throw and scooting home while the outfielders scramble to retrieve the ball. But he can't play now. He has to stay rooted to this spot until Ronnie shows up. The first bell rings, and slowly kids start breaking up their games and moving into the building.

"First bell," calls the vice-principal, who serves as playground monitor. "You got five minutes."

Tony ignores her. As he looks down the fencerow, flickers of bright blue jacket sleeve appear between the green posts. Finally.

"Hey, T." Ronnie flashes a quick smile. "You got it?"

Tony fumbles in his backpack. "I thought you weren't coming."

"Aw, little T worried I might leave him with the gun?" Ronnie laughs and shoves his hands in his pockets.

"Here." Tony hands out the plastic bag.

Ronnie reaches for the bag, then pauses. "You know, maybe I ought to leave the gun with you."

"What?" Tony feels suddenly hot in the middle of the icy morning.

"I mean, you one of us. Time you got ready to do a man's duty."

"No!" Tony hisses. "You have to take it."

"Just kidding, T." Ronnie looks past Tony's shoulder. "Uh–oh."

"What's this?" The vice-principal appears at Tony's side.

"Nothing." Tony drops the gun into his backpack.

"Can I see what you've got there?"

Tony looks back to where Ronnie was, and there is no one there, only a brief glimpse of bright blue jacket flickering between the posts at the end of the fence.

By the end of the first section, Giselle was taking the test personally. The questions bombarded her, each one trying to trick her, expose her ignorance. She broke the tip off her pencil over and over, she was scribbling so hard, burnishing the lead in her answer eggs until they gleamed.

Now she's free, dazed, numbed by the battle. She walks aimlessly around the campus, trying to clear her head. There are immense buildings on every side and she stands in the midst of them, trying not to put a specific name to the woozy feeling she gets imagining stepping into one.

There are young people everywhere, walking like they own these huge, lovely, open buildings. Backpacks, clogs, boots, stocking caps, patchy beards, ponytails. Nobody looks poor, and nobody looks like her. She walks all over the campus until she's found every building on her map—student union, liberal arts, education, day care, financial aid. She walks until the campus feels familiar.

Ronnie catches up to Tony as he leaves the school. "What happened, T.? Did she get the gun?"

Tony nods.

"Fuck, man. Why didn't you run?"

"Don't know," Tony shrugs.

"I guess you expelled now. You can hang out with Ronnie all day."

"They suspended me, but they didn't expel me yet. There's going to be a meeting where they decide."

"Didn't they call the cops?"

"No." Tony looks at the ground as he walks. Thin wafers of ice snap under his sneakers. "They said because it wasn't real they didn't have to."

"Not real? What you mean not real? They wasn't no bullets?"

"I don't know," Tony says, starting to cry. "They told me to go home. That's all."

Ronnie grabs Tony's sleeve. "I want to see the rest of those guns."

He makes Tony take him to the back yard and open the shoebox of guns. Ronnie holds one up to the sunlight and examines it.

"Don't wave it around." Tony pleads.

Ronnie peers into the barrel. The bore is only half an inch deep. The rest of the barrel is solid.

"Son of a bitch," he mutters. He turns the gun over a few more times, as a quietness settles over him. He sits down on the bricks and hands the gun to Tony. "Give these to your baby cousins. They ain't nothing but toys."

"What are you going to do?" The tears are threatening Tony's composure once more.

"They ain't no choice about what to do," Ronnie says, shaking his head. "It's only a choice of when."

Giselle sheds her overcoat and shoes. She has the whole house to herself for another twenty minutes before Germaine brings the babies back over. She wants nothing more than to drink a cup of hot, sweet tea very slowly while staring out the window at the blue-black sky of the early night.

Today she felt brave. In a way, she tells herself, it doesn't even matter if she passes the test. She took a leap for her babies and it makes her feel like an adult for maybe the first time ever.

She is about to fill the teakettle when she hears the sniffling. She follows the sound back to Tony's room, where she finds her little brother stuffing clothes into a small suitcase.

"What's up, Tone? Going on a trip?"

"Don't call me that," he sniffles.

"Okay, Mr. Anthony," she says, scrubbing his head with her knuckles. "Where you going?"

"I don't know." He puts his baseball glove into the case and zips it closed.

"You planning to tell Mom and Dad you're leaving?"

He shakes his head, flipping the pull-tab of the zipper back and forth with his thumb.

"Hey, come on, little brother." She tries to pull him onto the bed and tickle him out of his funk. But Tony pushes her off.

"You want to tell me what's wrong?"

"Nothing."

"Don't give me 'nothing.'"

He pulls a paper from his back pocket and hands it to her.

She glances at it. "You got suspended?"

He nods.

"For bringing a toy gun to school?"

He nods.

"Why in the world did you do that?"

"I don't want to talk about it."

"I think you'd better." She puts an arm around his shoulders and this time Tony doesn't shrug her off.

"Come on, Mr. Anthony. If you tell me, I'll help you figure out how to tell Mom and Dad."

Tony begins to mumble the story of how he met Ronnie, and as he talks, the words come faster, until he is telling her things he thought would be his very own secrets until he died—about the convenience store, about the hat, about hiding the guns in the back yard, and, finally, bringing the gun to school.

"Oh, baby," Giselle shakes her head. "You got yourself a world of trouble."

"I know."

"After what Pop and I did this year, I think Momma was counting on you to be the good one."

"I know."

"Listen." She pulls Tony close, and he isn't fighting her anymore. "Unpack that bag, and let's you and I figure out what to say to them."

"I don't want to."

"Hey, after all we been through this year, we can survive this."

"But what about Ronnie?"

"Don't you worry about Ronnie."

"But I think he wants to kill Jimmy now."

"Jimmy? Why?"

"He sold Ronnie the guns. You going to tell him?"

"Well," she says, slowly, rocking Tony against her side. "Jimmy's an idiot, all right. But he is the babies' father."

Thursday the 30th

Stacey Markowitz watches her husband doing the dishes. Will wonders never cease? He stacks the plates the way she has always asked him to, and uses the sponge-on-a-stick to get to the bottom of the beer tumblers.

"Honey, I'll finish those. You go watch the ball game."

Danny shrugs. "It's not the same anymore."

"I thought you would always be a Bulls fan."

"I am, I am. It's just these November games seem so pointless."

"Why don't they just start the season in April, when it means something?" She puts her arms around him from behind. Every time she does this, they both know she's noticing how much softer his stomach has gotten.

"I'm going to start doing sit-ups," he says.

"No way. I finally got some love handles to hang onto."

He turns and pecks a kiss onto her head. "These aren't handles. They're carry-on straps."

"Are you being gross? I think you are."

"I'll be out in the garage. I can listen to the game while I straighten the workbench."

When Danny gets reliable, Stacey starts to wonder what's going on. Since Thanksgiving, he hardly leaves the house. He goes to work, comes home and watches television, eats dinner, putters in the garage, and comes to bed. He even cuddles part of the time, when he isn't flopping outside of the blankets to escape the trapped heat. She feels perversely frightened by this side of him.

She follows him out to the garage. "Okay, buster. I'm not stupid, you know."

"Did I say you were?" He pulls out his Folger's can ashtray, and lights a Hava-Tampa.

"You didn't say. But if you think I won't know something's going on with you, then you must think I'm stupid."

"There's nothing going on with me. I'm just a little run down. No big deal."

"I'm going to take a wild guess, and if I'm wrong you can laugh hysterically, but if I'm right, you just stand there looking dumbfounded."

"What?"

"I think you've been seeing your ex-wife."

Danny stands there dumbfounded, and belatedly tries to laugh, but can't manage disbelief, much less hysteria.

"You are such a dope," Stacey says. "Come inside and tell me what's going on."

Ng is restocking the shelves and Leda ringing up the purchases of the last few customers when Sol Slivnick walks in.

Leda looks up under her bangs. "Hey, Mr. S."

"Did we have a good night?"

Leda looks in the drawer. "Pretty good. I haven't done the credit slips yet. Is that why you came by?"

"Actually, I came by to see our young friend here." He claps Ng on the shoulder and then withdraws his hand awkwardly.

"Is there something wrong?" Ng asks.

Sol looks around. "Um, Larry isn't here, is he?"

"No, he went to get a hot dog."

Sol takes Ng by the elbow and walks back to his office. He regards the paper strewn across the linoleum desktop, sighs, and drops into his desk chair. "Well, Ng, the thing is, I'm getting fan mail for you about your piece in the magazine."

"You are? You got actual letters? From people?"

"Okay, I got one letter. Well, one and-a-half. But that's still pretty rare. This guy from Holland who carries some of my stuff wants to know what else you have."

"What else?"

"Yeah, like poster designs, T-shirts, whatever. He thinks he could move some product."

Moving product. Ng likes the sound of that. "But I don't have anything. Between schoolwork and here, I haven't had much time."

"I know you've been drawing. There's ink on your hand."

Ng turns his wrist and sees the black smudge. "I'm doing a couple of drawings for a menu. For a friend."

Sol throws a legal pad on the desk. "Show me what you're doing. Just a quick something. Maybe we can do something with it."

"It's just a couple of doodles," Ng says apologetically, as he starts making lines without enthusiasm. But in a few seconds, a picture of his mother's face starts to emerge, and her chin just the way it should be: authoritarian, but feminine.

"Damn, I wish this weren't on legal paper," he says.

Sol watches him, chin in hand. "Say, you were a student of John Parsley's right?"

"Yeah." Ng is startled that Slivnick would have the remotest idea of this. But he's starting to accept that providence moves in ways he has no grasp of whatsoever.

"Did you hear he retired?"

Ng's hands pauses for a moment before continuing to sketch out the design. "I hadn't heard that."

"Guess he's having some personal problems. Health or something."

"So, you know him?"

Sol chuckles, running a hand across his bald spot. "We were crazy kids. Wanted to be anarchists back when it was fashionable."

There is a bump at the front of the store, and the door swings open. Larry O. Larry steps into the room, one cheek plump with macerated hot dog and bun.

"Well, well," he says, wiping a bright yellow streak of mustard from the corner of his mouth. "What have we here?"

Sol grimaces and mouths a single word in Ng's direction: "Busted."

Danny keeps looking around his car for a gift. You can't show up empty-handed for a thing like this. But there's nothing except greasy racing forms and empty malt liquor bottles.

He pauses the Impala in front of the diner where Soo works. Not re-opened yet, but showing signs of rejuvenation. That's one relief. It all seems so simple now that he's explained himself to Stacey.

That Stacey—not your average dumb blonde. She'd sat him down and listened to everything. And after all of it, she said only: "Men." And said it in that voice women use on TV, and with each other, when it doesn't really mean anything. But that was merely a place-holder until she'd thought of what she really wanted to say. And when she said what it was she really meant to say, it was in a voice stripped of all glibness. What she said was this: How she'd married a man with a son, and that was no secret. She'd been waiting for him to come to terms with it and maybe it was finally time for him to do the same, so they could be at peace with it. Together.

Maybe that old photo of him holding the kid when he was still a baby and Soo was such a little slip of a thing in a yellow sundress. He riffles through the pieces of paper strapped to the sun visor with a rubber band. Old insurance cards, parking lot stubs, fast food receipts. Where the heck did the picture go?

Everything he's done—staking out the house, selling the bike, roughing up the gangbanger—it was all a substitute for the one thing he doesn't want to do, the medicine he doesn't want to take. Stacey, it was like she was a mind reader, cutting through his words to something underneath. How is it women can do that?

Go to the kid's work, or wait at the apartment? He does a mental coin-toss and decides to head over to the apartment. Funny how good it feels to know Stacey knows where he is this time.

He pulls to a stop on the narrow street. Sheets of snow dust pinwheel down the asphalt. He can feel the cold wind thumping on the windows. He leans across the seat and rummages hopelessly through his glove compartment. Without another idea, he takes an old beat-up city map, folds it back to the southside, and, with the last gasp of an ancient felt-tip pen, draws a circle around the neighborhood where he and Stacey live. That says it about as good as he can say it. Better, even.

What a fucked-up day, Ng thinks. Mr. Parsley is sick, or depressed, probably because of him. People in other countries want to see what he is drawing. His stomach is stirred, uneasy, as from a carnival ride, as he walks from the bus stop to the apartment. All he wants to do is sleep. He shifts his portfolio to his left arm and gropes in his coat pocket for his keys.

That's when the man starts calling, "Excuse me!"

Ng turns and a man emerges from a large white car. A white man in a plaid overcoat with a Bears stocking cap slopped onto his head.

Whatever this guy wants, it can't be good. Ng tries quickly to unlock the door.

"Hey, Ng," the man says. "Wait up."

Ng pushes the door open, jumps inside, and closes it.

"Hey, come on," the man says. He puts his face up to the small, smeared window in the door. "Hey, I just want to give you something, that's all."

"Who are you? How do you know my name?"

"I'm sorry." The man steps back from the door. Ng can hear the sounds of him scuffling his feet on the stoop. Then the mail flap creaks open, and a folded map is pushed through the slot. Ng picks it up. There is a circle on the map, around a suburb Ng has never heard of—Midlothian—and next to the circle are the words *Danny and Stacey Markowitz.*

Ng looks out the small window. The man is hugging himself for warmth. Ng feels pretty numb himself. He opens the door.

"You're my dad?"

"Yeah," the man smiles crookedly. "Pretty disappointing, huh?"

Ng tries to come up with an answer to this question. He stands in the door, letting the bracingly cold air waft pleasantly against his suddenly overheated face. He breathes in a mouthful of the arctic breeze.

"Come in," he says at last.

December

Saturday the 2nd

After his suspension from school, Tony kept waiting for one of his father's dreaded belt whippings. The kind he got when he was six and wandered over to Jeffrey Avenue to watch firemen fighting a blaze on the train tracks. The kind that you wince to hear the belt snapping through the belt loops before Dad wraps his hand around the buckle and raises back like a tennis player catching a lob at the net. The kind where the sting follows the sound of the blow by a good two or three seconds, about the time the second blow comes, and the individual fires simmering on your bottom overlap and converge until you scream that you'll never do it again, and wriggle away covering your behind, getting the last stroke of the belt across the backs of your hands. The kind of whipping where Dad looks so sad, rethreading the belt into the loops, keeping his face down as he buckles the belt, turning it back into a harmless piece of clothing.

But the whipping never came. Instead, his father looked like he was going to cry when he heard about the suspension, grabbed Tony to his chest and kept saying how sorry he was, how very truly sorry. Everybody—Momma, Dad, Giselle, and Auntie Germaine—is acting like they are responsible for Tony taking the gun to school. Momma kisses him, Giselle rubs his head and plays video games with him when the babies are asleep. It's confusing.

Tony spends the days of his suspension watching TV. After school his cousins Johnny and Melvin stop by with his homework, handing it over with

371

wide-eyed caution, like Tony is dangerous or deathly ill. They refuse to come in and play video games. One day they've got tutoring, one day they go to music lessons, another day Melvin—it is always Melvin—doesn't feel well.

So Tony is bored. But he is afraid to go looking for Ronnie. Alphonse has warned him to stay near the house. Still, he imagines going to the hot dog place and eating fries and listening to Ronnie talk about the other gangs and how stupid they are. But he is also afraid Ronnie will take the King 5 hat back and kick him out of the gang for being dumb enough to get caught. In Ronnie's eyes, the worst thing you can do is get caught.

Jimmy turns to Lem and says around a mouthful of beans and beef, "Could the lord be any better to a righteous man?"

This good feeling has many sources. First of all, Jimmy is deep into a bowl of chili, chasing each spoonful with his second bottle of cold beer. Second, his wallet is fattening up again, plumped with a couple of successful poker games and a few deals with some fake guns he picked up in Chinatown.

The door opens, letting in two small figures and a blast of December air. A kid, the one who bought some of those Chinese guns off him, walks toward Jimmy with an exaggerated swagger to his step.

"Yo man," the boy says, "I got to talk to you."

This is how Jimmy knows he truly has fate by the balls. Fate is on its knees, whimpering. Here's how he sees it. If he hadn't fathered those two babies on Giselle, she wouldn't have called yesterday to warn him about this Ronnie kid threatening to pop him, and if she hadn't warned him, he might not have been packing today when Ronnie and his cross-eyed friend show up at Shug's Haven.

Jimmy looks around. "Do I know you?"

"Fuck yes," Ronnie says. "You know you do."

Jimmy nudges Lem. "Gimme a dollar. These boys must be selling band candy."

Lem chuckles behind his beer glass.

"Ain't no damn candy, yo." Ronnie tries to grab a handful of air and strangle it. "You sold me some shit."

"World's finest chocolate," Jimmy smiles. "I'll have an almond bar."

"Fuck you, man," Darol says over Ronnie's shoulder.

"Say what?"

Ronnie steps up to Jimmy. "He said fuck you. And I say it, too."

The bartender leans across the bar and points a large index finger at Ronnie. "You boys better take whatever it is outside. Now."

Ronnie swallows a reply. Then he says to Jimmy, "You heard the man. Let's us have a chat. Outside."

"Too cold outside," Jimmy says. "And I got to finish my chili." He picks up his spoon with his left hand while his right hand reaches across his stomach to touch the grip of the pistol nestled against his left hip. "You can wait for me outside. I'll be along, six or seven hours."

Lem nudges Jimmy, chuckling again.

"Man, I'm telling you, this here ain't one of your toy guns."

Jimmy looks over his shoulder. Sure enough, there is a good-sized actual Glock pointed at his head.

"Wait a fucking minute," says the bartender. "I'll get the cops in here."

"Don't worry," Jimmy says with a slow, spreading grin. He smoothly lifts the nose of the concealed gun toward Ronnie's midsection. He slips a finger around the trigger. "Now what's all this you fussing over?"

"You owe me some fucking money."

"We'll forget you dissed us," Darol adds, "if you return our money."

The bartender says, "That's it, I hit the alarm. Cops on their way."

Jimmy smiles at Ronnie. "Get out while you can, kid."

"Not without you."

"But I told you. My chili's getting cold."

"Fuck your chili." Ronnie lifts the nose of his gun to the center of Jimmy's brow.

Jimmy smiles patiently and squeezes the trigger of his concealed gun, which emits a metallic click.

"He got a gun!" Darol shouts.

Jimmy closes his eyes briefly, thinking, now fate shows her real colors, the bitch. He lunges from the stool, landing on hands and knees. The floor is sticky and pee-smelling. He crawls toward the door, smacking the balky gun against the floor and praying.

Ronnie fires. The gun jumps in his hands and the first shot shatters the front of the jukebox. Jimmy squeezes the trigger again as he dives for the door. The gun startles him by responding with a sudden burst of fire. Bottles explode into a mist of glass and alcohol. Ronnie wheels to follow Jimmy's diving limbs and catches him with two shots in the back. A third gun adds its booming voice to the melee and Ronnie lurches across the floor, falling into a stack of vinyl-padded chairs. Jimmy is lying in the doorway, half-in and half-out, blood from his head smearing the icy pavement. Lem is under his barstool, shrieking.

"I fucking told you," the bartender mutters, lowering his gun.

Darol stands in the middle of the room, swallowed in a cloud of glass particles, smoke, and atomized alcohol. A fairly small hole above his right eye belies the size of the exit wound in the back of his head. He falls straight backwards, eyes turned yellow-white in his head.

Giselle answers the phone while holding Jimelle on one shoulder. The only way to keep the infant from cramping up with post-feeding gas is to pat her vigorously after every bottle. The action has become automatic, something Giselle can do while cooking, cleaning, or picking out her courses for the January school term. She pats while she says, hello, and continues the soft motions while her body shudders with the news.

"He is? How did it happen? Oh, Lem. Dammit, Lem, why did he have to be that way?"

She stands, patting her child, holding the dead phone, smelling the baby spit up on her shoulder—patting, still patting the tiny shoulders—and begging her legs to continue to hold her up until someone can help her reach a chair.

Alphonse stands outside Tony's door. The boy's been in there for hours since the news came. He taps gently. "Son? Can I come in?" After waiting for a reply, he finally eases the door open. Tony is stretched out on the bed, one arm flung over his head, one arm across his stomach. His eyes are open, glazed, and the expression on his face is impassive as one of those giant stone statues on that deserted island.

"I heard what happened, son."

Tony's eyes flicker, and he shifts his face away from the door.

"Listen, I don't know if what happened makes things better or worse for you. That's all I'm concerned about. But I know they was your friends, and I'm sorry things had to go that way."

"They say Ronnie won't ever talk or move again," Tony mumbles through barely moving lips. "Darol was dead before the pair-of-medics could help him."

Alphonse puts a consoling hand on his son's leg. "You didn't make none of it happen, son. Don't feel like you did."

"If I hadn't told Giselle. If I hadn't got caught."

Alphonse gropes for a sentence that will eradicate his son's connection with these awful events, put it all back on god's will. "You didn't make them walk around with guns," he says. "You couldn't stop from them from doing what they wanted to do."

Tony turns his face to the pillow and shudders as the first tears come.

"No," Alphonse says, decisively. "They walked down their own chosen path, that's all."

Tuesday the 5th

Ellen rummages in a box of musty-smelling clip-on bow ties, feeling doom settle ever more heavily on her head.

"I'm sorry, there aren't any more paisley ones," she says to the man at the counter.

"Great," he says with pointed irony, "just great."

"Sorry," she says again, taking his disappointment personally.

Christmas is the most beautiful and poignant time for self-pity. Take *It's a Wonderful Life*. The most indulgently self-pitying story every written, and people watch it every year to get their cathartic weepies out. Sheesh.

As her father had predicted, Ellen's money had finally given out and she got a job as Christmas help at a vintage clothing store. It's not bad work, consisting mostly of folding and re-folding sweaters and reassuring shoppers that, yes, the clothes are dry cleaned before they go on the racks. Plus the mostly mindless work gives her plenty of time to pine for Alice. Get over it already, she tells herself. You blew it. Anyway, first-timers are always a dicey prospect. These are things she knows, but she also tells herself that it ain't over until it's *over* over.

Last night she stood outside the Lather rehearsal space, shivering in the cold just to hear Alice's voice and arguing with herself:

She probably changed her mind about me when the old boyfriend showed up. Maybe. But I want to hear her say that.

You don't get everything you want. Relationships don't always end nice and tidy.

"Excuse me, do you have this jacket in a large?" The questioner holds up a red sateen bolero jacket which, even in large, wouldn't fit one of her arms.

"All of our clothes are unique, ma'am, we don't get multiple sizes."

The woman makes a frustrated pout, condemning Ellen for this short-sighted inventory strategy.

Working for minimum, unloved, and without a future. If I threw myself onto the Chicago River, I wouldn't get a wingless angel and a tour through alternate realities like Jimmy Stewart did, she thinks. I'd probably just bounce off the ice.

Alice wipes steam from the mirror with a damp towel and takes a long look at herself. Stringy dark-wet hair dangling over pronounced clavicles, and bruise-dark eye sockets that are more sickly than brooding. It's like, since everything blew up with Ellen and Nathan, her body has run down while she wasn't looking. Her tan—the dark, exotic color cultivated all summer long—is gone. She is once again the fugitive pale of the Irish O'Learys, and in certain places—the crook of her arm, the sides of her breasts—the blue-white of skim milk. She sighs and begins combing out her wet hair. But the death of the tan is like the absence of the last vestige of Ellen in her life. All those August afternoons lounging on the rooftop, baking in the scent of sweet coconut oil. Maybe Ellen was a symptom of summer, a walk on the wild side, an attack of sun-madness that faded and disappeared with the overcast days of autumn. Maybe it wasn't meant to mean something. Still, she can distinctly recall certain touches that were entirely unlike any other touches she's ever felt.

Alice drops to the toilet seat, suddenly absorbed in a mental game she has played ever since she first kissed Ellen: like a statuette of blindfolded Justice, she places Ellen-sex in one pan of the scale, and Brad-slash-Nathan-sex in the other. Maybe the game is stupid. Maybe it's just sex. Why does who you fuck matter? Sex is sex. She's probably been screwing herself up by thinking it makes some kind of cosmic difference. Being happy is hard enough without having to follow so many rules that who knows where they came from.

She sighs, and a shudder of fatigue runs through her limbs. Time to go to work. She blow-dries her hair until it is blonde again. She can feel static electricity shimmering around her head like a halo.

She pulls on wool tights, wool skirt, and wool sweater. Now plump as a sheep, her shape is obliterated, leaving only flashes of pallid skin at the end of her sleeves and below her woolly hat.

The morning air charges at her, bristling with Canadian snow, a clean sharpness faintly undercut by bus exhaust.

Nathan is not so easily explained. Simple animal attraction? Is attraction, even animal, ever simple? The thought of that morning-after still turns her stomach. How could she have done that? Sure, it is good to be wanted by someone so beautiful, but once you act on that, it's gone, and you can't even savor the flirtation anymore. Plus not to mention the damage, lovers falling left and right like an arrangement of naked dominos.

Riding the overheated el is like being a piece of bread in a rolling toaster, until the doors open and she is popped out onto Belmont Avenue.

But Nathan is only the crowning glory of her life, after getting tangled up with Brad and Ellen—two other people who don't seem to have any idea of how she should fit into their lives. Queen of Bad Choices. That's me.

Ellen is waiting for her at the door of Urbs. She has a large box under one arm.

"Can I show you something?"

Since he returned to Chicago, Brad feels like a soap opera character who's come back from the dead after miraculous, appearance-altering surgery, aching for his former life but unable, for some dark and complicated reason, to take it back. Of course, it's all just an excuse for not doing the one thing he came back for—to re-join Lather. Although everyone was polite when Alice sprung him on the band at Thanksgiving, no one has asked him to take back his lead singer role.

He goes back to his apartment to red-circle classified ads for jobs he doesn't want. There's a small package in the lobby with his name on it, a padded mailer envelope postmarked from—Chicago? He steps down into his basement apartment and even before taking off his coat, tears open the envelope, finding inside a plain jewel case containing an unmarked CD.

A note taped to the front of the case reads: *Listen to this before you get any big ideas. Chipper.*

He shucks off his coat and takes the disc out of the case. It's one of those moments you dread, like seeing a former lover with a new partner. He puts the disc in his boombox and hits the play button. What comes out of the speakers is a sound not unfamiliar, but so different from the Lather Rinse

Repeat he left months ago that he gets a slight case of vertigo trying to make sense of it in his head. He sits down on his bed, closes his eyes, and lets it wash over him.

The only soundtrack is the bug-like whir of the projector, as the smoky shadows and creamy light swirl dream-like against the wall. Trees move silently, slowly, like genies emerging from long confinement.

Ellen stands against the wall, trying not to watch Alice watch the record of Ellen's watching her.

Alice sees herself—but not herself, an image achingly far away—pulling the camera through a city burned into lines of gray, white, black. She feels the passion, Ellen's desire, the eye's hunger. It is suddenly obvious, the beauty with which people walk, the graceful transfer of weight from foot to foot, how faces evolve at angles to the sun, how hands move, revealing the thought that moves them. It is a vision of life cooked down to an essence, intensified, like a miraculous French sauce. Alice feels goosebumps spread down her arms.

At the end of the film, a white square burns on the wall. "Oh, Ellen," is all she says. She feels unsettled, as though her clothes have been tugged askew.

Ellen keeps her eyes away from Alice's and begins to rewind the film. "I didn't really know," Alice whispers.

Ellen intently cleans the projector's lens with the tail of her shirt. "Well, now you know. It was important for me to know you knew."

Alice wipes her eyes with her sweater sleeve. "I have all these feelings," she stammers. "I don't know how to be—I can't promise you anything."

"You don't have to." Ellen's lips begin to tremble.

"Eventually I do," Alice says, "don't I?"

"Some day," Ellen replies, "you have to promise something to someone."

After the first song, Brad knows his hopes of returning to the band are over. There's no place for him—Lather Rinse Repeat is complete without him. The world he left behind has, in a few months, sealed up and left him on the outside. Starting over means just that—nothing that went before remains. He hits the play button on the boombox again. Alice's voice fills the dark room, and the melody they wrote together two years ago sounds completely remade and completely alive. He closes his eyes and lets the music fill his head like a perfume.

Tuesday the 12th

After Janie's visit, Robin fell back into himself. Claiming to still have shooting pains in his back, he began sleeping in the guest room, on a bed piled with ramparts of pillows and comforters. The bed never gets made, its lumpiness causing Nathan to feel as if it is somehow unclean, like a landfill poorly refurbished as parkland. But Nathan has found that, on the whole, he likes the new sleeping arrangement.

They have settled into a routine of being in the same rooms without speaking. You could cut the ambivalence with a knife, Nathan thinks. He makes little time for meals. Breakfast has become a bite of toast, a sip of coffee, and goodbye.

Robin limps over to the table, sloshing coffee out of the pot.

Nathan leans over his toast to keep the crumbs off his tie. "Shouldn't you talk to the doctor about that limp?"

"It's fine." Robin slumps into his chair.

Although he's technically healed, there's still something fractured about him. It's in the eyes, Nathan thinks. How do you talk about that? How do you describe it?

After Oprah, Robin cleans the dishes and walks around, straightening the odds and ends in every room. He pauses in the living room to dust off the battered, empty urn. One of the police divers had snagged it before it sunk too far into the river. Unfortunately, the lid had dropped like a stone. He could not convince anyone to go back for it. And the ashes, of course, were washed clean away. The urn, dented and dull, no longer seems worthy of its place of reverence. There's nothing of her left in it, but in a sense, it's all he has left. Maybe fill it with something that would remind him of her. Milkweed pods? Corn kernels? Pine cones? The emptiness of it is really too much to look at. He puts it on the top shelf of the linen closet. A clean, dark, quiet place.

Hanging up the phone after another one of Maddy's irritating come-home-for-the-holiday calls, Nathan feels a bright jolt of clarity, the kind of immediate emotional insight that has the neon of epiphany to it. He'd never allowed himself to put the thought into words before but it suddenly feels as though he has been thinking it for months. Stuck between his family on one hand and Robin on the other, Nathan has an opportunity to play both sides against each other. He can lie about his holiday plans and be neither at home nor with his family. It's vertiginously appealing, and feels in his guts just like the first articulation of his long-fermented desire to sleep with a man. He takes a moment to try and unthink the idea but he cannot, and the urgency of it causes him to leap from his desk and walk briskly out of the museum without his coat.

The grand flight of steps in front of the Art Institute appears as a cold and bright flow of gray ice as he clatters halfway down to the sidewalk. No one is lingering there as they do in the summertime. In the frigid air the stone rings with the hurried steps of people rushing to get in out of the cold. Nathan breathes deeply. The stone lions flanking the entrance are collared with holly. Giddy, Nathan runs up and leaps onto one like John Wayne. The stone radiates cold through his pants.

"What the hell are you doing up there?"

Nathan looks down to see the red cheeks and bright green eyes of Allen Overcamp and in that instant knows fate is stamping his epiphany with a fat, green authorization to "GO!"

"I'm posing for a holiday card?"

Allen Overcamp looks around. "Do you have a photographer across the street, sniper-style?"

Nathan slides down sheepishly from the statue. "I was merely trying the pose on for aesthetic appeal."

"It's a little late to begin designing your holiday message, Nathan."

Nathan suddenly feels the bite of the wind and hears a shiver in his voice as he says, "You're right. This whole holiday season just snuck up on me."

Allen purses his lips, watching Nathan hug himself for warmth. "It is quite subtle. You could easily miss the clues."

"Yes," Nathan catches the opening. "The Salvation Army bell ringers are dressed in some kind of, what is it, fur trimmed BVDs? And this holly," he gestures at the lions, "it has some kind of pagan significance?"

Allen heaves a majestic sigh. "There is so much to explain. Where to begin?"

Nathan points at the coffee shop across Michigan Avenue. "Begin with this 'egg nog.' It sounds very Easter, if you ask me."

"Gladly," Allen Overcamp says. "Shall we partake of some of this libation, the better to understand its complexities?"

"Let's." Nathan takes his arm and they cross the avenue under flapping banners depicting snowflakes in a variety of sizes and colors.

When Nathan gets home, Robin is on the couch with a patchwork of bills spread out on the coffee table. Robin holds up a hand while punching a number into the calculator.

"I realized today how it really should be my job to sort out all of the bills. My accident seems to have complicated things."

"It will sort out once you start working again."

Robin taps his pen on the checkbook in frustration. "It's going to be a lean Christmas. I hope you didn't ask Santa for a new bike or a pony."

"I always ask for world peace."

"And silk boxers."

"Call it a weakness."

Robin puts the pen between his teeth and grinds down on it. "Paying off the fines is going to keep me broke until the third millennium," he says through clenched teeth.

Nathan goes into the bedroom to undress. He feels as though he'll explode with tension until he drops his lie about going home for Christmas.

"I made lasagna for dinner," Robin calls.

"Okay." Nathan comes out in his winter evening attire: flannel pajamas and a flannel robe. "I was thinking about Christmas. Have you thought about getting together with Janie again? To keep the momentum going?"

Robin snorts. "Come on. You know she hasn't called since Thanksgiving."

"I just thought—"

"Honey, she's not even telling Dad she was *here*. She told me she made some excuse about a church retreat. I'm still a big black sheep, but she can tell all her bible school chums how she pulled a thorn out of my paw."

"That was a lion."

"Not that I'm not grateful for you getting her to come. It's still the best family moment I've had in the past twenty years." He brushes Nathan's cheek affectionately.

Nathan's ears burn with shame at what he's going to say.

Robin shovels a block of lasagna onto Nathan's plate. "But about Exmas, I was really sort of hoping we could, maybe you would consider, us going to your parents? Just maybe for one day?"

"I wish you wouldn't say Exmas."

"Well, it's not really about Christ, anymore, is it? Not that I care. I think the Ex means you can fill in whatever icon you choose. Anyway, I'll take that as a no."

Nathan pours a glass of wine and takes a large sip. "Maddy made her annual guilt-Nathan-for-Christmas call today. She's really putting on the pressure this time."

"Don't tell me," Robin says, dropping his fork loudly. "Another family holiday bash sans moi."

"My dad makes such a big deal about the family being together. He wants just immediate family. Recapturing the halcyon times, family only, blah blah blah. If I were married, it would be different, obviously, but as it is—"

"One more Christmas I have to suffer through like a leper on that island, wherever it was they sent lepers to."

"What do you want me to do? I'll be back in a couple of days, and we'll have an extended holiday together. Come on."

Robin stares at Nathan with venom, but feels his anger slipping away, replaced by the fear of taking this argument to the extreme he wants to.

"I really want you to make this up to me."

"Come on, sweetheart." Nathan comes around the table and cradles Robin's head. "Don't make this into more than it is. A few days. That's all."

Thursday the 14th

Elias stops himself before entering the diner, slightly stunned by the immense changes brought about in just a few weeks. The sign—a carved and painted oak panel designed by Ng—still reads "Sophia's," but that's about the only thing left of the sturdy, unassuming diner where Elias served food for two decades. In its place is a *restaurant*—a bright, pastel and wood-paneled room. Elias barely recognizes the place as his own. And when he opens the door, the transformation is complete. The new interior, washed with the morning's hesitant light, has the mild medicinal tang of paint and new vinyl. The kitchen—no longer separated from the dining room—is already at work, emanating odors of coriander, sesame, and lemon grass. The distinctive smell of tortillas on the *comal* underlines everything. No hash browns, no sausage.

The diner is now something strange, distinctive, and alive. Whatever his misgivings, Elias recognizes the unique voice of the space. Whether it succeeds or fails, it won't be just another diner. Elias smiles, trying to will his tide of worry to subside.

"Can a guy get a chili dog around here?" he calls.

Luis sticks his head out of the storage room. "A chili dog's not fancy enough for this place. Unless you top it with radish sprouts and *pinché* chopped peanuts."

"Come on, Luis, not today of all days."

The squat chef yanks off his baseball cap and fans himself with it. "This kitchen is going to be murder tonight. All I know is about two recipes, and the rest is got to be done by a waitress."

"She can cook, Luis, you've seen her. The recipes are great."

"We can argue about the recipes some other time. But what if we get bombed tonight, eight o'clock with a full house and a forty-minute wait? It could happen. Can she cook then? Are we going to be serving undercooked chicken, mushy noodles, and dried-out burritos? It's the little things, Elias, you know?"

Elias sighs and sits down on one of the new padded chairs. "We've put a lot into this, Luis. Let's give it a chance."

Soo walks in carrying a twenty-five pound bag of rice on her shoulders. "Good morning!" she says, smiling.

"Rice," Luis mutters. "Rice, rice, rice."

Elias actually feels a sense of vertigo when he flips on the neon OPEN sign. "Here we go," he says. And they wait.

Elias fidgets with an order pad. "Do we need anything? I can go out if we need something."

"No," says Luis.

Soo keeps busy at the burners, creating free appetizers. Luis plates them and places them around the tables.

A few people stop and read the menu on the outside, and then pass on by. Elias feels sick.

"It's early," Soo says.

Elias checks to make sure the door is unlocked. "Do we need anything? I can go out if we need something."

"No," says Luis. "Go have a drink, *please*. You're making me nervous."

Florence and Tommy walk in, and then suddenly the space is not virgin anymore. Suddenly there is business to do, and people to serve, and when Elias stops to assess the four full tables and the dishes being brought out of the kitchen, he is aware that something else is in the building—an energy that has no single source, but undulates with every opening of the door, every order, every bill set down in its plastic tray. He wants, like the mad scientist in the old movies, to wave his hands and shout, "*It! Is! Alive!*"

Ng is busing tables. Leda has arrived to help. Florence is greeting people at the door. Elias finds his instincts coming alive and does whatever needs doing. At nine o'clock, he goes to the store to buy coconut milk and sesame seeds. When he returns, there are no empty tables and five people wait, perturbed that there is no comfortable place to stand. Remembering Luis's fretful words, he hurries back to the kitchen to find his two chefs flinging sweat in their furious activity. Luis is glowering over a wok, flipping a tangle of noodles with a steel spatula.

"This is *comida loco*," he says. "Cheap bowl of noodles—how can anybody get rich?"

Soo says nothing, ignoring the remarks. She is finishing dishes at a blinding pace.

Ng is clearing a table for fresh customers, who turn out to be Mr. Parsley and another man.

"Hi," says Ng with surprise.

"Bit of a shock?" The art teacher settles himself into the chair slowly. He is pale and thin. He self-consciously touches a patch of rough, red skin at the corner of his mouth. Ng tries not to look.

"How did you know about the opening?" Ng asks.

"Leda invited me." He smiles at Ng. "Women can find gray where men only see black or white."

Ng supplies the men with forks and chopsticks wrapped in paper sleeves.

The teacher looks at Ng. "I supposed you had something to do with the sign."

"Yeah. And the menus."

"You're starting to get quite a bit of business."

Ng shrugs. "I did it for my mom and Mr. Kanakes."

"Listen. I've been thinking about your last visit, and I'm not happy how we left things. Do you think you could stop by next week?"

Ng's heart flops over in his chest. "Sure. Anytime. School's out."

Parsley flips open the menu with a flourish. "Great. Now, what's good?"

The silence on the sidewalks causes Elias to pause with his grocery bags, full this time of lemons and vermicelli. He stands across the street looking into the restaurant, which has begun to empty. The air has a freshness that makes him feel as if he has not breathed for many hours. Good or bad, the day has been exhilarating. They have fed people, lots of people, and he is in business again, with friends, and who could want more than that?

The chairs are upended on the tables, and Ng has volunteered to mop the floor. Leda is wiping down the counter. Elias has taken on the job that worries him the most: counting the night's receipts. Luis, dressed to go home in a down vest, decides to wait, sits down next to Elias, and watches him tally the pieces of paper against the cash register.

"She won't stop cleaning," Luis says, nodding toward the kitchen. "Everything is cleaner than it came, and she's scrubbing the grill front." He shakes his head.

Elias fights off a yawn. He suddenly has no energy left in his limbs. "It was a good night."

Luis shrugs. "Yeah, pretty good."

"It looked like rough going in the kitchen. Who knew it would open so big?"

Luis pops a toothpick in his mouth. "But will they come back?"

"Please, Luis, you don't have to voice my every worry."

"I'll say this—the lady knows how to work." The toothpick darts from side to side. "I think we could have fed twice as many. She don't waste time worrying, she puts her head down and goes."

"I told you so."

"Yes, you did, boss." Luis checks his watch. "I got to go. I like the late mornings, but these nights will take some getting used to." He stands up. "Hey, Soo," he calls.

Soo rises from her work on the grease-smeared grill, rag still in hand. Her eyes have dissolved into indistinct black smudges. "What?"

"You rock," Luis says. He holds up a fist, and then turns and heads out into the cold night.

"I rock?" Soo says. "What means I rock?"

Ng says something in Vietnamese, and his mother blushes, then silently returns to scrubbing.

"How did you translate that?" Leda asks.

"I said Luis called her the flower of the morning sky." Ng wrings out the mop. "It's about all the Vietnamese I know."

"That's pretty," Leda says.

Ng slops the string mop onto the floor, smiling shyly. "It's what she called me when I was a baby."

Sunday the 17th

The city appears dormant, closed up for winter on this early Sunday morning. Even down in the shadowed streets she can't see, inside the blank-eyed buildings, Florence senses a slumbering, or at best a slow wakefulness, as though everything is in hibernation, a time when the blood slows, and the mind settles into rags of semi-consciousness, coddled in the slanted, blunt winter light. Maybe she's projecting. She feels the coziness of being out early in the cold day, wrapped in a heavy coat, drinking take-out coffee from a Styrofoam cup while Tommy drives.

"You're quiet this morning."

"I'm still asleep," she says, clutching the coffee in both hands.

From Lake Shore Drive, she can see through the leafless trees right into the abandoned high-rise tenements, still only half torn down. All those empty rooms, some with Venetian blinds still hanging askew in the windows. Where did everyone go? How do so many people disappear into the bubbling stew of the city?

The coffee is still bitingly hot.

A small frozen pond at around 53rd Street bears the arabesque tracings of skates. Further down, the freshly renovated dressing house at the 63rd Street beach stands like an Old World bulwark confronting the flat, lifeless waters of the lake.

"I don't know how I would have found this place," Florence says as Tommy steers them through the quiet streets toward the church.

"When you deliver cheese for a living, you eventually see every part of the city."

"You've been down here before?"

"There was an old guy who made the most incredible sandwiches down on Cottage Grove. Used my mozzarella." Tommy smacks his lips. "He was a magician. This guy, one meatball of his was like a meal."

"What happened to him?"

"Neighborhood changed," Tommy shrugs. "He moved the business across Western Avenue and switched suppliers. The Manetti brothers own that part of town."

"That's a shame," Florence says.

"Easy come, easy go," Tommy says.

Florence watches him maneuvering deftly through the strange streets. Maybe it isn't properly independent of her to feel this way, but she has to admit she loves having a man to take charge of things again.

"I feel like we're starting on a long trip, being on the road so early." She snuggles against the door, her cheek touching the chilled window. "It feels full of promise."

"Maybe we are," Tommy says. "You never know."

Right after Jimmy's funeral, Giselle began insisting on having the twins christened. "You can't leave things to chance," she says repeatedly, not entirely sure what she means, but sure she is right just the same. So this morning she dressed the twins in sparkling white christening gowns and the family goes to church. Evander struggles inside his rustling finery so much that Giselle takes him out to the foyer, humming and whispering appeasements. Eloise follows her out, carrying Jimelle, who hates to be separated from her brother.

"You can't mess this up," Giselle whispers to Evander. "Baptism is a very important thing. It's an introduction to god."

Eloise walks beside her, bouncing Jimelle in her arms. "Relax," she says. "Babies get baptized every day."

Giselle continues to pace, staring fiercely at the linoleum floor. "I'm fine, Momma. I'm a little tired is all."

"You are not fine. You been like this since the funeral. Now let's get it out so we can do this baptizing in the proper frame of mind."

Giselle turns, still swaying Evander with a practiced rhythm of her shoulders. "When Jimmy died, I saw how close I was, Momma. I spent two years in Jimmy's world. Then I almost killed these two babies. If it wasn't for you and Daddy—" She sniffles, squeezing Evander until he squawks. "You never gave up on me," she chokes out. "I...I guess I just don't trust myself yet."

"Oh, honey." Eloise tries to hug her daughter without crushing the infants. "You on the right track. I'm telling you straight. Don't look back on that bad time."

"I just want to do this. Get them baptized like a good mother would do. Then that will always be there for them, some sign that I loved them."

Eloise touches her moist eyes with a handkerchief. "Oh baby, they going to be plenty of signs you love them. From today on, your love always going to be there."

Giselle tries to compose her face, for the congregation has begun the last song of the morning service. "Thanks, Momma."

"That's all right," Eloise kisses her daughter's cheek. "You'll do the same for them one day."

There's a small crowd on hand, with Florence Finkel and her boyfriend, and Elvin Wrightwood and—surprisingly—Lem. Even Giselle is surprised at how glad she is to see Lem. She gives him a warm hug.

"You don't mind me coming here?" he says bashfully.

"I'm glad you did."

Lem shuffles his feet. Giselle wonders what his world is like now, without Jimmy at its axis.

"Are you okay, Lem? Do you have friends to help you out?"

"I miss Jimmy. That might sound crazy, but he was about the only person who liked to have me around."

"Oh, Lem. Lots of people will want you around. You'll see."

Lem casts his eyes around furtively. "Listen, I brought you something from Jimmy." Lem feels around inside his overcoat. It is a thin, varsity-style jacket, with only two pockets, and Giselle briefly wonders what he is struggling with in there. He finally tugs something free. It is an envelope, heavily taped around all four edges.

"Put this somewhere safe," he says quietly. "It was Jimmy's, and I think you should have it."

Giselle squeezes the tightly sealed package. "But what is it?"

"Darling, come on," Alphonse calls. "It's time for the deal."

"Go ahead," Lem says. "You'll see."

The pastor is massive in a three-piece blue pinstripe, over which hangs a purple satin robe and a white satin chasuble. Florence thinks him terribly majestic.

She whispers to Tommy, "That's one thing I miss since Arnie. I never go to synagogue anymore. Not even for holidays."

"Mass," Tommy says, with a flip of his fingers. "I can't go anymore. It's an endless loop, always the same gestures, the same words. Any lifelong Catholic will tell you, it's like you enter a trance, doing everything by muscle memory, the communion, the Our Father, all of it. This, however," he adds, "is different."

The pastor steps forward, his voice booming out a call to the congregation: "We are here this morning to make these children god's children."

"Amen," says the organist.

"What is brought forth into this world, let god admit into the kingdom of heaven."

The pastor takes Evander into his large pink palms. With cupped fingers, he scoops from the baptismal font and pours the cool water generously over the child's head. Evander howls with sudden outrage. Jimelle launches in after him, their two voices tearing through the church with double ferocity. The preacher hands Evander to Eloise and takes Jimelle from Giselle's arms. The young mother's hands follow the child, as if reluctant to hand her over to this tender trauma. Oddly, the dribble of water calms the child, who returns to her mother wide-eyed, looking for an explanation. Giselle bursts into tears.

Tommy is pensive on the ride home. Florence doesn't pry into his thoughts. He's already mentioned how saying, "A penny for your thoughts" has always struck him as both intrusive and insulting. His thoughts, if they're worth anything, are worth more than a penny.

"I thought the buffet was quite good," she says.

Tommy pulls on his moustache.

"Delicious fried catfish," she adds.

He coughs. "Now don't take what I said about mass the wrong way. I believe in ceremony." He looks across the car at her. Florence pretends to be absorbed in the scenery.

"The baptism had, you know, *meaning*," he continues. "It wasn't something they did just for the sake of tradition."

"Mm-hm," Florence says. "I suppose."

"It's important to mark events, moments, important things." His tone is growing more forceful. "But you have to fight through the roteness of things. The birthday song. The communion. You can lose the meaning."

"Yes," Florence says. "Even funerals. Even shiva. You can do it, or you can do it with feeling."

"There's all the difference," Tommy says. He is really driving quite mess-ily at the moment, drifting in and out of his lane. Florence keeps her mouth shut. Where is this going?

"So what I'm saying is," Tommy says.

Florence waits.

"Well. What I'm saying." A car honks, and Tommy jerks the car back into its lane. "Whew. I'm getting all tangled up in this."

Florence decides to rescue him. "Didn't you think the hush puppies were divine? I could have eaten a dozen."

"Christ, I'm trying to ask you to marry me," Tommy says abruptly.

"Good lord," Florence says. Her face goes from ice cold to hot. She laughs in shock and, frankly, at how funny Tommy looks right now.

Tommy mutters to himself, "That was graceful. Nice job, Tommy. Nice and romantic." He is staring straight ahead, as if trying to make something out through a fog. Then he begins to laugh with Florence, and their laughter builds together until he has to pull off the road by one of the public phones set along the south part of Lake Shore Drive. They laugh until a police car pulls up behind them, and Tommy is forced to ask for directions to cover their flustered appearance. The cop waves them on. But when they are back on the road, the giggles catch up with them again.

After the children fall asleep, Giselle unpacks the baby bag that goes every-where with them—diapers, wipes, tissues, powders, toys—and she finds Lem's package. She struggles to pull off the tape—he has sealed it like a letter bomb. For a moment she pauses. He wouldn't give her anything stupid like some of Jimmy's leftover drugs. She tingles. A fat bag full of coke or heroin in this room with her babies. She almost throws the thing in the garbage. She feels through the wrapping again. It's too solid for any of that stuff. Probably love letters or old warrants or news clippings about his numerous arrests.

She rips it open and a handful of twenty dollar bills flutter to the floor. She looks at the wad of green still in her hand. There are fifties and hun-dreds, too, amounting to thousands probably. Or tens of thousands.

She lowers herself, shaking, into the rocker. She stares at the money. "Crazy Lem," she mumbles. "Should have been nicer to you all along."

Evander gives a quiet, moist chuckle, one of his standard sleeping noises, and pops his entire fist into his mouth and begins sucking noisily.

So somehow, out of all this stupid mess, the babies going to end up with two parents, sort of, she marvels. Who would have believed, last winter, that that could happen?

Wednesday the 20th

Alice and Shanklin arrive at the rehearsal a little late and find Molly and Chipper both glumly staring out into the new snowfall.

"What ho," Alice bellows. "I bring you gold and frankincense and glog."

"Ho ho ho," Shanklin says, prancing in front of them to make the fluffy ball at the tip of his Santa hat circle his head like a propeller.

Chipper and Molly stare at the insupportably cheerful bandmates.

"What up?" Alice says. "Who peed in your eggnog?"

"Chipped Beef Records," Molly says, giving a thumbs down.

"Lori blackballed us," Chipper adds. "We lost out again. Consequently, no one feels much like rehearsing."

"Not no one," Alice says. "I do."

"Don't blame me," Chipper says. "Our Christmas cheer must have leaked out of the container it came in. And Shank, I gotta say you look ridiculous in that hat."

Shanklin touches the red felt Santa hat defensively. "I get a lot of compliments."

"I would like to ask the Grinch what he did with my Christmas," Molly says. "And then I'd like to put a boot in his baggy green ass."

"I think you wouldn't have far to kick," Alice says, looking at Chipper.

"Nice," Chipper smirks. "Kick me when I'm down."

"You? Down? No one's buying that."

"How about this, then?" Chipper stands, wiping his hands on his jeans with metaphorical finality. "I quit."

"Whatever," Molly says.

"You wouldn't quit after getting the CD out and the holiday gigs coming up," Alice says. "I know you."

"Not buying it," Shanklin agrees.

"Well, chappies, I happen to be serious. I am out. No more delusions. No more skanky bar gigs and bullshit A&R whorefuckers. No more listening to radio in a jealous rage. I want to be normal."

"You can't be normal," Alice says.

"He's serious," Shanklin adds with amazement.

"Sure, but it's like he's declaring that he'll suddenly be handsome and wealthy by quitting the band," Alice says. "You can't just pull the plug on what you are."

"You're part of the band," Molly adds. "If you quit, you'll be defined by having left the band. You're a loser either way. A has-been or a never-was."

"I never thought of that," Shanklin says.

"That's crap," Chipper replies. "Sell the drum kit, or give it to the replacement idiot. I'm done." He walks dramatically from the room and closes the door with pointed softness.

"He'll be back," Shanklin says. "Right?"

"I hope so," Alice says. "Quitting now is not an option."

"And so the motivational baton is passed," Molly says, tossing Alice a drumstick.

Alice takes the drumstick warily. "Lo and behold the replacement idiot."

Leaving the bar where he spent the evening watching the Bulls lose yet another game, Brad sees Lori sitting in an instant photo booth, using the tiny metal mirror to apply a fresh coat of tangerine-hued lipstick. His first instinct is to duck his head and keep walking. And he does. But when he reaches the door, he pulls to a sharp stop. What is he avoiding? Should he cringe like a kicked dog? And all the events of the past several months emerge in his mind, swelling forth in all their grisly reality: breaking with the band, the loneliness of his squalid New York apartment, the unknown future. He backtracks in time to catch Lori blotting her lips on a lime-green band flier.

"Brad?" Her eyes flicker through several calculations. And then she squeals, leaping to her feet to throw around him a strong embrace heavily scented with cigarette smoke and patchouli. The scent immediately transports him back to the summer and the few splendid afternoons when he tasted these things in the sweat between Lori's wing-like shoulder blades.

"Oh my god, when did you get back?" She plants a freshly painted kiss on his neck. "Are you here for the holidays? Do you want to get a drink?"

She welcomes him as though nothing has happened, Brad realizes, staring in confusion. He doesn't know where to start with her.

"Are you joining back up with Lather?" she winks. "I'd still love to use my connections to—"

He steps forward suddenly, forcing Lori inside the booth. She stumbles back onto the fixed stool.

"Brad, hey, good christ."

Brad whips the curtain closed behind him. It's a tight fit, but that's all the better to soak up the reality of this woman who sent him halfway across the continent on a promise of her and then vanished into less than a promise—a dream, a vapor, a ghost-trace of an anonymous kiss in sudden darkness.

"I missed you," he says.

"I missed you, too," she says, misreading his tone, which is not pleading or sentimental, but merely factual.

"All those months. All that I left behind."

"You took a chance," she says, trying to squirm out from under him.

He fights the urge to bury his nose in her hair, just to smell it once more. "Was it hard for you? Did you fret over whether to come to New York or not?" His hand closes over her arm.

"Ow, let me out, are you crazy?" As it becomes clear that this exchange is not going in the direction she hoped, her struggles get more frantic. "I'll scream."

Brad forces a kiss on her, and she relents, and for a moment follows Brad into the kiss—this is the terrain where she rules, where men eventually succumb to her version of the world, and what better way to escape from this stupid photo booth? Suddenly, Brad pulls back. Lori opens her eyes and finds only the half-drawn curtain, and Brad hanging in the air, held up by his belt loops and shirt collar in the hands of a bouncer.

"And stay the fuck out," she hears the bouncer growl as Brad is ushered from view.

She re-applies her lipstick, goes to the bar and orders a double Dewars, neat.

"To losers," she says, lifting the drink in a general toast.

"Hi, it's me," Alice says into the intercom. "I needed a dose of Christmas cheer, and, lo, I happened to find a pint of mint chocolate chip ice cream in my backpack."

The door lock buzzes open.

Ellen's face inside a frayed nimbus of her carroty hair is bright, almost to the point of generating heat. Her smile creases her temples from eyes to ears.

Alice looks away. "Is this all right? I had a crappy day and I just needed—"

"Sure. I think so," Ellen says. "I mean, who knows?"

"It's just ice cream. I needed someone to share it with."

"Hey, there's no greater fan than me of mint chip."

"Two ice cream fans. Friends. That's all."

"Get your shivering butt in here," Ellen, says, tugging Alice's sleeve until she nearly topples.

"I'll get the spoons," she says, running to the kitchen.

"One spoon will do," Alice calls after her.

Saturday the 23rd

A small, elegant tree sits in the middle of Mr. Parsley's dining room table, which is covered with a snow-white, fleecy cloth embroidered with silver snowflakes. For decoration, the tree is hung with dozens of tiny gold stars.

"A teacher's joke," says Mr. Parsley, noticing Ng's gaze.

Ng smiles. "I like it. It's very Christmasy in here." He looks around at the gathering of paintings and pictures, many of them draped with tinsel for the season. "We haven't had much time to do Christmas. Mom's been absorbed in the restaurant day and night."

"It's a huge thing she's done. I hope you appreciate it." As soon as he's said it, the teacher clamps his hand over his mouth. "I'm sorry. I know I don't have to tell you that."

The teacher leads Ng over to a tray of tea and sandwiches. "I was in the mood for a formal tea," he says, bending over the pot as steam wafts over his face. "I hope you like it."

His moustache seems huge, but it is his face that is smaller. Ng remembers reading that fingernails appear to grow after death, as the flesh recedes, and he shudders.

"I made the sandwiches a touch exotic in your honor—cucumber and watercress are traditional—but I used a few different ingredients." He lifts one platter: "This is flaked tuna with cumin, chive, cilantro, and a drizzle of olive oil. The other bunch is hard-boiled egg with jalapeno and a garlic aioli. Mayo, to the common man." He pours some tea into a ceramic cup designed to look as if formed from leaves. The pot, shaped like a giant acorn, leaks through a re-glued crack down the side. "The tea is something I concocted, too, using pineapple mint from a little pot I keep in the kitchen—that and chamomile."

Ng tries a sandwich. His pleasure could not come close to that of his host, whose eyes squeeze shut with the intensity of the flavors. The teacher smiles apologetically, and his eyes appear moist.

"Pardon my reaction," he says. "Getting your holiday meals delivered from a hospice is just about the nadir of one's culinary experience. So this tastes extra fine to me."

Ng swallows the suddenly bulky bite of sandwich. He takes a sip of tea to wash it down.

The teacher does likewise, then dabs his lips with a linen napkin, and says, "Listen, I'd like to apologize again for my behavior on your last visit. It was a bad day for me. I didn't realize, I guess, until later, how hard it must have been for you to come to me and admit what you did."

"I didn't even want to. Leda made me."

"Don't absolve yourself of all credit. Part of what makes a good person is surrounding yourself with people who help you be good."

"Oh. Thank you, I guess."

"Don't be so modest, Ng. Look." Parsley stands and walks over to the wall, where Ng's painting hangs. "I put this up here never thinking I would see you again. Do you know what that means? I kept it because I liked it. How many times does a high school art teacher get to say that?"

Ng shrugs.

"The second reason I wanted to see you today was to ask you to be my student again." He gives Ng time to register his surprise. "No, don't answer yet. I won't be teaching again anytime soon, and it would mean a lot to me if I could have one talented student to work with. Part-time, one or two evenings a week."

Although a huge number of questions surge through Ng at the moment, he suppresses them.

"You're thinking, what can I teach you? And maybe you're right. But someone as bright as you can learn from almost anyone or anything. So think it over."

"I don't have to think it over. I'd like to do that. I would."

The teacher smiles over his teacup. The front of the cup, Ng can see, is chipped and stained from use. "We could work on whatever you want, or go to some galleries you should know about." He slaps his hands on his knees. "But I'm rambling. Think about it."

"I don't need to."

"Please." The teacher holds up his hands. "Also, as it's Christmas, I have this for you." He hands over a card.

"You don't have to."

"Oh yes I do. Open it."

The card is a piece of plain vellum on which is a watercolor of a deep blue night, spangled with stars, and one red dot, that emerges from the blue almost sneakily. He opens it, and there is only the word *Thanks*, and five fifty-dollar bills.

Ng hesitates. "I can't take this."

"It's your money. I used half of it to get the car a proper paint job. You can have the rest. Buy some really good Christmas presents for Leda and everyone else you care for."

"Did you make the card?"

"I always think of Rudolph's nose as a symbol of hope. Hope for the outsider to be accepted, hope for finding your way in the dark. Just—" he laughs, "plain old hope."

They finish the tea and sandwiches and Ng forces his teacher to accept an appointment in the first week of January to take his inaugural lesson.

Ng pauses outside and looks back through window, watching his teacher move slowly through the kitchen door with the tea tray. He fingers the card. There is one shopping day left before Christmas.

Monday the 25th (Christmas)

Everyone is dressed up, sitting on the couch in front of Alphonse's Christmas present: a new camera. Alphonse has set the camera on a stack of books on chair and is contorting himself to peer through the viewfinder.

The babies have on little suits—one pink, one blue— with sprigs of mistletoe on the caps. "So you can kiss them all the time," Giselle says.

Tony is back in the suit he wore to Darol's funeral, but this time with a bright new tie patterned with tiny baseballs and basketballs—a present received this morning along with a small box of monogrammed handkerchiefs. "You're old enough to get some adult presents now," his father said, right before bringing out the new bike that Tony had been afraid to ask for.

Giselle got a new calculator, a book bag, and a bottle of stay-awake pills to help her get through her first semester of college, starting right after the New Year. Some of Jimmy's money may be going for a computer, if she can find a good one used.

Tony fusses with the tie. How do people wear these things? It cuts off your air. He spent close to half an hour trying to tie it before he let his father, leaning over his shoulders, work it into place. It seems impossible that he will ever complete that triangular knot with his father's precision.

"Don't keep squirming around," his mother says. "That bike still be there when we get this done."

Eloise got a pearl necklace, which caused a predictable round of protestations from her and reassurances from Alphonse.

"I'm making decent money now," he says, "between the two jobs."

"I don't see how that figures, but it sure is pretty," she said, offering, in her stubborn way, the truce they both knew would come.

In a way, that's how the whole of Christmas day has gone: a reenactment of family rituals all of them had thought lost. His parents' battle over the pearls warmed Tony's heart—it was like his family's version of those manger scenes you see in front of churches—always different, but always the same, and each one both surprising and reassuring.

Eloise glances at her watch. "We best hurry, or Germaine gonna start dinner without us."

"I thought cameras had got simpler," Alphonse says from behind the book-stacked chair. "But this thing's got eleventy-two options for everything."

Tony walks over and points to a lever. "That's the timer, Dad."

Alphonse rolls his eyes. "I knew that. Now, everybody get into place."

He presses the lever and hurries over to the spot reserved for him in the middle, and throws on the same giddy, frozen smile everybody else has on—except the twins, of course, and especially Evander, who is screwing his face up for a peal of protest that will emerge just as the flash goes poof.

Tommy senses Florence's distress as soon as he opens the door.

"What's the matter?" he says, dropping his armload of packages on the floor. He embraces her silent, ghostly-white face.

Resting against Tommy's camel hair coat, Florence can smell the snow, the cold, the faint blending of aftershave, cigars, and the general comforting smell of a man.

She sniffles. "I called Louise and told her about us," she says into his chest. "I could tell she was upset. I feel awful about it." Florence squeezes her eyes shut against the tears.

"She was Arnie's sister. You'll have to give her time."

Duchess, hearing the strange sounds of distress, yips at Florence's feet, wagging her hindquarters anxiously.

"I'm just being an old crybaby," she says, wiping the corner of one eye. As you get older, the tears don't flow quite as readily. It's more like an emergent dampness, diffused through the wrinkles—no dramatic cascades of tears dripping from your nose and chin. "She said it seemed disrespectful to Arnie, too soon."

Tommy helps her settle on the divan, presents her with his handkerchief. "But you weren't entirely surprised by her feelings, were you?"

"No."

"Then I'm wondering. What do *you* think? Do you think it's disrespectful to Arnie to consider marrying me?"

"I've done more than consider it—I've agreed. And no, I don't think Arnie would take it that way."

He gives her a curious look. "You sound very sure."

"Oh." Florence suddenly realizes what she had been thinking as she was speaking. "Well, I was married to him for decades." She rises to move Tommy's packages to a table where the dachshund is unable to trample them, or worse. She pauses and turns. "I suppose I should tell you, however, that he used to visit me."

"His ghost, you're saying?"

"Yes. Several times until—until my stroke."

"You don't think he was maybe a byproduct of the condition that led to the stroke?"

She shakes her head vigorously.

"And it just stopped, like that."

"Yes," she says thoughtfully. She sits on one of the dining room chairs, reflecting. "It was as though he could only go so far, until he could be sure I would be all right."

"Do you think he'll return if he objects to our marriage?"

Florence smiles. "He hasn't shown up yet."

"Then I'd say we're pretty well in the clear. Unless you're worried about Louise conjuring him up to hex us."

"Oh no. Her bark is worse than her bite."

"That's good," Tommy says. "Her bark alone is nearly fatal."

It's like a dream. Nathan turns his face into the almost tangible cascade of honeyed sun pouring into the courtyard. He stretches, feeling the pleasant warmth of after-sex tumescence in his groin. The salad of musky, exotic fruits. The sweet, thick *café con leche*. He spoons up a bit of papaya, or is it guava? One thing it doesn't feel like is Christmas—despite the tinseled miniature cactus on the table. He admits to a slight twinge of guilt. But he argues against it. This is a trip outside and apart from normal time. Things could still go back to the way they were when he returns. It all depends on Robin's frame of mind. He tries to have no expectations—that's his new motto.

Allen Overcamp, a devastating curl of freshly showered hair curling across his brow, walks in and gives Nathan a quick kiss. "Isn't this just the best damn Christmas you ever had?" He sits and drapes his lap with a napkin.

Robin is never far from his thoughts, but Nathan pushes him aside to say, "Yes."

"Have you called home?"

Nathan shakes his head.

"Better get it over with."

"I can't tell him. Not over the phone."

"Of course not." Allen squeezes his hand. "I understand."

Allen: intelligent, handsome, stable. Robin: mercurial, beautiful, tragic. Holding a firework versus holding an Oscar statuette. There's not much of a choice, really, now is there?

"Apparently there's some kind of religious processional through the center of town today. Want to watch?"

Nathan wrinkles his nose. "Not for me."

"That's what I thought. So I asked around, and there's a spa about ten miles from here that's open today. A little dip, a little rub down, and then dinner?"

"That," says Nathan, "sounds like the best re-invention of Christmas I could imagine."

Ng's Christmas Day is a suffocating enclosure of four blank walls. Leda's family is with relatives in Joliet and Soo has been sleeping all day, leaving him to entertain himself. With what? The only thing on TV is the same movies you see every year that he can't bear to watch one more time. There's no place to go. It's a jingle bell prison. He has stared out into the street so many times he can see the scene with his eyes closed: the snow-dusted sidewalks, the ice-patched cars with dark fan shapes scored into the windshields, tree branches hung low with casings of clear, refrozen ice. It doesn't even feel like Christmas. But then he sort of missed the build-up anyway, the whole stretch of holiday furor from Thanksgiving to now has been so full of other events—the day arrived as an anticlimax.

Christmas has never been a big deal for Soo. She professes to be confused by the overlapping religious and secular imagery—angels, the baby Jesus, Santa Claus, wise men, and a flying deer with a red nose. She'd prefer to stay on the fringes of this holiday, thank you very much. And this year, she considers the full day off an opportunity for the greatest gift she could imagine: sleep.

After waking long enough to sheepishly admit she hadn't bought him anything—and to promise to shop tomorrow—Soo went back to sleep for several hours, waking at dusk to eat a few slices of turkey breast and some mashed potatoes that Ng prepared for her. No way was she going to cook today.

Ng feels letting her sleep is the least he can do since he didn't buy her anything, either. The only person he shopped for was Leda. A heart pendant with their initials on it. He imagines giving it to her, and the bounty of appreciative kisses he will receive. He pats the box he has been carrying in his pocket all day, as though keeping it near made Christmas more real.

Now Soo is wrapped in a blanket on the couch watching *White Christmas*.

He flops onto the couch beside her, huffy. "This is a totally lame movie. You do know that, don't you?"

"It very pretty. Pretty songs."

He pulls out the box and dangles the necklace.

"That for Leda?" Soo asks in a critical tone.

"Yes?" Ng says.

Soo shakes her head. "That things for little girl. No good for you girlfriend."

This is the first time Soo has used this word to acknowledge Leda, and Ng tries mightily to discern a critical edge to the usage.

"She likes necklaces," he replies defensively.

Still shaking her head, Soo rises and goes into her bedroom. Ng figures she has gone back to bed for the night. But then she returns and hands him an envelope. He opens it, and finds an old necklace of tiny, irregular pearls.

"Give her this," Soo says, and turns back to the movie.

Bing is riding in a one-horse open sleigh, singing his head off about snow. Ng looks at the necklace. It is a fine, delicate thing, still with the mark of handiwork upon it. The knotted silk between each pearl is impeccable. The clasp is a filigreed silver shell.

"This is too nice, Mom. Have you had this a long time?"

"Since you father give me for wedding."

"Whoa." Ng gasps, his head spinning. "I can't give something like that to Leda. It's, wow, it's way too much."

"You keep then. Give when is right time, right person."

"Mom, I don't know what to say."

"Merry Christmas," Soo says, and he catches the barest hint of a smile around her eyes.

Just then a voice outside calls, "Hello! Merry Christmas up there!"

Ng and Soo look at each other.

"Ho, ho, ho! Merry Christmas!"

Ng looks out the window. In the yard, wearing not red, but a black wool overcoat, is Elias, holding a bag in one hand and a bottle in the other.

Catching sight of Ng in the window, Elias calls, "Anybody want a Yuletide snack?"

Ng struggles to raise the window, finally cracking it free of the ice in the sill. He sticks his head out into the biting air. "Whatcha got?"

"Cheese, bread, egg nog."

"Who is it?" Soo asks.

Ng looks at Elias, his white hair tufting in the breeze, his cheeks reddened by the cold. "It's Santa Claus," he says, laughing. "And he brought treats."

Soo appears at the window. "Santy Claws," she mutters. "Buzz him in, before he freeze to death."

Tuesday the 26th (Boxing Day)

Each member of Lather Rinse Repeat came home after Christmas to find this ditty, sung by Chipper, on his or her answering machine:

"A band without a drummer/ Loses the beat/ But a drummer sans band/ Has no time to keep/ I may be a whiner/ a bonehead and hack/ I shot my stupid mouth off;/ Bandmates, please take me back."

Alice thinks: Brad could learn a thing or two about apologies from Chipper. And: Everybody has the right to freak out now and then.

Molly thinks: Saw that coming a mile away. And: Thank god he doesn't try to write songs.

Shanklin thinks: Is that to the tune of *Momma's Got a Squeeze Box*? And: Man, does Chipper have a shitty voice.

Fifteen…sixteen…seventeen… Robin watches the phone ringing, ringing. He'll never answer it. Never. Oh no, he thinks, I'm not that easy. Chinese and Italian food containers litter the apartment. He is half-naked, bearded, and smelly. He could unplug the phone, but then he wouldn't know if it were ringing. It has to keep ringing, or he will surely die. And he wants to milk that bell for every last ding. He wants the delicious, psychic pain of vibrations on his eardrums. If he could, he'd crawl inside that bell, surrounding himself in the sound, let it deafen him like the Hunchback of Notre Dame. He holds the phone to his ear. Come on, Nathan, give it to me one more time. Ah, here it goes again: *one…two…three…four…*

The decision to close the restaurant for the day turns out to be a good one. Elias wakes late with a fuzzy head and a desire to sit inside and watch football—a sport about which he knows almost nothing—on TV. The phone rings and he picks it up expecting Soo with a menu suggestion, or maybe Tommaso discussing details of his honeymoon planning. To his surprise, it is Sophia.

"Dad, hi. Merry Christmas."

"Hello. What a surprise. I called yesterday. Did you get the packages I sent?"

"Yes, Dad, but actually we never got a chance to open them."

"Did Elana—"

"Before you ask any more questions, let me tell you why I'm calling."

Two hours later, Elias knows the full story of Jonathan's leaving Sophia for his secretary and how the news, delivered with Jonathan's exquisitely bad timing over the Christmas breakfast of eggs Benedict and mimosas, had left Sophia feeling empty and confused. She told Elias how she looked at Jonathan's red eyes, drained her glass of champagne, and took Elana into the sunroom to play with the plastic kitchen set that Jonathan had assembled the night before with much cursing. She waited until she heard the front door close behind her husband and then she began to remove the tinsel and delicate painted glass balls from the tree. She had called, Elias realizes, so he could tell her how to feel.

"Just protect Elana," he keeps saying. "That is all you can do for now. Feelings will come and they will change. But the child, she needs all you have right now."

"But Dad, I don't have that…I'm not a mother like that." Sophia is sobbing now, with the permission that only a parent's attention can grant.

On TV, a red team had come from behind to beat a team in orange. Fans rush onto the field like slurry from a broken pipe. And though Elias has no idea how any of it transpired, the force of the event is undeniable.

It was Danny's idea to have Ng down to his house for supper. Leda and Soo pushed for it, too, even though Ng was not terribly enthusiastic.

"Doesn't anybody care what I want?" he whined.

"Be a man," Leda said. "Give your dad a chance."

"He try to help," Soo says. "Give him chance."

Ng wonders if they scripted their phrases to wear him down faster.

He rides next to his father in awkward silence as the white Impala speeds down the expressway, dusk settling quickly over the concrete ribbons of overpass and underpass, ramps up and down into the stream of blinking taillights. Danny flicks the radio between different sports talk shows, which are all discussing things that Ng has a hard time following. A trade that might happen, a high-paid player not meeting expectations. Danny's index fingers tap the steering wheel in time to an internal song.

"These guys are all full of crap, but I like to listen when they interview some of the old greats. Ditka was on last week and he—" Danny looks at his son. "You know Ditka, right?"

Ng shrugs.

"Oh brother." Danny is struck by the enormity of what his son has missed. He exits the expressway and rambles down a broad corridor of fast food stands, used car lots, and supermarkets before turning into a neighborhood of small houses with postage stamp lawns which, even under the snow, are obviously immaculate. The bushes in front of every house are geometrically perfect. Danny pulls up in front of a one-story house with stone facing. The roof line is outlined with the old fashioned bulbs, the big ones, blinking in slow alternation, so that the light appears to pass from bulb to bulb all the way around the house.

Stacey greets them both with demure cheek kisses. Her short dress is covered with a red Christmas apron.

"I'm very pleased to meet you, Ng. Dinner will be ready soon," she says, smiling. "Why don't you give Ng a tour of the house?"

From the outside, Ng had thought the house appeared generous, but inside, it feels even smaller than his mother's apartment. There is stuff everywhere: tiny vases, pictures, mirrors, statuettes, artificial flowers. His father moves among them like a man very afraid of touching anything. As if living in a you-break-it-you-bought-it store. The door to the master bedroom is closed. But when he peeks in the room across the hall, Ng freezes.

"Oh yeah," Danny says with some embarrassment. "Stace collects Barbies." The room is nearly a shrine, with well over two dozen Barbies in various styles of dress—Star Trek ensign, go-go dancer, nurse—standing pertly in their shiny, unopened boxes. These things are going to be worth a bundle some day. People go nuts for these things, especially in the original packaging. Not that she'll ever sell them. He nudges his son, acknowledging a joke between them.

"Wow," is all Ng can say.

"I can't really tease her about it. In a way, I got her started." Danny screws up his face, and then, seeming to come to an internal decision, pulls down a box almost hidden on the near wall. "See, I had this G.I. Joe when we moved in together. I had it to maybe give you someday. Anyway, she bought a Barbie to keep him company, sort of, and then all hell broke loose."

Ng takes the box from his father's hands. The cardboard has faded a little, and a fine dust settled across the chisel-faced figurine inside. "This was for me?" he says.

"Well, with an ex-Marine for an old man, I thought it might help you remember me."

Ng looks at the plastic soldier for several moments and then hands it back to Danny.

"Here, let me see something." Danny opens the tops and sticks two fingers down inside the box. "She'd kill me if she saw me do this." He wrenches something free and hands it to Ng: a tiny canteen, molded from silver plastic and diapered in its own miniature canvas holster.

"That's pretty much like the ones we used," Danny says. "You don't have to keep it if you don't want to."

Ng puts it in his pocket. "I want it. Thanks."

Danny smiles a smile that seems to go off in several directions at once. "So, let's go eat," he says finally, and his large, strong hand claps Ng squarely between the shoulders.

"Open carefully!" reads the handwriting on the outside of the heavy cream envelope. Alice? Ellen thinks, carefully peeling open the flap. Out flutter

several rather crushed rose petals. Oh well, it's the thought that counts. Wait a minute. There is a piece of paper stuck inside. The printed script reads: "You are cordially invited to a New Year's Eve bash at Urbs in Horto. Come as you are. Music by Lather Rinse Repeat. Food by Sophia's. A film by Ellen Kovacs." Underneath in Alice's handwriting: "*Bring the film, please! Xoxo, A.*"

It is several minutes before Ellen realizes what Alice has committed her to do, because her brain has been reduced to one mantra-like chant: "Exes and ohs. She gave me exes and ohs…"

Sunday the 31st (New Year's Eve)

Alice gives everything a last check. Six o'clock, and people are going to start arriving in about two hours. Food trays from Sophia's across the street: check. Movie screen and projector: check. Kegs and wet bar: check. We are ready to ring in the new year.

Ellen's film is running on one wall, with a soundtrack of whatever Shanklin happens to spin at the moment. It isn't a long film, and people stop and watch it all the way through, many of them looking over at Alice and wondering if it really is her in the film, and if so, whether it is an act of enormous ego to show it at her own party.

Leda is different tonight. Is it the momentum of the hour causing her to carry herself with less than the usual caution? Ng knows that there is still part of her, raised in what he thinks of as her family's special brew of half-pagan Catholicism, that fears these cosmic turnings. She has a small bottle of rum to mix in her Coke, and her kisses are growing more open, wet, and expressive. She is wearing the hand-me-down pearl necklace Ng gave her. She touches it often, and her eyes soften toward some imagined future connected to the object. Ng is enchanted, and alarmed.

Lather Rinse Repeat is playing an acoustic set in the midst of the flowers. Ellen is watching her film, with the band's new set for a soundtrack. The images of Alice flicker by. Ng stands next to her, and asks, "Hey, is this a video for the band?"

"Yes," says Ellen without a moment's pause, "Yes it is."

"That girl," Ng says, pointing at Alice, "has star written all over her."

Ellen does not reply, feeling, like Ng says, that Alice suddenly seems to be an otherworldly object passing through the atmosphere on her way somewhere better and brighter. She tries to recall what it was like to be close to that intensity, and now it seems unreal to her. Unreal compared to the rest of her life, which is now forever cracked into two parts—before and after Alice.

Carrying empty food trays from the party across the street to Sophia-Soo's, Elias stops on the yellow stripe in the middle of the street. Between the two places, sweltering with bodies, grill fires, and excitement, the frigid air feels good. There has been so much change lately, his life feels unlike the one he had even a few weeks ago. The windows exude light, as though the activity behind them were chemical reactions generating heat and illumination and he moves between them like some kind of, what is it, electron. He shifts the trays under one arm as a taxi passes by just behind him. He crosses on over to the restaurant, feeling with his free hand for the paper airline ticket in his pocket. Tomorrow he is going to Boston again—this time invited and needed. Changes bring more changes.

Robin rises slowly from the couch and stumbles through the ranks of empty vodka bottles scattered around it. He catches a glimpse of himself in the hall mirror: bathrobe askew revealing his hollow stomach, the cock drawn up into itself. His knee is killing him. Oh well, whatever the liquor doesn't numb, pills will take care of. He limps into the bathroom and swings open the medicine cabinet. The space where the brown bottles of pain pills used to be is empty. He finds the bottles, empty, in the wastebasket. Nathan flushed the pills, obviously, before he left. Some show of faith, eh? Can't call for a week, but still wants to control everything. The bastard. He limps out to the kitchen. Electric oven—no good. The longest, sharpest knives are missing. The apartment has been suicide-proofed. But Nathan couldn't lower it to the first floor. Robin walks over to the patio doors. Plenty of stories down to do the business, should he decide it needs doing. Not that there's any rush. He had survived the day when the phone no longer rang with Nathan's guilt. He'd survived how damn predictable it was, which was the worst part. Maybe tomorrow he will resolve to stop trying to change people. He looks from the ground up to the bleary sky filled with drifting puffs of smoke from expended fireworks. Tomorrow? What the hell does that mean?

In a sparsely attended service at the Club Azurri, Florence and Tommaso stand together before a judge, who is pronouncing them man and wife. They kiss.

"How will you tell Louise you eloped?" Tommy whispers as they walk beneath the drizzle of rice.

"Life goes on," Florence says. "And don't anybody forget it."

Ng has taken Leda outside, to snuggle in a darkened doorway far from the festivities. Leda takes his hand and puts it inside her sweater. Something wobbles inside Ng's chest, like a gyroscope compensating for sudden turbulence.

"Baby, you love me, don't you?" She is a little drunk.

Ng considers his response. "Yes." He swallows hard.

"I wanna be with you forever." She drops her head to his shoulder.

He knows that in her mind forever is a lot longer than a mere millennium.

"Me, too," he says anyway. And falls into the hot perfume of her kiss.

"Hi, it's me. For some reason I just keep thinking about you, wondering where you are, what you are doing. A year ago we rode the love train together, and it seems like a century ago. And, I was just thinking that if, you know, there is even a tiny chance you are thinking of me, I wanted you to know that it was reciprocal. Happy New Year."

Only once this evening does Larry O. Larry get up from the linoleum kitchen table which serves as his drafting table, and that is to get to cotton balls from the bathroom and stuff them in his ears. The blinds are drawn, the TV is off. More important than the celebrations racketing all over the city is the opportunity to spend several uninterrupted hours refining his craft. He adjusts the angle-poise lamp and leans back to the paper, willing his hand to do what is so strikingly simple that he is sure his desire will eventually lead him to execute the graceful lines in his mind.

The crackling fireworks and horns and shouts keep Tony from really getting to sleep. So he goes out to the kitchen for some water. He finds someone half-hidden inside the refrigerator.

Giselle straightens up and almost drops her plate of leftovers when she sees him.

"Lord, you gave me a start," she says, putting one hand over her heart. "What are you doing up, baby?"

Tony likes that she calls him baby sometimes, even though he usually pretends that he's too old for that. "I couldn't sleep."

"Me either."

She sets the plate on the table—remains of the supper: pork roast, black-eyed peas, and some cold mashed potatoes. Good luck food to begin the new year. Tony's mouth waters.

"I see that look. Come on."

Tony gets a fork, and they both nibble from the same plate.

"It's almost midnight," Giselle says. "Let's go outside and listen."

They step onto the porch in bathrobes and slippers, and in a minute a cascade of celebrations begins to burst in every direction, as the millennium begins, for everyone, at a slightly different point in time.

They hug instinctively, shivering.

"Gonna be a big time coming up," Giselle whispers in Tony's ear.

"I know," he says. "Everything's going to be different."

At the corner of State and Madison Streets—zero-zero on the grid established by city planners over a century ago, when the millennium was a futuristic illusion owned by French utopians and English dystopians—Brother Even steps onto a small valise and addresses the streaming crowds.

"It is here. The end. The beginning. The beginning of the end. Make this your resolution, brothersister: from this moment on I will heed no more moments. Give up on that one unstopping stopwatch ticking in your head. Give time back to itself. You pretend to own it. You say, 'I'm running out of time. I'll make time for this.' But you don't own it. It owns you. Time does to you what it does, the element beneath all elements. Time creates the wind. Time creates the river."

When he is done, he will pick up the valise and walk. He will walk down to the Chicago River, the one river running backwards in constant disagreement with time's demand. He will step into that river and taste what it tastes like when time swallows itself.

"What you don't understand about time is not expressible in words. Words require time. A story creates its own time. Time breaks apart, fragments, creates the world, remains whole. How would you know the earth beneath you without time to measure it? Is the world three-dimensional, then, or one-dimensional? I'll tell you, brothersister, the three dimensions you experience are all but subsets of the one: Time."

Will he buck the current and drift out into the lake? Or will he float out into the larger ocean, the flat plate of the continent, to be swallowed whole and then reborn in a ditch beside a field of wheat? God only knows.

"Give way, brothersister, it is the only way to hold on. Imagine the last moment. It will come. And it will never come."

The End

Acknowledgments

This book would not exist without my loving parents, Mike and Jane Winston, and my devoted sisters, Amy and Ann, who have always believed me capable of great things. Many writers—especially Donald Harington, Jack Butler, Donald Finkel, John N. Morris, and Ronald Harwood—gave me the gift of treating me like a writer. Mary Martens Phillips made the suggestion that unwittingly started this book. And most importantly, it is my great fortune to have a brilliant publisher and friend in Douglas Seibold, who, early in the first draft, bought me a beer and told me that he wanted to publish this book, not only several years before it was completed, but before there was even a publishing company to fulfill the vision. *Sláinte!*

About the Author

ANDREW WINSTON was born in Tulsa, Oklahoma, raised in Little Rock, Arkansas, and now lives outside Chicago. He is the past editor-in-chief of the *Chicago Review* literary magazine. *Looped* is his first novel.